The Bronze Box

Amy C Fitzjohn

Copyright © 2016 Amy Morse

All rights reserved.

All rights reserved. No part of this publication may be reproduced or transmitted in any form or by any means, electronic or mechanical, including photocopying, recording, or any information and retrieval storage system, without permission from the author.

This book is a work of fiction.

ISBN: 150021633X

ISBN-13: 9781500216337

FOR GRAHAM WITH LOVE

I write under my maiden name for my dad, who for more than 30 years has been tracing the footprints left in the sands of time by our ancestors.

Amy C Fitzjohn – © 2014

ACKNOWLEDGMENTS

Thanks to the very talented Lewis Fitzjohn for the new cover art.

I'd like to thank the group of writers at our King Bill critique group; Cheri, Hannah, Phil, Meg, Alex - who have helped me to improve my writing.

I need to make a special mention for Jo Reed, who always offers me great constructive criticism as well as moral support.

Thank you to my growing network of support from other writers.

A thank you to Dave Court who edited the first edition

Thanks to those diligent readers and sticklers for accuracy who helped by pointing out the errors from the first edit (oops)

Thanks to those who reviewed the first book too, both good and bad reviews, it all helps me to improve my writing,

Last but never least - thanks to my friends, family and colleagues, who have kept the pressure on with constant cries of
'I want to read your book, when is it out?'

Thanks everyone

SECOND EDITION
First edition published in 2013

This 2nd edition features:

- a new cover –

- editing changes –

- a new Epilogue -

- notes on the next books -

THE PAST

BYZANTIUM - 350 BC

'Our sins are more easily remembered than our good deeds.'
Democritus

"I have the package," he spoke in Greek.

"Shhh, keep your voice down! Come here!" Democritus pulled the Arab into a shady alleyway by the sleeve of his kaftan.

"Careful!" the Arab merchant stumbled.

Democritus chuckled, a nervous laugh, focusing his attention to everything but the young man.

"And my passage to Odessus - is it arranged?" he asked.

"You're sailing on the Majestic, it leaves the harbour at dusk," said the Arab.

Democritus pulled the hessian-wrapped package from the younger man's arms. It was heavier than it appeared. The old Philosopher, who felt himself getting frailer by the day, lost his balance and staggered back to take the weight of the box. An amused smile tugged at the Arab's lips when Democritus humped the package up under his arm, rested it on his hip, cursing the burden.

The Arab merchant slipped back into the crowded bazaar, leaving Democritus to do what he had convinced himself he had to.

The air was thick with dust and the smell of incense mingled with spice. Voices reverberated around the honeycomb of mud brick – he could pick out Greek, Latin and Arabic amongst the others and was unnaturally aware of every nuance of sound and the jostling of busy traders. He hurried through the labyrinthine corridors, dodging hustlers and beggars. The giddiness of the bazaar assaulted his senses - Dogs barking, insects buzzed, dust hung in the air like curtains of grit. Exotic music, the clattering of cartwheels and the noisy bartering of merchants, pulsed around him as he picked his way through. His mind brimming with a confusion of self-doubt and righteousness.

The Slavic snarl of a Thracian merchant caught his attention. The heavyset man, cloaked in layers of wool trimmed with animal pelt, bounded down the alley towards him, angrily grunting in a barely familiar tongue. Democritus clutched the package into his body, feeling its hard, cold weight in his gut. He looked back and forth, sweat beading on his face and trickling down his neck, sending shivers through his body. He picked up his pace, hurrying and sidestepping into another alleyway. He ducked under a crudely carved archway into a small courtyard, hoping he hadn't been cornered in this unfamiliar place, caught red-handed with the priceless box.

The locals were notorious for exacting harsh punishment on thieves. He felt sick at the thought of losing his hands and the humiliation of his life's work being exposed as a sham because of this package. These things terrified him more than death.

His heart crashed against his ribs, breath rasping. To calm himself, he closed his eyes and for the first time in seventy years, he prayed to Zeus for protection. The discovery of the box had shaken the foundations of his beliefs. If the box was real, the power of the Gods he had spent his life trying to deny could be true as well.

It seemed the King of the Gods was with him, as the Thracian thundered past and faded out of earshot, carrying the smell of sweat and animals with him. He could barely admit he was from the same region. They were both of Thrace but were completely different, to Democritus, the ruddy-faced man with his shaggy hair and a menacing gait, seemed wild and uncivilised. Democritus smiled to himself at the thought that; the man wouldn't have lasted a day in the pit of vipers of Athens. The frailty of humanity always amused him, it had earned him the rather undignified nickname of 'The Laughing Philosopher'.

His senses reordering themselves, he peered around the

archway, before stepping back into the dust and continuing his journey. He passed the Thracian again, wary, he glanced back. The bear of a man was shaking the wits out of a servant boy. Democritus was no pacifist but did believe unnecessary violence was inexcusable. Normally he would have spoken up against the ill-treatment of the boy, or perhaps even bought the handsome young man from his tormentor - he would have been a pleasing addition to the household. But on that day, he was simply relieved the Thracian had not been after him.

His whole life he had defended the truth of science and sought to demystify the fog of myth and legend crippling the Greek people. There was logic in the inexplicable world; why resort to worn out superstitions and excuses?

He had fought ridicule and scorn for such radical ideas - convinced his work on atomic theory would one day be vindicated. But now this – the box. A myth made true. In all his endeavours he had never encountered such a paradox.

What unholy arrangement of atoms could harbour such power? And what truth is this? We dare not unleash the box on the world.

He followed the ideas around in his mind. Surely only some higher power could change the nature of atoms in such a terrifying way all empty space around them becomes filled with the essence of death itself.

He had considered destroying the box, but told himself mighty Zeus alone knew what a terrible curse may befall humanity if he did. He chose to hide it in a place of death, where it belonged, and somewhere it would never be disturbed. He told himself it was for the good of mankind, to keep it safe from dangerous hands. The fact that concealing its existence would also protect his work was of additional benefit. He was a pragmatic man, but for the first time in his long life, he found himself wondering about the point of it all. To Democritus, a man of science, a seeker of truth, it was the worst feeling of all.

VARNA, BULGARIA – 1998

June

"This site was first uncovered in 1972 by a digger operator excavating a trench for cabling. No one suspected such riches lay by the city. They found what seems to be the oldest worked gold in the world here. Thousands of years older than the Pyramids."

Sasha's eyes widened and she focused on Dr Thornton as he spoke, his voice filled with enthusiasm. She barely noticed the dry heat pressing in on her as they surveyed the patch of waste ground that could change the world's view of history.

"What do you mean, 'the oldest worked gold in the world'?"

"You'll be aware from your studies, this site is from the Chalcolithic Period, better known as the Copper Age. A time after the Neolithic but before the Bronze Age, when people began experimenting with metallurgy."

"Of course," she shrugged.

Sasha Blake was impatient to get to work now, having landed at Sofia in the small hours then been buffeted along by a soviet leviathan of a train for six hours to get to Varna. She had managed a few stilted hours of sleep between the flight and the train and was pumped with the adrenalin of finally making it here, having untangled her way through a maze of red tape.

Thornton cleared his throat and cast an eye up and down her. She was self-conscious, like he was sizing her up.

"This period demonstrates the earliest development of complex societies. When, following a brutal Ice Age, Neolithic people started to cultivate the land – a new system spread from the Middle East, called farming," he offered her a wry smile, "As the climate continued to warm people migrated further north. It means Chalcolithic sites in Southern and Eastern Europe are generally older than those in Northern and Western."

"I've seen a lot of evidence though my studies this period of history is more advanced, in a sociological sense, than was previously thought," she said, having her own theories about the Copper Age.

She was an Archaeology graduate, here as part of her Masters and had been following Dr Thornton's work. As she looked out over the excavation, she shielded her eyes, then caught the glint of the razor wire fences around the perimeter. She had never seen a dig site with such security.

"How can you be sure of the period of this site?" she said, "I understand you believe it could date back to between 4000BC and 5000BC?"

"I do, yes. It was in 1975 that Ivan Ivanov excavated here and first suggested the gold dated back to 5000BC. We can estimate the period of this site from the discovery of rudimentary weapons and everyday tools close by, as well as household items such as pottery. It's fairly typical of the period. Please."

He beckoned her to follow him on a tour of the Varna Necropolis site. As they picked their way around the rubble quietly she heard the innumerable songs of birds and the low buzz of insects. She swiped away a fly and swatted a bug on her arm.

Thornton brushed down his khaki slacks, pushed his wire-rimmed glasses up his nose and strode forwards, as if he were about to ascend a great mountain. She shrugged her rucksack onto her shoulder, batted away a hoverfly and followed. As they walked, Dr Thornton continued, "What isn't typical about this site, however, is the vast wealth of gold buried in these, what we assume to be, warriors graves. It's solid evidence these people were not as primitive as we have previously believed." Thornton peered over his glasses at her and grinned.

"Why did the archaeologists stop work before?" she asked.

Thornton flicked his floppy brown hair out of his eyes and

adjusted his spectacles.

"Money – as always with these things. That and the Soviets."

He was speaking so fast he barely took a breath, as if he held so much knowledge it was bursting to escape. He was even more impressive in real life than she had imagined from reading his books.

"It was Churchill who first coined the term 'Iron Curtain' you know - 'From the Baltic to the Adriatic an Iron Curtain has descended on the continent' he said. The bloody Soviets did that."

She smiled, she had never imagined her idol would be so down to earth. She had been star struck since she was accepted onto the placement, hardly able to believe she would be working alongside one of the greatest minds in Neolithic archaeology. She was surprised at how attractive she found him, with his confident swagger and searching gaze.

"This way," he waved her onwards. She tripped over a loose rock and with swift reflexes, Dr Thornton reached for her arm before she fell.

"Watch your step," he said.

Their eyes met briefly. She was absorbed by how kind his eyes seemed - deep crow's feet forked into his temples and he had an innate charisma about him. She felt roses bloom on her cheeks, thanked him and adjusted her white cotton blouse, paranoid the buttons around her breasts would let her down. She fumbled in her satchel for a notebook and pencil.

"From my understanding," she gesticulated to the wilderness surrounding them, "This necropolis dates from the same period as the Pločnik site in Serbia. I studied the site as part of my degree. Although I have a feeling this place will be even more significant."

Thornton raised an impressed eyebrow, "Indeed."

She felt vindicated. Despite it, he still corrected her, "I believe this site is a little earlier than Pločnik. The people of Pločnik were from the Vinča people, descendants of the Starčevo culture. The people who created this site have been named the Varna Culture, but based on bone spatulas found close by, I think they are related to the Starčevo people. That said, the society who created this cemetery is still not fully understood."

She capitalised on the moment, eager to prove herself, "I assisted at the Windmill Hill Causeway site near Avebury. I realise it's a more recent site but it is still Chalcolithic Age. It was a field trip as part of my Archaeology Degree."

"What were you involved in at the site?"

"Mostly cleaning up and cataloguing of finds. It was a valuable insight into the period. I wondered if rather than metallurgy being spread from Eastern Europe, it could have sprung up independently in different places and eventually, as populations spread, their techniques merged?"

Song birds chirped on the breeze and the occasional seagull cawed overhead, as if there were cheering her on.

"Interesting. There is evidence to support that. But it's good you're experienced at cataloguing finds. Good, good." Thornton muttered and trailed off, "Should we continue?"

Eager, she followed him and looked him up and down. His clothes were surprising clean given the nature of his work.

Sasha imagined, from having read his books, he saw himself as a great adventurer, a modern day Indiana Jones, who dug up the past in wild and exotic places. She suspected in reality he was rather more bookish, judging by his neatly pressed and spotless trousers.

"I have taken the liberty of speaking with my associates at the Varna Archaeological Museum," he said, "They have agreed to increase my funding so you can be comfortable while you're here. I'm staying in a hotel, I would ask no less of my staff."

She smiled to herself.

"That's kind of you Professor, thank you." She wasn't about to say no to a warm bed and her own bathroom.

"Not at all. And you may call me David. It makes things easier. I've arranged accommodation at the Odessus Hotel. It's where I'm staying. The décor is a bit 70s I'm afraid. Not that you'd remember the 70s," he chuckled, "But it is comfortable, and convenient for town. Plus it makes things easier if all the site workers are at the same place. Did you know Odessus was the Classical Greek name for Varna?"

"I did, yes."

"Oh," he grumbled. He seemed disappointed she wasn't impressed with that nugget. They continued the tour of the partially excavated remains of the Varna Necropolis.

"I estimate we have so far uncovered less than half of what is here," he said, "It's a significant find. Just one of these graves contained more than two pounds of gold. Plenty for thieves to get their hands on."

She raised her eyebrows - it explained the security cordon around the site.

Thornton crouched awkwardly over a broken stretch of wall to get to the lower level of the site then held up a hand to help her down.

"You know," he continued, a distant look in his eye, "I have a daughter not much younger than you. She's never shown much interest in my work."

"So what is your daughter into?"

Sasha was careful to watch her step this time and followed Thornton through a weaving path of over grown rocks towards a line of shadowy rectangular excavations.

"Georgie? She's studying business – it's all very dry!"

"Do you have any other children?"

"A son, he's an Accountant," he laughed.

"Over here are the first graves we found."

Thornton stretched his arm in the direction of the pits. Sasha's heart raced with a morbid curiosity.

"May I?"

She edged closer, eager for permission.

"Carry on!"

She half walked, half jogged, gripped with excitement, then leaned over and gazed into one of the pits.

Thornton moved alongside her. She was sure he had been eyeing up her backside, she didn't mind, she was flattered, and glad she had worn such figure hugging jeans.

"It's empty!" she said, unable to disguise her deep disappointment.

"Not all of the graves have a body. And those that did, Dr Kamel's team have taken the remains away for forensic examination. I trust Kamel. It is an unfortunate truth there are unscrupulous people in our industry who sell stolen pieces of history to line their own pockets," he offered her a small smile.

"Were the artefacts also removed to prevent theft?"

He smiled, "Since the 1970s it has been known there is gold buried here."

She gave a considered nod.

"How long have you worked with Dr Kamel?"

"More years than I care to recall," a smile flashed across his face, "He and I have a similar outlook on things. The man may be a bit prickly but he knows his stuff, and like me, has worked all his life to preserve human history to educate future generations."

"And his team have taken the remains back to Istanbul?" she said, flatly. So close yet so far from coming face to face with Europe's ancient ancestors.

"He has. They are at his lab at the Istanbul Archaeological Museum. I'm sure you'll get the chance to see them. It's important they are preserved and treated with dignity."

Sasha stood tall and smiled, "So when do I get started? I've even bought my own tools," she said, tapping her satchel, "Where are we digging next?"

"Over there, to the east, by those trees," Thornton pointed to an audience of walnut trees, "We think," he added.

"Think? Aren't you sure then?"

"Well, we've done some shovel tests and believe the outer wall runs along that low fold but the geophysicists will be here on Wednesday with some gear. Come on, I'll show you what we'll be doing until then."

Thornton tracked between crumbling walls and dodged thick weeds, sun faded scatterings of litter and patches of rampant nettle. He kicked over a rock and a bright green lizard scuttled across his path. He jumped back and Sasha stifled a giggle.

"It's just a lizard, for a moment I thought it might be a snake."

She smiled, seeing the residue of panic in his eyes. They walked back up to the higher lever of the excavation and towards a portable site hut. It looked like a recycled cargo train car.

"*Zdrasti!*" he called over as they approached the cabin.

"What does that mean?" she whispered as a roughly shaven, portly man emerged from the hut.

"It means hi," he said, smiling.

The two men shook hands as they came together and she stood quietly while they exchanged some words in Bulgarian.

The man, dressed in grubby jeans and a fake Manchester United football shirt, jabbed a podgy hand at her, his face sullen.

She took his hand, it was coarse and stiff – a labourer's hand.

"Drashty!" she said, trying to imitate Thornton.

The Bulgarian labourer's face brightened and a gap toothed smile opened it up.

"You speak Bulgarian?" His tone suggested he was teasing, but she was keen to make a good impression.

"No, no. You speak English though?"

"Dr David, he teach me words. No school Anglish."

He seemed pleased with his efforts.

"Well I think you speak English very well."

"You're doing all right aren't you, Tsvetan?" said Thornton.

"I hope," Tsvetan said, looking coy.

"This is Sasha Blake. She's a student archaeologist."

"Then you learn Bulgarian, yes," said the site assistant, "It help. We have big history here," he opened his arms wide, as if he wanted to hug his whole country with pride.

"I suppose," she reluctantly agreed. Languages had never been Sasha's strength and from what she had seen and heard, Bulgarian seemed to defy any logic.

Tsvetan was an intimidating bear of a man with a heavy brow and wild ebony hair. His clothes smelt faintly of sweat and tobacco and his breath of alcohol, poorly disguised with mint. He waved her into the shabby hut and she followed him up the rickety rusting steps.

"This our, how you say…" he looked at Thornton for a clue. Thronton's face was folded with confusion, not sure what Tsvetan was trying to say, "*P'chifka*?"

"Ah!" The spark of realisation ignited and he translated, "*P'chifka* is rest, this is our rest area."

"And *officy*," added Tsvetan.

"I see," mumbled Sasha, peering in.

The air was stale with tobacco smoke, a brown film creeping over every surface. Papers, bulging cardboard boxes and dusty tools were scattered everywhere. There was a velour settee just inside the door, its springs collapsed into a mushy heap of 70's fabric, a couple of wonky old melamine desks, and a wheel-less operator's chair in front of a crusty beige computer. On the sill of the small grimy window was a row of bottles of mysterious looking sprits and some sticky cups. Below the window was a brown filing cabinet, the drawers buckled and uneven and opposite was an ancient looking wood stove, a black kettle perched on top of it and a mismatched pipe zig-zagging up the wall.

"You don't have any other women working at this site do you?" commented Sasha, screwing up her face.

"No. Why?" asked Thornton, oblivious.

"Oh, just a guess."

"Rakia?" chirped Tsvetan, "Yes – you have Rakia, you must!" he nodded, reaching for one of the bottles on the sill. Thornton smiled widely, as if the two men were forming a secret pact against her. Wise to it, and game for a laugh, she could handle her drink.

"Why not!" she grinned.

Chuckling to himself, Tsvetan took one of the cups from the shelf, wiped the rim with a grubby cloth, something more off-putting to her than the thought of the drink, and he sloshed a generous measure into the cup. With a big smirk, he offered it to her.

She examined it, looking for obvious dirt, then lifted it to her lips, paused, and knocked back a mouthful. The harsh liquor burned around her mouth, her lips tingling. She held it in her throat for a moment, trying not to gag, then gulped it down. It burned down her gullet like hot acid and she winced at the strangely pleasant sensation.

"My, how you say," Tsvetan looked to Thornton for assistance with the language, "*Brat?*"

"Brother."

"Yes – my brother. He make. Is good?"

"Mmm, yes," she exaggerated.

"More?" Tsvetan eagerly grabbed the bottle and was about to top up the cup but she put a hand over it and shook her head.

"Perhaps later."

Tsvetan seemed confused and tried to force more liquor into the cup. Thornton intervened and waved Tsvetan back, muttering some words in Bulgarian.

"In Bulgaria they nod for no and shake their head for yes."

"*Oh!*" she realised the confusion then felt guilty for refusing his hospitality as Tsvetan's eyes dropped in disappointment.

"We keep the smaller artefacts in here," said Thornton, back to business. He thumped the top of the filing cabinet.

"Oh right," she replied.

Tsvetan waved her onto the couch and she smiled politely, as the cushions folded her in, like an enormous marshmallow mouth.

"We could use some help cataloguing it all. Do you think you can do that?"

"Sure. Where do I start?"

VARNA, BULGARIA –1998

August

"Is Tsvetan not joining us?"

Sasha slid into the chair opposite David Thornton and he watched, enthralled, as she set her handbag down on the white linen tablecloth. A suspicious look on her face. He tried to hide his deceit but was conscious she could read it in his eyes.

"No. He couldn't make it," he said, and glanced away looking for a waiter to use as a distraction.

His student glanced around at the lavish surroundings of the Bistro.

Lush feathery palms licked up the corners of the room and a constellation of flickering candles lit up the islands of tables laid out for two.

Had he gone too far? Was it too romantic here?

"You didn't ask him did you David? Go on, admit it," she sounded severe. He twiddled his thumbs together on the table and looked down, preoccupied with the weave of the tablecloth.

"No. No Sash, I didn't," he admitted, forcing a smile. His face burning up.

What the hell are you doing? His inner chatterbox yelled.

"I see," she frowned.

David took a breath and found the courage to look at her. He could see in her eyes she was flattered by the gesture, like a beacon behind a sheet of ice. His shoulders loosened, it seemed his gamble had paid off.

"I wasn't sure if you'd come if you knew," he confessed, brushing his hair from his face and fiddling with the arms of his spectacles.

"Why wouldn't I come?" said Sasha, taking her bag off the table and offering him a smile.

For weeks the pressure to confess what he was feeling had been building. Every synapse had been screaming to him this was a bad idea yet his rib cage throbbed under the weight of it. She was beautiful, fresh and adoring. He felt like she understood him, and could see her potential. A quality he found appealing.

Ann had always been there for him, loyal and loving, but in their years of marriage he never felt she was a match for him on an intellectual level. They had long been leading separate lives. But Sasha was here, right now, and he was sure she wanted him too. He had batted the possibilities around in his mind for days and necked a couple of glasses of Tsvetan's homebrew before coming out tonight. He was a decisive man, and now was the time to act, before he lost his chance, or his nerve. He let it out.

"I feel so foolish doing this, but I love every moment we have together, Sash. You make me feel ten years younger. I know I'm old enough to be your father and everything, but I feel so, I don't know – alive - when you're around."

He was breathless from the confession, it had been building for weeks.

Sasha blushed and giggled at the compliment. He watched, captivated, as she swept her unruly blonde curls behind her ears and rested her peachy pert cheeks in her hands.

"If I'd known you were asking me on a date David, I would have made more of an effort."

"You always look beautiful Sash."

He finally said it, then fell silent, waiting for her reaction. The social overtures played out. It was a relief when the waiter sidled over and jabbered in Bulgarian at the couple, and broke the deadlock.

"I got the word 'menu' but…" Sasha held a hand out to David, encouraging him to take over. He enjoyed her submission, he liked that - attractive and willing to allow him to take the lead. He responded to the waiter in stilted Bulgarian, keen to impress her. Acknowledging him, the waiter bowed and then scuttled off.

"What did you say?" asked Sasha said with a polite smile, changing the subject.

"I asked if they had an English menu. He said they don't get asked often but he'd go and find out. In the mean time he's going to bring us a wine list."

"Oh, okay." She folded her hands across her lap and sat back in the chair.

He was nervous again, wondering if he had overstepped the mark, "Is wine okay?"

"Sure, why not. It's not really the kind of place to ask for Kamenitsa is it?" she said.

He laughed, "You can have beer if you want?"

"No, no. Wine's good."

"I like Bulgarian wine," he said, "I'm surprised it's not more widely available actually, but I don't think they produce enough of it for export…" he stopped himself and hung his head, "Sorry – I'm a boring old git, I know."

"Don't be silly," her voice was chirpy and encouraging, "You're not boring at all. You'd be excellent in a pub quiz!"

"Oh cheers."

He sulked. In his work, he was always supremely confident, but when speaking to young women, his quiet insecurities crept into his thoughts.

"No I mean it," she unlaced her fingers and drew a hand onto the table to reach for his. He stiffened, surprised by the affection and she withdrew, giggling, "Sorry."

"Don't be," he smiled. Her empathy was heartening, she seemed to sense his insecurity but wanted him to be relaxed around her, it filled him with hope. For a moment their eyes fixed across the table, before he looked away, intimidated by the intensity of the moment. The awkward silence was broken into by the waiter approaching, waving a leather bound booklet at them. David offered a polite smile, took the menu from the waiter and thanked him in Bulgarian.

"Is that the wine list or the English menu?" asked Sasha.

"Both!" he said, waving the booklet at her, and then spread the pages open on the table. He ran his eyes down the front page and selected a wine, checking only whether Sasha wanted red or white and assuming she knew little about wine. There was nervous silence as they exchanged glances, allowing telling little smiles. They decided on food, ordered and waited.

"Did I miss much this afternoon?" David resumed the conversation.

"Nothing much. While you were at the meeting at the Archaeological Museum I finished cataloguing those pot shards we found earlier in the week."

"That was quick. Well done," he hoped he hadn't sounded condescending, he was aware he was predisposed to it, having dealt with so many students who seemed more interested in drinking than learning. Sasha was different, she impressed him more than any other student, and on many levels.

"I thought it would have taken you much longer than a couple of days, there were nearly 200 individual pieces there," he said, trying to make it sound like a compliment.

"I methodically worked through them, piece by piece. In fact, many of them fitted together. I believe most of the shards were from only about 20 individual pots and urns, many stained with tannin from wine."

"Very impressive Sash. You'll have to show me tomorrow. Still, that was quick work."

She looked like a frightened. He wondered if anyone had ever complimented her, she seemed so uncomfortable accepting them and offered an excuse for herself.

"I was always good at jigsaw puzzles. I like taking small pieces, finding a pattern and putting them together to build a larger picture, it's satisfying work."

"Well, it seems you are certainly more than cut out for the work of a professional archaeologist. I have high hopes for a future Doctor, Sasha Blake!" he wasn't exaggerating. If only he had met this extraordinary young woman years ago, his choices would have been different.

"Doctor? I'm still only part way through my Masters."

"Well, rest assured you will certainly receive a glowing report from me towards your thesis," he said.

Sasha blushed, "Well, thank you David, that's kind of you."

"Nonsense," he said, irritated she thought he was being kind, he wasn't, he was being honest.

"It's not about kindness, you've done well."

The waiter strode over, arms spread wide and loaded with silver platters of colourful clay dishes, steaming with the inviting smell of fresh cooked meat and vegetables. The warm scent of spicy tomatoes and paprika drifted over the table. They both thanked the waiter in Bulgarian as he slapped dish after dish between them with a clattering flourish. Sharing the vegetables and potatoes, they tucked in.

They ate quietly before Sasha picked up the thread of conversation.

"Tsvetan said the geophysics team returned yesterday with magnetometers?"

"That's right. With a Chalcolithic Age site, and given the amount of precious metals found there, I thought it would be a useful way to survey other parts of the site to determine the full extent of it."

Sasha nodded, finishing a mouthful of potato,

"He said you believe the site is bigger than we first thought?"

"Hmm," nodded David, chewing through a forkful of meat, "There seems to be another burial on the eastern edge of the site. It's unusual because it doesn't fit with the established pattern of the other graves."

"Tsvetan said a distinctive shape showed up on the magnetometer – it looked like a box?"

"It's too small to be a casket for an adult."

David trailed off, he had already said too much.

"So do you think it's a casket for a child then?" Sasha finished his sentence.

He fidgeted, trying to keep the unease off his face, before looking away, "Possibly, but if it is, it's the only one."

"Maybe the child was particularly special? Nobility perhaps?"

He could see in Sasha's eyes she was getting wrapped up in

the excitement of a potential discovery and her enthusiasm was infectious.

"But why single out one burial in a casket? It makes no sense. There are no other caskets at the site. Copper Age settlers don't typically bury their dead in a casket. And judging by some of the burials and the riches found with the remains, there are some far more important people interred there."

It was a useful diversion, but he had been hoping to find the box. If it was the box he had been searching for his entire career - it seemed to fit. He had thought he was close before, only to have his hopes dashed. It didn't hurt to speculate over what else it could be.

"Is it possible the grave is later?" Sasha asked, she sounded incredulous.

They both knew if there was a later burial at this site, it was a huge discovery. There was no documented evidence anywhere in the Bulgarian archives making reference to the Varna Necropolis. All he had was what had been given to him and Dr Kamel. He knew there was no reference in Russian or Ottoman texts either, all he had was theory and superstition. Everything pointed to the first evidence of the site being discovered in 1972, which meant a later burial begged the questions; who put it there? Why? And why did they make no mention in any texts about the discovery of the site?

"It's an interesting find."

Conscious his words were inconsistent with his flat, emotionless tone. He saw the familiar flutter of anticipation in Sasha, he had felt it himself so many times in his long career.

"Interesting?" she chirped, "It's incredible! When are we going to dig it up?"

Thornton let out a small laugh, the last thing he wanted was to involve her.

"One thing at a time," he said, "We still have a lot to do at the existing excavation pits, without digging up more. We haven't even got permission to dig there yet. It could be weeks before it comes out of the sausage machine of Bulgarian bureaucracy."

Sasha slumped back into the chair like a sack of potatoes. David felt awful for crushing her enthusiasm, but he needed to curb it. The consequences were too frightening to contemplate, and he had already made plans for how she would fit into the mix.

"There are still discoveries to be made. Patience. You've done well so far. In fact, I think I can trust you with other responsibilities."

Sasha blushed again. She had spent most of her time in the office with Tsvetan cataloguing finds and piecing together tiny bits of pottery and he hoped the promise of other responsibilities and opportunities would keep her occupied - she barely had any dirt under her manicured fingernails.

"Thank you," she muttered and shoved a forkful of meat in her mouth to hide her face from him.

"I mean it," he reached across the table and stroked her arm. Her skin felt so soft and supple, he longed to find out if all of her skin was like that. He watched as she noticed his rings glint in the candlelight, noticing he was wearing two rings on that finger. He drew his hand away, partly feeling guilty about Ann, but also to avoid any awkward questions.

"Is that an eternity ring?" she asked, brushing her finger along the engraved surface of the heirloom.

"Sort of," he flashed an awkward smile. He blinked away, and concentrated on the last morsel of food on his plate. He wasn't ready to tell her about that ring – perhaps one day, when this was all over.

After they had eaten, and drank some thick syrupy coffees, he was impatient to leave. He could feel his desire for Sasha swelling and knew if it didn't happen tonight, it probably never would. Their lives would be taking different courses after tonight.

"Should we get the bill?" he asked.

"Sure. I'll ask for it though, I could do with the practice."

David waved over the waiter and Sasha asked for the bill in the best Bulgarian she could manage, "*Smetka molya.*"

"Very good," he threw her a smile, worried he sounded

patronising. He glanced across the restaurant several times, to hand over a wedge of notes so they could make the most of the time they still had together.

They walked back down the boulevard to the hotel, arms linked. David guided a tipsy Sasha, who staggered and giggled for much of the walk in the warm evening air. When they arrived in the hotel reception they hesitated by the lift, each waiting for the other to make the next move.

"Did you want to come up for a drink?" Sasha broke the tension. There was no hesitation in his response, he had wanted this so much and until that moment, didn't know if she felt the same. His arousal swelled and he cast his eyes up and down her exquisite form, imagining how she would look sprawled naked in front of him.

VARNA, BULGARIA – 1998

Friday

"Morning!" chirped David as Sasha trudged across the site towards the cabin. David and Tsvetan were stood in the shade of the hut, looking at a crumpled map of the excavation.

"Morning," she said. She felt vulnerable and small and slid towards them with heavy feet.

"You not well? You seem not good today?" asked Tsvetan, his eyes narrowed with genuine concern. She usually arrived at the site each morning with a spring in her step but she couldn't summon the energy.

"I'm fine, just a little tired," she told him, forcing a smile. He shrugged and stepped into the hut.

"Chai?" Tsvetan shouted, offering them all some tea.

"No thanks," mumbled David and Sasha in unison. David flashed a smile at Sasha, but she refused to return it. Her stomach wound itself into a knot. Alone together, David folded the map up, dropped it onto a faded plastic chair by the door and took a tentative step towards her, extending a hand as if he were about to pull her into his arms. She shrugged away, as if a thousand microscopic insects were trailing across her flesh.

"What?"

He seemed irritated. That had been the intention but causing him only a minor irritation hardly seemed sufficient after he left her feeling so humiliated.

"Never mind."

Sasha launched up the steps into the hut to join Tsvetan, sure that David was scrutinising her every step, searching for any clues to her sour mood. She wanted him to feel guilty for what he'd done, perhaps even doubt his sexual prowess. She had given herself to him and now she had never felt so cheap and dirty.

She allowed herself a furtive glance towards him, wondering what he was thinking, if he even cared. He was serving an agenda that was his alone. She watched him shrug, pick up the map and walk to the eastern side of the site, confidence in his stride. It took all her willpower not to run across to him and slap his lying face.

She stepped into the cool interior of the site hut, glad of the shade. Even this early in the day the heat outside leached her energy.

"So you not want chai?" asked Tsvetan again, offering her his familiar kind smile. He may have looked intimidating, but over the past weeks she had learnt he was far from it. All he ever wanted to do was to help and serve others. He took great pleasure in helping his elderly mother with her smallholding at weekends and often bought produce in for the team - that day he had bought in some goats' cheese and bread. When Sasha entered the hut she was met with the welcoming smell of freshly baked bread. It made her smile.

"Go on then. I'll take a chai to go with some of your mother's bread."

Tsvetan flashed a broad smile at her, pleased she'd accepted his hospitality.

"You sit, you sit. I do breakfast," he waved her into the squashy couch while he fussed about cutting the bread, boiling the kettle and finding some relatively clean plates.

Sasha sat, gazing out through the open door across the site. For a moment, she forgot her cares and smiled to herself. She was actually here, she was at the Varna Necropolis. It lifted her spirits to remind herself of that.

A few minutes later, Tsvetan joined on the couch, a little too close for comfort. He was balancing a plate and two tea cups in his hands. She took one of the cups from him and he set the plate down on her lap. Two fat doorsteps of bread perched on the plate like scavenging gulls, a wedge of goats' cheese on each.

"*Molya* (please)," gestured Tsvetan, and Sasha took one of

the chunks with a grateful smile.

"*Merci* (thanks)," she bit down into the soft warm bread with a satisfied hum. They sat quietly, enjoying the bread for a moment, exchanging smiles with Hamsters cheeks.

"So, Doctor David," Tsvetan's mouth still full, crumbs sparked with his words, "He say you leaving?"

Sasha was used to Tsvetan's horrible table manners now and ignored them, more concerned about what he had just said.

"I'm not planning on leaving. What makes you say that?"

"There," he pointed at the desk, a card wallet printed with the British Airways livery was strategically placed on the keyboard in front of where she always sat, "This not yours?" he seemed confused.

She frowned, set her plate aside and stretched across the hut. She reached for the ticket wallet and hesitated. A dull ache throbbed through her, as if her heart was pumping acid into her veins. She sat in the wonky operators chair and peeled open the flap. Sure enough, a one way ticket for her to Istanbul, the flight was leaving that evening.

The acid turned to fire, burning an engulfing rage through her. She leapt out of the chair and stormed out. In her mind she played out the scenarios – what could she say to hurt him? The desire for revenge was both painful and empowering in equal measure.

Tsvetan stared at her, so shocked he stopped mid-mouthful and a dollop of cheese fell from his lip and landed in his lap.

She jumped the steps out of the hut, landing awkwardly on the side of her foot. She winced but ignored the discomfort and half jogged-half limped across the site.

Now it made sense to her. The coward had slid silently out of her bed on Saturday night, then spent 24 hours ignoring her and working out the best way to get rid of her. Now she realised he couldn't face breaking the news to her, and he was avoiding her, taking refuge in the far easterly corner of the excavation.

He was turned away, gazing into the distance, surveying the

terrain in the area around where the mysterious box was buried, seen only through the magnetic eyes of technology, deep in the earth.

"Hey!" she shouted, power walking towards him, her arms long and stiff like oars propelling her along a river of rage.

He leaned around, looking over his shoulder. A ghost of a smile fluttered across his face.

"What the fuck is this?"

Sasha threw the ticket wallet at him - an insult personified.

"Calm down. It's not what you think."

Turned to face her now he wafted his arms like palm leaves as if he could cool her down.

"Calm down? Don't tell me to calm down!"

David hunched his shoulders, as if her voice was scraping up his spine, like fingernails on slate. He winced, she felt like slapping him, but lost her nerve.

"So this is why you snuck out in the night? What was it, hmm? Wham bam thank you ma'am? You bastard. I'm not your fucking whore you know!"

She wanted the words to cut deep.

"That's not fair Sash, come on, be reasonable…"

How dare he tell her how to behave?

"Reasonable, my arse! What's reasonable about packing me off to Istanbul the moment you got your shag?" she knew how cruel it sounded and was glad of it, anything to get a reaction, "How many other students have you lured to bed with you then sent them packing?"

"It's not like that!" his voice raised an octave, almost pleading.

His pathetic stoop, floppy hair and big kind eyes. They conspired to work their magic on her.

How did he do that to her?

He had made her feel so good, his fingers so gentle between her thighs, his lips so warm and inviting, only to toss her aside when he'd had his fill.

"Then what is it like? Hmm? I thought this meant something," her eyes moistened, "You know. I thought there was…a chance…more than…" she sniffed back a tear and cut off. Her heart was tearing itself apart.

How could he be so callous?

"It is!" he reached a hand towards her, blinking sympathetically.

"Don't," she shrugged him off, the anger rising once more. Whatever they both felt, she wanted an explanation, she deserved that at least. She stared at him in a wordless request, trying to stay focused.

"I promise, one day I'll explain all of this to you, and I hope you will understand why I sent you away from this place. There is a dark shadow here, a demon. Something beyond nature lurks in this dirt. And it knows I'm here," he swirled his foot around in the dry dusty earth, his eyes glazing over as he stared out into the distance again, out to the horizon as if the answers would come trotting over the crest on a brilliant white horse. Instead the sun beat down its intensity and baked everything around them. Her head throbbed as her brow crinkled. The sun licking its fiery tongue on her unprotected arms, uncomfortable in her own skin. David was speaking in riddles and she was losing patience. She'd been dumped before, but never because of demons, it was the worst dump line she'd ever heard.

"Fine!"

Sasha stomped back to the hut. It still made no sense, but right then, all she wanted was to get as far away as possible from the bastard who had used her.

ISTANBUL, TURKEY –1998

August

Sasha took a deep breath, her fist poised, then rapped on the tall oak door before pushing it open.

"Dr Kamel?" She called out as she leaned around it, "The door was ajar.

"Are you here?"

She gingerly stepped in, her trainers squeaking on the lino. The room had that familiar academic feel. A beautiful old building, functional 1960's melamine and caustic strip lighting shoehorned into its former grace. The sound of a chesty smokers cough burst through the silence and she span around.

"Hello?"

Sasha walked deeper into the gloomy network of partitioned offices.

Despite the feelings of betrayal that dogged her, she had come this far and intended to make the most of her trip to Istanbul. She had long been an admirer of Dr Kamel's work, and had she not been so bitter about David, she would have been more excited about meeting another of her professional idols.

Her relationship with David had gone past the point of no return now. Feeling used and rejected, part of her was glad to get away from him, but she was already missing him more than she could stomach.

"Come through," a gruff, heavily accented voice cut through the thick air and she followed it.

Past one of the partitions she saw a stout little man with a leathery complexion and narrow eyes. He waved her forwards, not bothering to get up from behind the thick wooden battlement of his desk. Stacks of books surrounded it like ramparts. In front of him was a computer monitor, stained brown from tobacco smoke. The room smelt like a stale ashtray. A dirty half-light seeped through the buckled venetian blinds that covered the row of long sash windows, making the room seem more squalid.

"So you must be the girl?" A glint bloomed in his eye like a dying ember, "Hmmm, now I see why Thornton favours you," he chuckled to himself, which then broke into a cough. Sasha's skin crawled, realising the chubby Turk was staring directly at her breasts. She tugged her vest top higher to cover her cleavage.

"Come in, come in," he barked.

"Dr Kamel?" She wanted to be sure it was him - part of her hoped it wasn't.

"What do you think?" he rolled his eyes, "Come on then, come here so I can look at you," she shuffled deeper into the wolfs lair. He hummed to himself and stroked his small pointed beard, his eyes travelling up and down her body. It was as if he was eyeing her up to trade her, like a prized goat or donkey. She felt grubby, and not just from the flight.

"Sit then!"

His face was pained with irritation. This wasn't the reception she had expected.

"Thornton said you were a good little cataloguer? Good with spread sheets and files. Very organised. Yes good, very good," he seemed to be having the conversation with himself as his voice trailed off. She wondered if there was a question in there somewhere. She angled herself into an uncomfortable looking old school chair on the opposite side of the desk and fidgeted like a bird pattering around on a thin branch, before forcing herself to sit still.

"I enjoy puzzles yes. I like to put the pieces together to build up a bigger picture," she said, trying to sound enthusiastic.

"Yes, yes, very interesting," muttered Kamel. Clearly not interested. He looked down at his desk, losing contact with his guest utterly. She painted a smile on her face, expecting feedback from a man who was supposed to be teaching her.

He fumbled around on his desk, itself a dig site of layers of debris, collected over many generations. Paper covered the entire surface and with increasing urgency he peeled back the layers searching for something precious. He laid his hands on it and his whole demeanour loosened with relief. Sasha, in misplaced hope, wondered if he was about to reveal something fascinating to her, but instead he excavated a crumpled, half empty cigarette packet from under the rubble. He slid a cigarette from the packet and gripped it between his lips like he was sucking on a wounded finger. Then he slid a cheap plastic lighter out of the packet and unapologetically flicked it a couple of times until it burst into life. He took a couple of satisfied puffs and returned to reality, eyeing her suspiciously. A billow of smoke circled her head like a demonic halo. She held her breath so she didn't cough, the last thing she needed was to give him further excuses to be irritated by her.

"So - what do you want to know?"

A wave of rediscovered tolerance seemed to breathe through him with the nicotine.

Her smile softened, "Well I was hoping to get an insight into the forensic examination of the bodies from the Varna Necropolis?"

Kamel let out a burst of guttural coughing, choking on her words as much as the smoke.

A cruel smile gouged across his face, "I don't think that would be appropriate, dear. Do you?" he phrased it like a question, as if Sasha had a choice. She tried to hide her disgust and disappointment behind her stoic smile. Really she felt like telling him to fuck himself, then storm out and take the next flight back to the comfort and safety of the student house she shared with her friends in Fulham. Instead she swallowed it back, almost gagging on a taste of his second hand smoke, and forced all her courage to the surface.

"Why not professor? I am sure I can be of some help."

"I don't think so, dear," he hauled his fat laden bones up from his seat and walked towards the window, keeping his back to her. Behind the protection of the table, and while there was no chance he would, see she flicked him the bird and mouthed 'fuck you'.

Kamel teased apart a gap in the venetian blind, as if he were opening a moldy sandwich to check if the innards were worth salvaging, and squinted into the early evening sunlight. A chink of buttery sunlight filtered in. He partially turned to face her, the limp cigarette blinking a red glow through the sludgy gloom.

"No, no. I think I shall have you in the archive, sorting and cataloguing some pot shards."

More bloody pot shards and still no corpses, she thought.

"Did Dav…Dr Thornton, tell you about the work I had done piecing together some shards in Varna?"

The cigarette glowed brighter for an instant, then went out, a thread of smoke curling up from the stump. He coughed before responding, almost spitting the dead stump from his lip where it was stuck by an invisible tether.

"He did. Why else would I assign you the task?" He sniffed. He tugged a crumpled grey handkerchief from his pocket and spat a mucus ball into it. She tried to hide her contempt, but her eyes narrowed.

"You must start somewhere my dear. We can't all be professors," he scoffed and fired a condescending smile as he turned away from the window. His chubby fingers let the blind drop then he tugged the dead shriveled finger from his lip and dropped it into a waste bin on top of a small mountain of other charred and discarded filter tips.

"Now then," his voice was muffled. He had his back to her and rummaged through a cardboard filing box behind his desk, "I know I have a notepad in here somewhere," he muttered.

Sasha folded her arms, closing them around herself as a protective shield.

"Ah. Here we are!" he span on a heel and flung a dog-eared spiral notebook across his desk towards her. A raft of papers slid with it, teetering on the desk like a car skidding towards a cliff edge.

She flinched, half expecting a heap of tobacco tinged paper

to land in her lap. Kamel nodded towards the book with a crooked frown, failing to even attempt to make eye contact with her as he barked information at her.

"Write all this down. I don't want you forgetting any of it and bothering me with petty questions, I'm a busy man."

She nodded.

Busy my arse. Busy smoking maybe – said her internal chatterbox.

"Of course Doctor Kamel," the insincere smile that accompanied her obedience was transparent, but Kamel was too wrapped up to notice.

"The archive room is in the basement. The lift is at the bottom of the corridor on the left. At the basement level take the 3rd door on the right. NOT the others. Stay away from the other doors. Is that clear?"

Sasha nodded.

"You are writing this down aren't you?"

"I can remember."

"No – write!"

She fixed her eyes on the page and scribbled nonsensically in the book.

"The key code for the door to the archive is 7-1-2-6. Got that?"

"Yes."

"Repeat it back."

"7-1-2-6"

He huffed and continued, "The cabinets are labelled up, in Bulgarian and Turkish. You do speak and read both languages I assume?"

Sasha's eyes drifted.

"Oh for goodness sake. Learn," he barked. He offered no more assistance than that and she silently seethed.

"Ca…" she began before being cut off by Kamel's blade-like tongue.

"I am not finished. Do not interrupt me," Kamel drew in a deep sigh and she clamped her lips shut before she blurted out something she may later regret.

"Now. You will find the pot shards concerned in a clearly labelled and referenced set of boxes. Since you have not bothered to learn the basic language of the countries that you are permitted to work in, you will need to cross reference the box numbers with the card index in Dr Elmas's office. Fortunately for you they were started by Dr Thornton and are also translated into English."

"And whe…" Kamel cut her off again by lifting his hand and swatting it through the air as if trying to outsmart a housefly.

"Let me finish. How will you ever learn anything if you do not listen?"

How will I ever learn if I can't ask questions? She thought.

"Dr Elmas is also a busy man. He is my superior and the head of the three Museums; Archaeological Museum, Museum of the Ancient Orient and Museum of Islamic Art. He is usually in his office on a Friday before Jum'ah."

"Friday payers?" Sasha interrupted to make sure she understood.

Kamel fired a withering look, nodded and continued, "He is very busy with the opening of the Thrakia-Bithynia and Byzantium display saloon which is about to be unveiled in the new building. Many of the artefacts from the necropolis feature in this exhibit so you are restricted to the unclassified works. Is that clear."

"Crystal."

Kamel grunted.

The trill of his desk phone gate-crashed their conversation. Kamel picked up the receiver, "*Selam.*"

He waved the back of his hand at her. Her eyebrows knitted together. He glared at her as he listened to the voice on the phone.

He was a vampire - he had a way of sucking the soul from you with a single, withering look. Kamel waved more furiously at her until she realised he was expecting her to leave.

She didn't hesitate, the seat was burning, she was so desperate to get out. She snatched up the notepad, waved goodbye, but by now Kamel was looking at his desk and ignoring her. She might as well have been a ghost.

Sasha stepped back out into the sterile corridor, carefully pulled the door to behind her and took a deep breath. She loosened her shoulders, shook her hair and tousled it lose. It smelt like a night club and she screwed her face up in disgust, already dreaming of getting back to the hotel that evening and stepping into a warm shower.

The screech of her trainers echoed down the grey corridor as she walked towards the lift. She pushed the call button and heard it rattle up the shaft, before announcing its presence with an optimistic ping. In the lift she slumped against the speckled mirror, drumming her fingers on the paneling beneath it, staring at the mustard carpet as if it held some long sought secret. She let the vibration of the floor soothe her as the lift jerked slowly down.

With a ping, the lift shuddered to a halt and the doors slid apart. A cool flow of air washed in making her shiver. She stepped into a dimly lit corridor, whitewashed to make the most of what little artificial light was available. The ceiling was low, slung with a maze of crooked pipework and a shallow hum seemed to vibrate down its chiseled walls.

She took a deep breath of the musty air and stepped out of the lift. She glanced left and right into the narrow corridor, both sides fading away into a lifeless murk. The opposite wall was lined with anonymous doors, each with a code keypad. She took the third door on the right as instructed, wondering what could be hidden behind the other doors that Kamel seemed so keen for her not to find.

When she tapped in the code, she entered another world. She stepped out of the barren corridor and down into a dark hole. A light automatically buzzed into life, illuminating a barrel vaulted stone cell in the bowels of the old building. She stepped down four heavily worn stone steps into the chamber. It smelt of damp stone, like a medieval church. The room was small, with no natural light. The florescent strip light was incongruous with the ancient space. Plastic trunking fed the parasitic 20th Century light, and clung precariously like a tape worm around the belly of the room. It could have been a wine cellar, bunker or a dungeon in a former life. The back wall, a few metres ahead, was lined with a regimental row of grey steel filing cabinets. Each the same, at three drawers high, their tops level with her chest, like a miniature firing squad lined up to face her. There was nothing else in the room except an old school desk with a faded plastic chair tucked under it.

Her heart quickened as she stepped closer to the cabinets. Each was labelled in Bulgarian and Turkish, she didn't know enough of either language to even make an educated guess. She gave way to her impulsive nature and opened a drawer at random. She had chosen a middle drawer in a middle cabinet. She leaned over to peer in. Inside was a carpet of crumpled up evidence bags, filled with muddy chunks of history. The warming energy of discovery flowed through her veins. She reached into the frothy plastic soup and took out a bag.

She tried to remember what Kamel and told her about the record keeping system. She cursed being too stubborn to write it down as he had instructed. She was also pleased to have defied him, despite it being to her detriment.

"What the hell are you doing?"

A deep male voice reverberated like a shotgun in the tiny cell. She had been so absorbed, she hadn't heard anyone come in behind her. She felt herself flush red, then cursed that it made her look guilty.

"I...I..." the words defied her.

"Who are you? You have 10 seconds before I alert security."

"I'm..." get a grip Sash, she told herself. She swallowed hard. "My name is Sasha Blake. I'm a student on the Varna Necropolis dig."

"Ah! So you're the girl," the burly man's voice softened. He was tall, heavy set and bursting through the seams of his expensive suit. He had thinning, unnaturally dark 'just for men' hair. His eyes were small and cold as he examined her. He too made her feel dirty, as Kamel had, although not from cigarette smoke, there was something more malevolent flickering behind his coal eyes.

"I suppose I am," she swallowed, trying not to look afraid.

He bounded forwards. His chins wobbled with each step. She cringed. Then a wide grin covered his face. His mouth was full of innumerable yellowed teeth. He held a stubby hand out, each finger laden with a gold ring, like knuckle-dusters. Cautiously, she accepted his hand. He grasped it tightly and shook it so vigorously she was afraid her arm would be tugged from its socket.

"I am Doctor Osman Elmas. You, my dear, may call me Osman," he turned her hand in his and planted a damp kiss across her knuckles with his fat lips. She felt a bead of vomit gather in the back of her throat. She pulled her hand away, slowly enough to be polite and fast enough to ensure minimal physical contact with him.

"Apologies for not being available to meet you earlier. I see that Kamel has told you some of the basics?"

She wondered if the question required an answer, but Elmas was too fond of the sound of his own voice to allow her time to formulate it.

"I trust he also told you the pot shards you are to assemble were in labelled boxes?"

"He did."

"Then why are you looking in the drawer containing artefacts from another site?" he raised an accusing eyebrow, "You should have come to me first and I could have shown you which drawer the boxes were in. Were you going to continue to rifle through drawers that do not concern you?"

She wasn't sure what to say. Perhaps she should have apologised? But she wasn't sorry so why bother. As if he sensed the thought he huffed.

"No matter," he continued, "The boxes you want are in that drawer."

He waved to indicate one of the cabinets on her left.

"Thank you," she said and moved towards the drawer.

Elmas stepped into her path. She swallowed again,

everything about the man made her uncomfortable. She wanted to scratch herself all over, her skin crawling.

"My dear. Without having the reference cards from my office how will you know what is what?" he offered her a condescending smile, "Come on, we will go to my office where I can assist you." The haughty smile became oily, his dark eyes glowing.

She wandered if in his head the sentence finished 'I can assist you… to remove your clothes.' The thought made her stomach churn, but what choice did she have? She was a guest in his museum. If she upset him, he could make life difficult for her. He was a man of reach.

She offered a compliant smile.

He ushered her out, a plump hand drifting dangerously close to contact with the small of her back, which encouraged her to move.

She stepped back out into the antiseptic corridor, Elmas close behind her. He moved to her side, brushing against her and went ahead to get to the lift before her. They stepped into the confined box his thick frame filling half of the space. The heat of his fishy breath and sweat, poorly disguised with sickly cologne, filled the lift. Beads of sweat formed down her neck and spine, her skin still itching. She wanted to run to the nearest shower, barricade herself in, tear off her clothes and scrub herself raw. Instead, she pressed the button for floor three as instructed and stood quietly, avoiding eye contact.

Elmas cleared his throat.

'Oh god he's going to speak to me'

"So, how are you finding Istanbul?"

He clasped his hands behind his back and rocked back and forth on his heels.

"Fine."

"Have you been exploring yet?"

"No."

"I can show you around some of the city's sights of you like?"

Normally, the idea of having a personal tour of a city so

steeped in culture and rich in archaeology from arguably one of its foremost national experts, would have been a dream come true.

"I don't think I'll have the time."

'I'll be washing my hair', she smiled to herself as she thought of it.

"I can arrange time if you want. After all, this is my museum."

He raised his arm with a flourish, "I can make a slot in your workload, I'm sure it would be of benefit to your studies?"

Shit, how would she refuse now?

"That's kind of you, but I know how busy you are. Especially with the launch of the Thrakia-Bithynia and Byzantium display."

He insisted, "I can delegate that work. I have done my part now."

"Still, I wouldn't want to inconvenience you."

The oily smile returned. He unwound his arms and slithered a hand out to rest nonchalantly on the side of the lift. She cursed how slowly it was travelling as it trundled and shuddered up the shaft.

"My dear," she cringed at his instance on calling her that, inside she was screaming 'I'm nobodies dear, least of all yours', "You could never be an inconvenience."

'Ping' and she was rescued by the lift. When the doors opened, she stopped herself from leaping out of it and running away, like a bird, released from its cage.

He dropped his hands to his sides, shook out his suit and slid his hands into his pockets. He stepped out and walked alongside her and rummaged his hands in his pockets. She wondered if it was a nervous gesture or if he was touching himself. The bile surfaced in her throat and she shook the thought away.

"This way."

He stepped ahead, slowed and took a hand out to reach for the door. He held it open for her, but stood in the frame, forcing her to slither past him to get in.

He gestured her deeper into his lair.

"I keep the card index in my desk. Come, come," he waved her forwards, "And shut the door," she stepped back to shut the door. It creaked and slammed like a prison door.

"I'm sorry about the mess. Do take a seat."

She looked around. The only seat had a pile of books on it. She hesitated by it.

"Go on, just put those on the floor and bring the chair closer," he sounded breathless as he searched his desk drawer.

She did as he asked and noticed he was momentarily distracted by her bending over and stretching to pick up the old wooden chair and bring it closer to his desk.

"You work out do you?"

"I'm sorry?" she said, horrified.

"You seem very fit and muscular. Slim. Almost boyish," he said, leering at her, undressing her with his soulless eyes.

"I beg your pardon?" Sasha's voice cranked up an insulted notch.

"Forgive me," he shrank back a little, like a snake withdrawing, seeing she could defend herself.

"My English clumsy." He deliberately omitted grammatical structure in his words, just to prove the point. "I observe that this work, it normally done by young men. I see few women Archaeologists," she tried to hide her offence, "It good. It a good thing. There need more women in the job," he cleared his throat and blushed.

"You know, Plato said that if we are to treat women the same as men then we should educate them in the same way," he said, as his words reverted from pervert to expert, his English miraculously improved.

"He was a wise man," she said, flexing her eyebrows..

Elmas chuckled, his chins wobbling, "The very wisest of men."

No she'd seen the two sides of the man. She liked to think she was a good judge of character – although maybe she'd been wrong about David? Of Elmas she judged that; he was an expert in his field, a man of great knowledge who deserved the respect of his contemporaries, but there was a seedy aspect to his character, an underlying sadistic force that guided part of him. The way his eyes stripped her naked, the way he compared her to a boy and said 'young man' with such adoration in his voice. His attempts to be charming by kissing her hand and pandering to her femininity with his references to the need for more women in the profession. She got the impression he wanted more women in the profession so he could leer at them, not because he valued their contribution. She wondered if Kamel was seeking to emulate the man, they both seemed of a similar disposition, but Kamel seemed tame in comparison, once you got past his lack of social awareness, he had none of the malevolence of Elmas.

Sasha shifted from foot to foot, as if she were limbering her legs up to run away.

"Can I offer you a drink?"

"No thank you sir."

He gave a small laugh.

"Please. Osman is fine. I only have tea or water anyway. If you were expecting me to ply you with alcohol you are mistaken."

His tone turned mean, her heart quickened, "Allah does not allow such sin."

His emphasis on the word 'sin' was sharp and defiant, as if he were in conflict over its meaning.

"Bring the seat my dear. I want to show you something."

Sasha warily pulled the crooked wooden chair closer to the desk. Elmas levered himself into a high backed leather chair and squeezed under the desk. He fumbled about in the top drawer while she waited, both curious and suspicious.

Before he continued, there was a loud knock at the door.

"Come!" he shouted. She jumped in her skin.

Dr Kamel came rushing in. His face slicked with sweat, his hair ragged, his tie twisted and shirt half untucked. He didn't even acknowledge her.

The two men exchanged some furious words in Turkish. Elmas looked unimpressed. Kamel looked desperate.

"Wait here," Elmas barked the order at her. With that he unplugged himself from behind the desk, furiously gestured and chattered to Kamel in Turkish and they both left the room. The door slammed. She listened to their footsteps moving down the corridor at speed.

She sat for a few minutes, it felt an age, her foot bouncing. She crossed her legs, huffed, drummed her fingers on her knee. She dropped her head into her hands, growled and tugged at her hair.

Fuck it, she said to herself and jumped out of the chair as if it had just electrocuted her.

She buried her hands into her waist and looked around the room. It was bright. A row of tall sash windows lining a wall that overlooked the gardens below. She stepped over to look out, bright sunshine penetrating everywhere, tempered only by a film of yellow smog in the air. She pulled one of the windows up and let in the impatient cacophony of car horns. She breathed in hot polluted air and slammed the window shut. She turned and leaned against it, folding her arms, resting her hips against the glass and looked around the room.

It was tall and spacious. The old decorative plasterwork and architraves were peeling, cobwebs and dust covering every surface that could not be easily reached. It would have been a splendid baroque space once, but at floor level it was covered with the clutter of a modern office. Filing boxes, reams of paper, filing cabinets, bowing shelves of books and mismatched melamine furniture. She looked at the layers with the eyes of an archaeologist. The earliest strata was the building, with all its crumbling finery. The partition wall that split off this part of a large former gallery into a big office looked 50's. On the floor, a threadbare carpet, unchanged since the 60's. The tables from the 70's, the filing cabinets from the 80's. The microfiche machine in the corner from the 70's. The PC next to it from the 90's.

She wanted to unpeel the layers and make another discovery. She was interrupted.

Elmas stormed back in.

"What is it?"

"It's the Police."

"Here? Why?" She was confused, feeling guilty but she didn't know why. She had thought about going through Elmas' things but hadn't done it. Thinking something wasn't against the law. At least, in Turkey, she didn't think it was.

"What do they want to know?"

"They are asking about Thornton," Elmas was breathless. He went to his desk and dug through the drawers once more. "Dammit!" he cursed.

"What?"

"I can't find the card index."

"What about Thornton? And why do you need the card index?"

"Because until you have tapped the information into that, it's the only record we have of the artefacts at the Varna site!" He prodded a fat finger towards her and then to the PC as if he had asked her to do something and she had refused.

"Why Thornton? What's he done?" She was surprised at how worried she was for him – Was he okay? Was he in trouble?

"It seems he left Varna unexpectedly," he paused and looked at her, defeat painted all over his face, she almost felt sorry for him.

"They have reason to believe he has stolen an artefact from the dig site."

Shock gripped her like stone, "Stolen? David? There has to be a misunderstanding? He has always been vocal about his hatred of antiquities smuggling. I can't believe he'd take something from his own site. For what purpose?" She couldn't comprehend it. She was confused and frightened. If David could do such a thing, the world could collapse in on itself and swallow her whole.

"I know! It makes no sense. Where the fuck is my card index. I bet that blundering fool Kamel has it."

It was as if they were having two separate conversations. More worried about covering his own back by finding the only comprehensive record he had of the artefacts than the fact the world had lost its senses if a man like David Thornton could turn rogue.

"You must excuse me. I need to follow this up." Elmas emerged from behind the desk with more agility than Sasha thought was possible for the overweight old man, and he made for the door.

"Where are you going?"

"Out."

"Should I come? Perhaps I can be of help?"

"No, no. It wouldn't be right. I need to speak to some…people. They don't appreciate… westerners…" He paused, looked her up and down with a sneer, and curling his lips he elaborated, "…especially women."

He left the room and slammed the door behind him.

"Dr Elmas!" she called after him, knowing it was futile. Sasha cursed to herself, stamped a foot then slumped into the chair to gather her thoughts.

The police? Stealing antiquities?

She let the thought's swim around in her head.

Now what was she supposed to do?

M4, JUNCTION 19, ENGLAND – SEPTEMBER 1998

"You've scarcely spoken David. What's on your mind?" asked Ann.

"Hmm?" David took his eyes off the road for a moment to look at his wife.

"I asked how your trip went. You told me all about the nightmare of a flight and the delays at the airport and how you had to take a detour in Amsterdam, but never told me how the dig went."

"Oh. Yeah. It was fine I suppose," he muttered, turning his attention back to the hypnotic columns of light flicking past in the drizzle.

"Fine I suppose? Is that it?" she pressed, "David. You were so excited about the dig. What went wrong?"

"Nothing went wrong, as such. I just don't feel like talking about it."

"Oh, all right then," Ann shrugged.

"You did remember to put those keys in my desk drawer didn't you?" He asked, anxiety rising in his stomach.

"Of course!" Ann responded with a shrill and critical tone. He had called her from overseas to remind her to do it. He didn't mean to be condescending, but he needed to be sure, "Thanks," he mumbled.

Ann changed the subject.

"Did you manage to catch up with Michael in Amsterdam?"

"Only briefly."

"Is he all right?"

"Yeah, yeah – he's fine. Rich, and stupid as ever." For the first time he offered her a smile, albeit a wry one. Ann sniggered. It was a family joke that David's brother Michael was such a pompous oaf but had all the luck in the world when it came to money.

"Do you want to hear what I've been up to in the weeks you were away?" Ann said. She seemed irritated.

"Sure," he said, with forced enthusiasm. The least he could do was pretend to be interested in the minutia of his wife's life, even though his head was filled with far more pressing concerns. She had driven for four hours to pick him up from Heathrow – for all his distractions, he did appreciate the inconvenience she had gone to.

"Well," she began, "I promised I wouldn't say, but I just can't help it. I have some exciting news for you."

"What's that?"

"Danny asked me what I thought of Sarah and how I would feel about having her as a daughter in law."

"Oh right," David processed the unexpected news.

"Don't you care? Your son is planning to get married!"

"I care about the credit card bill!"

He turned and offered her another sly smile and she slapped him playfully on the arm, "Da-vid!" She chided.

He watched her furtively as she settled back in the passenger seat. He always liked to drive and she was happy to be a passenger on the journey home. She was used to being a passenger in his life. He took it as acceptance of his nomadic ways. If nothing else, he had a duty to the mother of his children. She gazed out at the meandering rain flicking against the window. The only sound was the rhythmic thrumming of the engine and whooshing of the wipers. Outside the world was a bleak shade of grey.

His eyes fixed on the expanding yellow beams at the end of the bonnet. He was the first to break the contemplative silence.

"When we get home, I'll ring Danny and Georgie and arrange a family get together. How's that?" David offered the concession, feeling the need to appease his wife who seemed, rightly, suspicious of him.

"That'd be nice," Ann's response was stilted. Perhaps she knew he was hiding things from her?

His mind swam with thoughts of the beautiful and doting young student he had left behind. It had been years since any woman had showed him such affection, and the promise of it was tantalising. The guilt of abandoning Sasha into the care of his old friend and colleague, Dr Hakan Kamel, ate at his guts and left him nauseous. He longed to see her again, he closed his eyes briefly to picture her beautiful soft face and remember that sweet smile of hers. He ran his tongue across his lip, remembering how she tasted.

What had he done?

He had severed every moral fibre of his being. He had searched all his life for the box, and justified his behaviour by reminding himself of the importance of the mission and of the promises he had pledged. When he left the dig site, it was in the dead of night, taking the artefact with him, knowing it was wrong but fearing the reality of the box and the consequences if it fell into the wrong hands. He had to protect it, he had to hide it. And he had to protect Sasha, which meant removing the one true threat to her safety – himself.

He turned to capture Ann's eyes, for the first time he noticed them. They looked weary and sad, bruised with exhaustion. He had done that to her.

"Ann? Have I…"

The moment was interrupted by screeching tires. Stopping mid-sentence, he looked in the rear view mirror.

A lorry had jack-knifed on the wet road and the tail end of it was careering towards their car at an alarming rate. Instinctively, he jerked the wheel to skid out of its path, but it happened too quickly.

"Oh shi…"

On impact, the back of David's skull travelled out through his face.

THE BRITISH MUSEUM, LONDON - 2004

"Darling, you are only saying that to humour me. Go on, tell the truth. They're hideous aren't they?"

Gregory flapped his hands dramatically and affected a forlorn look. He had drunk far too much champagne and his usual flamboyance was magnified, but he loved the attention and the guests flocked around him.

"Oh don't be so silly!" Sasha leaned into him with a big performance of a hug, joining in with the theatre.

"Really. If your paintings and sculptures were hideous why would the Arts Council have backed the exhibition? Hmm? Everyone loves it. And everyone loves you. Enjoy the moment. It's been years in the making. You deserve it!"

"Oh sweet-heart," his eyes began to glaze with moisture, "You made this possible, it's such a boon, hosting my opening party here at the Museum. I'm blessed to have you as a friend."

Gregory always got emotional when he was drinking. Sasha folded her arm into the crook of his elbow and led him out of the crowd.

"Do excuse me. I…I…" he pressed the back of his hand into his forehead, careful not to touch his perfect sculptural quiff. Sasha apologised to his guests and ushered him to a big lip-shaped seat in the corner, fussing over him.

"Perhaps you should have some water Gregory?" she advised, pressing him into the couch and stepping away.

"Wine darling!" His tone changed to an exuberant one again and she rolled her eyes as she walked away.

Gregory Lepton had studied fine art at the same University as Sasha. He struck up a relationship with a wealthy businessman to sponsor his art, in exchange for 'certain favours' that were to be kept in the strictest of confidence. Gregory had been desperate for a break, and it was a trade-off he was willing to make. It was finally paying off. Sasha, at the time, had made a big fuss about how he 'should never compromise himself' but she was quietly pleased to have the opportunity to hob nob with the rich and famous. He always promised her he would get her an invitation to his first big-break exhibition, and she had pulled a few strings with her contacts at the museum to host it. The glass-covered courtyard was hired out for the occasion. Gregory was reveling in the attention.

She returned to his side a few minutes later with a glass of water but it wasn't long before he was distracted by a well-wisher who approached them to congratulate Gregory on his success. Sasha excused herself and stepped away, glad of the space to breathe for a moment. She was tired of the sycophants who swarmed around Gregory like flies on dung. She had had enough of the evening but felt that it was too soon to leave - so she mingled about in the glasshouse, weaving between the guests. She felt a harsh jolt against her back and stumbled forwards, almost tripping over her impractical shoes. She tried to stay upright forgetting her glass of champagne, until she felt a wet, cold, impact on her foot. She silently cursed and turned around. Behind her was a tall man with dark hair, chocolate eyes and a serious frown.

"Oh, I'm so sorry," he said in a velvety voice.

"It's all right," she grumbled, but permitted herself a small smile.

A sympathetic look tugged at his emotionless face, his eyes hinting at the smile first.

"No. No it's not," he said, sounding apologetic, "Allow me to at least get you another drink?"

She hesitated. His voice was hypnotic. He spoke with a crisp accent, well enunciated words and an even tone – Oxford English, like most of the grey old academics she was used to working with who had hardly left Oxford and were trapped there by its educational institutions. But this man was far from grey. She made a conscious effort not to stare at the man while she cast her eyes over him, drinking him in.

He was wearing a beautifully cut black suit, a crisp white shirt and a black pencil tie. His hair was cropped short at the sides with thick chestnut curls on top, almost military style. He turned his head towards the bar and began to slowly move away. She noticed a spiral of cable snaking down his neck from his ear and disappearing under his jacket collar.

"Security eh? Perhaps you should have been paying more attention?" she said.

At an event full of rich businessmen, she falls for the security guard. Welcome to a life with no money. A little smile escaped onto her lips as she thought it.

"Quite!" he smiled ruefully, as if he'd read it in her eyes. He held an arm up and ushered her towards the bar.

"People will think I'm being escorted out for causing trouble!" she smiled, and the man let out a small laugh.

"Come on. I insist."

She yielded. His arm was a breath away from the small of her back as she followed him. For an indulgent moment she imagined what such a powerful arm would feel like wrapped around her.

The man glanced back and an illegible smile danced across his lips. He was almost head height taller than her. She tucked in behind him, apologising and smiling as they cut through the crowd congregated around the free bar. She felt like that motorist who pulls in behind an ambulance to jump the traffic. The man excused and shouldered his way to the bar and waved to the harassed looking barman.

"Hey Tom!" the barman called, acknowledging the man. Sweat leached from the barman's forehead as he slapped a couple of full pint glasses down in front of another customer then turned his attention to the man.

"Drinking on the job are you, Tom?"

"You're a funny man, Mitch," replied Tom with a sarcastic grin.

"What can I do for you, mate?"

Tom turned to her, "What would you like to drink?"

She smiled at the barman, who had a wide smirk on his face.

"House red?"

"Coming right up!" The barman thumped Tom on the arm as he turned away. She leaned on the bar, watching the him uncork a bottle of wine. She glanced aside to see Tom watching her. He flicked his gaze away, as if he was embarrassed she had caught him staring. A small smile escaped from her lips. She took the opportunity to eye him up more closely. He was slender, with narrow hips and a round tight bottom that flexed appealingly as he leaned on the bar. She followed the seam of his jacket up his spine to his broad shoulders. Through the corner of her eye, she saw the barman approaching and they exchanged a polite smile.

"What time do you knock off?" the barman asked Tom. Tom drew back his sleeve to expose an expensive looking watch.

"About five minutes ago," he stood tall and triumphant.

"Can I get you something then, mate?"

Tom glanced at her, then back at the barman, as if having a conversation with himself.

"Perhaps you could join me? Unless you are in a hurry to get home?" She wasn't sure why she said it but there was something about the handsome security guard that appealed to her.

Tom glanced back and paused. He seemed to be taking in every detail of her. She silently congratulated herself for taking Gregory's advice and choosing such a figure hugging and expensive dress for the event.

She thrust a hand at him, "My name's Sasha. Sasha Blake."

"Tom," he said, gripping her fingers lightly, "Tom Sheridan."

The barman coughed deliberately and Tom turned his attention back to him.

"Drink Tom?" he said, glaring over the bar.

"I'll grab a glass of house red too thanks, Mitch."

Mitch mumbled in the affirmative and went about his business.

Tom leaned a hip against the bar. She saw anxiety dart across his eyes, yet his face gave nothing away. She took a sip for courage.

"Don't you have someone waiting at home for you?" she fished.

"Only Patch."

"Patch?"

"My cat," he confessed, embarrassed, "He has this funny stripy patch over his right ear and eye. It's as if someone has picked a tabby cat up by the ear and dunked him in white paint," he chuckled then clamped his lips shut, as if he felt foolish. She giggled.

The barman interrupted the awkward exchange to hand Tom his drink. Tom gestured to Sasha to move away from the bar and thanked Mitch as they slipped towards a free table in the corner.

"What about you? Didn't you come with a boyfriend? Or perhaps some friends?"

"Sorry?" she gestured to her ear then wove between a couple of guests to get to his side. He slowed down so she could catch him.

"I asked if you had come alone or with friends?"

As he asked, they reached the table. With an unexpected burst of energy he stepped into her path. She gasped, but then realised what he was doing. He pulled a chair out for her then slid around to sit opposite. They set their glasses down and pulled the heavy wooden chairs in under them.

"I just accompanied Gregory."

"The artist?" as he asked his eyes scanned the room. Gregory was busy draping himself over as many of his guests as he could.

"Yeah. He's the only person I know here tonight," she said, disappointment lacing her voice - this was what she was reduced to.

"You mean you're not with Gregory?" he said.

She raised an eyebrow and they both shared a small laugh at Gregory's expense.

Tom lifted his glass to Sasha and they chinked their glasses together with a stereo chorus of 'cheers'.

They settled and Tom continued the conversation.

"So how do you know Gregory then?"

"We met at uni, and were housemates for a while."

"So are you an artist too?"

"No. An archaeologist," she said.

"Really?" Tom's reaction was more animated than expected..

"Yeah. Why? Are you interested in archaeology then?" For a moment she thought she'd struck gold - handsome, fit, muscular and a fellow archaeologist? It was a rare combination and probably too good to be true.

"I dabble," he replied with a coy smile, "So do you work here at the museum?"

"Sometimes."

"Sometimes? What does that mean?" he set his elbows on the table, folded his hands together and rested his chin to steady his attention. It made her nervous, often the moment she admitted to being an Archaeologist people would offer polite platitudes and change the subject but he seemed interested.

"I work with different institutions on various projects."

"So what about at the moment? Are you working here now?"

"I am as it happens," her tone lifted, excited about the latest project and happy to be asked about it.

"What are you working on?"

She smiled widely.

"We've just had a breakthrough actually. We used radio carbon dating technology at Oxford Radiocarbon Accelerator Unit, to determine the age of the graves at the Varna Necropolis. I'm just helping out, the project is a collaboration between institutions in the UK and Bulgaria."

"Varna? Bulgaria?" Tom interrupted, his voice filled with intrigue.

"That's right." She nodded.

"I've heard about it. Isn't that where they discovered graves filled with gold artefacts?"

55

Her heart seemed to stop for a moment, amazed he knew what she was talking about.

"That's the place. It's fascinating. We've determined they date from 4700-4200 BC. It proves my late colleague's theory the gold found at the site is the oldest in the world."

"Late colleague?" he narrowed an eye and tilted his head, as if he could sense there was a story there. She wasn't ready to talk about it, it was too raw.

"The whole project has something of a cloud over it. It's always felt cursed to me, so I feel kind of vindicated. If that makes sense?" he looked confused, "Probably not. Yeah, you're right. You know what. Never mind."

He looked bewildered and it made her edgy. She took a deep drink and changed the subject.

"What about you? I know most of the security guards here but I've not seen you before?"

"I work for a contract firm. They sent a few of us in for tonight's event."

"But you know the barman?"

"He works for the same company - the agency specialises in events support."

"Oh, I see," she mumbled. Sipping at the wine and letting the silky notes of his voice sweep over her.

"So you said that archaeology interests you, is that why you took this job?"

He raised an eyebrow but there was no other change in is passive expression, his Adams apple twitched.

"Yeah. I've always been interested in art and history. European art and history in particular. I've studied it in the past and my father was a professor at Oxford. It's in my blood, whether I like it or not," a smile flickered across his face, "There may be more detailed investigative work here at the museum in the future so I said I'd work tonight to get my foot in the door. You may see me around a lot more."

A sense of satisfaction filled her. She made a mental note to look for a professor Sheridan in the alumni records next time she was at Oxford.

"So you know Gregory and you do bit of work here, did you set up this event?"

"Me, no. I just put a word in with the Museum Director."

"Oh, I thought perhaps you had set this up and connected some of the people here up?" he sounded surprised. She was apprehensive.

Maybe he was too good to be true and she was being naïve? She gave a guarded response.

"No. I put a word in, but Gregory's agent did the rest."

"His agent?"

"Yeah?"

"Who's his agent?"

"Why?" she found herself instinctively backing away. She'd had a few people, reporters mostly, pestering her recently to get more information on Gregory – his artwork had been causing quite a stir. Perhaps Tom wasn't all he seemed? Perhaps he was one of those undercover reporters for a tabloid with a hidden camera?

He seemed to notice her change of tone and let out a small laugh.

"I'm sorry," he said, "I'm off the clock now. Remind me to stop thinking like a security guard and start being Tom again!"

She asked herself if she was being paranoid.

He offered her a wide smile that lit up his entire face. She was under a spell. She enjoyed a quiet moment to watch him sip at his wine with his thin, shapely, lips. Whatever his agenda was, we all have them. She thought.

Hers was to get laid.

She talked herself back into trusting him - Who was she kidding, she was a nobody. he was probably a nobody too. In her mind she constructed a narrative: He was a history nerd who worked in security because the pay is good and for tonight, the two worlds met and he was somewhere he wanted to be. The alternative could have been patrolling the perimeter of some boring old warehouse, so tonight he was making the most of the perks of being at a party to have a drink with a girl, who hopefully, he quite fancied too.

"So, do you live near here?" she asked, hoping to continue their conversation before she scared him away.

A cheeky grin played with his lips at the innuendo. Realising how her question sounded, she felt her cheeks burn red.

"Sorry," he chuckled.

"You do that a lot."

"What?"

"Apologies," she said, turning the embarrassment onto him.

"Story of my life!" he said and drunk deeply from his glass. She sensed there was a story there, one she'd like to hear.

They sat in comfortable quiet for a moment, both thinking about which direction to take the conversation. His comment he 'dabbled' in archaeology had been bothering her She broke the silence to indulge her curiosity. "So what's your interest in archaeology then? Aside from providing security services for artefacts?"

He laughed mysteriously to himself.

"Actually, you have hit the nail pretty much on the head."

"How's that?"

"I've always been interested in history, and have some specialist knowledge about works of art and antiquities. When I was stationed in Germany I was part of a unit who specialised in repatriating art looted by the Nazi's."

"So you were in the army?" It explained the muscles and the haircut. He nodded and sipped the last of his wine.

Maybe when he left the army the only job he could get was in security? She thought, remembering a couple of mates from school who had done just that.

"Oh, okay," she felt she should say something but was stunned to hear Tom's story. She thought for a moment about what she could follow that comment with, "wow. That's pretty cool," she took a deep drink and asked, "So how come you left the forces?"

His mood visibly shifted and his voice darkened, "It was mutual. I don't want to talk about it."

A strange sort of sadness came over him as he said it, like

there was a deep hurt there. Her curiosity was peaked further but she didn't want to pry, so changed the subject. Their conversation was taking each of them down painful pathways, yet there was a magnetism that kept them talking, despite skirting on the edges of what each of them were willing to reveal.

"I went to Berlin last year actually," she remarked. The conversation link was tenuous but Tom seemed happy to run with it.

"Oh yes. Was that business or pleasure?"

"Business, mostly."

"Mostly?" he raised an eyebrow and flashed a wicked grin. She giggled flirtatiously. She wished there had been some holiday romance at the talk on Neolithic societal boundaries, but the only other delegates were crumbling old professors or spotty teenagers. It kept him guessing about her though, which meant he must be interested, she reasoned.

The exchange was interrupted by a waiter clearing away their empty glasses.

"Would you like another drink?" he asked. They exchanged an enquiring glance and something in each other's eyes made them both decide to take a second drink.

"I don't want to keep you from Patch if you have to get away?"

"Believe me, all you are keeping me from, Dr Blake, is another tortuous night in front of the TV!"

"Well Mr Sheridan, if I can save one person from the evil that is reality TV, I'm happy to oblige!"

They laughed together. As their laughter trailed off he broke the momentum.

"What about you? I wouldn't want to keep you from the rest of the party or from your old uni mate?"

"I doubt Gregory has even noticed I'm missing. He's in his element. Actually, I'm glad of your company. I was getting bored being a wall flower. Before you spilt my drink in my shoes I had been contemplating sneaking out."

He chuckled, "Well, if you ever need anyone to ruin your

shoes again, I'm your guy!"

After they had finished the next glass of wine, chatting about more light-hearted topics, they dispensed with the glasses of wine and ordered a bottle, and talked and drank late into the night, eventually being among the last to leave the party, long after it was over.

*

Tom held a hand out to Sasha. She took it lightly and he lifted her from the chair. She slid tantalisingly close to him, so close he could smell her hair and felt her warm breath on his neck. He tilted his gaze down, lost in the landscape of her eyes, before flicking away the surreptitious look. She was dressed in a long midnight blue dress that flowed down her lithe frame like a waterfall. It was the first time in as long as he could remember that a beautiful girl had spent so much time talking with him. Despite making some stupid, clumsy reference to Patch.

Maybe she was a cat person? He thought.

And now it was that decisive moment - Behind the bar, Mitch was flicking out the spotlights and a cleaner was swooping around the room with a wide broom – Tom told himself to be cool, not to act like a jackass. If he did this right he wouldn't be sleeping alone tonight.

She shuffled her feet back into her heels, brushed down her skirt and offered him a small, uncertain smile. He read her eyes for clues. Her blonde curls bounced around her porcelain white shoulders, scooping around the delicate lines of her neck. He watched, mesmerised, hardly believing he was in this moment. It was up to him to make the next move. Her long lashes blinked slowly around her big bright eyes.

"Shall we leave then?" he said, then silently cursed himself for blurting it out. He always said something stupid or inane when he first met girls. His inner chatterbox was shouting idiot at him and he lamented the fact that this was probably the reason why he was still single.

She offered him a mysterious little smile, then looped her arm into the crook of his elbow.

*

Sasha woke up, scratching her tickling nose furiously.
'Meow'

The cat was rubbing itself up to her face, padding and pacing around on her pillow. Sniffing, she pushed the white ball of fluff away and it clambered up onto her and purred and pawed at her chest.

"Morning."

His smooth voice filled the room and she felt a rush of contentment wash through her like warm honey. She rolled onto her side to look at him, Patch leapt down with an irritated mew.

"I think he likes you," said Tom with a soft chuckle. He was laid on his side, resting on an elbow, gazing down at her with his deep chocolaty eyes.

"Hey," she smiled back, running her eyes up and down his bare chest. Unable to resist a touch - as if she was checking he was real and not a dream. She stretched a hand closer to him and brushed her fingers through his curly chest hair and across a jumble of old scars that puckered his abdomen. The smoothest skin was scar tissue. She wanted to ask how they came to be there, but assumed they were from his time in the army, a subject he had been uncomfortable talking about. He leaned across and stole a soft kiss from her lips then pulled himself upright and clambered clumsily off the side of the bed.

"Coffee?"

"Sure," she said, the thought of coffee was appealing.

The thick fog of red wine was starting to drum on the inside of her head and her mouth tasted like she'd been eating mud.

She watched his white naked bottom as he stepped into his trunks and studied the sinuous muscles of his back and legs as he slipped out of the room.

He hesitated by the door, turned, looked at her briefly with a wide smile, then went through to the kitchen at the opposite end of his apartment.

She let the soft mattress swallow her and slid down the sheets.

She pulled the covers up around her chin and breathed in his smell. Closing her eyes, she remembered the previous night fondly. She sucked her lips to taste him on them once more, and then slid her hand across her bare breasts and down her naked body. She slid her fingers between her legs and remembered the feeling of him there, imagining his warm body against hers.

Her moment was broken into by the sound of heavy feet padding across the carpet in the hallway. He stepped into the room, set the coffee cups down on the dresser and stood at the foot of the bed.

She studied his beautiful toned body as he slid his trunks off once more then watched with delighted anticipation as he climbed up the bed, dragged the covers aside and stalked up her body.

He stretched the length of her, brushing his hard penis along her thigh and cupped his hand around her head. Her skin came alive as he slowly ran his hand along her curves. He pressed his lips hard and deliberate into hers, his kiss demanding. Her whole body convulsed with arousal. His fingers circled and danced. Her consciousness clouded and she allowed the sensations to devour her.

EXETER, ENGLAND – 2012

"Are you all right?" whispered Rees into Gina's ear, glassy eyed, resting his hand on her shoulder softly.

She nodded and continued to stare into the deep rectangular hole at her feet. Her ears tuned in for a moment, but her vision was blurred with fading memories.

"Ashes to ashes, dust to dust…" the vicar's words drifted out of her consciousness once more, became little more than white noise. She tucked herself into Rees, who pulled her into his arms and cradled her. She couldn't cry. She should be crying, but mostly she felt numb.

The coffin seemed unreal in the grave at her feet. She couldn't imagine her mother lying in it. She looked away, and scanned the faces of people she had known all her life encircled in a black clad embrace around her sleeping mother. Her uncle Mike had been doing the same and their eyes met. A slim smile tugged at the grey jowls of his face. He dragged his fingers through his wiry blonde hair and without thinking she tousled her mousy brown, neatly cropped hair in a mirroring gesture, only for a cold gust of wind to rustle it.

After the ceremony, hushed and shuffling guests congregated in the lounge of the Golf Club, in a state of limbo, drifting somewhere between the comforts of the bar and the buffet table.

Gina left Rees entertaining some of her mother's friends and wandered aimlessly around the room.

"Hello Georgina," said a familiar voice and she turned around, cringing at the sight of Mike.

"Hi Uncle Mike."

"I'm sorry about your mum."

"I'm sorry about your sister in law."

He gave a small laugh.

"It's tough once your parents are gone. You always believe they are immortal, but hey, your grandparents were no more immortal than your parents. I miss them too, but we carry on regardless," he took a deep gulp of scotch, dribbling some of it along the deep creases around his podgy lips. Nothing about Mike reminded her of her father, which was the last funeral she had attended.

Seeing the different emotional currents around her mother since his death, she was surprised she hadn't given up sooner. She was sure that part of her mother had died with her father. The concealed grief of losing him had eaten at her mother - Perhaps she had suffered a broken heart?

Gina smiled politely, but was slowly becoming irritated, knowing Mike's tendency to be condescending with just about everyone. Her gaze drifted around the room, searching for a point or person of interest to focus on. Her cousin Bobby shuffled past. He, strangely, did remind her of her father. Something about the way he carried himself. He had that same spindly frame and nervous tension as her father had had.

"Hey Bobby," she waved at him.

"Hey G," he waved back with a wide smile. He then gestured to her if she wanted a drink and she nodded.

"Well, you know, in these times, things can be difficult for a family. First your dad and then your mum. Our family is getting smaller," Mike droned on and she pretended to be interested, shuffling back and forth on her feet. "I suppose there are a lot of affairs for you and Dan to sort out. Where is your brother anyway? I've not seen him and his gorgeous little lad yet. What a sweet little chap our Alfie is. Bet you love being an auntie? I know I love being an uncle," he paused to breathe and smiled down at her as she shrunk away, "You know you and Reed…"

"Rees," she corrected.

"Yes, yes," Mike's jowls wobbled and he gulped at his whisky again, "You and your husband. You know you are always welcome to come and stay. Ursula and I would love to have you. Have you ever been to Amsterdam?"

"Ye…" before she could complete the word Mike continued talking, apparently oblivious to everyone else in the room, "Of course, of course. You know you really must come and stay. We have a lovely house on one of the canals on Mozartkade, close to the Museum District. We have plenty of room, in fact we have 3 spare bedrooms, all en suite. We can show you around the city and I can give you a tour of the Diamond House?" he nudged her arm, as if he was offering her an exciting incentive, his eyes looking very pleased with himself, "It's really very fascinating working with the diamonds. The process of getting the raw diamonds, assessing them and cutting them into exquisite little sparkles of art. Of course, I don't get involved with that work," he sounded almost dismissive, "but I do have full access, being one of the Directors," he said, boastful and rather pleased with himself, as ever - then backtracked, "You'd like it. Every girl loves diamonds."

"Thanks uncle Mike but I'm really not…"

"Oh stuff and nonsense," he interrupted, his tone accelerating, "Please don't tell me you are one of those goody-goody types with a fig up your arse about the evils of the diamond trade. Surely not, Georgina?" Mike snorted and gulped the last of his whisky, his face reddening. The awkward exchange was interrupted by Bobby.

"Here dad," he wriggled his way in between them and handed Mike another Whisky, "G," then passed a glass of white wine to her with a wry smile.

"Oh cheers Bobs you're a star," she said, "I'll leave you with your dad; I'd better go and rescue Rees and talk to some of the other guests," she offered Bobby a sly smile and he mouthed 'No'.

"See you later Uncle Mike."

He muttered something approximating a 'seeya' and Gina melted back into the crowd gathered around the buffet table - scrabbling for the remaining scraps of sandwiches like pigeons in Trafalgar Square.

"Hey you," a bony arm pinched around her shoulders.

"Hey Danny Boy."

"Oy," Danny punched her on the arm, "You know I hate

being called that."

"Exactly. Shitbag," she responded.

They paused, exchanged a few more insults then wrapped their arms around each other and held there for a while, allowing silent tears to flow for a moment at the loss of their mother. Now it was just the two of them, no mum or dad to rely on.

"Mum would have told us to pack it in had she seen us play fight like that, like she always used to," said Danny.

"The difference is, we're adults now. She'd have screeched at us to grow up!" the sadness broke into smiles and they looked each other, recalling the fond memories of growing up together.

"You all right kid?" asked Danny, a sympathetic look in his bloodshot eyes.

"Kid?" she thrust her hands into her hips and gave him a sharp look.

"Come on smelly. Let's go get some fresh air and have stroll shall we. I'm sick of all these people," he said, clutching his arm around her shoulder and pulling her away from the buffet table.

They shouldered through the crowd, excusing themselves and bustled out to the terrace.

Danny snatched the glass of white wine from her and took a sip.

"You didn't get me one?"

"So sue me! Actually, sue Bobs, he bought the last round in."

They followed the daffodil lined path around the fairway. It had become a fresh day, as if the gloom had lifted now the worst part of the funeral was over. The sky was creamy, thick with swirls of cloud but a damp smell of mud and rotting leaves filled the air.

Now it was a new beginning and Gina found herself breathing the crisp spring air deeply into her lungs, surveying the vista of manicured rolling green.

She glanced back at Danny, he seemed overcome with

sadness for a moment. She stretched an arm out and gripped his bicep. He held her hand there for a moment and gave her a weak smile.

"You were right, we ought to be able to have an adult conversation by now," he said, "We could banter and think up stupid insults for each other until the cows come home. But we need to talk about what to do next."

"What do you mean; what to do next?" she said, her voice laced with a sense of denial.

"About the house. All of mum and dad's stuff. Should we get lawyers and stuff? How do these things work? I just don't know G, Mum handled Dad's affairs when he died, I was at Uni."

"Neither do I," she dropped her hand away and looked to her feet for an answer. Danny rubbed her shoulder reassuringly.

"I wouldn't expect you to know, you were just a kid when dad died. But you know who does know about legal mumbo jumbo?" he said.

"Ah man. I know. Doesn't he handle all the legal stuff for Castell Diamonds?"

"Uncle Mike, yeah."

"Oh crap, that means we need to go and talk to him I suppose."

"We do. But not today."

"He's pissed anyway. He's been knocking back the scotch like it's going out of fashion, " she said, rolling her eyes.

"Tomorrow then?"

"I suppose. But first, I guess we need to go back the house and start sorting things out. We'll get Mike to come and meet us at the house tomorrow and we can deal with it as a family."

"Come on, let's get our asses back in there," said Danny, trying to keep positive, "They'll be bringing the cakes out soon."

Gina quickly drank the last of her wine, "I'm off to see who I can tap up for another wine!" she jabbed him on the arm, as if she were challenging him to a race back to the buffet table and then headed back across the terrace.

Danny picked up to a jog to catch her up, "Nice little sis. I like your style."

"Hey, our inheritance has paid for the food they're all scoffing in there, the least they can do is get us both a sympathy drink."

*

Danny laughed softly.

"What is it?" asked Gina, looking up from where she was sat on the floor, piling books into a cardboard box.

"Do you remember this?" he held up the picture frame in his hand.

"Oh yes!" she chuckled, "Wasn't that the day you fell into that big pile of horse manure?"

Danny stuck his tongue out at her, screwing his nose up. He carefully laid the picture frame on top of the books he had just filled a box with. He took a final look at the sunny picture of the two of them, flanked by their parents, all smiling in front of the stables Uncle Mike had owned when they were children, and folded the flaps of the box over it. Another memory of their childhood trussed up in cardboard to be stored away and forgotten.

"Here we are guys," said Rees, walking back into what had once been the living room of Gina and Danny's parents' house, carrying a tray of steaming mugs. The hazy smell of fresh coffee cut through the somber atmosphere, and he set the tray down on top of a packing crate.

"Ah cheers mate," said Danny, sweeping up a mug as if it were a welcome pint of beer.

"Thank you sweetheart," said Gina. She stood, pulled an arm around Rees and planted a kiss on his cheek, nuzzling into him.

"Has anyone gone in there yet," asked Rees, tugging his wife into his side gently and looked towards the door in the far corner of the room.

Nervous glances were exchanged between the siblings.

"Not yet," a wave of fresh sadness seemed to weigh Danny down as he said it, his eyes flitting over to the locked door of their father's former office, "No one has been in that room since dad died. Mum didn't want anyone to disturb dad's stuff. It became her quiet memorial to him."

"Well," Rees drew in a breath and released Gina from his grip, "We need to empty the room. After tomorrow, this is no longer your house, guys," his face fell into a sympathetic frown.

Going into that room would be the final goodbye for Danny and Gina. They fixed an uncertain look on each other. She nodded empathetically at Danny, "It's all right Dan, we'll both do it. Are you ready?"

"As I'll ever be," Danny's face crumpled with anxiety. He taped up the box he had finished with and walked towards the door, gesturing her to follow him. She turned the key in the lock and slowly pushed the door open. It groaned, stiff with age and cramp, and a bloom of dust, undisturbed for years, billowed up from the parquet. A swirling cloud of sparkling particles, caught in the sunlight from the voile-covered window.

The slightest glimpse into the room and memories of their father flooded back to her, welling in her stomach as sorrow.

It was a large room, the original purpose would have been that of a dining room, but had always been their fathers' office, for as long as she could remember. When he had been alive, she and Danny had never been allowed in the room unsupervised and part of her expected her father to come in and yell at them for going in without permission.

The room was dominated by a massive antique wooden desk. Behind it were floor to ceiling display cabinets full of crumbling books and dusty ornaments. A brown leather chesterfield settee grinned at them from across the room, presiding over an oversized threadbare Persian rug. Pictures, wall hangings, tapestries and framed certificates covered every inch of wall. Gina stepped onto the old rug, as if it were about to disintegrate under her feet, and headed for the desk. The surface was clear, except for a stack of shabby Moleskine notebooks and a British Museum souvenir mug stuffed with chewed pens and pencils.

"Are you coming in?" she waved over Rees and Danny, who both looked afraid to follow her, like something frightening was lurking in the office, ready to pounce.

Danny found some courage and bounded over, going behind the desk and slumping into the squashy old leather chair behind it.

"Bagsy I have this chair," he said, crossing his legs widely, putting his hands behind his head and tipping back in the seat, "No wonder dad spent so long in it, it's proper comfy."

Gina raised a disapproving eyebrow and leaned over to scoop up the notebooks, "What do you think dad's written in this lot?"

"There's only one way to find out," said Rees, moving silently behind Gina and resting a reassuring hand on her shoulder.

She looked into Rees' adoring eyes, "It feels like a violation, reading these," she said, feeling strangely guilty.

He pressed a kiss onto her forehead and spoke softly, "It's all right. I'm sure your father would want these to stay in the family, whatever they are. The fact he left them on his desk shows he expected you to find them one day. Take them with you, read them another day and reflect on them in your own time. Perhaps they are even meant for you and Danny."

"Hey, G G?" Danny interrupted the couple's tender moment and rattled the desk drawers, "Are their keys on that bunch for dad's desk?"

"Are you going to go through his private desk?" her voice rose an octave.

"Well, it's no good to dad now is it? Besides, we need to empty the desk so we can move it."

She sighed, realising he was right, but not ready to accept it. Their father had died some years ago, but he had spent so much of their lives away with work that while his office lay undisturbed it still felt as though he would be coming back. He had always come back, even when his job had taken him to the other end of the world for months on end, they knew he would always come back, and always with some weird and wonderful gifts for them.

She rustled the keys. There was a smaller ring, crammed with little keys attached to the main ring and she shook it free of the others, "Try some of these," she passed the bunch over the desk to Danny.

Danny went through the keys, dismissing them one by one and until finally, "Eureka!" The top drawer of the desk groaned open.

She couldn't contain her curiosity and slid around the desk. She leaned over the open drawer, "Oh."

"What is it?" asked Rees, seeing her disappointment.

"There's a few quid in loose change, but otherwise just sticky old paperclips, a calculator and some old receipts." Danny was just as dejected. He scooped up the cash and trickled it into his trouser pocket, "Well guys, at least the three of us can have a final beer on dad!" he said.

Danny sifted through the contents of the drawer, to see if there was anything worth salvaging before he pulled it out and tipped into a bin bag that Rees had brought in with him.

"Hang on," Gina stopped him before he tipped the drawer up, "We should take the receipts' out and make sure they're not important."

"15 year old receipts?" Danny threw a sarcastic look. Undeterred, she snatched the receipts, rescuing them from the bin bag and gathered them up on top of the notebooks. Danny shrugged and carried on tipping. The weight of the drawer shifted in Danny's hands and with a thud, something fell into the bag, "What the…?"

"What was that?" she said.

They joined Danny and he reached deep into the refuse sack pulling out the drawer and a sheet of plywood. They dragged the bag flat on the rug and spread the contents out.

Danny looked up at the others, his face mapped with

bewilderment, "There's a false bottom in the drawer."

"What? Are you sure?" asked Rees. Danny glared at him and Rees backed away with a shrug.

"Why would dad have a false compartment in his desk?" she shuddered, got down onto her knees and rummaged among the black plastic and confetti of paper and lint. She reached further into the bag and scooped out an A4 brown envelope. Both Danny and Rees were now sat on the carpet with her, congregated around the bag like a campfire.

She rattled the envelope and a small weight shifted and sagged the paper. She studied the envelope, suspicious.

"Open it then!" said Danny, leaning over in anticipation. Rees watched the siblings, his brow heavy.

She slid her finger under the flap and tipped out the weight. It was cold in her hand, "What do think this is for?" she held up a small key.

"Is there anything else in the envelope?" Asked Danny.

"Oh, hang on," she slowly slid out a sheet of paper, "Anyone read German?"

"German?" Rees looked more confused.

"I didn't know dad spoke Germen? Let's have a look." Danny reached for the page. As he looked over it, his face crumpled, "I don't know any German but this is the headed paper for a bank."

"A bank?"

"Can I see?" Rees waved to Danny and he passed the sheet across, "It's a Swiss bank, look, the address is in Zurich." Rees showed the others.

"Why the hell would dad have dealings with a Swiss bank?" she asked, to no one in particular, as if the answer would drop out of the sky.

Danny shrugged, "Well, I guess we should keep it, we can look into it another time."

She took the page and carefully slid it back into the envelope with the key, then added the old receipts to the package, "I'll keep all this together, you never know, these receipts could be related to the account. Danny, did you say you'd found an old shoe box in the hall?"

"Yeah, hang on, I'll go and grab it," he ducked out of the room, leaving her and Rees to pick up the mess from the refuse sack.

"What do you think this all means, Rees? And why the hell would my dad have a safety deposit box at a Swiss bank? I'm afraid to ask what he was up to."

Her stomach back flipped at the thought of it.

"We'll put it all together in the shoebox, along with the notebooks and keep it somewhere safe," he replied, shaking his head. He rested a reassuring arm across Gina's shoulder while they were crouched over the rubbish bag, "Let's not think about it today. We can deal with it another day, perhaps that would be helpful."

THE PRESENT

PROCTORS BOOKSELLERS, OXFORD STREET, LONDON – PRESENT DAY

June

Dr Sasha Blake glanced up at the big round clock by the front door, the minute hand was tantalisingly close to the end of the shift. The steady line of customers waiting to get their copy of the book signed or have their picture taken with her, had dwindled to a couple of stragglers.

A sweaty young man in a fur lined anorak was grinning at her from the opposite side of the table.

"Can you write 'To Eddie' please?" he grinned, his eyes wide and expectant.

She danced the nib across the page and tried not to make eye contact with him.

Being at a book signing sounded far more glamorous than the reality. She flexed her aching fingers and willed the minutes to pass.

The work she had done six years ago as part of the team responsible for radio carbon dating the artefacts from the Varna Necropolis had cemented her reputation as an Archaeologist. She had published those findings and the work was widely read by archaeology students the world over with dreams of making that once in a lifetime find.

The work had opened the door for her to step into fiction writing - 'The Thracian Queen' was her first novel, loosely based on her work at the excavations of the ancient Pliska fortification north of Varna. It had taken her three years to write and sitting in a dusty old bookshop all day with a false smile on her face hardly made it seem worthwhile.

She looked at the clock again, the hands seemingly frozen in time. Feeling herself fade from a lack of caffeine, she cursed

Toby, the over enthusiastic assistant manager, who had ducked out to fetch them coffee from a street vender half an hour ago.

It was then she noticed the well-dressed gentleman hovering in the shadows of the reference section. As the last customer made for the door he approached.

"Dr Blake," said the stranger with a wide smile and an outstretched hand. She still couldn't get used to the way 'Dr Blake' sounded. She eyed the man and his broad palm suspiciously.

"My name is Milton Harkett. I have followed your career for some time."

She didn't want to be rude to the man; he was a potential customer after all. As she stood, leaned across the desk and stretched out her slim fingers to meet his. He shook her hand firmly, a real sense of authority in his gesture.

She was intrigued – he was perhaps mid to late 50's, his suit clearly expensive judging by its exquisite cut and quality pinstripe. He was average height and build, but had gravitas about him. Clean shaven, she imagined he would have been very fit at one stage. Former military? She thought. His silver hair was tinning at the temples and was neatly swept back, his eyes pale blue and clear as water.

"Pleased to meet you. What can I do for you Mr Harkett?" she responded, polite yet formal.

A wry smile sideswiped his face, "Immediately to the point I see," he remarked, as if sharing a private joke with himself, "And please, you may call me Milton."

She crinkled her brow, unsure if he was mocking her or complimenting her. She forced an expectant smile, furtively eyeing him up and down.

"Would you like a signed copy?" she gestured to the small pile of books in front of her.

The man responded with a small laugh, as if she had asked a silly question. She glanced away and neatened the stack of books to avoid making eye contact that would betray the offence she had taken.

"Apologies, Dr Blake. I am certain the book is excellent,

however, that is not the reason I'm here."

"Then why are you here sir?" she offered him an insincere smile.

The suited man took a deep breath, then fixed Sasha with a steely gaze.

"Dr Blake, I work for a specialist agency. Your work over the past few years, especially your work on ancient Balkan archaeology, has not gone unnoticed. May I?" He gestured for her to retake her seat behind the desk then drew up a chair opposite. She nodded and he continued. He shuffled into the chair, tugged at the thighs of his trousers to get comfortable then crossed his legs and folded his fingers together on the desk in front of him. He seemed serious, speaking with a deep authoritative voice, it reminded her of the way her professors had spoken to her. For a moment a memory of Dr Kamel resurfaced, the way he carried himself was similar to how Milton moved - assured, confident.

"Specialist agency? What do you specialise in?"

A mysterious smile played at the corners of his mouth.

"That is not important. What is important is that my business partner and I need your help. We could benefit from someone with your talent in our organisation."

"My help?"

"Indeed, Dr Blake. You see, a client has employed my agency to locate an artefact, and your name came up."

"Excuse me, Mr Harkett…"

"Milton," he interrupted.

"Milton…" she took a deep breath as she considered the words, "It sounds as if you are offering me a job?"

"Indeed I am," a wide smile opened up his face.

"I don't understand?"

"Listen," he unthreaded his fingers and moved to touch her but stopped short of contact when he saw her shoulders stiffen with discomfort, "How about we set up a meeting and we can discuss this in more detail?"

Part of her was freaked out by him, but part of her couldn't resist the mystery. She wanted to find out more about him, and a job offer meant money - something she was definitely short of.

"Okay?" her head was filled with uncertainty and curiosity; she never could resist a discovery. She thought of her late mother, who had always told her that curiosity would kill the cat, as if that should have been an important life lesson. She'd never listened.

"I would need to call my agent to set up a meeting."

"Your agent is not required."

"But I have an agreement with …" he cut her off with an irritated wave.

"This is not about your writing career doctor. This is about your unique expertise."

"What do you mean? And why me?" She was perplexed, but intrigued.

"You and I have, had," he paused, a sadness interrupting his flow, "A mutual friend. Dr David Thornton," he offered a smile, waiting for the impact of his words.

Then it hit her. Like a punch to the chest. David. A connection to David. She had to find out more.

She thought back to that phone call from the police while she was in Istanbul, then a week later finding out about his death. What had happened to him in the days before his death? Could she have done anything to prevent it?

She had always carried an inexplicable guilt. The last words she'd exchanged with him were in anger and she'd always regretted it.

"You knew David?" The words filtered out as she dropped back into the present. Her heart was folding in on itself, like she had forgotten to breathe, "How?"

"He helped my organisation out from time to time," he shrugged, like it meant nothing.

It took her a moment to compose herself.

"You need an Archaeologist?"

"We need an expert. We need you," he undid his jacket button and reached inside. He took out his mobile phone and his fingers danced across the touch screen to pull up his calendar, "Now. I have put you in my diary for Tuesday at 2. Is that acceptable for you?"

"Urm, I…" she was lost for words at his presumption. She searched the inside of her head, "That should be fine, but it would depend on where you would like to meet?"

"You will be in London, yes?"

"Yes, yes I think so," she was confused for a moment, it was almost as if the man already knew her itinerary, he spoke with such confidence.

"Excellent," he said triumphantly, "I shall have a car pick you up on Tuesday at 1.45pm from your hotel."

"I'm staying at…"

"The Premier Inn," he interrupted.

*

June – A Few Days Later

"Here we are Dr Blake," announced the driver, bringing the car to a stop just off Regent Street, "Mr Harkett is waiting for you inside."

The black Mercedes had arrived five minutes early at the hotel. Sasha was quivering with nerves as she shuffled back and forth on her feet in the Reception. She had changed three times before finally settling on a dress suit. Conservative yet elegant. A thousand questions fogged her mind.

What kind of interview would this be? What the hell was she doing, meeting this man? Did he really know David, or was he manipulating her? What was the job? Who was Milton Harkett, could he be trusted and why had he sought her out?

The driver had pulled up outside an exclusive looking restaurant and she felt under dressed in her off the rail suit while beautiful people in designer clothes swept in and out of the shiny revolving doors.

The driver stepped out and opened the door for her, tipping his hat. She felt like a movie star.

"Thank you," she muttered, swallowing back her nerves, her thoughts scattered.

She stepped from the street into the cool interior, her low heals echoed around the marble shod atrium.

"May I help you madam?" a sour faced host shuffled out from behind a podium.

"Urm, yes. I'm Sasha Blake, I am meeting with Milton Harkett."

"Ah yes!" the concierge's tone lifted an octave and a mirthless smile threatened to crack his stony façade.

"If you will follow me, Dr Blake."

She followed while he meandered between the diners that populated the sparkling set tables and led her towards the window. She glanced, the room had a high ceiling with towering windows. Flock wallpaper and fine frescoes covered every inch of wall. Soft ripples from the grand piano in the corner mingled with the low rumble of conversation and occasional clink of cutlery. Inviting smells of roasting meat drifted from the kitchens.

By the window, a silver haired man was sat at a round table and stood to greet her.

"Ah, Sasha. Thank you for coming," Milton opened his arms then stretched a hand out to her. She shook it, far less hesitantly than the first time they had met. He waved her into the chair opposite his.

"I took the liberty of ordering some wine. A fine, fresh, Chablis, I trust you approve," he announced as he retook his seat.

"Thank you," she mumbled and shuffled into her chair, resting her hands in her lap. She was ready to listen to what he said, they were in a public place so if she didn't like what she heard she knew she could walk away.

Milton snapped his fingers above his head and a waiter was in attendance. The waiter proceeded to pour the wine, one hand behind his back, the other draped with a crisp napkin.

With a flourish he replaced the bottle into an intricately decorated silver ice bucket on a stand beside the table and backed away.

Milton lifted his glass and gestured to Sasha, she lifted her glass and nodded it towards him.

"Cheers," he announced, clinking his glass into hers.

"Cheers."

"So, Sasha. I'm glad you came. I see that my offer has intrigued you?"

"It has," she smiled, "I must admit, I have never been head-hunted before!"

He let out a pleasant laugh. She was starting to warm to him, despite him being such a cliché.

"You are a very talented archaeologist, Dr Blake. One worthy of note. It is about time you were rewarded for your expertise."

"That's very kind of you. But like most archaeologists, it's not about money or glory, it about the thrill of discovery," she wrapped her lips around the glass and sipped at the cool fresh liquid.

"A noble sentiment. And one I can understand. But what if you could be paid handsomely for that knowledge?"

"Well, it would depend on the circumstances."

She swirled the syrupy liquid around in the bulbous glass, the clean scent of fruit and flowers drifting from it. Part of her was shouting, *yes, yes, take the money, pay off your debts, get a proper job* – however, she wasn't about to make any rash decisions or come across as desperate. She fixed her poker face firmly in place and hoped he would do most of the talking.

"Are there not some questions you would go to any lengths to have answered?"

"I'm not sure what you mean?" she watched the liquid cling to the inside of the glass, then sipped again from it, buying herself some thinking time; What was he getting at?

"Should we order?" he changed the subject by waving over the waiter. Leaving her contemplating the implication of his words.

The waiter appeared with menus and recited the specials list in a well-rehearsed robotic manner. Sasha tried to hide her shock at the prices, but he caught sight of it and offered his reassurance.

"Order whatever you like. The Agency is settling the bill."

She wasn't about to pass up a free lunch, but was wary about what he'd expect in return. She needed to know more. This was probably the weirdest job interview she'd ever had, and she still didn't know what the job was. Milton danced his way around her, giving nothing away – she could play along, she wasn't bored of the waltz yet.

They took a moment to consider the menu. He recommended the Lemon Sole, which she ordered, to avoid having to make a decision, it all looked delicious to her.

They placed their orders and paused for the waiter to depart before resuming the conversation.

"You asked me whether I would go to any lengths to answer certain questions. What did you mean by that?" she said, frustrated at how evasive he seemed.

"Have you ever wondered what it was that Dr David Thornton removed from the Varna Necropolis before he died?"

"How do you...?" she stopped herself, starting to realise that Milton had extensive contacts and the question was futile, "Of course I have."

"And wouldn't you like to know why he did it? Why, the man who spent his career bringing history to life, went against all he stood for to steal some of it?"

"I have asked myself that many times over the years."

He had tapped right into something deep inside her she had tried to ignore all these years. The weight of it pressed on her lungs and her breath sharpened. Every time she thought of David she experienced a raw physiological response. It was painful and coarse and until Milton appeared from the shadows, she had boxed it away. He was a dark echo of her conscience, challenging her to face the questions in her past. Perhaps that was what drove her to give his offer, such as it was, serious consideration?

Despite her fears about his agenda he seemed somehow sincere, like he knew her. She could feel herself trusting him. The apprehension dispersed like vapour and was replaced with a visceral need to find answers.

"My agency has access to extensive resources to help you to answer these questions that have dogged you for all these years."

Her inner cynic reared its head once more, "For what purpose? Why would you do that?"

"Because our client wants the box."

"The box?"

"The artefact Thornton took from the necropolis. A box."

"What box? And what do you mean, your client?"

"The identity of our client, I'm afraid, must be kept confidential. And the box - Why - it is the key to everything."

"Mr Harkett…"

"Milton…"

"Milton," she heaved a great sigh, bewildered and overwhelmed. None of this made sense to her, "What do you mean the key to everything? And why me? Why now? I don't understand."

"You will come to understand, in time. But all that remains to be said today, is will join my team?"

"You haven't answered my questions."

A frown creased his face.

"We chose you because you came highly recommended and all of your questions will be answered in good time. What do you say?"

"I don't know what to say," she confessed, her voice laced with incredulity. He was asking her to trust him based on no information at all. Part of her wanted to walk away, but the temptation to know more was irresistible. It kept her rooted to the seat while she studied Milton for any signs of deception.

"Perhaps this will change your mind."

He reached into his inside pocket. She was half expecting him to bring out his mobile phone but instead he pulled some paper out of his pocket. He placed a crisp ivory envelop in front of her.

"What's this?" she leaned forward and hesitated.

"Open it," he smiled, with a firm nod. She set her wine aside and reached for the envelope. She slid her fingers under the sticky flap as Harkett watched her, almost intimidating. She couldn't hide her surprise at how much he was offering her, and counted the zero's just to be sure.

"Consider this an inconvenience fee. Whether to you decide to join the agency or not, the money is yours. I know you have some student debts. If you join my team, I will make it worth your while, for as long as it takes to find the box. And I know you want to know these secrets. I know you long to understand what David died for and why he did what he did. That alone should be enough of an incentive. Clear the man's name, solve the puzzle and settle your conscience."

Sasha stared at the cheque. It would almost wipe out her debts, and this was just an initial payment. It seemed too good to be true.

David had never been far from her thoughts, even after all these years. She had been infatuated with the man, and he had betrayed her. The desire to know why had weighed heavy on her mind.

Why had he gone against all his principles to steal an artefact from the site? Where had he gone with that artefact? What had he taken? Where was it now? Was there more to his death than a car accident?

Milton was offering her the chance to answer these questions that had plagued her, and the money was irresistible.

"What do you say? Are you with me?" his question broke into her quiet moment of contemplation. She examined his eyes. She was tempted to follow her impulses and say yes there and then, but sensible Sasha was telling her to proceed with caution.

"Let me sleep on it and I'll call you in the morning with my answer."

SECRET LOCATION SOMEWHERE IN LONDON (PART 1)

July

Milton Harkett opened his arms and clamped his hands on both of Sasha's shoulders, "Welcome. Welcome, Sasha. I'm glad you came."

She shrank back, not quite comfortable with the contact, her breath shallow. She still wasn't sure what to make of the mysterious Milton and he was a little too over familiar for her liking, as if they were the best of friends.

They were in a small, bland waiting area. She had just been whisked into a gleaming lift, then ushered through what she could only compare to a series of airlocks.

"Thank you, sir," she said.

"Please. As I said before, Milton is fine. We may be a professional organisation, but we're a friendly team. Do come through."

He dropped his hands away and escorted her out of the room down a flight of steps and into a short dingy corridor with a set of oversized double doors at the end of it. At the door he looked into a retinal scanner, tapped in some numbers and showed her through. He gestured towards two leather couches facing each other in the centre of his plush and expansive office. Antique books sat on walnut shelves lining the room, and beyond a large Persian rug, was Milton's enormous desk, presiding over the room. No windows, so far she had seen none in the complex, leading her to believe she was underground.

"Can I offer you a drink?" he asked, as Sasha took a seat while he made his way towards an antique writing desk. He rolled open the front, it was filled with bottles of spirits. He poured himself a scotch, neat, and nodded the bottle towards her.

"No thank you," she said. Crossing her legs and threading her fingers together around her knee, she glanced at her cheap leather watch. She couldn't imagine drinking scotch at 11 O'clock in the morning and tried to not to show her surprise. He sat on the chair opposite with a satisfied smile on his face.

She reached for the jug of water on the coffee table between them and poured herself a glass. Milton took the jug from her and carefully tipped a couple of drops into his glass, "These aged scotches are beautifully smooth with a dash of water," he said, then sat back into the settee, crossing his legs.

"I am sure you are eager to get started, but before I introduce you to your partner, tell me how your orientation week went?"

Sasha took a sip of water and thought about how to sum up the most intense week of her life. It was how she imagined an army boot camp would be, but indoors and less physically strenuous.

"It was fine," she said.

"Fine?" Milton raised an eyebrow, knowing there was a story behind her comment.

She did have some stories, and had learned a lot, but this wasn't the time – she was there to do a job and was keen to get on with it.

"I'm not sure what I was expecting but I surprised myself at how accurately I could shoot and learned some new self defence techniques I'd never used before!"

That was the thing that lodged in her memory. She had done an introduction to karate at university once, mostly to keep her friend company, and had sat through some personal safety awareness training once, but last week had been the first time she'd ever held a gun. It scared her. It shouldn't be so easy to take a life.

Milton chuckled, "Good. Hopefully you won't need to use those skills! As an archaeologist your abilities as an investigator and puzzle solver exceed those of many of our agents. I have chosen a highly experienced partner for you. He's ex-military – special forces – and is also a historian, so he will understand your point of view but he'll also, have your back, so to speak. You'll be brilliantly mismatched," a smile crept along his face, "Do you have any immediate concerns before I introduce you and get you set up?"

There were a million things Sasha wasn't sure about, least of all her nagging suspicions about the cloak and dagger nature of The Agency.

Who financed this operation and why was the security level so high? What were they hiding, or protecting?

The comment she and her partner would be brilliantly mismatched intrigued her. She wondered what sort of Neanderthal she'd have to work with.

"No, nothing at the moment," she responded, smiling politely.

Milton raised an eyebrow in disbelief.

"I will endeavour to answer your questions in good time, but for now, I'm encouraged that you seem so keen to get to work," he paused, knocked back the last of his whisky with a refreshed sigh and began to stand. She followed his lead, part excitement at the potential for discovery, part apprehensive over what she was about to do.

"Please," Milton raised a hand to direct her. Reaching past her to open the door, he led her onwards.

Back out in the narrow grey corridor, Milton showed her up the steps and turned left into another anonymous corridor. Still no windows, just endlessly repeating closed doors. Dark blue carpeting absorbed their footsteps, giving way to the muted sounds of phones ringing, muffled conversations and keyboards clicking behind blank walls. She wondered how many people were working down here, unseen by the world, running some, quite literally, underground industry, deep in the bowels of the city.

The corridors wound and twisted in a warren of dim tunnels and she could get no sense of the scale of the place as Milton led her right and left along numerous passageways. She read the numbers on the doors, but otherwise there was no signage or writing to indicate what went on behind any of them. Stopping abruptly, Milton knocked once on door number 127 and let himself in. She glanced up and down the corridors, noting for the first time the lights had dimmed further down, plunging them into murky darkness and making it impossible to tell how far they stretched.

"This is you."

She followed him into a larger office. It was a wide room, lined with filing cabinets, printers and office paraphernalia. No one was working here and the small meeting area, lay unoccupied. More anonymous doors led off the room, this time with frosted glass panels, a watery suggestion of movement beyond. Again there was no natural light, everything corporate shades of grey and blue. It smelt and felt sterile.

"This is my office?" she asked, bemused.

Milton let out a small laugh "No, no. This is a communal resources area, you'll be sharing your partners office, through here," she felt foolish and tried not to blush. Milton lifted a hand towards one of the frosted glass doors. A tall rubber plant stood in a tub next to it.

"I'll introduce you to your partner and I have arranged for you to meet IT later to sort out your equipment allocation. Your partner will show you the way."

He knocked once and stepped through the door. As she brushed past the rubber plant, she realised it was plastic. Everything about this place seemed somehow artificial. She wondered how far underground she was, and asked herself how she would find her way out again.

A low step down and they entered another office. This room was partitioned off with the same grey walls on three sides, but the last wall was whitewashed concrete, it seemed like the outer wall of the complex. The room smelt musty and of unwashed clothes, like the bedroom of a teenager. It was a cramped, untidy space, barely big enough for the single occupant who was sat hunched over with his back to them, entrenched in a stack of bulging folders. Surrounding him were cardboard filing boxes, stacked on the floor and every available surface, brimming with documents, pictures and cuttings. On one wall were pictures and maps with pins in them, linked with string in a web of investigation that looked as if it had been consuming him. Behind the wall of paper on his long desk lay an idle computer, the mouse resting on a box file and keyboard askew on a heap of newspapers.

Milton gave a deliberate cough, "Agent."

"Hang on," mumbled the man in a gruff voice, "Just…here it is…ur…" the man scrabbled around on the desk for a pen and finally laid his hands on one. He scribbled furiously, swore and threw the pen aside, then repeated the process twice more before finally getting a pen that worked.

Milton folded his arms, flashed an impatient eyebrow at Sasha and drummed his foot on the raw concrete floor. For all his conviviality, she got the distinct impression that Milton was an impatient man who didn't suffer fools gladly.

"Agent," he repeated.

"Okay," said the man, then slowly sat up and turned around.

Sasha stepped further into the room, getting ready for the formal introduction. As the man's face fell into the light pool of the desk lamp a sick feeling balled in her stomach. There had been something familiar about him and his low voice, as if from a long forgotten dream, but it was when she saw his eyes she knew it.

He looked up, doubt flashed across his face, then disbelief. His features hardened until they looked like they had been cut from stone.

"Agent Sasha Blake. I would like to introduce you to your new partner, Agent Tom Sheridan," Milton served a welcoming smile between them, seemingly oblivious to the tension.

"Agent Blake," nodded Sheridan.

"Agent Sheridan," nodded Sasha.

"Okay," Milton clapped his hands together triumphantly,

"I'll leave you two to get acquainted. And for god's sake Sheridan, clean up will you," he ordered with a sharp smile.

Sheridan pursed his lips. Milton turned on a heel and bid them good day before leaving them alone. There was a cold silence as the realisation struck and the mundane pleasantries ended.

"I didn't expect to see you again," Sheridan stood and held a stiff hand out to Sasha.

"Likewise," she replied, offered a forced smile and shook his hand. His face registered no emotion, his eyes icy and vacant. He was dressed like a problem teenager from a rough estate in scruffy jeans and a baggy sweatshirt. His chin coarse with several days of growth, his hair longer than she remembered and flecked with grey. He looked older, weary somehow, like the world had dragged him down as it passed him by.

They studied each other briefly, it was Sasha who took the initiative, they had to make this work. Mismatched, yes, but brilliantly? she wasn't so sure.

"So what's all this then?" she waved at the web on the wall. It looked complicated, a sea of pictures, clippings maps and scribbled notes.

Sheridan excused himself past her, giving her a wide berth and started to explain.

"I'll take you through all the files and information we have gathered so far but the map is a good overview."

She nodded, listened and scanned the images more closely.

"Why do you have my graduation picture here?" she pointed to a picture of herself, a heavy feeling in her stomach. It disturbed her he had had a picture of her on his wall all this time yet could barely look her in the eye. Had she hurt him that much? In it she was smiling and wearing a mortar board, it bought back fond memories. She felt the apprehension rising – What was going on? What had she walked into?

"You're part of the puzzle. I knew I would be getting a partner, but Milton never warned me it would be you," he said accusingly, "But I can understand why he wanted you here."

"I see," she mumbled, although she wasn't convinced she did.

"In August 1998, this man, left the Varna Necropolis dig site unexpectedly and at the same time an unreported artefact went missing," Sheridan pointed to a picture of Dr David Thornton. She cast her eye over the image, her stomach tying itself in knots. "And you were sent to Istanbul? Is that right?"

"Yes. That's right. I was with this man, when the Police called the Istanbul Archaeological Museum to speak with him." She pointed at a picture of Dr Osman Elmas – a cutting from a Turkish newspaper.

Sheridan edged up an eyebrow, the only response his stony face had given to her since they met. She read it as a new piece of information she had just provided him with and held onto the idea. She already felt better for having contributed something, however small, to the investigation.

"48 hours after he left Varna, a man matching Thornton's description was recorded on CCTV at Budapest airport." Sheridan waved his hand over Budapest on the map and a blurry picture of Thornton.

"And was he on any flight manifests?"

"No. There is no record of his passport passing through the airport."

"Did he have any known alias's?"

Sheridan flashed an eyebrow at her, and the vague suggestion of a smile. In his eyes she could see she had impressed him and inside she was congratulating herself.

"We are trying to figure that out," he said.

"Any idea where he could have been flying to?"

"None. But 48 hours later a car registered in his wife's name was involved in an accident during bad weather on the M4 westbound, just outside Swindon. Suggesting she had picked him up from a London airport, probably Heathrow, to return to their home near Exeter. Ann Thornton survived the crash with minor injuries, but David Thornton was killed instantly at the scene," she could feel her face draining of colour as he described it, "A lorry behind them had jack-knifed and a scaffolding pole from its load came free, broke through the back window of their Ford Focus and impaled Thornton through the back of his head. He never stood a chance. Fortunately Ann Thornton had been knocked unconscious from the impact and didn't have to see the gruesome scene that met the emergency services."

Tears lanced at her eyes and she choked them back. She had never known how Thornton had died, only that it had been a car accident. Sheridan had just been so matter-of-fact in the description that part of her wanted to be sick.

"In the accident report there was the suggestion of faulty brakes on the Thornton's vehicle," he added. The sick feeling rose in her gut. Had it been an accident? She didn't want to think about it yet, she needed more information. Swallowing back the bile she looked at another section of the map.

"So," she began, "Do you know what was stolen from the site? If indeed it was a simple case of theft?"

"What else could it be but a theft? If Thornton had nothing to hide, why did he try to conceal his whereabouts?" Sherdian's face remained impassive, but she detected the strain of incredulity in his voice, as if he thought he had already figured it all out.

"I didn't say Thornton had nothing to hide," his assumption irritated her, "But you can't be sure it was a simple as that, can you?"

"Do you have another theory?"

"Not yet, but I don't have all the facts yet. So I am not jumping to any conclusions until we have a better idea of Thornton's motives."

"Spoken like a true investigator," he said, with a hint of a smile.

She was pleased she was starting to ruffle his feathers. She stared back and said nothing. Sheridan narrowed his eyes.

"The artefact stolen was a box, made of bronze."

"A bronze box in a copper age site?" Her face fell slack with bewilderment. She had suspected it and the memory of discussing it with David in the Bistro in Varna came rushing back to her; "interesting."

"Indeed," he raised an eyebrow.

"Do you have any other leads?"

"Perhaps."

She glared at him. Would he always be this difficult?

"Who are these people?" she said, focusing on another part of the map - around the Middle East and the Mediterranean.

"These men work for a terrorist organisation led by a man known only as 'The Libyan'."

"Terrorists? What the…?" words failed her. This conversation was about to veer off on an unexpected tangent.

"Do you have any idea how much weapons and munitions cost?" asked Sheridan.

"A lot, I suppose," she shrugged.

"Have you got any idea how much organisation and expense it takes to put on a display like nine eleven?"

"Nine eleven?" she screwed up her face.

"Terrorism is an entire economy, bank rolled at the highest levels of business and politics. There is far more to it than extremists bombing civilians because they are driven by some twisted ideology. For the foot soldiers on the ground, brainwashed into strapping a bomb vest to themselves or hijacking a plane, it may be as simple as that, but at the top of the food chain it's big money."

"What's any of that got to do with this?"

"Nine eleven was just an example," he sounded quietly irritable, "What it's ultimately all about is money – or rather, the world's distribution of wealth."

"And this bronze box? How does that fit?"

"Why are Allied Forces in Afghanistan?"

"Excuse me?" she was becoming more tangled the more she listened.

"Afghanistan. Why are NATO troops there?"

"To stop the Taliban?"

"And?"

"Because they are a threat to global security?"

"And?" he repeated, trying to get her to say it. She sighed, wishing he'd get to the point. She was finding this little dance rather tiresome. It was like he was trying to psych her out and she was in no mood for such games.

"Because of the drugs trade?" she shrugged in irritation.

"Exactly. The flow of drugs around the world is a key source of finance for terrorist operations. Any idea what else can command such high profits?"

"Enlighten me," she pursed her lips and folded her arms. He hummed, his brows knitted.

"Art and cultural artefacts," he said.

"So you think the box has gone into the black market trading of stolen antiquities?"

"Precisely," although his expression didn't give anything away, she could hear the triumph in his voice.

"But that doesn't make sense," she was annoyed now, "David would never have sold artefacts on the black market. What possible motive could he have to go against everything he believed in?"

"Agent Blake, I know you were close to the man, and it's hard for you to accept, but it's a fact that most artefacts taken from archaeological dig sites are taken by site workers," his tone was condescending. She had heard this argument before, people often made unfair assumptions about her profession and it infuriated her. She held her breath, told herself to calm down, but every fibre of her being was screaming out that David would never have sold an artefact to terrorists.

"Agent Sheridan," she stiffened, her arms crossed tightly around her chest, "What you are saying is utterly ridiculous. There is no reason why David Thornton would do that. Is there some evidence he was in debt or needed the money?"

"Not really," he conceded.

"Well then. There you go. Think about it for a moment. With respect, Agent, I think you are jumping to a convenient conclusion."

"With respect, Agent, I think you are too emotionally invested in this to be objective."

"Emotionally..." she stopped herself, took a breath and

released her arms, she wasn't going to allow this to become a tit-for-tat, "Where do I get a drink from around here?"

"Outside, second door on the right is a kitchen," he waved dismissively at the door and turned back to his desk.

"Do you want anything?"

He looked at her, a note of surprise in his eyes.

"No thank you."

"Fine," she huffed and made for the door.

"Fine," he was determined to have the last word. As she stepped out, she flexed her fingers, imagining herself slapping him. She enjoyed the thought.

She found the kitchen, poured herself a glass of water from the tap, downed it and poured a second. She rested on the sink for a moment, composing herself before facing him again.

When she walked back in, taking a full glass of water with her, she found him facing away, buried deep once more in the mountain of paperwork on the desk.

As the door opened, he span around, almost stunned she would come back so soon. Before stepping down into the office, she leaned into the doorframe, holding the glass in both hands.

"Okay, so, leaving aside any preconceived ideas we each have, let's look at this objectively shall we?"

"Agreed," he said, turning the shabby operator's chair he was sat in around and folding his arms. She cast an eye up and down him, trying to read his body language. His thick biceps pressed on the fabric of his sweatshirt, his jeans tugged in all the right places. She was reassured he hadn't completely let himself go since the first time they met.

"So, we have a missing box. We have a network of terrorists. We have former colleagues of Thornton's…"

"Yourself included," interrupted Sheridan, a suspicious glint in his eye.

"Myself included. Who else is involved?"

A hint of a smile curled his lip. He unfolded himself, like a spring releasing and reached for a folder on his chaotic desk. He fished around in the file and produced a photograph.

"We have her," he waved the picture at her like a flag of surrender.

She closed the door behind her and moved closer. She leaned across to get a better look.

"Who is she?"

The picture was of a young woman, perhaps in her early thirties, close to her age. She had soft features and a friendly face that seemed endlessly apologetic. Her hair was dark, smooth and cropped in a tidy frame. Her eyes stared back at her, as if they were looking into her soul.

"Her name is Gina Morgan. The only reason we came across her was because we acquired some intelligence indicating The Libyan was trying to find out more about her."

"Acquired some intelligence? What does that mean?" she cocked a hip and raised an eyebrow at Sheridan. He said nothing, but his Adam's apple twitched minutely.

"That's not your concern. What is important is that if the Libyan is looking for her, she must have a connection to the box."

She felt sure Sheridan was hiding something, but played along, "And how do we find her?"

"She's in Bristol."

"Bristol? Should we go and talk to her?" she sighed, gulped down the last of her water and leaned against the desk beside Sheridan, dangerously close to his territory, "How does it work?"

"What do you mean?"

"Are their particular protocols we adopt, a procedures manual? Anything like that?"

A minute smile stretched his lip, but his eyes told her more, "Protocols? You really do have a lot to learn! Milton wants results. He leaves his agents to decide how they operate. All he asks is that we behave with discretion, and keep it low key. Rule number 1 - don't draw attention to yourself. Aside from that, I report in regularly and the Agency provides any resources we need. From there, it's down to us."

"So let's get this show on the road shall we?"

"One step at a time. Let's get you set up with a laptop, phone and firearm…"

"Wait a minute. A firearm?" The sick feeling returned.

"What?" For the first time he showed some real emotion, however faintly - it was disbelief.

"I'm not carrying a firearm, Agent Sheridan."

"Why not? What happens if we're in trouble and need to defend ourselves?"

She gave him a withering look, "What are you, paranoid? And what about rule number 1 – Nothing draws attention like a gun."

"One gunshot will go unnoticed. People will second guess themselves and explain it first – a car backfiring, something heavy being dropped. As long as there are no witnesses. Two shots will arouse suspicion and three is 999 time. There is a time and place and rule number 2 is – protect yourself, don't take any unnecessary risks."

"More people in America are killed by their own guns than someone else's," she said. He stared back, refusing to take the bait.

"I still refuse to have a firearm," she said, "We're in a basement somewhere in central London - what could we possibly have to defend ourselves against?"

SECRET LOCATION SOMEWHERE IN LONDON (PART 2)

July

She followed Sheridan to the Black Mercedes. It was one of a row of identical cars whose number plates were all the same but for the last letter. Sasha couldn't help but feel she was walking towards a defining decision. She just wasn't sure what kind yet. Sheridan reached into the pocket of his jeans, the dimly lit underground garage flamed orange and the squeal of the car alarm disengaging bounced off the concrete columns.

She slid into the passenger seat and before she had time to clip her seatbelt into place he had twisted the ignition, and screeched out of the parking bay with a jerk of the steering wheel. Fumbling around as the car moved, she finally strapped herself in. She fired a critical look at him, which went unnoticed. The tyres screamed against the concrete, the growl of the engine, like a panther, reverberated off the low concrete ceiling. Up a ramp, around a corner, through a series of up and over doors and down a dark tunnel and eventually they emerged into daylight. He gunned the accelerator and swept out of the junction, hardly stopping to check the route was clear. Her heart rate quickened. Where had this guy learned to drive, Silverstone?

They sped down a maze of empty back streets and lurched onto The Strand. A chorus of horns blared around them, some directed at them, as they weaved between the slow churn of vehicles and onto a clear stretch of road. She wondered if he got a kick out of being the world's most inconsiderate road user, but if he did, he never showed it.

Grey clouds gathered, the wind buffeted the car and a gloom leached through the air. They slowed for a set of traffic lights, but he balanced the clutch and revved the engine. A plump blob of rain landed on the windscreen, then another, and another. He flicked on the windscreen wipers and stared accusingly at the traffic lights. Outside, men and women in sober coats and suits scurried along the crowded pavements, pulling their collars up, opening umbrellas, and rushed through oily puddles. At least it was warm and dry in the car, she thought.

"Are we in some sort of hurry?" she asked. He fired an impatient look at her, as if sarcasm did not compute. He pumped the accelerator as soon as the light switched to green. Her head was forced back into the chair and she huffed.

They settled into a rhythm as they hit heavy traffic and he was absorbed in the driving. She stared silently out of the window, running the images on the map through her mind and trying to piece them together.

"This girl," she began, "What's her story?"

"She works for an alternative investment company."

"What does that mean?"

"That she helps rich people to invest their money wisely."

"Do you think she is involved in the smuggling of antiquities?"

"Let's find out shall we," he pressed the accelerator harder as they hit a 40 zone, the speedo edging towards 50.

"So what's your plan Agent Sheridan? Are you going to knock on her door and say excuse me, have you smuggled any stolen antiquities for terrorists recently?"

"There's no need to be sarcastic, Agent Blake," his tone was uncompromising and she twitched, as if the chair had nipped her.

"Well what then?"

"We need to find out more about her. She'll respond better to you. She might be more inclined to trust a woman close to her age. I want you to build up a rapport with her, see if you can get the measure of her."

"You want?" she raised an eyebrow. His response was a disproving hum.

They fell into contemplative silence once more.

He elbowed the car onto the Hammersmith Flyover and wove through the congestion to a clear stretch of road. She cringed as they narrowly missed wing mirrors, cones and barriers. She watched the Victorian terraces, 60's squat blocks and gleaming office buildings whip past until gradually they were replaced with trees, hedges and verges.

She had always hated long car journeys and boredom quickly set in. Her mother had always thrust a book at her when she showed signs of boredom and she wished she had something to read now. She fidgeted, fumbled with the radio, tugged at the constricting seat belt, occupied herself by watching the concentration on Sheridan's face as he drove, and broke the silence.

"What's in the satchel?" she asked, leaning between the chairs and exploring the backseat.

"My laptop, and a few files."

"What files?"

"Files about the case."

"Talking to you is like getting blood from a stone."

He made a low guttural growl in his throat, as if he had more to say but had trapped it behind his teeth in the name of diplomacy. Sasha rolled her eyes.

"You're a man of few words, Agent Sheridan."

"Unless you can improve the silence, sometimes it's better not to say anything at all." It sounded like an accusation - to avoid more futile questioning, she satisfied her curiosity by reaching around the chair and tugging the satchel onto her lap.

"What are you doing?" he asked, his eyes never leaving the road, his tone impenetrable.

"I was going to read through the files while you drive, since you're not in the mood to talk."

Another icy hum issued from his lips. She ignored it and took the files out of the heavy satchel. She pulled a folder out and lifted the flap. Inside was a series of pictures.

"You've been gathering a lot of information, I see."

"The Agency has, yes. We have researchers working on contracts across the world."

"Has anyone from the Agency ever approached her, or questioned her?"

"Not yet, why do you think we're on this road trip."

She shuffled through the images, turning them over and reading notes on the back of them, "None of these pictures are dated back more than about a year?"

"We've just come across her."

"But how long have you been investigating the case of this missing bronze box?"

"About 7 years now. Well I have anyway."

"What do you mean I have, how deeply are The Agency involved in this?"

"It's only since you came on board that a client has come forward to pay the agency to locate the box. Before then, it was just something I had taken an interest in when there seemed to be a link to a wider network of strategic art thefts from some of the world's greatest art and antiquities institutions."

"Institutions like the British Museum?" she said, waiting for a reaction from him. He cleared his throat and ignored the reference.

"So you believe there is some wider conspiracy at work here?" she asked.

"Don't be naïve, Blake. There is an entire hidden economy in stolen art smuggling. It's big business. And it's a business that has been well funded and organised since the Second World War."

Angered by his accusation, she was determined to set the record straight, she was not as ignorant as he seemed to believe. It frustrated her she would need to prove herself to this man throughout the course of this case.

"I'm not being naïve, Agent. People have been profiting from stolen art since communities have been trading. Egyptian tomb robbers, invasion forces picking up the spoils. You yourself alluded to the fact that most artefacts stolen from archaeological sites are taken by the workers. I'd appreciate it if you didn't speak to me as if I'm stupid."

He hummed irritably, "I'm simply trying to point out that we are dealing with a global industry, it goes deeper than one man stealing a box. It's important that you appreciate the context we are working in. If you were stupid, Agent, you wouldn't be here, and I'll ask you to show me a least a little respect as your colleague. Believe it or not everything is not always about you, Agent Blake," his tone remained flat and emotionless, but she could see from his descending brow line he was irritated.

She let it hang for a while and seethed silently – she didn't remember him being this arrogant?

She focused on the world flashing past outside, avoiding the tension inside the car and having to communicate with him further. Only as she saw how far behind they were leaving the other traffic did she realise how fast they were travelling. She glanced at the speedo, it was approaching 90.

"Where are we?" she enquired, affecting a passive tone.

"On the M4, approaching Swindon," he mumbled, veiled animosity in his voice. As they passed under a series of foot bridges, it dawned on her they were now on the stretch of motorway where David had died. Although it had been over ten years ago, she couldn't help but feel saddened. A lump of grief formed in her throat.

Why was she even here, in a speeding car, with an arrogant and overbearing man who's only redeeming features seemed to be physical?

She distracted herself with the pictures once more. Flicking though various blurred landmarks in Bristol with the young woman, in sharp focus, engaged in various activities. Sipping a cold beer with a man she seemed close to, chatting on her mobile while laden down with grocery bags, laughing in a group of other women her age, all dolled up for a night on the town.

Had Gina ever suspected that a stranger working for some

shady organisation was following her around capturing intimate snapshots of her life?

"Who's the bloke?"

"Hmm?" Sheridan hummed, not even bothering to form a polite response.

"In this picture. The one having a beer on the harbour front with her?"

"Her husband."

"What do you know about him?"

"Nothing much. His name is Rees Morgan. He's a lecturer at Bristol University."

"What's his subject?"

"Business studies."

"Anything dodgy about him?"

"Nothing. He's never even had a speeding ticket. He's squeaky clean and frankly, a bit boring," Sheridan kept his emotionless eyes on the road. Answering only what she asked and not engaging in more conversation than that. It suited her fine - right now, all she wanted was facts from him. She had to work with him, she'd stay civil and as long as he did the same she'd be happy.

CAFÉ NOIR, BRISTOL

July

"Hiya. Single espresso please."

"2-39 please," Gina had £3 ready in her hand and gave it to the barista who rang it into the till then handed her a trickle of shrapnel.

"Pick your drink up at the end. Have a nice day. Next."

Gina shuffled along the counter and waited at the end, eyeing up a jar of biscotti. A handsome young man with an Italian accent handed her the drink with a twinkle of a smile. She watched him for an indulgent moment. She loved her husband but there was no harm in window-shopping.

Deciding against biscotti and distracted by the man's lyrical voice, as he chatted to his colleague, she turned away from the counter and was hit from the side.

"Shit!" she cursed to herself and shook warm coffee off of her hand and brushed her suit trousers in a futile attempt to tackle the spillage.

"Oh, I'm so sorry. Here. Allow me," a tall woman with mid length blonde curly hair dabbed at her with a handful of scrunched napkins. Annoyed at the intrusion on her personal space she snarled at the woman. In the true spirit of English politeness she apologised, even though it wasn't her fault.

"I'm really sorry. Please, let me buy you another drink." responded the woman.

"No, no, it's fine. Don't worry about it," she hissed, trying to remain cordial but seething she barely had a drop of coffee left in the cup.

"Please," pleaded the blonde woman, "I insist."

She looked the woman up and down. She had fearsome emerald eyes but a kind face. She had the inexplicable sense that this woman would be important to her but she didn't yet know why.

The woman offered her a rueful smile.

"All right," she relented, feeling somehow drawn to her.

The café was almost empty and the woman waved her over to the counter where she was served a new espresso. The woman ordered herself a cappuccino.

"Why don't you join me?" offered the blonde.

"It's fine, really."

"Please," smiled the woman, "I hate sitting on my own and the least I can do is keep you company after wasting your drink for you!"

She shrugged. There seemed no sense in fighting it. She wouldn't usually talk to random strangers but something in the woman's demeanour was strangely familiar. She led the way to a table by the window and the two women sat on tall stools beside each other, looking out to the busy street beyond. The sun was warm as it cast a buttery glow through the plate glass window.

"So are you on your lunch break then?" began the blonde woman, starting a polite conversation.

"Yeah. You?"

"In a way. I'm visiting the area on business, I'm killing time between meetings."

"Oh right. So what business are you in?" asked Gina.

"I work for a specialist agency. What about you?"

"I work for an alternative investment company."

"Oh really? That sounds interesting. What does that involve?" the blonde blinked at her, looking interested in her line of work. It was something she rarely encountered. Normally she received a sneer that she worked in finance and all the associated grubby money grasping that came with it.

"I account manage business clients who are looking for alternative ways to invest their money. Instead of the usual stocks and shares."

"Oh, what, you mean like, art and things?" the woman asked, then blew on her cappuccino and took a long sip.

"Yeah. Art, wine, jewels, property, things like that," she

elaborated.

"I have a friend who is an artist. He's a sculptor, you may have heard of him, Gregory Lepton?"

"Oh yes! Didn't he win the Turner Prize last year?"

"That's right."

"How funny that you know him. Just last week one of my clients sold a Lepton piece and made a tidy profit," she commented, intrigued by the apparent connection to the blonde stranger.

"Oh how funny," the blonde sipped her coffee and watched as Gina drank her espresso deeply.

"So what does specialist agency mean? Is it a temp agency or something?"

"Not quite," responded the blonde with a wry smile, "We work at a high level. Recruiting specialists for specific projects on behalf of corporate clients who value their privacy. We have to practice discretion at all times."

"That sounds a bit cloak and dagger!" she laughed nervously. The blonde laughed too, but her laugh was stilted somehow, leaving her feeling guarded.

The woman slid her purse from her handbag, snapped it open, "here," and she handed her a business card.

She fumbled the card in her fingers. It was good quality, glossy, but all it had on it was a name and mobile number.

"This card says nothing about what you do? Or who you work for?" she commented, her face craggy with reservation.

"Like I say, my clients value discretion."

"Well. It's nice to meet you…" she hesitated and re-read the name on the card, "…Sasha."

"You have me at a disadvantage?"

"Oh, yes, sorry. My name is Gina, Gina Morgan. Hang on, I have a card here somewhere," she fumbled in her handbag and pulled out a dog-eared business card. As she passed it to Sasha she noted how cheap it seemed in comparison and was momentarily ashamed of it.

"Thanks," smiled the blonde as she got up. She glanced at a simple leather wristwatch then back down to her.

"Please excuse me Gina, my next meeting is in a few minutes. If you ever find yourself in any trouble or in need of help, give me a call."

The way Sasha said in any trouble disturbed her.

"I will do," she said, hesitantly, "Thank you Sasha. And thanks for the coffee."

"No problem. I'm sorry I wasted your first one."

With that Sasha stood and began to turn away out of the café. She glanced back at Gina.

"I'm in Bristol for a few days. If you want to catch up for a drink or something?"

She smiled at the woman, the invitation felt genuine.

HARBOURSIDE, BRISTOL

July

"I got you a beer," said Sheridan as Sasha approached the table.

"Oh. Cheers," she smiled, pleasantly surprised by the gesture. From what she'd seen of him so far, such an act of generosity seemed uncharacteristic.

Perhaps he was trying to make peace? She thought.

Sheridan had found a table for them under the dappled shade of the trees behind the Arnolfini Gallery. She dragged a director's chair across the cobbles and sat opposite him.

He'd changed and freshened up at the hotel and she caught the musk of his fresh citrus aftershave on the breeze that licked along the harbor, impressed at how well he scrubbed up.

Perhaps he was making an effort to impress her too?

The last golden strip of sunlight clung to the city skyline, gilding the cranes along the Warf and the masts of the pleasure boats. The harbourmaster periodically bobbed by, his spluttering two stroke engine carving a lapping wake that disturbed the resting seagulls and swans.

"So what did you learn from her?" he asked, a faint foam moustache forming on his top lip. He licked it away, a motion she found fascinating.

"I found out she drinks Espressos!" her eyes smiled at him over the rim of her glass, condensation dripping onto the table from it.

"Do you ever take anything seriously, Blake?" his eyes looked severe.

Defiant, she took a swig of her beer and flashed him a smile.

"Okay, I'm sorry," she said half-heatedly, "Gina confirmed she trades in art on behalf of her clients…"

"Interesting..." he interrupted, raising an eyebrow.

"But she and I have a connection."

"How so?" he sipped at his beer, his dark brown eyes filled with curiosity.

"It's a bit tenuous, but it could give me an in. My friend Gregory Lepton won the Turner Prize last year. His stock value has increased massively. Gina told me a client of hers had recently sold a Lepton piece and made a significant profit. The thing is, Gregory has something of a niche for his work."

"I remember it from the exhibition at the British Museum. I seem to recall it being particularly erotic."

"It is. That's why it was so controversial when he won the Turner Prize."

"I remember seeing it on the news. I thought of you..." he cut himself off and buried his lips into his beer. She thought she detected a flush of red in his cheeks and was quietly amused. Every time she provoked a reaction from Sheridan it gave her that giddy thrill she felt when she was close to a discovery. Perhaps working with him wouldn't be so bad after all - if only for the entertainment value.

A busker struck up a tune on his guitar and the satisfying beat prompted them both to gently bob their heads as they quietly drank. The low rumble of voices and clatter of heels on cobbles seemed to follow the rhythm of the music. Couples, students, runners, young families, pensioners and office workers trickled back and forth.

"Two more?" the friendly voice of a waitress interrupted their contemplative moment. As she swept up their empties, they exchanged uncertain glances.

Sasha relented, "Sure. Same again please."

Sheridan didn't protest. They were both comfortably slumped, gazing over the silvery water.

"So now that I've made contact with the girl, any ideas about what we should do next?"

"I believe this woman is somehow linked to the missing box, but I'm not sure how yet," replied Sheridan, "I've been thinking we need more information at source."

She narrowed her eyes, "What do you mean?"

"I've been going around in circles for so long with this. There is only so much I can do remotely. I've been close to this for so long now, I've lost my focus."

The Waitress returned with fresh beers for them, they paused their conversation to thank her.

"Then perhaps we need to go back to the beginning. Lets' go back to where all of this started. I still have some contacts," she suggested.

"Bulgaria?"

She nodded.

He sat upright, animated, "I'll make the arrangements."

BISHOPSTON, BRISTOL

July

"Was that the door?" Rees put his steaming mug down and leaned around the settee, expecting to hear the doorbell. There was a heavy bang on the door as it pulsed violently in its frame.

Gina got up slowly and edged towards the hall. Again, the door pulsed inward with a sharp thud, then again.

"Oh God," terror filled her body. She felt nauseous.

"What's happening?" Rees's eyes were glazed with bewilderment, as if he were disorientated in what should have been a familiar space.

"Someone is trying to break in," Gina said, hardly believing the words had come from her mouth, "We have to get out of here."

She dashed into the hall and grabbed her handbag before catapulting herself back in to the lounge towards Rees.

"What the hell!" Rees stared towards the hallway, frozen. He looked straight through her as she returned to his side.

"Come on, we need to leave," she tugged at his arm, "We have to go."

"How? There's only one door to the flat," he was sluggish to react, his face grey, and sheer frustration gave her the strength to get him moving.

"Just shut up and follow me will you. Now come on!" she clenched Rees's hand and pulled him towards the window. With the other hand, she drew the sash up and climbed out.

"What the fuck, Gina. We can't get out that way!"

As he said it a heavy boot thudded against the front door. With a bang, it smashed open. In stepped a man wearing a hoodie, zipped to his chin, the hood shadowing his face.

"Shit me!" shouted Rees as he was dragged out of the open window. They stepped down onto the roof of the flat below, a space they had used as an occasional balcony in the summer. Gina was leaning down, judging the distance to the roof of next doors garden workshop.

"Where the fuck are we supposed to go from here, Gina, hmm?"

"We can make it, come on!" without further thought or argument, she bent her knees, rocked back on her heals, psyching herself up, then jumped.

"Gina!" he called after her with a horrified cry.

"Come on!"

She had landed with a square footing, as if she'd done it a thousand times, and waved him to follow.

She watched, as he glanced behind him, looking for an alternative. The hooded burglar was leaning out of the window behind him.

Rees hesitated, not accustomed such urgency, "Oh fuck. Fuck me, what am I doing?" he cursed and then jumped.

He landed with a thud on both feet beside her and tapped himself down, as if he was making sure he had actually made it. His eyes relieved and reassured. She crouched onto all fours, negotiating her way off the side of the workshop roof onto a low stone wall a few feet below.

Shaking his head in disbelief, Rees followed. He took one final look behind him at the open window of their flat, as if he were hoping he had just imagined this and everything would be fine.

It wasn't.

From the window they heard crashing and banging and saw the assailant getting ready to jump down after them. Behind him, another man in a hoodie with an indistinct face was in close pursuit.

"Shit," Rees cursed and followed in her footsteps as she tight-rope-walked along the low wall, before leaping down into a neighbours flower bed. She brushed herself down and dashed across the lawn to the next fence. She glanced back and was relieved to see Rees following her. A weight lifted and adrenalin kicked in. She had to keep moving.

They vaulted over the low fence to next garden along the terrace. Gardens were on both sides and they were walled in by the backs of endless terraced houses, a domesticated fortress.

"Gina," Rees panted, she glanced back as she negotiated the next low garden fence and paused to allow him to catch up.

Rees reached for her hand and pulled her over the next fence with him. They ran, hand in hand over Mrs Johnson's prized lawn and through her herbaceous borders and clambered over the whitewashed garden wall, leaving muddy scuff marks down it.

"Sorry Mrs Johnson," Gina shouted, just in case.

It was getting darker now, the twilight giving way to inky blackness. A smoky world swallowed them as they kept moving. Vaulting over fence after fence in some twisted nightmare of a hurdle race. As exhaustion caught Gina, the icy air seemed to freeze in her lungs.

"We're almost at the main road," Rees panted, in a frail attempt to reassure them both that it would soon be over. In the deepening gloom behind them, grunting and the pounding of footsteps seemed to be more distant now, but they had to keep moving. Over one more fence was the inviting glow of orange and the increasing sound of traffic.

They helped each other over the final wall and clambered down onto a side street. They stopped, crouched down and clutched their knees, gasping for breath.

"Now what?" asked Rees.

"Where did you park?"

With hardly the strength to lift his arm, Rees pointed back towards Gloucester Road, "That way."

"Come on," she said, clamping him on the shoulder.

They half-walked half-jogged to the car a couple of streets away.

"Shit," swore Rees.

"What?"

"My keys are in my jacket. Fuck," he punched the roof of the VW Beetle in frustration.

"I've got my set," she grinned. At least one of them had

had the foresight to bring their bag with them. She never went anywhere without her handbag, even when running for her life she couldn't be without it. She unlocked the car and handed Rees the keys. They climbed in, sat back in their seats relieved, and quietly took stock.

She saw movement in the interior mirror, "We have to move," and fired an urgent look at him. Two hooded men were heading their way, like swooping ravens they moved ever closer.

"Fuck," Rees twisted the key in the ignition and swung out into the road. They turned into Gloucester Road and joined the never ending chain of traffic, just another anonymous link in the circle of vehicles that choked the city. There was nowhere to overtake down here so while they were part of the mindless flow they were safe.

"Now what?"

"Just drive," said Gina, wringing her fingers for comfort.

"Where are we going?"

"I don't care, Rees, we just need to get out of the…oh shit."

"What is it?" Rees flicked a concerned look.

"I see them. Two cars behind. A black BMW. They're following us."

"Shit. Hang on. I'll try to lose them."

Keeping an eye in the mirrors he wove between the lanes as they approached the junction at Stokes Croft. He peeled onto the roundabout, indicated left then swerved into the middle lane. Tyres screeched and horns blared in every direction. The BMW was still there. As they negotiated the lanes around The Bearpit, Rees swerved across and briefly stole a space between some busses, right now a fine for being caught in the bus lane was the least of their problems. Using the side of a double decker to hide from their pursuer, Rees weaved around and along the Haymarket. He jumped a red light, again inviting a hateful tirade of horns. Glancing in his mirror, he could still see the BMW, but it looked disorientated. They'd gained an advantage.

Around the parabola of Colston Avenue, the tyres howled against the cobbles. Dodging between the endless stream of buses, they lost them. Gina looked from mirror to mirror and stretched to the back window in a desperate bid to make sure they were no longer being followed. She cursed the day she had fallen in love with such a distinctive convertible VW Beetle.

The traffic lights seemed to be on their side as a green wave opened up ahead of them. They surfed it up Park Street and a gap soon appeared behind as the pedestrians, like guardian angels, kept the pelican crossings red behind them.

"Now what?"

"Keep driving," Gina barked, more single word communication.

"But where are we going?" His tone flicked to sarcasm, "Here's a thought. How about we go to the fucking Police Station Gina, Hmmm?"

"Hey. There's no need to swear at me," she said, wounded.

"Sorry babe, it's just, y'know," his tone softened and he glanced a smile at her.

"I know," she said with a rueful smile.

Rees fixed his eyes to the road ahead as they swung up into Clifton and headed for the Suspension Bridge.

"What just happened?"

"How would I know!"

Rees pulled into a street side parking bay and knocked the gear stick to neutral. The car throbbed as the engine purred, like a big cat about to pounce. Rees turned in the seat to look at his wife.

"We're trapped in the Bourne Identity and we don't know why?" he said, frustration thick in his voice, "You seemed to know what the fuck was happening at the flat!"

"What does that mean?" she turned to glare at him.

"I don't know. That whole climbing out of the window stunt, it was like you had already planned your escape."

"Are you telling me you've never thought about how to get out of the flat in an emergency?"

Rees shrugged. She smiled to herself, and gazed out of the window, seeing the majestic iron arms of the bridge reaching across the gorge. She rummaged through her handbag, pulled out her purse and rifled around in it with a growing frown.

"Do you have 50p?"

"Hmm?"

"For the bridge toll," she reminded him calmly and gestured to the barriers, "Do you have 50p for the bridge?"

"No I don't have 50 fucking P. Funnily enough I didn't think to bring my loose change when I was being bundled out of a third floor window!"

"All right! Don't be like that!" she undid her seatbelt and got out of the car.

"Where are you going?"

She slammed the car door behind her. Seconds later she heard his raised voice again.

"Gina! Don't do this!"

She looked back, her brow furrowed and saw him leaning out of the open window, his hands poised on the steering wheel.

"Don't just leave me. I'm sorry babe, all right, I didn't mean to be shitty with you!" she smiled to herself and turned back.

"I'm not leaving you, you moron, I's sweet talking the Toll Collector!"

Every now and then Gina's adoptive Bristol accent crept in.

She pulled her arms around her chest against the biting wind that periodically whipped through the gorge and strode towards the luminous jacketed man at the barrier. Turned away, the guard was chatting to his colleague as she approached the barrier.

She swallowed hard, rehearsing her sob story in her head, when she glanced down at the change machine. There, a silver nugget sparkled in the floodlights, was a 50p piece, lying in the cradle under the reject hole.

"Yes," she said to herself, swiped the coin and dashed back to the car. She handed the coin to Rees and they drove over the spine of the bridge, its glowing iron ribs stretching up either side, framing the twinkling view down the gorge. Beyond the bridge Rees pulled into a lay-by, fringed with grasping trees. He twisted off the ignition and turned to look Gina in the eye.

"All right," he began, "I'm sorry I got upset with you earlier. But what the hell just happened and why are we here and not at the police station?"

Gina felt her eyes moisten, "I remember something I read in one of dad's journals. It was almost as if I should have been expecting this. He always used to say 'no matter how fast you run, the past will always catch you'. This is something to do with him, I can't explain it, but this isn't just a random attack. Someone is after something that dad left behind. Something he knows, something he's done."

"But that makes no sense? How can you be sure?" Rees sounded irritated, "Those thugs who broke in to our apartment, who were they then?"

"I don't know. I'm sorry Rees."

She began to sob. Her head throbbed, every bone in her body seemed to ache with weary tension.

"Hey, hey. Come here," Rees undid his seatbelt and leaned across the car. She allowed him to take her in his arms and hold her a while. "It's all right. We're safe now," he said in a soothing voice.

"No. No it's not all right, Rees," she pulled out of the embrace, sniffed back her tears and creased her face with frustration, "This isn't over. Something is going on here," she wiped her cheeks on the back of her sleeve.

"So what do we do then? We can't go home?"

"We need to go to Exeter and I need to see Danny."

"Danny? Is your brother likely to have any answers?"

"I don't know," she confessed and slumped in defeat. She picked mascara from the corners of her eyes with a neatly manicured fingernail and lost herself in her thoughts, trying to find reason in the madness.

"If this is about dad, maybe Danny will have some ideas," she muttered, as if her subconscious was given a voice.

"We should still go to the police."

"I'm not sure Rees. Dad was into something, I want to find out more before we involve the authorities."

"Gina, that's daft! We just had our flat broken into and got chased through Bristol. When does that kind of shit happen to normal people like us? Why not go to the police?"

"They'll just take a statement and offer us platitudes – I want answers Rees. What do they think I have? Whatever it is they are looking for, it doesn't seem like them finding it will end well for us? Whoever they are? Let's go to Danny first - we'll call the police later."

Rees threw a doubtful look, and then reluctantly nodded.

Something unknowable deep inside her made her not want to contact the police, not to trust them, although it made no sense. If someone was after something she had, this wouldn't stop until they had it.

"The box," she mumbled.

"Box? What box?" she looked back at Rees, his face looked strained and weary. She rested a reassuring hand on his knee.

"The shoebox. Maybe it's something in the shoebox."

"Shoebox?" Rees' eyes were narrow with confusion now, as if all logic in his life had died and he was being reborn into some strange world he had no hope of comprehending. She offered him a soft smile.

"The shoebox with dad's notebooks in and that envelope. I read something in one of dad's books that was in that box. Something about powerful men wanting to know the secret and stopping at nothing to get it. Never to trust the authorities, trust your instincts."

Her eyes glazed over as she thought back to the day after they had cleared out their parents' house. After finding those books and the envelope and putting them in the shoebox, she couldn't sleep. She had tossed and turned, curiosity getting the better of her. She sneaked down to his study in the middle of the night and opened one of the books. She'd read a few pages, then freaked out and put it all back in the box, realising she wasn't ready to see what her father was up to. But now it had been forced on her. She had to know. What use would going to the police be if she didn't at least have a vague idea what was going on? It would just be put down to another burglary in the city - Another crime number and insurance claim. There was more to it, she knew it, and she had to get to the bottom of it. Danny might know.

"Danny has it. The box is at his place. We need to get it, and make sure he's all right."

Her heart quickened as she realised the implication. If someone had found her, perhaps they could find him too?

"You realise how you sound don't you?"

"What do you mean?"

"You sound crazy, Gina. And you make your father sound like a criminal!"

She rolled her eyes, "Just give me the benefit of the doubt, please Rees, just once!"

He shrugged, "Fine - for now!" He raised a critical eyebrow.

She stroked his cheek, and he offered her a resigned smile.

"Thank you," she said.

As she played out the scenarios in her mind, looking for some logic, she tried to make connections. Despite her fears, she knew they needed help. Only one thing made sense to her. It was too much of a coincidence. Her father had always said 'I don't believe in coincidences' and sometimes she had to agree with him. The words echoed in her mind; If you ever find yourself in any trouble or in need of help, give me a call.

"Hang on," she said and rummaged around in her handbag with a renewed urgency. Could this be a solution?

She pulled out her phone.

"What is it?" asked Rees impotently.

She took out her wallet and slid out a business card, "A woman I met last week, I think she can help."

It felt right. She tapped in the mobile number and called Sasha Blake.

ROUTE 9, NEAR BANYA, BULGARIA

July

"How far did you say it was to Varna?" Agent Sheridan shuffled in the driver's seat, fumbling with the levers to get comfortable.

"About 60 miles, but the route takes us up over the leading edge of the Balkan Range Mountains before they fall away into the Black Sea so it's a winding route and can be quite slow. Especially if we get stuck behind one of those ancient lumbering Soviet cast-off trucks. I can drive if you'd prefer?"

"No, no," a forced smile reminded Sasha he liked to be in control. "So a couple of hours then?" he asked, twisting the key in the ignition.

"More like hour and a half - all being well. The views are good though, the highway follows the coast line."

Sheridan clunked the gears in the tinny Fiat Panda and stretched around the driver's seat to back out of the parking space, while Sasha watched in the mirrors, knowing that his driving could be erratic. She was always far more cautious, edging out of parking bays, but he stamped the accelerator and sliced his way into the thoroughfare.

"Remember to drive on the right," she said. He responded with an irritated grimace and a growl. It amused her how easily she could wind him up now and she smiled to herself, hiding the expression from him by gazing out at the hazy sky beyond the soft slopes of scrubland.

They pulled out of the airport car hire parking lot and slotted into the stream of traffic behind a rusting bus that belched out black swathes of smoke.

"So you know this route well do you?"

"I've travelled it a few times yes, but I usually fly into Varna or Sofia instead of Burgas."

"If there's an airport at Varna, why the hell didn't we fly into there?"

"Because they don't fly from Bristol to anywhere in Bulgaria but Burgas, and it was such short notice. It's only one road though and we needed a car anyway."

They filtered out into the highway and the traffic thinned as most of the vehicles leaving the airport took the turning for Burgas city centre.

They travelled in silence for a while, cruising along the long and empty road. The terrain levelled out, salt flats stretching out either side of them, the azure sea glistening in the sunshine to the right of them.

"I've worked in Russia before but this is the first time I've been to Bulgaria," said Sheridan, taking in the wide vista around them, "I somehow didn't expect the landscape to be so dramatic. I know a lot about history but I know very little about this part of Europe."

Sasha threw him a knowing smile, "That's why I'm here though isn't it?" she replied.

"That, and you have first-hand knowledge of what it is we're looking for."

"True, but at the Varna Archaeological Museum you'll be able to see some of the artefacts I helped to recover for yourself."

"Are these the ones you helped to Carbon Date?"

"Some of them. There is still a small collection at the British Museum too."

"And this box, it was never among this collection?"

"I never saw it, except on the computer model, based on what the geophysics and magnetometer data showed. The technology was quite new at the time, today's computers could have given us a much clearer picture of the composition of the box.

'From what we knew at the time, we could determine its size and density and that it was a metal alloy, we assume that to be bronze. The Varna Necropolis is a Chalcolithic Age site."

"Chalcolithic, what does that mean?"

"It comes from the Ancient Greek khalkos meaning copper and lithos meaning stone, commonly known as the Copper Age."

"Then why not say that?" hissed Sheridan.

"Sorry. I forget that you're just a historian and not an Archaeologist."

"Just? …Never mind."

She fired him an irritable look for breaking up her flow with pettiness.

"The Copper Age was before the Bronze Age, which makes the box a curiosity as it couldn't have been buried at the same time as the bodies and treasures interred there. It made no sense. I'd like to say it is an Out Of Place Artefact but that phase conjures up images of kooks, crypto zoologists and pseudo archaeology."

"What do you mean?"

"Out Of Place Artefact or OOPArt was coined by an American Naturalist to describe things that seemingly don't belong where they were found. A Norse coin found in an American Indian excavation. It's the kind of shit hoaxers and Creationists and generally idiotic people use to drag down the good name of proper archaeology."

"But it sounds like it's exactly that. Something that doesn't belong?"

"I know. And it messes with my head, frankly," she screwed her face up like yesterday's newspaper at the thought of it.

"But you said that you and Dr Thornton had reason to believe the artefact was buried there later?"

"True. We had our suspicions at the time but it bore out later in 2004 when the artefacts were carbon dated. The Necropolis dates back to 5000BC, the earliest known Bronze Age sites were 2000 years after this."

"The box was never carbon dated though?"

"Well no, of course not, it had gone missing years before. Keep up!" she fired a wry smile, and he kept his eyes on the road but curled his lip in contempt.

"As a consequence, not knowing the true genus of the missing box, we cannot be certain. The most common and popular metal alloy used in classical antiquity was bronze and remained so for centuries before alchemists started to experiment with what we now know as the elements."

"But the alchemists were trying to turn lead into gold?"

"They were, but in the process made many valuable discoveries about the nature of the building blocks of the planet and later, paving the way for Dmitri Medeleev to invent the Periodic Table in 1896," she responded, "Medeleev was Russian, they're a resourceful lot out here on the edge of Europe. And did you know the first scholar to come up with the theory of everything being made up of atoms was a Thracian?"

"That was around here was it?"

"This area is part of ancient Thrace, yes, but Democritus was from Abdera, which is in modern day mainland Greece. He was known as the laughing philosopher because of his lively temperament. They call him the father of modern science. Plato hated him by all accounts."

"So you know about classical Greece too?" Sheridan edged up an eyebrow.

"I know enough. Of course, that was the first time in the history of humanity, really, where we have written historical records. More your thing I guess?"

"To a point. Historians have to rely on the written record but I'm no expert on classical Greece - but it is the birthplace of modern Europe, and it is European Art and history that I know more about."

"And the coastal area of Thrace is now part of modern Greece. But these border lands and tribes are all interrelated in this region, the country borders we recognise today have only existed since the 20th Century. For millennia these lands have been conquered, invaded, fought for, won and lost by civilisations and empires that we have long forgotten. That's why this part of Europe fascinates me so much. It's largely undiscovered by the western world. It's the very birthplace of

European civilisation yet so much of the ancient history of the region remains a complete mystery. Bulgaria hides many secrets. There is archaeology out here hidden under these vast stretches of wilderness, just waiting to be discovered. People have inhabited these lands since the dawn of time. The first ever known market street was uncovered in Bulgaria you know?"

"Market Street? You mean the Bulgarians invented the High Street? So we have them to thank for retail industry do we?" he offered her a thin smile. She relished it for a moment, a rare glimpse of emotion from him. He fixed his attention on the road, slowing for a junction.

"I suppose so," she returned the smile, "It was Karanovo, very close to here in fact, just inland from Burgas. This whole region was part of the ancient land of Thrace, in Bulgarian Trakiya. Before being conquered by Macedonia."

"You mean Alexander the Great?"

"So you do know something about the history of this area?"

"Not much, just Alexander the Great," he said.

"Although, much evidence suggests the Thracians actually joined Alexander and accompanied him as allies during the Persian wars," she added, "Thracian was still a recognised ethnic group right into the early 20th Century, when there was ethnic cleansing during the second Balkan Wars. Anyway, this is all much later than the Necropolis and the Chalco...sorry Copper Age."

"Hur," murmured Sheridan, "ethnic cleansing – every time I hear those words I think of Serbian monsters butchering Kosovans."

Sheridan's whole demeanour shrank. She picked up on the change of atmosphere, like a suffocating smoke had filtered in.

"You served during the Yugoslav wars didn't you?"

"How do you know that?"

"You're not the only one who checked up on their partner," she flashed a wolfish grin at him but he seemed unmoved.

"What of it?" his shoulders stiffened, fangs bared.

"All right – sorry I bought it up."

"It's none of your business what I did in Yugoslavia. Anyway, it's irrelevant."

"Fine, fine. No need to get your boxers in a bunch."

Sheridan growled, took a breath and changed the subject, "So the Necropolis. Is it one of many such sites, thousands of years older than the pyramids?"

"Certainly. As I say, much of the country has been fallow and wild for centuries, there is hidden archaeology everywhere."

"So I see the excitement for you here. I guess the biggest buzz you get from Archaeology is discovering something new. Much of the history of Europe is well documented and the land has been worked and reworked for centuries. There is almost an expectation that you'll find undiscovered secrets in Bulgaria, when you know where to look."

"Precisely," she beamed, satisfied her companion understood why this place held such a fascination for her.

"If the box is later than the Necropolis site, can you estimate at least when it might have been buried at the site?"

"I would guess it would be around the time of classical Greece."

"How do you know the box is from classical antiquity? What do you base that assertion on?"

"It's merely an educated guess. The site reports indicate the strata of the soil makes sense for it to be that time. In the period between 7th and 1st century BC, Varna, then known as Odessus, was a recently established settlement and strategic port for Thrace, the emerging Roman Empire and Greece. It's reasonable to suppose that during this time of great upheaval where Greece and Byzantium were jostling for position, the Necropolis was known about. It was later, as the city grew, that many ancient sites fell into disrepair and were stripped of any useful building materials. The treasure there was well buried, and the Thracians had no reason to know what riches lay under their feet. Or perhaps they viewed it as sacred and forbidden? The site was forgotten. And whoever hid the box, I suspect chose the site for this reason. A land of the dead. In a superstitious time, people were too afraid to tamper with ancient burial sites, for fear of releasing unwanted spirits. For someone who was not of a superstitious disposition, it was a perfect hiding place."

"But who was not of a superstitious disposition at that time is history?"

"A scholar? Remember, we border Greece and Turkey here, we're at a crossroads of classical learning and philosophy. Any student of Plato or who studied at the Academies of ancient Greece would be of such a disposition. In classical antiquity there was a renaissance of ideas. Many people were starting to become sceptical and curious. Accepted explanations of Gods and monsters began to be questioned by an emerging educated class."

"But they would need to be of means to be able to travel to Odessus? Why would they want to hide knowledge of a box anyway? Surely they were all about discovering the truth of the world around them, not smuggling boxes of treasure through the Byzantine empire and burying it in a graveyard in some backwater Thracian port?"

"Who said it was a box of treasure? Why bury a treasure box in the largest cache of gold in the ancient world? And you're right. Then, as now, an education equals status and with that, wealth."

"But you said there was no reason to realise there was gold there? If there was, the site would have been looted long ago?" Sheridan pointed out.

"True, but that's not the point I'm making. The point is; it probably isn't a box of treasure. We're not talking about pirates burying a treasure chest under a palm tree. If whoever buried the box had the means to go to Odessus, a, as you put it, backwater Thracian port, why bury treasure there? It makes no sense."

"So what is in the box then?"

"We have no way of knowing. But something important, or

terrifying, enough to hide. When it was found we didn't have the technology to find that out without physically digging it up and taking a look inside."

"Do you think Dr Thornton opened it up and looked inside? I know I would have."

"But would you? I'm not sure I would have. If it's not treasure in the box what is it?" he shrugged at her question, despite its rhetorical nature, "If I have my doubts about the contents, the chances are David did too. I don't think he would have opened it."

"So what would he have done with it?"

"Isn't that what we're trying to find out?"

The car slowed, approaching a bottleneck of traffic moving in and out of the Sunny Beach resort. Ahead, the road narrowed and the looming green folds of the Balkan Range stretched ahead of them. Green waves of trees crept up the hillsides in the distance.

"Okay, so, what would you have done with it?"

"Me?" she said, "I probably would have taken it to the Varna Archaeological Institute for examination."

"Is that why we're going there, to find out if Thornton did the same?"

"In part, but also to speak to the experts and find out what they know."

"And this contact you said you were linking up with, who is he?" asked Sheridan.

"His name is Tsvetan, he was Thornton's right hand man at the site. I lost touch with him years ago but the geeks at HQ tracked him down."

"Did he know about the box?" he said.

"That's what I want to find out. He would have known as much as I did and seen the computer models, but whether he knew more than that, or helped Thornton to take the box, I don't know."

"Is it possible he in fact took the box and we're investigating the wrong person by going after Thornton?"

"You surprise me Sheridan, I thought you'd already made

your mind up about Thornton?"

"To echo your sentiment in London, I'm not jumping to any conclusions," he glanced at her, his face momentarily cracking into a smile. Pleased she was exerting some influence over him.

"It is possible that it was Tsvetan, but doubtful," she said.

"Why doubtful?"

"Do you really think he would have been so willing to talk to me if he was the thief? Besides, why else would The Libyan go after Gina? As far as we can tell she has no link to Tsvetan."

"But we know she is linked to Thornton and we know the Libyan is aware of her."

"Exactly. So the prime suspect in the theft of the box remains David. The question is why?" she said.

"So from what you knew of the man, did you ever have any reason to suspect he would remove and artefact for his own gain? You seemed upset when I accused him before?"

"I've had time to think since then. But still, I have to say no. And that's the crux of it. He was a successful professor and author, he owned several properties and had substantial investments in the Diamond trade. So he didn't need the money. If you read any of his work he was passionate about preserving history, not selling it to the highest bidder. The whole idea he would deliberately remove an artefact is completely out of character."

"So what about Tsvetan? The cloak and dagger nature of this meeting suggests he knows something?" said Sheridan.

"Perhaps. It's the best lead we have right now."

Sheridan dropped his gaze briefly. It seemed like he was hiding something, "It wasn't hard for the geeks at HQ to track him down," he said.

"What do you mean?" her brow furrowed at the implication.

"We've been monitoring him for some time."

"You've what?" her voice tripped up an octave, "Why tell me this now?"

"Need to know, Blake. Until you set up this meeting with

him, you didn't need to know."

She heaved a sigh of frustration, just when she seemed to be getting through to her partner he closed the door on her again.

Sheridan fought with the gears as they climbed further and further into the mountains and the little engine struggled to keep up with the strain. Whining in 2nd gear, they crested the hill. From the plateau, the views were breathtaking. They both fell silent and paused to take in the vista of vineyards, woodland, and rolling pastures that fell away into the sea.

"What else do I need to know then Sheridan, hmm? The Bristol girl is the only other lead we have so far. Is there anything I need to know about her?"

"Not at the moment," his Adam's apple twitched, "How did you get her to trust you anyway?"

She drew in a sharp breath, sure he was hiding things from her. Could she trust this man? The thought was too frightening to dwell on.

"The old spilling a drink trick!" She tried to make light of the rather transparent technique she had used to get the attention of her mark. Only then, when she heard herself say it, did a memory resurface. A sick feeling hit her - How could she have been so stupid? She fell silent for a moment and stared out of the window, watching the greenery of the woods flash past as she collected and reordered the memories.

"You did it to me didn't you? The Agency wasn't just monitoring Tsvetan, it was monitoring me too," she turned to Sheridan and glared at him.

"*That's how Milton knew so much about me…*" she muttered to herself, voicing her new found clarity.

He glanced back at her, his Adam's apple twitched. It was something she had noticed about him, while his face gave nothing away, he would swallow if he was trying to hide something – that was his tell.

His silence spoke volumes.

"Don't lie to me, Sheridan. Tell me, be honest!"

"I didn't even say anything and you accuse me of lying!" he

erupted. It was a diversionary tactic she clocked immediately.

She looked at him severely once more, "Come on, Sheridan. Don't avoid the question. You did it to me didn't you? That night, at the British Museum?"

It all made sense to her. It made her nauseous to think about how vulnerable she had made herself.

"Was I your mark? Was the wine and the sex all a ruse to get my attention and entice me into revealing something?"

"Hey, hey! Hang on a minute," he said with raw, unmistakable anger. For her, it was a clear signal she had caught him out. He tried another diversionary tactic, and said, "Why? Do you have a guilty conscience? Did you have something to hide?"

"Just answer the damn question!" by now she had shifted 90 degrees in the seat, a withering look on her face, her arms folded.

"Oh for gods' sake, Blake. That was years ago. And it was you that left me, remember? What does it matter?" he hissed, as if he had no time for these games. His eyes looked stony and cold, dark and foreboding, like he was so focused on their objective and didn't need these indulgences, her feelings didn't matter. Did anything matter to him, except the job?

"It matters to me! I was your mark wasn't I? You weren't a security guard were you? You were working for The Agency weren't you?" his silence inflamed her, "Tell me!"

He sighed theatrically.

"Look," he began, "We have a job to do here. Just as I had a job to do then. All of this shows me how inexperienced you are as an Agent, Blake. You can't take these things personally. You need to learn this. The moment you do, the more successful you'll be. If you don't this job will screw you up. How long until we're in Varna?"

The red mist rose at the way he patronised her.

"It's nothing to do with my inexperience as an agent!" she spat the words, "What this is about is whether or not I can trust you, Sheridan. You're my partner, I need to be able to trust you. I need to know you'll have my back."

"All right!" he growled, "You were my mark…"

"I fucking knew it!" she interrupted. Then she let the implications of it sink in, "You used me. You…"

Before she could finish the sentence a stag leapt into the road from between the trees.

"WATCH OUT!" she screamed.

Sheridan had seen it too, and as she was shouting, he was already swerving to avoid the massive lumbering animal in their path. He slammed at the brake pedal, it barely responded. Realising it would not be enough, he jerked the wheel to avoid the collision. The car skidded and he turned into the swerve, attempting to ride through it. Sasha just hung on, her knuckles white against the dashboard.

It would have worked, until they encountered a deep ragged pothole in their path. The Stag had safely leapt out of the way and gamboled off into the vineyards opposite as if nothing had happened. Sheridan struggled to regain control of the car. Snatching another yawning pothole the car slid into the ditch along the side of the road. There were no crash barriers on this section of road; along the entire length of route 9 the barriers were intermittent. As he fought with the steering wheel, the car began to tumble. She braced herself. Determined, he wrenched the wheel back and forth and pumped the accelerator to force the car out of the ditch, but its momentum was too great. Gravity and inertia conspired against them and the car began to tumble beyond control. It tipped and rolled down the hill. Over and over, a tangled ball that gathered speed before being abruptly stopped by a grape vine.

VARNA, BULGARIA

July

Sasha looked up at the edifice of Varna Hospital as she went back inside. It was a crude lump of soviet concrete, spilling out into wooden prefabricated huts. She knew enough Bulgarian to make herself understood by the receptionist, with the help of a few charades. The receptionist, a slight woman with home-dyed red hair, directed her in.

The ward Sheridan was on smelt of new paint and disinfectant. The walls bore a fresh coat of magnolia, the floors were shod with rubberised turquoise linoleum. It was brightly lit by a row of large UPVC windows and the caustic glare of strip lights suspended from a skeletal mass of pipes and wiring. By contrast, the furniture and equipment still seemed dated, like something transported from the 1950's. The occasional trolley of modern medical equipment dotted the room, with flashing lights and beeps, as if an alien spacecraft had landed.

Sasha's practical flat shoes squeaked as she walked the length of the ward, between the rows of beds, to the one at the end of the room where Sheridan lay.

He was tucked into a turquoise waffle blanket, like a pea in a pod. His arms were outside the covers and a clear plastic tube snaked up from one hand to a rusty old drip stand. The covers rose and fell steadily, he seemed so peaceful.

She pulled up a molded plastic chair and fidgeted her hips to get comfortable on the clammy seat. An air conditioning unit clattered dramatically at a nearby window, blasting a welcome relief from the hot and dusty city streets.

Her inner chatterbox was debating whether or not to disturb him. She was itching to talk through what she had learnt from the curator at the Varna Archaeological Museum a couple of blocks away.

Settling beside him, she watched him sleep for a while. Only then did her head remind her how handsome he was, it was usually preoccupied with how infuriating he could be, especially after their fight earlier. Yet despite it all, she felt an inescapable attraction to him.

She cast her eyes down his quiet form. The fine lines on his face mapped his history across it. Unshaven, stubble cluttered his chin and neck, emphasising his Adam's apple, which twitched periodically. He was wearing a hospital gown, his Special Forces tattoo partially hidden by it. His thick biceps and shapely arms were tanned and dusted with fine dark hairs and led to big, long fingered, hands. She slid her fingers under his, unable to resist the craving to reach for him. His fingers felt warm and reassuring. She squeezed a little tighter - it was enough to rouse him. His eyes blinked open and his gaze drifted towards her. A long smile stretched his face, activating his high cheek bones.

Embarrassed, she drew her hand away and said, "Hi!"

"H…" his voice failed, he cleared his throat, "Hey," he began, "How long have you been sat there?"

"Just a couple of minutes."

"You should have woken me."

"I just did."

He let out a small laugh.

"How 'you feeling?" she asked.

"Aching but fine," he said.

"You had me worried for a moment there," she chuckled to herself, "I'm still pissed off with you, but I was afraid I was going to lose you," she confessed, then stopped herself from saying more and risking further embarrassment.

"You won't get rid of me that easily," and he winked, an expression that confused her.

She had walked away from the crash with only cuts and bruises. After an all clear from the doctors she had wanted to see him as soon as he was bought to the hospital, to sit with him and be with him. She was afraid he would die, just as David Thornton had. The last words she had exchanged with

David all those years back had been in anger, but she had loved him, and had held the burden of that regret to this day. She had feared that history would repeat itself with Sheridan.

The doctors had prevented her from seeing him and she was made to wait until official visiting hours, since she was not a relative. It angered and frustrated her - she had to know he was okay, had to see it with her own eyes.

"Do you know how long they're keeping you here?"

"Because it was head injury, they wanted to keep me overnight for observation, but I should be fine tomorrow."

"Well that's good news at least," a relieved smile stretched across her face and she loosened her shoulders.

"When were you meeting your contact?"

"Tomorrow evening. So we can both go. He wants to meet me at Primorski Park," replied Blake.

"Primorski Park? Where's that?"

"The sea garden."

"Oh, why not just say that," he sighed, "Isn't the hotel close to the gardens?"

"It overlooks them, I know which bench he means as well, and it's in a quiet part of the gardens, next to the military museum."

"Couldn't you just get him to meet us in the hotel?" he asked, his voice laced with frustration.

"It was his insistence. He's worried the hotel might be compromised."

"That sounds like a load of paranoid crap to me. He obviously has something to hide."

"Or something to protect."

"Hmmm," he sounded unconvinced, "How long have I been stuck in this god awful place?"

She glanced at her watch, "Well it's 3pm now."

"What? Christs' sake," he fidgeted and shuffled up the bed. "*Woah.*"

"What?" she gripped his hand.

"Head rush."

"See, you need to take it easy, Sheridan. I'll let you get some rest."

She began to pull away but Sheridan stopped her, grabbing her hand.

"No wait, Blake. I've been bloody sleeping for nearly a day, rest is one thing but since you're here, you'd better give me an update."

She sat back down, fussed with the blanket briefly and began her tale.

"I went to the appointment at the museum this morning. The doctors wouldn't let me in to see you so I thought I'd make myself useful. By the way, Georgiev, the Curator..."

"Georgiev eh?" teased Sheridan.

"Pack it in," she chided, "Georgiev asked after you."

"That's good of him."

"He's a nice bloke. And he said that if you wanted to make another appointment to see the artefacts from the site, he'd be happy to arrange it. Anyway, we talked at length about the Necropolis site and the stories that have built up around it. The missing bronze box has become something of an urban legend in the Balkan archaeological community. I felt like a minor celebrity actually, Georgiev was thrilled to meet me and ended up quizzing me over a couple of coffees about my time at the site..."

He faked a cough.

"Sorry," she said, "We took out some of the artefacts and re-examined the reports. He didn't have copies of the computer models of the box. It seems they too were missing. A state of denial was in place after the incident and many conspiracy theories have grown up in the scientific community as a result."

"So there was a cover up?"

She nodded.

"Any idea what happened to the computer models?" he asked.

"He wasn't sure, but suspected they had been filed away by Dr Hakan Kamel."

"If I remember rightly from the case files, he was the

Curator at the Istanbul Archaeological Museum?"

"And still is. But he has an influential boss, Dr Osman Elmas. He's the Director of the Istanbul Archaeology Museums. There are three of them; 'Archaeological Museum', at which Kamel works, 'Museum of the Ancient Orient' and the 'Museum of Islamic Art'. Elmas is also a well-respected cultural advisor to the Turkish Government."

"You mentioned him before. You were with him when the Police called about Thornton. The same names keep cropping up don't they? And I don't believe in coincidences."

"David used to say that," she said, melancholy at the comparison. She snapped herself out of it, nodded and continued, "Whenever there is any cultural discovery of note in Turkey, Elmas seems to be the resident expert the media roll out for the cameras."

"And you worked with him?"

She nodded again.

"And?"

"I didn't trust him then, I sure as hell don't now," she hissed, her skin crawling at the very thought of the fat old letch.

"He was your mentor for a while wasn't he?" asked Sheridan, "So why don't you trust him?"

"He's a sweaty and unpleasant, woman-hating little man. Both Elmas and Kamel are cut from the same cloth."

"Those are strong words. Both men are a well-respected scientists."

"But both are also obnoxious."

"So you're not keen on returning to Istanbul then?" asked Sheridan, a smile threatening to crack his serious expression.

"You could say that!"

"So what about these conspiracy theories? Any of them credible?" he asked.

"I couldn't say. There were only a couple that Georgiev could recall."

"Which were?"

"That Osman set up the theft, but Thornton was supposed

to bring him the box. Instead Thornton sold it to the highest bidder. That Osman is part of a terrorist network and Thornton was trying to prevent the box from falling into his hands."

"So Osman's not especially popular among his colleagues then?"

"Apparently he rules with an iron fist but he knows his stuff. The most outrageous theory is that Kamel and Thornton were part of some ancient brotherhood sworn to keep the box hidden from the world and he knew it was there all along."

"And what do you think?"

"That the truth is probably somewhere in the middle."

"So you think there is mileage in all those theories do you?"

"I was chewing it over in my head after he said it. On my walk over here from the museum I remembered the excuse David gave me for packing me off to Istanbul. He said something about 'a dark shadow, a demon beyond nature that lurks in the dirt and it knew he was there'. He was gazing right out over the area where the box was found as he said it, it was as if he was trying to protect me from something. It was creepy."

"Demons and shadows? That sounds like a load of bollocks to me. But it does sound like he had some preconceived ideas about the box that may have motivated him to act in such an out-of-character way?"

"Exactly," she chirped, "That's what I thought."

"What about Osman? Do you know much about him?"

"Only his CV, which reads like a who's who of archaeology; three masters degrees, a doctorate, award winning writer, highly acclaimed lecturer – but also, there were some claims of corruption that were swept under the carpet a couple of years ago."

"Our intelligence also suggests he has potential links to known terrorist organisations," interrupted Sheridan, "but it's unproven."

Sasha raised an eyebrow, shocked but not surprised. "He is also an outspoken anti-Semite, hater of Kurds with religious views verging on extremist - he has publicly denounced Western interference in the Middle East."

"He sounds like piece of work," said Sheridan, "Our intelligence suggests he has also looked complicit in the theft of several priceless works of art in Serbia, Romania and here in Bulgaria. Rumours abound he and Kamel have links to the black market smuggling of art."

A cold shiver shook through her, as if pieces were falling into place.

"I hate to perpetuate a cliché about my industry, but it's often the ones who are supposed to be protecting cultural heritage that profit the most from it."

Was Thornton just a patsy for the shady Turkish masterminds he worked with? She thought.

"Now you're talking my language." An unmistakable smile flashed across Sheridan's face, as if he were thinking the same thing at the same time and read it in her eyes. "We've been watching Osman Elmas," he continued, "He's known to have met with international criminals. He's already on the Agency's radar."

"Well that's interesting," she looked out into the middle distance, allowing the pieces of the puzzle to reorder themselves in her mind and start to slot together.

"What?" asked Sheridan.

"Hmm? …Oh sorry. I was just thinking about something."

"Which is?" searched Sheridan.

"I was thinking about Elmas. Trying to remember some of my conversations with him. When he got the call about David's disappearance, he panicked. He was desperate to get somewhere and do something and was insistent that I didn't come with him."

"So you suspect that Elmas is more involved in this than may first appear?"

She slowly nodded in realisation, "Up to his fat neck."

PRIMORSKI PARK, VARNA, BULGARIA

July

A dim streetlight cast a rusty orange glow among the shadows of a majestic tree. Under it, a park bench, a lumbering silhouette hunched over on it.

Sasha's heart quickened in anticipation. Tsvetan had been kind to her at the site. He had appreciated her work and done what he could to be a good host. She had eaten meals with his family, spent many leisurely evenings in beachfront bars sharing beers and laughter with him. They had become friends. He was dependable, loyal and always seemed happy – Except when Manchester United conceded any goals!

Over the years they'd lost touch. An initial exchange of letters fizzled out as their lives took different paths. After funding for their dig ran out she had heard he had gone through a series of temporary labouring

jobs at many of the new shopping malls and apartment blocks that had sprung up from the dirt of the city since Bulgaria had joined the EU. Money, and with it opportunity, had spilled over from the rest of Europe - The opportunity to turn that western money into more money, and not always through legitimate means. She wondered what manner of man he had become, and if they would even recognise each other after all these years.

"Is that him?" She glanced over at Sheridan as he asked. His face was fixed with a serious frown, he seemed guarded. It instinctively put her on edge.

"I think so. This is the place we agreed to meet," she said.

*

Sheridan slipped his hand inside his jacket and felt the cold reassuring steel of his sidearm in its shoulder holster. He pulled it free, flicked off the safety and held it at his side.

They exchanged one final glance before moving closer. He tried hard not to show apprehension. This was the first time they had been in the field and potentially in harm's way. He needed to be strong for her, authoritative so she didn't freak out. Over the past few weeks they had worked together he'd seen how emotionally erratic Sasha was. Rule number one, don't draw attention to yourself.

A scream roared up her throat and she cupped her hand over her mouth to stifle it.

He stepped closer to her, to reassure her but also to see it for himself.

"Jesus Christ," he cursed, "I'm guessing that's him? Or what's left of him?"

She nodded, her hand still over her mouth, her face whiter than the sands of Varna beach.

"Are you sure?"

She dropped her hand away, "Fake Manchester United Football shirt – it's him," her voice was a whimper.

He reached for her, stepped ahead of her and clamped her on the shoulders.

"Keep it together, Blake, " he ordered. It was important he keep her under control, they couldn't afford to make a scene. They may be being watched. She nodded slowly. It was fortunate she was being passive and allowing him to take point. He'd done this before, he knew the drill. He checked their exit points, "We need to move."

He flexed his fingers around his gun, reminding himself he was armed, his soldier's instincts kicking in with adrenalin. He wrenched Blake away but her feet were concreted to the spot as she stared at the gruesome sight.

He glanced at the figure on the park bench, curling his lip in disgust. It was a neat, professional job but still a bloody mess. The dirty stain of the streetlight shone through the back of Tsvetan's head and lit up the contents of his skull, pooled in his lap.

"He's been executed. Clean and quick," said Sheridan, compartmentalising his emotions, something he had trained himself to do instinctively these days, it was the only way he was still sane after all the shit he'd seen and done.

"Clean!" she screeched, "His brains have been blown out!"

"Keep your voice down," he hissed, "Come on."

He pulled her hard, and snapped her free, dragging her behind him.

"Where are we going?" she protested, as she stumbled along the uneven path behind him.

"Back to the hotel."

He felt her tighten herself and she moved alongside him. He was glad she was being rational and following his expert lead.

They rushed from the park across Boulevard Primorski. The horn of a truck blared and spotlights lit them up in the twilight as they wove in front of the traffic.

MUNICIPAL POLICE, VARNA, BULGARIA

July

"There! Rewind a bit. Stop there. See it?" speaking in Bulgarian, Detective Vladislav Violinov prodded at the blurry monitor as his more computer savvy colleague, Sergeant Hristro Bolev, operated the machine.

"Where?" Hristro responded in Bulgarian, his eyebrows knitted together as he squinted to see what Vladislav was seeing.

"There!" He hissed, poking the screen so hard the LCD bowed in like a warp in space, "Pause it. Can't you zoom in a bit?"

Hristro's fingers danced across the keyboard and clicked rapidly at the mouse. Windows flashed up and switched from across the screen and the image magnified.

"It looks like a male and a female?"

"The truck driver seems a bit pissed off, he's had to jab his breaks. The two of them are clearly in a hurry."

"The timestamp fits with the window of the victim's time of death," pointed out Hristro.

"But we do have to account for the fact that decomposition is more advanced in hot weather. Our window of opportunity is relatively wide," cautioned Vladislav.

"I'll rewind it, switch between cameras and see if I can find where they came from."

He nodded once and sat back in his chair while Hristro clattered the keyboard.

Vladislav Violinov was aware of his reputation around the precinct for being impatient, he couldn't deny it. He stared around the room, while Hristro hummed to himself and disappeared into an electronic bubble. Vladislav's chair squeaked in protest as he tipped it back to its extreme. He crossed his legs and drummed his fingers on the side of his made-in-china leather shoe, echoing the sound of the ticking clock. He blew air through his lips, then chewed on his bottom lip. He picked at the Nicotine patch on his left bicep like a scab.

"Aha! ...Boss!" Hristro stretched around in his chair his face wide with excitement as if he'd just opened a fabulous gift.

"Let's see," Vladislav wheeled his chair closer and shoved himself in front of the computer.

"There," Hristro pointed at the screen, careful not to touch it.

"Do you see?"

"What am I looking at?"

Hristro clicked furiously at the mouse and the image zoomed in closer. The image slowly loaded as the circuits of the computer ground angrily like an anchor being hauled in. The pixels smoothed out on the hand of the man frozen in mid-run and Vladislav's eyes widened. He fumbled in his jacket pocket for his mobile. His fingers danced across the keypad

"Allo. Is the Chief Inspector their? Tell him Hristro Bolev and I may have found the shooter."

MODUS HOTEL, VARNA, BULGARIA

July

"Are you all right?" asked Sheridan, his voice even and reassuring.

"No I'm not fucking all right! I've just seen a fucking dead body! My friend has been shot to death in a public park. What part of any of that would make me fucking all right?" she paced around the hotel room, holding her stomach and shaking her head.

"*Hey*," said Sheridan. He reached for her and with his hand resting on her forearm she froze. He was perched on the edge of the bed and looked up, his eyes infinitely dark and empathetic. Something snapped in her, like a tightly wound cord, breaking loose. Her eyes moistened and she turned away, shrugging him off. She rubbed her eyes and raked her fingers across her face, as if she could claw away the terrible memory.

He stood and moved closer to her, not put off so easily.

"Come on," he said, taking her arms and pulling her around to face him. Her eyes were throbbing and sore, her face felt hot and damp. She let him pull her into his arms and relaxed against him, letting him share the burden, it was too much to carry alone. His arms were comforting and warm around her. He pressed a gentle hand onto her hair and drew her into his shoulder, giving her permission to let out the grief.

He held her and allowed her to cry for a while. She shuddered in his arms, sobbing quietly. He pulled her in close.

"I'm sorry about your friend," he whispered.

They stood together in the embrace for a while, Sheridan occasionally shushing. Neither said what the other was thinking.

Gradually the tears stopped. Sheridan's musky smell, his warm arms and velvet voice were soothing and despite the sorrow, she was contented to be in his powerful arms.

She slid out of the embrace, "Thanks," she smiled, masking her embarrassment. She'd always thought she was an ugly crier and would never have wanted him to see her so vulnerable, it was enough of a battle proving herself, without him viewing her as some pathetically cliché damsel in distress.

"We should both get some sleep," he said, his manner almost dismissive.

She wanted to object, how did he expect her to sleep after this, but she remained quiet, offering a defeated smile instead.

"I'll take the sofa," Sheridan pulled one of the folded sheets off the end of the bed, and reached for a pillow.

"Oh no you won't. Sheridan, you've just come out of hospital. You take the bed and I'll take the sofa."

She wiped her eyes on her sleeve, and forced herself to put the fear and pain to the back of her mind. She felt as if she was floating, like observing a nightmare from someone else's perspective.

However flimsy, she had something to cling to, a purpose. She wasn't the only one who needed supporting - mothering him took her mind off what she'd witnessed. He tried to protest but she fired a stern look. He stood fixed to the spot, not quite knowing what to do with himself, and she snatched the sheet from him. She knew he was trying to be a gentleman, but she wasn't allowing it.

"Go on!" she gestured to the bed, he didn't argue and skulked across the room. He tugged his t-shirt over his head and undid his jeans. She blushed and forced herself to look away, then occupied herself by arranging the sheet over the sofa. A soft lump thumped her in the back.

"Sorry!" he laughed, having flung a pillow across the room to her. She turned, trying to look severe but a smile escaped.

As he climbed into the bed, she watched. He had stripped to his trunks and his sinuous muscles flexed under his tanned skin. The moment was broken when he threw himself onto his back and the bedside lamp cast a lemony glow across his chest. Old wounds peppered his stomach and side, like a braille code of battle scars, paired with black bruises on his ribs and shoulders from the crash.

He'd never spoken about his days in the army, always tensing up when it was mentioned. For the first time since relying on him to train and protect her, she considered how vulnerable he may be. Those old scars went deeper than the surface, she was sure of it - why else did he always hide his feelings from her? He was protecting himself as much as her.

He flicked off the lamp on the bedside table, "night," he mumbled.

"Night," she responded, in a watery voice.

The only light in the room was from the desk lamp by the settee.

She glanced at his t-shirt crumpled on the floor by the bed and for a moment contemplated wearing it to sleep in. His warm smell was fading since their embrace and she longed to cling to its reassurance. Instead, she dug into her carry case and pulled out a t-shirt of her own. She quickly changed and curled up on the couch.

Her satchel was on the table beside her, bloated with documents and pictures. Across the room, the rate of Sheridan's breathing changed subtly and she glanced over. He was sleeping. Part of her was amused by how quickly he could switch off and sleep, part of her was envious.

She bundled the sheet around her and sat up. She dragged the satchel onto her lap and a raft of photographs slithered out into the folds of the cover. She cursed under her breath and caught the cascade. Scooping up the pictures, she arranged them into a neat pile on her lap. The top picture stared back at her with cold eyes.

"What are you up to Kamel?" she said to the image, as if he would give her an answer. She began shuffling through the pictures like a deck of cards, pausing to look at each of them. In the handful of images were pictures of the Bristol girl - Gina Morgan, Dr Elmas, surveillance images of anonymous men in suits who were yet to be identified but were somehow connected to the Libyan. For a moment she amused herself by comparing them to the unknown men in red uniforms who always got killed in Star Trek. She stopped when she got to a picture of Dr David Thornton, stood next to Hakan Kamel on a golf course with big smiles on their faces. A ball of sorrow lodged in her throat once again. She swallowed it back and traced her finger along the shape of his face, as if she could reach to him from beyond the grave.

"And you," she whispered to the image of him looking happy and carefree, "What are your secrets? What were you keeping from me?"

In the years that had passed she had told herself he had sent her away because of the box, because he didn't want her to know what he was doing, instead of it being something she had done. But there was always that element of doubt and that sense of betrayal. Somehow the fact that David had been friends with Hakan Kamel coloured his character. If he could be friends with a chauvinist like Kamel, what kind of man was he really? Had he just charmed her to get laid? Had he preyed on other vulnerable girls who had been his students?

A loneliness engulfed her, like her insides had been scraped out leaving a hollow husk.

The more she looked at his picture, the more she remembered the kindness in his eyes. What had he left behind? A wife, two children, grandchildren he'd never meet, and a string of unfulfilled promises. Life seemed so cheap and fleeting.

"What was it you said to me that morning I left?" she asked herself out loud, at the time, she had viewed it as a cowards way to dump her.

She looked around the room, trying to dredge up the memory. She set the small pile of pictures on the table and reached into her satchel for her notebook and pencil. She jotted a few words in the centre of a blank page, hoping to draw out the memory; 'dark', 'shadows', 'devil' – she crossed out 'devil' and wrote 'demon'.

"Shadows and demons," she muttered to herself, chewing on the end of her pencil, "Beyond nature."

She studied his eyes more closely, as if she could glean something more. "What were you trying to say? You promised me that one day you'd explain," she sniffed a laugh, knowing it was a promise he would never keep. The first and last of many perhaps?

She looked at Kamel next to him in the picture. His crooked brown teeth burning a decadent smile through the image.

"You know more than you're letting on, don't you?" she said to him, eyeing him with suspicion. She studied the two men, wondering if there was anything in their body language. It was then she noticed something; "hang on," she mumbled - verbalising her thoughts always helped her to organise them, especially when she was tired. She lifted the picture closer and squinted. "You're not married. Why the ring?" Kamel was wearing an intricate gold ring on his ring finger. She had seen one like it somewhere before. She turned her attention to David, remembering his two wedding rings from the night they had slept together, "What the…"

She swept aside the covers and tiptoed across the room to her jacket, draped on the back of a chair. She took her smart phone out of the inside pocket and laid the picture on the desk. Her fingers danced across the screen and she lined the camera up to take a picture of the part of the image that had caught her eye - their hands, resting on golf clubs in the foreground of the picture.

She pulled up a photo-editing app and magnified the section of the image. Her suspicions were confirmed, both men wore identical rings. She captured the image and stored it in the phone to show it to Sheridan in the morning.

She sneaked back across to the settee, flicked off the table lamp and bundled back under the sheet. She curled down into its warm embrace and closed her eyes. Sleep was illusive as she writhed and twisted under the sheet. The couch springs were harsh along her spine, the arms folding her in. She dragged herself out from under the sheet and sat up. The sheet slid down her T-shirt, clung to her nipples before cascading away.

A septic green glow filtered around the room from the digital clock blinking on the hotel TV. She glanced at the lamp and toyed with the idea of switching it on work, but she was dog-tired. Tired of staring at anonymous pictures, tired of seeing the exploded face of Tsvetan each time she closed her eyes, tired of replaying every moment she and David had been together, combing the memories for any scrap of a clue to his intent.

Sheridan was still sleeping. He had slept where he had thrown himself. The only noise was the occasional car passing in the distance and Sheridan's rhythmic breathing, a dream-bound mutter sporadically floating from his lips.

She tucked her heals under her hips and clasped her ankles. Like a frog on a rock she watched him silently, preparing to plunge into the unknown.

In the clammy heat he had kicked the counterpane to the foot of the bed. A sheet was wound between his muscular thighs, his underpants bunched up. Her eyes searched the contours of his sleeping form, the calculating gaze tracing the outline of the sheet. She felt an overpowering urge to take its place, wishing those powerful thighs were wound around her.

Had it just been work to him, all those years ago? It lasted a few months, their funny little affair, there had to be more to it? Did he still feel it too - that heat that passed between them whenever they touched? She'd led a virtually celibate life since those passionate nights in London. Were the memories still as vivid for him too? Had he missed her, the moment she had walked out, the way she'd missed him?

She pondered the outcome of such an act and settled for a compromise.

The bundle of blankets barely flinched under her light touch as she stalked from the foot of the bed towards him. Like a cat come in from the cold, sneaking in to snuggle up to its owner. Careful not to make contact, she was a hairs' breadth from his bare flesh as she slipped into the bed beside him. Slowly, cautiously, she rested her head on the pillow beside him, hardly daring to breathe, her eyes never leaving him.

His breathing changed and she froze, a child caught with their hand in the sweet jar. She held her breath. Part of her was terrified he would catch her, part of her exhilarated he would wake and sweep her into his arms. In her mind she speedily played out the scenarios; what would she say if he woke in confusion, or anger or lust? How would she handle each situation?

He muttered incoherently and fell silent again. She breathed deeply in relief and settled down into the soft wide bed. Lying on her side, she watched him sleeping. Hearing his breath, smelling his sweat and the remnants of his cologne. Feeling his warmth radiating around her, watching his powerful chest, gleaming with a thin film of sweat, calmly rising and falling, his strong features softened in sleep. She wanted to wrap herself around him and feel protected, to smell his skin against hers, to feel him inside her, but settled for the thought of it, the tantalising promise of pleasures yet to come. The sleep that eluded her soon took hold.

*

A loud bang in the street shocked her from sleep. She blinked her eyes open, thrust herself upright, her heart racing.

"Morning," Sheridan's smooth voice drifted into the void between sleep and consciousness.

He was stood by the window, a steaming cup in his hand, wearing a crumpled T shirt, "It was just a car reversing into a bollard in the street."

She yawned and stretched, "What time is it?" she asked and rolled over, clinging to the comfort of the last shreds of sleep

"About eight. Cuppa? I've just boiled the kettle?" He offered her a compassionate smile.

"Yes please," she said and sat up in the bed.

He dropped the curtain he was holding back from the window and padded across the room, his threadbare socks barely making a sound on the polished wood floor. She watched him stride across the long and narrow hotel room, enjoying his nimble movements, then felt self-conscious - embarrassed she had sneaked into bed beside him and had such lurid thoughts. She dragged the sheet from the bed and wrapped it around herself like a Toga, covering the skimpy T-shirt and lacy knickers she had slept in. In her half-awake state she struggled to decide what to do with herself so got up and followed him across the room.

He sensed her approaching and turned to look at her. The refreshing aroma of coffee encircled her.

"Here, still white without I assume?"

She took the cup from him with a grateful smile, "Spot on, thanks T...Sheridan," Sasha corrected herself, self-conscious about almost dropping the formality of their professional partnership.

A smile played with the corners of his lips, "So, did you sleep well last night?"

Sasha felt her cheeks turn vivid red and edged away, making for the protection of the settee.

"Yeah. In the end," she mumbled, "The sofa was uncomfortable," she sipped at her coffee, affecting a casual expression.

"If you wanted to swap you should have said. I wouldn't want to be accused of not being a gentleman."

She threw him a faint smile and returned to staring into the swirling brown liquid for answers.

*

Sheridan laughed to himself. Part of him wishing she had disturbed him last night so he could gauge her reaction to him indulging his urge for female company. Shaking hands with the bishop in the shower just wasn't the same.

He rested a hip on the counter over the mini fridge and sipped at his coffee. He remembered the feel of her in his arms as she shuddered with sadness. He closed his eyes and remembered her warmth, her perfume, her breath against his neck while he had comforted her. He longed to hold her again, to wrap her in his arms and protect her from the reality of their mission. He had seen death before, been the bringer of it in Germany, Russia and Kosovo. He was trained to handle weapons, to defend himself, to kill, and to cope with the consequences - she wasn't. She didn't belong in his world, yet he knew he needed her. He needed her knowledge and skills for the mission, and he needed her to remind him of his own humanity. He was more than what his years in the army had made him, but feared sharing himself with anyone who could not understand what it meant to have lived that life. Sasha was his connection between that and having a normal life – A family of his own, the love and understanding of a woman, someone to pull him from the brink of this hunting and death that represented his life.

Did she still think so fondly of those nights, back in London all those years ago, as he did? What had he done to drive her away? How could he convince her that it had been more than just a mission for him? That there was more to him? And should he even try? Was it right? Could she be that for him? Could he trust that? Could he trust himself not to drag her over the edge and dash her to the cliffs below in his wake? Perhaps it was safer to push her away?

He had been watching her dainty little movements silently while he contemplated this unseen reality, his arousal swelling. He wanted her, needed her but something held him back. A sense of duty? Fear perhaps? He'd been in warzones and been less afraid than he was now. But it wasn't a fear for himself - but a fear of what he would do to her, of what she would do to him, if he dared share his true feelings with her.

She sipped at her hot coffee, her gaze drifting into the distance. To know her mind, to know her heart, he desired nothing more.

"What are you thinking?" he asked. He had never been a man to beat about the bush.

*

Sasha looked up and smiled at him. He looked contented. What was he thinking? If he could ask it, why couldn't she?

It was his forthright approach and unflinching confidence that formed part of the package that appealed to her, and the question gave her the reason she needed to get her head back in the game. They were here to work. The hotel room may have booked in their aliases as a married couple, but that was only ever a ruse, there were boundaries to respect.

She processed the question, forming a non-committal answer and glanced back at him; "I was wondering where we should turn to next. I can piece together puzzles but first I need the components."

Sheridan's stomach growled and she let out a small laugh at the sound as it vibrated through the silent room.

"Hungry are you?"

"Ravenous," he said, his cheeks flushing. She'd not seen that before.

"Come on," he said, "Let's get dressed, grab some breakfast and go through the files together. I think much better once I've refueled."

*

After a brief debate about who should use the bathroom first, Sheridan sat on the end of the bed and picked up the remote while Sasha had a shower.

He flicked through innumerable foreign language channels then hesitated when a scene flashed on screen of Primorski Park, roped off with police tape. Bulgarian commentary, that made no sense to him, accompanied the pictures. The scene changed to a stretcher with a body bag on it being carried past the police tape and towards what looked like a coroner's ambulance. A deep dread knotted his stomach.

He leapt off the bed, anxious to understand what was being said. Unless someone else had been murdered in the park last night, it had to be Tsvetan. He hammered on the door to the bathroom.

"Hang on!" a voice muffled by the hiss of the shower called back.

His gaze flicked back to the TV. The story was still going, but the scene had changed again to some frightened locals being interviewed by reporters against a backdrop of forensic officers scrabbling around covered from head to toe in paper overalls.

"Blake. I need to you translate something on TV," he pressed himself against the door and shouted. The door slid inwards. Realising she had left it unlocked he gingerly pressed it open.

"I'm coming in," he warned, making a show of turning his eyes away to protect her modesty.

"Oh!" she squeaked, shocked to see him at the door.

"Sorry. Sorry."

"Dammit, Sheridan, what is it?"

She hid behind the shower curtain and reached for a towel.

He tried not to allow himself to be distracted by her naked skin clinging to the opaque curtain, like a plaster cast of her perfect shape. He blinked his eyes away, telling himself not to get aroused.

"Tsvetan's murder is on the news. I need you to translate."

Huffing, she lifted her leg over the side of the bath. Long, supple and slicked with shining water, he tried not to stare. Following him out of the room, she tugged the towel around herself. She perched next to him on the end of the bed, like a nervous bird on an unstable branch.

The reporter was talking into a big microphone that looked like a massive foam lollipop.

He felt his face crumple with frustration, there was nothing worse than not being able to understand what was being said. It sounded similar to Serbian, a few words of which still echoed in his memory from the war, but not quite – he couldn't be sure, "What is she saying?" He glared at Sasha, willing her to have the answer.

He watched while she mumbled to herself, translating the words as best she could, "Sorry, I'm a bit rusty. She's speaking quickly. Urm," she paused, her lips fluttering as she thought the words and then silently processed them. She verbalised them, and it came across like Morse code, all dots and dashes, "Politsia. Looking for. Have questions. Suspects…shit."

The scene changed to some grainy CCTV footage of two people, a man and woman, dashing from the park and across the road in front of a passing truck that flashed its lights at them.

As soon as he saw it Sheridan reacted; "We can't stay here. Get dressed, and pack up your stuff."

She clutched the towel to her breast, as if it would protect her, "Where are we going?"

"Istanbul."

ISTANBUL, TURKEY

July

"I'll drive."

Sheridan snatched the keys from her as they left the hotel. They needed to get out of Varna quickly, he didn't have the patience for a slow and meandering journey to the airport. Agent Blake could make the arrangements on the way. The journey was short and swift, but not so swift as to attract attention.

Using their false ID's 'Mr and Mrs White' dropped off their hire car and taking only hand luggage, boarded the first flight to Istanbul they could get. He wasn't happy about having to leave his sidearm in a locker at the airport but at such short notice, there was no time for the Agency to get a jet out to them.

Sasha turned to him, once they were buckled into their seats and had sat through the safety announcements; "So, 'Mr' White," she began, offering him a wry smile.

"Yes 'Mrs' White," he flashed his eyebrows, prompting a musical giggle from her, he enjoyed the sound of it. The last few days had been emotionally turbulent, for both of them, and it lifted his spirits to see her smile.

"I have to be honest..." she paused, confused for a moment, "Tom... That feels strange."

Tom gave a low laugh, relishing in the sound of his own name, as they crossed an unseen barrier, "What is it, Sasha?" He enjoyed forming her name almost as much.

"I have to be honest," she repeated, trying to find the point she was originally going to make, "I don't think we'll get anything out of Hakan Kamel."

"Why do you say that?" Tom narrowed his eyes. They needed to get out of Varna until the heat was off, but he was mindful their trip to Istanbul shouldn't be a waste of time.

"Because he's evasive, pig headed and chauvinistic," she said.

"But he knows you. He knows you're part of the puzzle. I'm no one to him."

He needed her to focus, he couldn't do this without her.

"But I still think you should lead," she said, looking physically uncomfortable at having to see Kamel again.

"Okay, but you need to be there with me. There's no reason for him to speak to me, but if he sees you, he may be more inclined to trust me."

"Trust? The man trusts no one. Least of all women!"

*

They landed without incident and strolled through customs, looking like low level business people in their smart / casual dress. In the arrivals hall, Tom paused to switch his phone back on and saw a missed a call from Milton Harkett. He held a finger up to Sasha to indicate she wait and he picked up the voicemail. A satisfied smile broke his serious façade as he listened to the message. Relief he couldn't hide.

"What is it?" mouthed Sasha.

He ended the call, slid the phone into his jacket pocket and looked at her.

"That was Milton. We're all clear."

"All clear? What does that mean?" her face pinched with confusion.

"It means I sent a code to HQ to make them aware of the suspicions of the Bulgarian police and Milton has made the allegations disappear."

Shock had her in its grip, "He can do that?" she said.

"Of course!" Tom grinned. He'd worked for Milton long enough to know the score, and knew better than to ask questions, all that mattered was they were okay, she would be okay, "Come on. We need a car."

He drifted a protective hand into the small of her back and

led her across the terminal following the signs for the car hire desk.

"I can drive this time if you like?" offered Sasha.

"No, no. I'll drive," insisted Tom. She rolled her eyes. Several near misses on the streets of Varna, not to mention the fading wound above his eye from the car accident, had done nothing to shake Tom's confidence behind the wheel. They swerved out of the car park and screeched into a thick swathe of traffic on the motorway that led into the city.

The streets were choked with cars. A cacophony of car horns, tyres shrieking and the bustling chaos of Istanbul hemmed them in like a fog as they inched their way to the waterfront and turned onto Kennedy Avenue.

They found a Best Western that had a room and where they accepted cash - waxy and fresh from a neighbouring cashpoint - and checked in under their pseudonyms. The hotel didn't seem to mind that Mr and Mrs White were vague about how many nights they would be staying, they were just glad of a booking.

*

Having dropped off their bags and freshened up, they stepped out onto the hot and dusty street and back into the cool cocoon of their hire car. It was a short drive through heavy traffic to the main Museum building, where they parked.

They ascended the short flight of stone steps, past the tall colonnade and into the Romanesque style atrium. Their feet rang against the flagstones and the sound circulated against the decoratively carved stone work and vaulted ceiling. A modern wood and plastic cubical had been slotted into the corner of the ancient space and a barricade squeezed into the archway that welcomed visitors.

They stepped up to the reception kiosk. A tall, gaunt, girl with heavy eyeliner and pointed features was fiddling with her mobile phone at the desk. Her long bejewelled finger nails clicked against the buttons while she concentrated on the glowing screen.

Tom drummed his fingers on the desk, the young woman ignored him. Then he faked a cough. Still, she was oblivious, engaged in some fascinating conversation via text message that took precedence over her customers.

Sasha leaned over the desk and the girl noticed her.

"Excuse me," she said.

"Salem – hello," said the girl, her eyes still distracted by the lit up phone.

"Could you tell me where we can find Dr Hakan Kamel?"

"Who to asking? Then if he available I call him?" she spoke in clear, if disjointed, English but all of the notes and letters scattered around her desk were written in Turkish.

"I'm Dr Sasha Blake. I've done some work with him in conjunction with British Museum. He's an old friend," she said, offering the receptionist a convincing smile.

It took the girl a few seconds to process and translate the response, "He in his office. Shall I call him for you?"

"I'm sure that won't be necessary. I'm just in town for the day and would like to surprise him."

"Of course, Dr Blake. Go through, but I need you both first pay to the admission ticket, unless you have guest pass." The receptionist rang up the price of two tickets into the till and held her hand out. Tom took out his wallet and paid her.

"Thank you. Enjoy your visit," chirped the girl and went back to playing with her mobile.

"One more thing," said Sasha.

"Yes?" the girl looked up.

"Has he moved offices recently?"

"No, not since he working here, in the east part of building, floor two."

"Thank you."

They nodded courteously to the receptionist then shuffled through the turnstile and into the museum.

"This way," indicated Sasha, and Tom followed her up a processional staircase, past commemoration plaques and posters advertising out of date exhibitions.

"The staff area is through a couple of the exhibition halls at the end of the building," she led the way, ignoring the nagging dread in her gut at seeing him again and focusing on the task at hand. They bypassed meandering tourists, past lit up glass boxes displaying colourful assortments of pottery, gleaming trinkets and crumbling sculptures. The rooms seemed suspended in a state of hushed reverence, the only sound, whispering voices and footsteps on creaking floor tiles. The air conditioning swirled the smell of dust and old masonry around on a cool breeze. Visitors glanced up disapprovingly at the two people in business suits marching through their contemplative moment with history.

At the far end of the last exhibition hall was an anonymous door next to a wall cabinet displaying some small Grecian figurines. Sasha pushed the familiar door open and Tom followed.

They stepped out of the public theatre of the museum and behind the scenes into an empty utilitarian corridor. Strip lights buzzed overhead and the comforting smell of the exhibition hall was replaced with the pervading stench of cleaning chemicals. Sasha felt nauseous, and couldn't decide if it was the smell or the memories.

They rounded a corner and stepped down into an older part of the building. They walked side by side along the dingy corridor, their footsteps echoing in the tall, narrow passage. Layers from many years of repainting were peeling from the mucky beige walls, the feint smell of mildew accompanying them.

"Where is his office?" asked Tom, his voice hushed.

"If I remember rightly, it's just down here on the left," she said, like a pair of cat burglars they moved noiselessly along the backstreets of the complex.

"Here it is," she stopped at an anonymous door, paused and took a deep breath - preparing herself for what was to come - and knocked.

"Evet (yes)," a muffled man's voice said from beyond the door. They exchanged a wary glance.

"Dr Kamel? Are you here?" she called out as she opened the door and stretched around it. She waved Tom in after her. He straightened his tie and strode in, dripping with confidence.

They swept past a curtain of stale smoke and found Dr Kamel sat behind his enormous desk, studying some documents through a magnifying glass. She felt heavier, weighed down with the burden of unpleasant recollections.

"What is it?" grumbled Kamel, without looking up.

Friendly as ever – Sasha said to herself.

They approached the fortress, and Kamel glanced up from behind his parapet.

He squinted at Tom, then saw Sasha behind him. His eyes widened and he sat back in his chair, a self-satisfied smile on his face. The chair groaned in complaint.

"Good afternoon Dr Kamel," Tom held a hand out to him. Kamel glared at the gesture.

"Yes?" he said in a thick Turkish accent and narrowed his eyes. A second short of Tom's arm aching, Kamel heaved himself out of the chair, leaned across the desk and took his hand. He shook it weakly, leaving a clammy paw-print that Tom tried to erase by sliding his hands into his pockets. Kamel slumped back into the chair and folded his hands behind his head, damp stains covered his arm pits.

"My name is Agent Tom Sheridan, I am an investigator."

"And who do your work for?" Kamel eyed him with suspicion.

"We work for a private client."

"And I am assisting Agent Sheridan with his enquiries," said Sasha, with an emotionless smile, using Tom as a human shield.

"How nice to see you again Ms Blake," said Kamel, oozing false courtesy.

"Actually, it's Dr Blake," corrected Tom, aggrieved on her behalf by the slight.

"I know," he replied.

She curled her lip into a polite smile and gritted her teeth, remaining silent. Kamel looked a lot older than she remembered. His letterbox of hair clumped in woolly curls around his ears and his face was brown and saggy like a wet paper bag. He had always been portly, but now he seemed to get out of breath with the slightest exertion. His mouth was wrinkled and pinched, a cigarette never far from it.

He sat forward in his chair and folded his hands on top of the desk. His thick pink fingers stacked on top of each other like two crabs mating. "What brings you to Istanbul?" he said, his voice sullen.

"We are investigating an artefact that went missing from the Varna Necropolis a few years ago," said Tom, displaying a fine salesman's smile. Sasha had never seen it before, but the twitch of his Adam's apple showed her that it was all an act.

"I see," Kamel looked away from them, and rummaged around on his chaotic desk. He pulled a crumpled packet of cigarettes from under a stack of unopened letters, put a cigarette between his lips then lit it with a cheap plastic lighter. He sucked on the shriveled white stick like a dummy and puffed curls of smoke around them.

Sasha stifled a cough, to which Kamel seemed oblivious.

"I can't help you with that," he said.

"Dr Kamel," she broadened her false smile and folded her arms across her chest, daring to move closer to him, "With respect, I think you can. You know the site and the artefacts as well as I, perhaps better."

"Perhaps?" he said, screwing his nose up as if he was smelling something unpleasant.

She pandered to his ego, "Indeed. So you know the site and its finds better than I, do you?"

"I knew the finds that I've catalogued. This box you're searching for, however, I know nothing about that."

"I never said the artefact we were searching for was a box," said Tom, leaning back against the windowsill beside the front of Kamel's desk, his hands still in his pockets.

Kamel's eyes enlarged. He coughed, almost spitting out the cigarette, but it clung to his flaking lip with determination.

Once he had composed himself he shrugged and said, "I

just assumed you were referring to the box. As far as I'm aware it was the only artefact unaccounted for during the excavation. And I have my doubts about whether in fact it even existed. We have no evidence of it ever being found. All we had were some computer models based on magnetometer readings, and they proved inconclusive."

"So I understand. What happened to the computer files?" asked Tom.

"They were corrupted."

"How convenient for you," said Sasha, unable to hide her disdain.

"I fail to see how that is convenient, young lady. It was most unfortunate. We had a power surge and it affected quite a few files."

"And you had no backups?" said Tom, narrowing his eyes.

"Our IT person had some problems and we had to let him go."

"Did you ever do any shovel tests in the area?" she asked.

"No."

"Did anyone else ever excavate the area?" she pressed.

Sheridan remained silent and affected a causal stance, but watched Kamel's reactions, looking for any clue about his complicity.

"My dear, you know full well the only team to work on the Necropolis site at the time was the one assembled by David Thornton - Allah rest his soul. Why do the two of you come here bothering me with these ridiculous questions?" he fluttered his hands in the air irritably and shifted his bulk in the chair. It creaked in protest.

He threw an accusing look at Sasha.

"You and I both know that a team returned to the site with the police, when Tsvetan reported the theft, and studied the alleged location of the missing box," she continued, "Soil samples were taken but they were dismissed because they were not old enough to correspond with the date of the Necropolis site. And you know that I am aware of the date of the site because you know that I was part of the team that radio carbon dated the finds. So don't give me that!"

"My dear, are you trying to accuse me of something?" Kamel offered an insincere smile.

"Should I be?"

"This is absurd," Kamel thumped the palm of his hand on the table top, which jumped, as if shaken from sleep. The cigarette glowed like a white hot needle between his moist lips, he drew on it furiously.

Tom and Sasha stared at Kamel, waiting for a punch line that never came.

Kamel calmed himself and said, "Everything eventually ends up in the ground. It is always a question of when," he glanced at Sasha, "As archaeologists, you and I know the best we can ever do is make an educated guess. We cannot know the minds of people who died thousands of years ago leaving no written record," he heaved an exasperated sigh, "Are you going to sit down?"

Kamel waved to two guest chairs on the opposite side of the desk. Tom and Sasha exchanged an enquiring look. Tom shook his head and rested back on the windowsill, but Sasha pulled out one of the chairs and perched on the edge of it.

For all his hostility, Kamel seemed reluctant to let them go.

"Well you have been a busy young lady haven't you?" Kamel fired a condescending smile at her then wrapped his legs together like tentacles. He licked the dry patch on his lip where his cigarette had hung, like a snake tasting the air.

"And you?" he glared at Tom accusingly, "How did you get mixed up with this?"

"I'm a former soldier and a historian. I do this because our history is not for sale," he folded his arms over his chest and grimaced at Kamel, "This is no ordinary box. There is a something special about it. Something men will kill, or die for. I think you know what it is?"

Kamel twisted a gold ring on his finger contemplatively then a wicked grin streaked along the side of his face before he flicked his eyes away.

"I don't think there is anything further I can assist you

with," he peeled himself off of his chair, "Now, if you would both excuse me, I will ask you to leave. I have another appointment to attend."

Sasha and Tom got up.

"Perhaps if you are unable, or unwilling to help us, your boss, Dr Osman Elmas can," said Tom.

Kamel looked unmoved, "I am afraid he is out of town. He has meetings in Bulgaria this week," he held up a hand, waving them towards the door.

"If you could pass on the message to Dr Elmas that we would like to see him, that would be appreciated."

"Of course," Kamel threw an insincere smile, as if it were a kick in the guts.

"We can see ourselves out," said Sasha, edging towards the door.

"And take the public stairs will you. I wouldn't want you to get into any mischief."

Tom held a hand out to Kamel, "Well thank you for your time sir," he said.

Kamel stared at the hand like it was diseased before shaking it limply.

Sasha asked herself if Kamel had enjoyed the opportunity to torment her once more, or if he was just a rather sad and lonely man. Whichever it was, she was relieved when they left.

Their footsteps echoed down the worn stone steps. Anger pulsed through her.

"Where the hell does he get off? He's still the bastard I remember. Why do people have to be like that?"

"Very few people mean to be a bastard, it's doesn't mean they aren't."

She smiled at his comment.

"Did you see his ring?" asked Sasha as they descended.

"Urhuh," nodded Sheridan and flashed her a smile, "The same ring from the picture. The same kind of ring as David's, but the design was subtly different."

"He has to be hiding something," she mumbled.

"Well that much is obvious," said Tom, exasperated.

At the foot of the stairs, the cold steel tongue of the turnstile spat them out into the street.

"So now what?" she asked as they trudged back across the dusty car park.

"I was expecting you to say *I told you so*," Tom flashed a grin, "I wonder where he's going?"

"Shall we find out?" She smiled broadly, desperate for an opportunity to catch Kamel out. Tom nodded.

They waited in the welcome air conditioning of the car for Kamel to emerge from the building. They watched his beaten up old Fiat opposite them in the car park, poised to react.

Kamel trotted down the steps, glanced around, then got into his car.

"Here we go," said Tom.

He waited for Kamel to start his car first and begin his manoeuvre, before twisting the key in the ignition. They slid out of the space and slowly followed Kamel out of the car park, keeping an unobtrusive distance. Falling back behind a rattling old taxi, they followed Kamel down a maze of narrow back streets. The tyres rumbled on the rough cobbles. An orange haze gathered around the rooftops as the sun dipped below the skyline. The call to prayer rang out and echoed down the winding passageways of the city.

"Listen, Sasha," began Tom, his tone earnest.

"What is it?"

"I've not been fair to you. And I've said some things that I shouldn't have. I thought you should know."

Tom kept his eyes on the road. Sasha leaned forward, trying to look him in the eye. He flicked a distracted look at her then fumbled with the levers to switch on the sidelights.

"Tom Sheridan, was that an apology?"

"I'm not sure I'd go that far," he replied, the corners of his eyes creasing into crow's feet, hiding a smile. She laughed musically.

Careful to stay out of Kamel's wing mirrors they snaked around the city streets a few cars behind him.

"There's something I'd like to talk to you about too."

"Oh yeah... Left, he's going left."

Tom followed her instruction and seemed to lose the thread of the conversation as he carefully watched the little Fiat weaving between lanes ahead of them.

"I was thinking about what you said just before the accident," said Tom.

"I was too. Listen, I'm sorry. I shouldn't have had a go at you. I was being unreasonable. Maybe if I hadn't ...we...you..." she said.

"*Shh*. Stop that. The accident wasn't your fault. Don't apologise. You were right about the job. But...there's something else...I..."

"Hang on. Hold that thought, Tom. Kamel is turning in."

Kamel then indicated, the light flashing and bouncing off the neighbouring buildings, and slid his car between two crumbling old houses and through a gateway. Tom drove past the opening, glancing over to see where Kamel was going. Kamel had parked up in an empty courtyard and turned off his engine. Tom manoeuvred back and parallel parked into a space almost opposite the gateway, then turned off the side lights and engine. They watched and waited.

It was getting darker now, but there was still enough light to make out what was happening. Kamel's manner seemed distracted. He knocked on a rusting metal doorway to a disused mechanics garage and waited for a response. When no answer came he knocked again, increasingly desperate. A crack appeared in the door and a figure stepped out of the darkness. The silhouette appeared to shake hands with Kamel and something indistinguishable was passed between them. Something small.

"What do you think that was?" whispered Sasha.

"He can't hear us!" Tom whispered back, then said, "It looked like paper. Either a note, or money?"

The shadowy figure disappeared back inside the building and Kamel stepped away cautiously. Robed in increasing darkness, he did not notice the black Ford Focus parked opposite with a man and a woman sat inside.

He got back into his car and pulled out of the courtyard. Keeping their distance once more, the agents followed. Back through a honeycomb of backstreets. It wasn't long before Kamel stopped again. This time he pulled into the driveway of a modest house, dripping with rambling greenery. They drove slowly past and watched Kamel take a key from his pocket and let himself into the house.

"Hang on, what street are we on?" asked Sasha.

Tom glanced around for landmarks then tapped the screen of the built in SatNav.

"Utangaç Sokak."

"That's where his house is."

"Oh," Tom sighed, "Well, we may as well head back to the hotel then."

"We can go back through some of the files, see if there are any other connections to be made?" said Sasha, trying to sound hopeful.

"Or we can find something decent to eat?" said Tom, glancing a small smile her way.

"There are a few restaurants down on the waterfront by the bridge," she said, "I'd like to freshen up quickly back at the room first."

Tom started the car and turned onto the deserted street. Night had blackened the windows by now and the city was closing its doors. They wound their way back through the side streets, following the robotic commands of the SatNav as she barked orders in an irritating American accent, until they reached the hotel.

"I'm going to park the car. I'll meet you inside."

Tom dropped her off at the Hotel reception and parked the car in a side street. She was sat flicking through a two day old copy of The Times when he stepped in from the dusty street, sweat leaching through his shirt, tie loosened and his jacket tossed over his shoulder.

She looked over the crumpled page, indulging in the view for moment. In a well cut suit and clean shaven, it was easy for her to pretend to be his wife.

"They have started the campaigning for the Libyan elections," she said, pointing to the article on an inside page.

He flicked up an eyebrow and commented, "Then time may be running out."

The hotel Receptionist glanced surreptitiously towards them. Tom and Sasha exchanged a look, it was a silent agreement to take their conversation up to their room.

Inside they felt able to talk once more.

"Drink?" Tom made straight for the mini bar, pulled out a can of Effes and waved it at Sasha. She hadn't even thought about taking anything from the mini bar but the promise of a chilled beer in the humid early evening made her mouth water. She nodded, held out a hand and Tom gave her a can and took another for himself. They both perched on the end of the bed next to each other and snapped open the beers. Almost in unison, they knocked the cans together with a stereo chorus of cheers and drank deeply.

"That bastard Kamel. What's he up to?" It was Tom that broke the silence, not expecting Sasha to respond.

"I told you he was evasive. There's something going on at that Museum. Something dodgy."

"I can see why you dislike the man. He seems to have no redeeming features whatsoever," he flashed a grin at her.

She took another refreshing sip before saying, "Sooner or later he'll be visiting his fence, especially if he thinks we're on to him."

"Unless he just paid them a visit?" interrupted Tom, an eyebrow pinched up.

Sasha frowned for a moment.

"Even the brief time I worked in that museum the record keeping systems were flimsy at best. The management hasn't changed so it's reasonable to assume that procedures are just as lax. It would be easy for someone with the right access to remove artefacts from their archives, especially something that could be easily carried out."

"Do you think that's what Kamel is doing? If he is, he doesn't flaunt it, in his scruffy old suit and rusty crap heap of a car," Tom took a long drink from his can and let his remark hang there for a moment.

"Perhaps. But he's a clever man," she said.

"But not a criminal mastermind!"

"Then what is he hiding?"

"An ancient box," said Tom

"Do you think he was working with David?"

"I'm sure he was - the ring tells us that much."

"David and Dr Kamel had worked together for many years. But those rings, they wore. I wonder what they are?" she mused.

"Do you think it's relevant?"

"Is it irrelevant?" she countered.

Tom gave a considered nod, "The question is, why? And does he even know where Thornton took the box?" Tom slurped the last of his beer from the can, and shook it with a disappointed scowl.

"So what do you think we should do next then?" asked Sasha, also finishing the last remnants of beer, sipping from an echoing can.

"We need to try again. We'll follow him, perhaps we'll get lucky? Tomorrow we should stake out the museum and see if he goes anywhere."

"All right," she nodded thoughtfully, "speaking of following Kamel, when we followed him earlier, what was it you were trying to say to me in the car?"

"It doesn't matter," his gaze drifted away.

"Well it seemed to matter to your earlier?"

"Did it?" he replied, "never mind."

Sasha studied his expression. It gave nothing away. His Adam's apple twitched, which roused her suspicion.

He fell silent for a moment, then brought the subject back to work, his tone sounding more purposeful, "Well Thornton is dead, Kamel is being evasive – the girl in Bristol is the only other lead we have now. Perhaps she can take us to the box?"

As Tom spoke, Sasha's mobile chirped and vibrated against the table she had thrown it onto. They exchanged an uncertain look. She reached for the phone, "Oh my god. You won't believe who's calling!"

"Who?" said Tom.

"It's the girl – It's Gina…"

THE OUTSKIRTS OF BRISTOL

July

"It's Gina Morgan, I…" her voice crumbled into a succession of sobs.

"Gina. Calm down. Take a breath. It's all right," replied Sasha, "What happened?"

Gina clenched the phone to the side of her face for comfort, "I don't know why I…I just thought…well no I didn't think…I…"

"Gina! Stop. Tell me. I might be able to help."

Sasha's firm tone brought her back into sharp focus. She wiped her eyes on her sleeve, took a breath and composed herself, "You can. For some reason I'm sure you can, but it makes no sense."

"What happened, Gina?"

"Two masked men just broke into our flat."

"Are you hurt?"

"No, No. Rees and I escaped out of the window."

"Where are you?"

"We're at the motorway services, Rees has gone to get coffee. We had to leave. I think they are trying to find something, I don't know what. They trashed the place."

"Does Rees have cash?"

"What? Why?"

"Would he pay for coffee with cash or card? Or does he plan to go to a cashpoint?"

Sasha sounded grave and she felt the fear escalate, "I don't know. Why? What does it matter?"

"Because if he uses a card he'll leave a trace."

A cold slick of sweat covered her skin and icy lumps of fear flowed through her veins. Why hadn't she thought of that?

"They can find out stuff like that?" She was shocked and

now second guessing what Rees would do.

"It depends who they are – but it's not worth the risk. You need to start covering your tracks."

"Sasha, this is all...well I don't..." the words were stifled by fleeting thoughts and fears, she was well out of her depth.

"Look, never mind that," Sasha's voice sounded more urgent now, "Getting away from the city is the right thing to do – it's difficult to hide among witnesses and easier to spot someone following you when there is no one else around. Where are you going?"

"Can I trust you Sasha?"

"Of course you can. And the phone I'm using is secure, but we can't talk for too long, your phone won't be. Do you have any idea who they were?"

"None."

"Were they familiar in any way? Any distinguishing features?"

"No. But something in one of Dad's journals made me think."

"What do you mean?"

"In a notebook among the things my father left for me he wrote about ghosts in his past who would follow everyone he loved. Thugs who would be searching for the key to his work."

"You're not making a lot of sense Gina."

"I know I sound crazy," her breath was becoming shallow. She felt like she had somehow violated her father's trust.

Why would her father write such things unless he wanted them to serve as a warning?

She and Danny had had conversations about how they thought that their dad was a spy and his business trips abroad were some kind of cover. She tried to calm her breathing and quell the mounting panic. Maybe she should have called the police first? But Sasha's remarks about them being tracked had put her off all the more.

"I knew that my father had secrets. He used to say he was away on business, but I never understood what that business was. Business didn't seem to be the type of word to associate with what he did. He was scared of something. Or someone. As if there was a spectre that was never far behind him in his past."

"Okay," said Sasha, her voice laced with uncertainty, as if she had decided to humour her, "What else can you tell me?"

"All I know is that something defining is about to happen," she said, knowing she still sounded like a crazy person.

"Defining?"

"Yeah, you know. One of those defining moments in your life that changes your course, based on a sometimes seemingly arbitrary choice."

"And you think this choice has something to do with me?"

"It seems like too much of a coincidence. My father always said he didn't believe in them. I don't either. You reached out and offered me help, right when I need it the most. Tell me, do you believe in coincidences Ms Blake?"

Sasha seemed to evade the question.

"I'm a long way from Bristol, Gina. But I can be with you tomorrow. Where are you going?"

"Exeter. I'm going to my brother's house."

"Okay. Then I'll be with you tomorrow. We can sort this out together. Don't contact the police yet."

"Why?"

"We don't know who these people are working for or what access they have. Don't worry Gina, we can protect you."

"Who's we? And don't you want the address?"

"It's fine, I can find the address."

"How can you find the address? You don't even know who my brother is?"

"The Agency know."

"The Agency? Who exactly do you work for?"

Her suspicion peaked.

"As I said before, our clients value discretion. All that matters is that I'm on my way and The Agency can help."

ISTANBUL, TURKEY

July

"Yes, yes, I know that," he mopped the sweat from his brow with a crumpled flannel handkerchief. He fumbled around on his desk for the comfort of his cigarettes but his hands were shaking so much he lacked the coordination to slide one from the pack.

The well-articulated English voice on the end of the phone barked at him again; "You keep saying you know Kamel, but what do you know? Hmm? Someone knows something and all I seem to be getting from your people is a wall of silence."

"I'm sorry, but Dr Elmas is not returning my calls, I don't know what I can do to help with your enquiries."

The caller sounded agitated now, "Hakan, are you telling me that you have no idea where the pieces are? That Osman is the only one who has access to your files?"

"No sir. I have access to the files, but they're not there," as he spoke, his tongue felt thick and his throat constricted, realising how inadequate it sounded.

"What aren't there?"

"The statues."

"How can three priceless ancient Greek statues just disappear?"

"I don't know," Kamel tugged a cigarette from the pack with his moist lips and gnawed the filter. He couldn't understand it, he'd seen the statues last week and knew they had been returned to the right collection.

"They must be in the wrong collection or filed in the wrong place?" he said, unconvincingly.

"So you are telling me that you are incompetent, is that it?"

"I don't know what to tell you Dr Brightman. They were there last week and now they're not."

Brightman heaved a deep guttural sigh down the line, Kamel could imagine his head shaking in disgust. He'd always thought that Brightman was arrogant and the idea of his disdain being levelled silently at him from 2,000 miles away infuriated him. This wasn't his fault, he knew it, and he wasn't going accept the blame for it.

"We would never tolerate this at The British Museum and our collections are much vaster than yours," he said. Kamel felt the anger rising - he could sense the stiff and pompous Englishman *tutting* him. How dare he?

"With respect, Dr Brightman, our collection may be smaller than yours but it is no less significant. Istanbul is the birthplace of European civilisation, my ancestors were farming this land while yours were still living in caves. And don't forget, these pieces were on request to be loaned to your institution. You have no claim over them."

"Why does everything have to be about your insufferable ego Kamel? I have no time for your quarrelsome little lecture on European History – I am simply trying to locate some artefacts that your office seems to have lost and I would like to know what you intend to do about it?"

"Brightman. What I intend to do is to reject your request for these artefacts and get back to work."

He slammed the phone down and smiled triumphantly to himself, then sat back in the chair and lit his cigarette.

SHERIDAN AND BLAKE – M5 SOUTHBOUND, UK

July

"I must admit, I have my concerns about the girls' credibility after what you've told me. She read about ghosts in her dad's diary? That's just odd," Tom rattled through the gears as he turned onto the motorway onramp.

"Perhaps we should try to obtain her medical records – make sure she's not some crazy person? But she doesn't seem to be. She has a good job, a husband, a flat, a happy, normal life."

"She wouldn't be the first person to live a double life. On the surface she seems normal but there is this strange, other reality, she inhabits. The bitter irony of most mental illness is that sufferers often do not realise they need help."

"But she is asking for our help."

"And we're responding to her. But I will contact Milton and put in the request. I expect he will email the information to us."

Tom dabbed the accelerator, thrusting them back into their seats, and weaved into the fast lane. Sasha didn't dare glance at the speedo but suspected it was close to triple figures.

"As we are in the area," began Tom, "There's someone else I'd like to see."

"Who's that?"

"My Uncle Frank. Well, he's not actually my uncle; I've just always called him that. He was my father's best friend."

"You have parents? Wow. I thought you were grown in a lab!"

"Funny! She's a comedian now as well," his face twitched into a brief smile. She relaxed back in the passenger seat and chuckled to herself.

"So why your Uncle Frank? Is it a social call, or business?"

"Both. He's in a nursing home in Exmouth. He was a Monuments Man in the war."

"Monuments Man?"

"The Monuments, Fine Arts and Archives section of the Allied Armed forces – men and women from 13 Allied nations with expertise in art, architecture and antiquities whose job was to preserve the world's cultural heritage during the war."

"I see. You're starting to make sense now Sheridan – I get it. You wanted to follow in his footsteps. You admired him."

"A comedian and a shrink. Is there anything you can't do, Agent Blake?"

She was sure she detected a wink when he said it.

"You don't have to be sarcastic! Do you think he can shed some light on the bronze box?"

"There does seem to be some evidence the Nazi's were searching for a mysterious box, several actually, some containing Holy Relics. The Third Reich's Einsatzstab Reichsleiter Rosenberg (ERR) was a special unit organised in 1940 under Reich Leader Alfred Rosenberg, initially to collect political material in occupied countries. Reichsmatschall Hermann Goering assigned the ERR the responsibility of confiscating *ownerless* Jewish art collections. The extravagant and vain Goering kept what he wanted after the Führer had taken his share. But other high ranking Nazi's were obsessed with collecting antiquities and looting archaeological sites in the pursuit of proving Aryan supremacy by writing their own version of history."

"It seems like a long shot, but all right," she said.

"How good of you to grant me permission, Agent Blake. But I was going anyway, it's up to you whether or not you want to join me."

"Again with the sarcasm, perhaps you are human after all," she flicked a smile like a warning shot, "I'll come with you, I'm sure he has some interesting stories to share."

Tom slowed the car and steered into the nearside lane, indicated and swept off the motorway, barely slowing down for the roundabout. The SatNav squawked directions and they passed through a narrow corridor of trees along a lonely road for some time before turning down into a hedge-fringed lane.

They rolled past a couple of gateways leading to little stone cottages, "It's one of these houses," mumbled Tom as he craned to look for the numbers.

"There it is," said Sasha, pointing one of them out.

They turned into the driveway. Gravel sparked under the wheels and they drew up in front of a little stone building that was dripping with wisteria.

Before they had even turned off the engine the front door was opening and out stepped the familiar figure of a short haired brunette with bird like features and lively eyes.

Gina stood in the doorway under a pitch-roofed porch with her arms wrapped around her middle. As Sasha slid out of the car she hesitated, shocked to see a man behind Gina who looked so familiar. Like a ghost from a long forgotten dream.

She waved at Gina as she approached the house. A gust of wind sent a flock of leaves across her path. Under her feet the gravel crunched like eggshells. Gina didn't move, but from behind her, the young man stepped out into the low autumnal sunlight and held up an arm to greet her.

"Hi, I'm Danny. Gina's brother. You must be Sasha?"

"Hi Danny," she said as their hands came together, "Sasha, Dr Sasha Blake. How do you do," she turned to peer over her shoulder.

"This is my partner, Agent Tom Sheridan."

"Agent?" Danny's face folded with confusion.

"Perhaps we should come in. I have some explaining to do," she offered an empathetic smile and Danny stepped aside. Gina disappeared back into the cottage without a word.

Sasha and Tom followed them down a narrow passageway to a cozy sitting room with a low beamed ceiling and large open fireplace.

"Please," Danny waved them toward the three piece suite. Sasha and Tom sat in separate armchairs, "I'll put the kettle on. Tea, coffee?" his voice fading as he left the room.

As requests for tea and coffee were offered Gina joined them, sitting on the settee opposite an oversized wooden coffee table.

"So who do you really work for?"

Tom and Sasha shared an anxious glance.

"Shall we wait for your brother?" said Sasha. Gina looked impatient and fidgeted but she agreed.

The three of them sat in awkward silence. The clock on the mantle thumped like a metronome, counting the rhythm. Nervous smiles were exchanged.

Sasha looked around the room. There wasn't a single right angle in the place. The small square window was sunk into a deep recess suggesting the thickness of the whitewashed walls. A couple of framed watercolour landscapes hung from bass picture hooks and in the triangular space under the stairs were narrow shelves, crammed with books. The flooring was wide wooden planks coated with layers of thick dark varnish. It was a quaint room, and could have been the same for hundreds of years, had it not been for the thoroughly modern three piece suite and big TV with its single lifeless eye starring at them from the corner, guarding over its brood of DVD player, amplifier and satellite box, all connected by an impossible spaghetti of umbilical cabling.

Danny came back in, the floorboards creaking under foot, carrying a tray of steaming mugs. The scent of fresh coffee wafted in and swirled around the room. He set the tray down and distributed the mugs before sitting on the settee next to his sister.

"You have a lovely home," said Sasha, making polite small talk. She lifted the mug and enjoyed the feel of the warm steam under her nose.

"Thank you,' said Danny, "These are old farm workers' cottages, it's been here since the 18th century. I keep meaning to go the Public Records Office in the city and find out about the history of the place, but you know, life, it gets in the way," he offered an uneasy smile.

Sasha could sense Gina throbbing with impatience.

"Now will you tell us what's going on? And who you work for? It feels like you know what this is about and why I have been targeted," said Gina. Stifling an outburst, she sipped at her coffee and cradled the cup in her hands for comfort.

"I'm going to ask you to suspend your disbelief for a moment and humour me. Can you do that?" responded Sasha.

"Okay," said Gina, shifting uncomfortably.

"Agent Tom Sheridan and I work for a covert organisation, The Agency, who specialise in tracking down missing cultural artefacts for private clients."

"What does that mean? That you trade antiquities to the highest bidder?" Gina went pale and looked as if she was about to be sick.

"No," said Tom, "That's not what we're about. We are trying to disrupt the supply of stolen artefacts. Most of our clients work for highly respected institutions or the political elite who want to repatriate looted cultural artefacts. Often they do not have the resources to do it themselves, and that's where we come in."

"I see," Gina relaxed in the chair, looking more convinced, "But I still don't understand why some scary blokes broke into our flat and came after us?"

"There is a possible link to Agent Sheridan and I's current investigation. That's why I found you."

"What investigation? What link?" Gina sounded frustrated now.

"We are trying to locate an ancient box that was stolen from the Varna Necropolis," Sasha spoke softly in the hope of keeping Gina calm.

"The Varna Necropolis? Wait, that was the dig where the oldest gold in the world was discovered? Even older than the pyramids. Dad raved about it in his letters to us. But he never came home."

"I worked with your father once. That's how I got involved in this case," Sasha turned to Danny, "you look a lot like him," she flushed with embarrassment.

"I've been told that," he replied, a sadness in his eyes.

Gina seemed to drift off into her own reflective world for a moment. Sasha was dredging up painful memories, it seemed to her that Danny and Gina hadn't talked about their father in years.

"My dad used to call me Georgie. I was sixteen when he was killed. I've been Gina ever since."

"He talked about you," she offered Gina a sympathetic smile and touched her hand lightly.

"Really?" Gina pulled her hand away, "How funny he never mentioned you?"

Tom flashed a warning eyebrow at Sasha, as if she needed a reminder to keep the siblings on side.

"Well, I only worked with him for a few weeks. I was just one of a number of students he mentored. I wouldn't have expected him to remember me."

"When did you know him?"

"It was right at the end of his life."

Gina's eyes narrowed. It was Tom who stepped in to break the deadlock.

"Do you have anything of your father's that might help us? You mentioned a book?"

"Help you with what? I still don't see what this has to do with my dad?"

"In 1998, an ancient box left the site at the same time as your father. He dropped off the grid for a few days then ended up dead."

"Wait a minute, are you saying my father stole from a dig site!" Gina's tone was incredulous.

Sasha lifted a reassuring hand before Gina lost her temper.

"All we know is the box went missing at the same time that your father left the site. There is no suggestion he was a thief."

"But that's the implication. Agent Sheridan said the box was stolen…how dare…"

"I know," she interrupted, "it looks suspicious. Some believe he stole it. Personally, I believe he was protecting it. Help us clear his name."

Tom shot her a severe look.

"I know my father was no thief. He spent his life protecting the world's cultural treasure from thieves."

"I agree with you, Gina. That's why we need your help," repeated Sasha. Keen not to alienate her, they were already walking a fine line between trust and suspicion. She smiled sympathetically at Gina, ignoring Tom's eyes scowling at her from across the table.

"The shoebox," interrupted Danny. He jumped out of his chair as if he'd just been electrocuted, "It's in my filing cabinet."

With that he darted up the stairs.

"Shoebox?" she wrinkled her face at Gina.

Something seemed to change in Gina, her mood shifted as if she'd been reminded of the reason she'd called Sasha in the first place.

"When we cleared out our parents' house, we found a false bottom in dad's desk. Inside it was a key. The only thing he had left on his desk were some Moleskine notebooks. We put them in a shoebox for safekeeping and Danny has kept them locked in his filing cabinet ever since."

Tom and Sasha exchanged an encouraging glance.

"And you've already looked inside the notebooks?" she asked.

Gina's shoulders slumped and her eyes saddened, "Not all of them. I flicked through a couple, but I've not been able to bring myself to look at them. I don't know about Danny?"

Behind them, the stairs creaked and Danny bounded back in, carrying a tatty and faded Nike box. With a triumphant flourish he dropped it on the coffee table between them, before retaking his seat.

"Have you been through this box?" Sasha asked Danny as he joined them. He shook his head without hesitation.

"Who else knows about this?" asked Tom, leaning forward to open it.

"Just Rees."

"Your husband? Where is he?" asked Sasha.

"He's had to go to work."

"He's at work!" Tom's eyes were wide moons, "Have you spoken to him today? Is he at his usual place of work?"

Panic flicked across Gina's face at the urgency in his voice, "Why?"

"Why!" Tom rolled his eyes, "You've just been chased from your home, did you not think that if someone was trying to find you the next place they would look would be at work?"

The colour drained from Gina's face, and Sasha fired an angry glare at Tom. Sasha leaned across the table and touched Gina's hand.

"Do you know where he is?" she asked, her voice calm and soft.

"He's not in Bristol. He's at a conference in Plymouth today. We thought he'd be all right because he wasn't following his usual routine. It's an important event for him that had been planned in for weeks. He didn't want to miss it."

"Okay," she nodded, "Listen, don't worry. It's good. It's good he's broken his usual routine. If someone has been watching you both they wouldn't expect it. But he can't go back to work after this. Neither of you can go back to your life until this over."

Gina's gaze darted around the room. Tom's face was set in a serious frown, unwilling to be drawn, as ever, he nodded slowly, backing up his partner.

"Then what is she supposed to do?" asked Danny casting nervous glances.

"Danny," began Tom, looking to Sasha for help, who looked back sternly. He kept his tone neutral, "It would be advisable if you change your routines too. Where are your wife and son?"

"My...?" Danny looked bewildered, "Sarah has taken Alfie to nursery, she'll be back soon."

"I would suggest the three of you take a holiday. Do whatever you like, just stay inconspicuous. Avoid using credit or debit cards, stay off the radar. Take your car and drive to somewhere remote and lay low," said Tom. Danny nodded, his eyes moist with fear.

Danny traded a frightened look with his sister, who shuffled up the settee closer to him. Gina tipped her head and Danny pulled her in close with a protective arm around her shoulders.

"What about Gina?" he asked.

"Both you and Rees need to do the same. It's up to you if the four of you stick together or if you split up. We don't know who these people are or what their plans are for you and it's not worth the risk to hang around and find out," his cold eyes reinforced the warning while he stared at the siblings.

"May I?" Gina and Danny nodded at Sasha's request and she reached across the table for the shoebox.

Tom dragged his chair closer to Sasha and looked over her shoulder as she lifted the lid. She reached in and took out the contents, feeling the familiar surge of adrenalin that struck whenever she was about to make a discovery.

Inside was a brown envelope with something small rattling around in it and four A5 notebooks, held together with an elastic band.

Tom reached over and she passed him the envelope while Sasha tried to separate the books. The elastic band snapped and gave way, perished over time, and the books loosened, as if they were able to breathe again.

Danny and Gina watched, fascinated.

The crinkling of paper being separated broke the stillness and Tom reached into the envelope. He slid out a sheet of paper and squinted as he read the information.

"It's in German," said Danny, with an inane smile. Tom threw him an irritated glance, "I can see that," he said, trying to sound polite, "I am fluent in German."

Sasha glanced at him, surprise burning in her eyes, "I was stationed in Germany for the British Army for some years," he said.

"What does it say?" she asked. Her hands were holding the notebooks reverently. Inside these books were precious pieces of the life of a man who's death had bought these strangers together. A man she had cared about. A man who had betrayed her and everything he stood for. She couldn't escape the thought that inside these books could be the secrets he needed to share from beyond the grave. She lacked the courage to open them yet, and the envelope held a welcome distraction.

"Hold on…." Tom was scanning the page, before looking up and capturing the eyes of his audience, "It's an agreement for a safety deposit box at a bank in Zurich."

The four of them exchanged uncertain glances.

"What about the notebooks? What are they?" asked Tom, looking at Sasha expectantly.

She drew in a deep breath and carefully peeled open the first book. She flicked through some of the pages, her face craggy.

"Notes, scribbles, sketches. There doesn't seem to be any logic or narrative," her heart sank, feeling cheated by David Thornton once again.

"Are they all like that?" asked Tom, he too sounded disappointed, but his reasons weren't as personal as Sasha's.

"They seem to be," she replied, flicking through the books. She put them back in the shoebox.

"The section I read was like a diary. I put it down quickly. It didn't feel right reading it," interrupted Gina, her eyes moist.

Tom placed the key and the letter back in the envelope and put everything back in the shoebox, then closed the lid.

"Can we take this with us?" he asked, pulling the box towards him. Gina reached forward and clapped her palm on the box.

"Do you really think this is what those men were looking for?"

"Unless there is something else your father left, then yes, I do," said Tom firmly.

"Then you can take the box, but wherever the box goes, I go." Gina tugged the box towards her and dragged in onto her lap where she cradled it like a kitten.

Sasha and Tom exchanged wary glances.

"I'm afraid that will be difficult."

"Why?" protested Gina, "These are my things, left to us by

my father. Why should I trust you with them?"

"You called us, remember," countered Tom.

"But you've not told me anything. How do I even know that you're not working for the men who broke into our flat?" Tom glared at her, his lips pursed.

"Gina," said Sasha in a reassuring tone, "I know that you know that's not true. Please let us help you."

Sasha let it hang for a moment, holding her breath in the hope the bluff would pay off.

"All right," said Gina, "But I can't sit here doing nothing. I need to know what this is all about, and perhaps I can help."

"I can't see how," said Tom. Sasha's glared at him, kicking his foot. He scowled back at her.

"Have you got some ideas you can share?" asked Sasha, her tone conciliatory. They needed those books, and the key. They were the only clues that David Thornton had left, everything else was anecdotal.

"Well what about the safety deposit box?" interrupted Danny.

Tom shrugged, "What about it?"

"Hang on a minute," a thought had just occurred to Sasha, "He's right. Gina can help. As his daughter you'll have inherited whatever is in that box," she offered a victorious smile to Gina. "With Gina, we can access the box."

"All right then," agreed Tom, his bottom lip crinkling in consideration, "At least we know you'll be safe with us. But think carefully about this Gina. Are you prepared for this?"

"What's to prepare for?" Gina folded her arms.

Tom pointed a warning finger at her, "If you come with us, you need to do as we say and follow our instructions. Is that clear?"

Gina nodded enthusiastically.

"He's right," reinforced Sasha, "We have no idea what's waiting for us in Zurich. Agent Sheridan and I are trained investigators, we're paid to do this. We will be responsible for your safety. You must work with us and do exactly as we say, for your own safety and that of your family," Sasha sent an uncompromising look around the room, "Do you understand, Gina?"

"Of course."

"All right then," Tom pressed his hands into his knees and stood up, "Danny?"

"Yeah?"

"Take your wife and kid and go somewhere else. Take your brother in law with you," Danny gave a mock salute and Tom hummed curtly, "Gina?"

She looked up and blinked acknowledgement.

"Make sure Rees knows what to do. It might be safer if he sticks with Danny and his family, at least you can all protect each other."

"Okay, I'll call him."

"Right," he continued, "Pack a bag. We'll set it up and pick you up from here later. Wait for our call."

ISTANBUL, TURKEY

July

"Do you speak English?"

The screen of the smart phone slid around on his cheek, skidding on a warm puddle of sweat.

"Yes. Angleeski okay," responded the heavily accented voice on the other end of the phone.

"Is this Detective Vladislav Violinov?" asked Kamel.

"Moment. I get him."

Kamel gnawed on the cigarette between his lips while he waited on hold. He flicked his gaze around. He couldn't trust anyone at the museum. It could have been any of them. Instead, he took his mobile down to the car park and sheltered under the arms of a massive lumbering tree.

"Violinov," said the voice on the other end of the phone.

Kamel spat out the stub and ground it into the floor with his cheap leather shoes, relieved, he blurted out his concerns, "Detective Violinov. I didn't know who else to call. This may not even be in your jurisdiction..."

"Who is this?"

"Kamel. Dr Hakan Kamel of the Istanbul Archaeological Museums."

"Istanbul? This not my place. How you have my number?"

"We spoke about five years ago. You were asking about some artefacts that went missing from the National Archaeological Museum in Sofia. And before that, about an artefact that was reported missing from the Varna Necropolis."

"Da. These things not solved. There have been developments in these cases, I still have investigating. What is it I can do for you?"

"I have to report a theft. In fact, a series of thefts and I believe they are related to the artefacts missing from Sofia."

"I listen, what missing?" Violinov's disjointed English was beginning to annoy Kamel by now. He considered switching to Bulgarian but his Bulgarian was rustier than Violinov's English - he gritted his teeth and persevered.

"The most recent theft is three classical Greek statues, but I have been looking back through the records and have found more artefacts that are unaccounted for."

"Why you think thefts are linked?" asked the Detective, who sounded like he was taking notes.

"The items that have gone missing are all related and are from collections of particular value. There is one man who I can place at both locations at around the time the items went missing."

"Who is the man?"

"Dr Osman Elmas."

"Dr Elmas? He an important man and this a serious allegation." The Detective sounded surprised.

"I realise that. I don't say this lightly. I have proof. I have been collecting evidence for some time as I was suspicious of differences between his records and mine. I keep the files at home on my computer because he has access to the computers at the museum."

"Can you send this information to me?"

Kamel took a cigarette and lit it, pausing before responding.

"Yes. I will use the email address on the card I have of yours. I'm on my way home soon and will send the files this evening."

He pulled on the calming warmth of the cigarette, relieved he'd finally set things in motion – maybe it would be over soon?

"Thank you Dr Kamel. Once I looked at this I ring you and we can arrange to meet. I can be in Istanbul later this week, but first I have work in Sofia. I think your information help me with work in Sofia so you send quickly, yes?"

"Of course. Thank you Detective. I should go. I don't want to draw attention to myself. We'll speak soon. Ciao."

"Ciao," replied the Detective and hung up.

Kamel slid his phone into his shirt pocket, looked around and scurried back into the building to collect his things.

EXMOUTH, UK

July

"I'm still unhappy about it," said Tom, his eyes fixed on the road, his voice grim.

"I don't see what other choice we have. There's no way she'd have let us have this if we didn't let her tag along," Sasha tapped the shoebox resting on her lap and pulled her seatbelt tighter while Tom accelerated onto the dual carriageway. They sped past a blur of cars, caravans and lorries, the road opening up ahead of them bounded by majestic hills, barren fields and bulbous trees spread out under creamy clouds.

"What time is the flight?" she asked.

"We leave Bristol tomorrow at midday so we have plenty of time. As long as we get back at a reasonable hour tonight."

She nodded contemplatively.

"We could take the shoebox and do this without her?" one of Tom's eyebrows flashed up as he suggested it. She chewed it over in her head.

"There's no way we'd get away with it. We need her for Zurich. We'll get whatever is there and send her home. It'll be fine."

"She's just an office girl, she's not prepared for this."

"Sheridan, can't you give someone the benefit of the doubt, just once!" she scowled. He made a low resonant hum and focused on the road. The atmosphere cooled and Sasha stared out of the window, watching the greens and browns of the Devon countryside flash past. After a few miles of reflective silence, Sasha broke the impasse,

"Do you see your uncle Frank much?"

"Not as much as I'd like to."

"He's known you all your life?"

"That's right."

He fixed his concentration on the road, engaging in basic courtesy. Sasha could feel the frustration rising as he cut her off.

"He lives alone?" she asked.

"He does."

"In a nursing home?"

"Correct."

"He's pretty healthy and coherent?"

"Yep."

"Does he have any other family?"

"Just me," he said, never looking at her throughout the whole thread of conversation. She ran out of small talk to make at that point and let the silence consume them again. It infuriated her, sometimes she felt like she was talking to a machine.

She fiddled with the stereo, twisting the dial through hisses of white noise until she landed on some inane talk show chatter for company.

Tom's nostrils flared and he huffed. She flicked the volume higher to spite him. It gave her a warm sense of satisfaction, doing little things to get a reaction from him.

*

Tom led Sasha though the double doors into the lobby of the care home. If it hadn't been for people in medical uniforms walking past, they could easily have been walking into the lobby of a country hotel.

They walked up to a sweeping mahogany reception desk, gleaming under sunken spotlights. Their footsteps scarcely registering on the patterned runner that led from the door, like a carpet welcoming Royalty. Hushed voices rippled around the wide reception room. He stepped forward and leaned his elbows on the high panel separating the receptionist from the rest of the room.

"Hello. My name is Tom Sheridan, I'm here to see Frank Fitch."

A mature woman with blonde hair glued into pristine curls by enough hairspray to supply a small country, and wearing a similar amount of make-up, looked up with a polished smile.

"Ah yes. Mr Sheridan. Bridget said you were due to visit today. Frank always enjoys your visits, although he does get rather overexcited afterwards," he felt a little like he'd been scolded and offered a rueful smile.

"And do you have a guest?"

"Yes. This is my…friend…Sasha Blake"

"I see," replied the receptionist, with a tone that implied there was more to their relationship than he had inferred. Part of him wanted to blurt out that Sasha was someone he worked with who seemed to get perverse pleasure from winding him up - instead he smiled politely and reached for a shackled pen, knowing the signing-in procedure.

They walked into the subdued sitting room at the back of the building, with its wide picture windows overlooking the gardens and then the seafront beyond.

There were armchairs set up around the expansive room, encircling small tables, and a scattering of elderly people spread among them. Tom scanned the sterile room, all shades of dirty brown and magnolia, the only concession was some vases of chrysanthemums – it smelled like a funeral. Sat alone, in his usual spot, where the sun pooled in through the window, was Frank. Tom showed Sasha across the room and they weaved between the mostly empty tables.

Frank's wispy white hair was neatly swept back from his face. His skin was so pale and flawless that it was almost translucent. From behind the thick lenses of his spectacles burned a pair of keen blue eyes that didn't miss a trick. He looked up from the newspaper folded on his lap, away from a half-finished crossword, and smiled widely as soon as he saw Tom's face.

"Tom!" he was animated and stretched part way out of the wing-backed chair that framed his small body.

Tom shifted quickly across to him, not wishing the old fellow to over exert himself, and clasped his bony hand between his.

"Uncle Frank."

He perched on the table in front of Frank. Never letting go of his hands and offered a smile filled with genuine affection. He loved the old man, in many ways he'd been more of a father to him than his own. He glanced back at Sasha behind him, and was surprised to see her eyes rimmed red. She smiled broadly at him. It took him a moment to register her reaction, then he realised she was touched by his affection for the old man. He felt his cheeks warm and part of him wished she hadn't been here to see this. Tom knew he always got emotional around Frank, and didn't want Sasha to see him so vulnerable. It was bad enough for his credibility she'd already sat vigil at a hospital bed for him.

"Uncle Frank, it's good to see you. Are you well? Are you still chasing the nurses around and finding ways to get them to bend over?"

Frank chuckled and gripped his shoulder.

"How else can an old man like me get his kicks eh my boy!' a wolfish grin flashed across his face.

"Let me introduce you to someone," he waved Sasha over, "This is Sasha Blake."

"Nice to meet you," Sasha leaned over and shook hands with Frank then stepped away to seek out chairs for them both.

"Ah, you've done well there my boy, she's a looker," said Frank, the moment she was out of earshot.

He laughed out loud. Sasha looked over and came closer, a chair under each arm. She had a wide smile on her face. He was aware that it was another thing Sasha had never seen him do before, she seemed to enjoy the sound of his laughter and it made him feel awkward.

"No, no, Frank, you cheeky bugger. I work with Sasha."

"Ah," Frank raised his unruly eyebrows and his whole face seemed to stretch, "shame," he mumbled, not quite under his breath, "'bout time you settled down lad. Life's too short to be lonely."

"I'll keep it in mind," he replied in half-hearted assurance.

When it came to relationships, Tom was master of analysis paralysis. There was nothing in his life he couldn't turn his back on at a moment's notice. His life was lonely and austere, a world of vanilla and no commitments, it all formed part of his protective shell. Nothing but his work - but now, increasingly, Sasha.

She joined them and arranged two chairs in front of Frank, they both sat.

"So. What's the occasion?" said Frank, "I got all excited then, thinking you were about to tell me you were getting wed or some such, only to have an old man's hopes dashed! Still, it's nice to see you lad. It really is," Frank reached for Tom's hand and squeezed it. Affection that Tom relished. He had nothing but admiration for the old man, but he knew that Sasha was enjoying stripping back the protective layers and seeing below the surface, like she was unpicking his seams - he wasn't prepared for that yet. His mouth pinched, eyes wary, he was ill at ease.

Back to business, he told himself.

"I wanted to talk to you about some of your experiences during the war."

"Ah. Is that all?" Frank's eyes dimmed and he looked away, "Not thought about that in a long time. I'd rather not, if you know what I mean."

"I do know, Uncle Frank," said Tom with an unspoken earnestness.

"You do, lad. I know that. I know you're in a unique position to know it. Still, make's it no easier to think about, even if you've been through the like."

"I know," said Tom, resting a reassuring hand on Franks shoulder.

"Have you seen any action?" Frank looked at Sasha with his inquisitive eyes.

"I've not," she said.

"Keep it that way," said the old man, his gaze steely, "Nothing but misery and evil. War brings out the worst in people."

Frank drew in a wheezing breath, and pulled himself upright.

"What did you want to ask me about?"

"It's actually not about the war, as such, more about your work with the MFAA," said Sasha, her voice chirpy, "I ask as a fellow archaeologist and all round history nerd."

"Oh really," Frank's stature grew with renewed optimism, "The Monuments Men - Now there are a few stories I could tell!" he flashed a grin at her.

"Keep it clean!" warned Tom, winking.

Frank chuckled to himself and began.

"I don't know how much you know about what we did in the war, young lady," he began, addressing Sasha directly, "But the Monuments Fine Arts and Archives section was set up in 1943. Made up of 350 or so of us, from 13 Allied nations. It was the most ambitious effort in history to preserve the cultural treasure of Europe. It was the foundation of later United Nations programmes and legislation to protect our heritage from those who seek to profit from or destroy it."

"How did you get involved with them?" she asked.

"Before the war I had worked at Oxford as a professor of Classical Studies. I used to teach the work of the great thinkers who shaped our view of the world. The first scientific and comprehensive written records from Ancient Greek civilisation. I taught Plato, Homer, Aristotle, Socrates, Democritus, Plutarch – I picked the fact from the fiction in the great stories and odysseys."

"You taught me a thing or two about history too Uncle Frank," chipped in Tom

"That I did son. In truth, Tom here was a good boy. One of my best students."

He offered Tom a proud smile and he felt himself blush, sure that Sasha would see it too and get some smug sense of satisfaction from it.

"I'd been out in Greece and the Greek Islands advising archaeologists and helping to piece together our past. When I was drafted, it wasn't long before I had a call from a colleague across the pond, Mason Hammond."

'We had no resources, no authority and no jurisdiction and muddled along begging favours and garnering the support of local people in occupied territories. The Nazi's were engaged in the greatest theft in history, and we ended up on the greatest treasure hunt in history. The Nazi's stole and transported millions of cultural objects and a good many of them are still missing to this day."

Tom and Sasha exchanged a knowing smile while Frank paused to take a sip from a glass of water on the table in front of him.

"Most of the Monuments Men's resources were tied up in western Europe, trying to find art and antiquities that had been stolen by the Nazi's. Hitler had these grand plans to build the world's greatest art museum in Linz and started the cult of the Third Reich. But elsewhere in Europe was damage limitation. The Nazi's had influence all over the world. They were obsessed with proving the supremacy of the Aryan race. They took symbols and interpreted history from all over the world to further their cause and anything that didn't conform to their ideals was destroyed. The swastika was a symbol they stole from illegal excavations in Troy and Himmler was obsessed with the occult and used rune marks in his symbolism."

He paused for breath, and offered a smile to Sasha, "as an archaeologist you'll appreciate this – did you know that one of the earliest known uses of the swastika symbol was by the Vinča culture?"

The colour drained from Sasha's face.

"What?" Tom saw her reaction and was anxious to understand why. Had they missed something?

"I've studied the Vinča culture, but I didn't know that."

"Who are the Vinča culture?" Tom hated being on the fringes of the conversation.

"They are a Neolithic people, from South Eastern Europe. Chalcolithic Age to be precise, from Serbia."

"Chalcolithic, that's Copper Age isn't it, like in Varna?"

Sasha nodded, her eyes glazing in thought.

"We were fighting a whole other war. One unseen," Frank continued his story, "While fires tore through cities and millions of people were slaughtered, the Monuments Men were fighting an idea, an ideology. We were fighting to keep the cultural identity of our ancestors and protect some of the greatest works of art in history."

"What did you do?" she asked, edging forwards on her chair.

"My first mission was in Sicily, with Mason. He moved on with campaigns in Italy and Germany, I was to join another planned campaign in Greece following the Casablanca Conference in 1943, after the failed Greek Campaign in 1941."

"Did you have a particular objective in Greece? Anything of note?" asked Tom.

"There was something. I only got as far as reading the intelligence reports, smuggled out of Greece by the Greek Resistance. Following the Battle of Greece where the Axis powers occupied the country and bought it to its knees - the occupation was split between the Italians, the Germans and the Bulgarians. The Germans were in a bureaucratic wrangle with their Bulgarian Allies over possession of the strategic city of Thessaloniki. The Germans held Thessaloniki, but approved the foundation of a Bulgarian military club in the city. The Germans had reason to believe there was a site of special Archaeological significance. Something about an ancient burial site close to an important port on the Black Sea."

"But Thessaloniki's not on the Black Sea?"

"But it did provide a strategic staging post for the Germans, and a route to the Black Sea through agreeing concessions with the Bulgarian's."

She nodded, starting to see the pattern.

"The Germans were planning a raid on a Bulgarian port?" she said.

"It seems that way. But it was far more efficient to get the Bulgarian's to cooperate than to force their way in, much of Germany's resources were tied up in France at that point," said

Frank.

"What were they looking for?" asked Tom.

"Well, It was when the Reichsführer for the Waffen SS, Heinrich Himmler, showed a particular interest in the area that Allied intelligence started to ask why. Now let me think," Frank glazed over and stared out of the window, "it was some sort of ancient box. A box that had the potential to be a Wunderwaffen."

"A wonder weapon," said Tom, even though it was unnecessary for him to translate.

SOFIA, BULGARIA

July

"More champagne?" asked Osman, pulling out of the exquisite kiss between he and his lover.

"Mmm, yes please, handsome."

Osman always booked the Presidential Suite at the Sheraton Hotel when he came to Sofia. The concierge was discreet for a handful of Leva and it was as if when he landed in Bulgaria and climbed into a limousine, he gave himself permission to be with the one person who made him feel good.

His marriage to Zaneb had always been more of a show to hide his true passions and he spent as little time with her as possible. Sending her regular gifts and transferring chunks of cash into her account whenever he could. He knew he was buying his way out of the guilt, but saw by his wife's extensive and expensive wardrobe she didn't seem to mind. But with it, she seemed to always demand more of him. Money for this, money for that, school fees to pay for their only daughters' education – Zenab's insatiable thirst for wealth and status was stifling. He needed these excursions to find himself again, as well as keep the cash flowing.

It felt safe here, surrounded by fine fabrics and antique furniture, swallowed by the warmth of a soft bed. And it felt safe in his lovers' arms.

Osman leaned out from under the quilt and reached for the champagne at the bedside. Rubbing himself along his partner, he topped up their glasses and settled back against the pile of cushions they had dragged to the bed-head during their love making.

He felt a soft hand caress the curve of his spine. He moaned with pleasure at the sensation, feeling his arousal swelling once more. He turned onto his side, eager, moist, lips waiting to receive his. A slim arm followed the line of his arm and around his plump belly and settled there among the salt and pepper hairs swirled around his navel. Their lips met. Osman's full lips and long tongue exploring the mouth of his lovers', deeply. The skinny fingers of his lover danced down his stomach and slid between his legs. He was hard once more and felt the warmth of desire slick through his veins like hot syrup.

Their lips parted and his lover danced kisses along Osman's roughly shaven, thick neck, trickling up to his ear.

"I love the way you taste," whispered his lover, who then nibbled on the fat lobe of Osman's ear.

Caught up in the moment, he was ready to allow himself to surrender to the pleasure, but the intimate moment was interrupted.

Osman's mobile phone buzzed and shrieked like a squawking raven.

He pulled back, stiffening his body and lurching towards the phone.

"Oh leave it, handsome," pleaded Gregory.

It had started a few years ago as a favour. Gregory was looking for a sponsor for his erotic sculptures and Osman was looking for an Escort. A slim, young, boyish man – just his type. At first it was just business – sex for money – the oldest business in the book, then it became an addiction. For a reasonable price, he could have whatever sex he wanted, live out any fantasy, Gregory was satisfyingly suggestible.

"It's business. I can't just ignore it," hissed Osman and he reached for the phone.

"But baby," pleaded Gregory, blinking his big blue puppy dog eyes, "Just a moment. That's all it'll take. I'll make you feel amazing," he smoothed his hands across Osman's chest and slid them over his stomach.

This was business. Gregory needed to understand that. He shook him off with ferocity.

"Hey!" protested Gregory.

All the time the phone blared. It scorched his ears, filling him with irritation. Gregory reached for him and tried to pull him back to him as he lifted the phone to his ear.

Enraged, he swiped the back of his big, powerful hand across Gregory's face, hitting him with such force that it almost knocked him off the bed.

"Fuck you!" he spat.

Osman ignored the slight, for now, and answered the call.

"Selam!"

He glared at Gregory, who was laid spread-eagled on the bed. Flaccid, and bleeding from a split lip; the sight of the scrawny little man looking so pathetic disgusted him. As he took the call, he thought about how to deal with him, picturing the scenarios in his mind's eye.

Gregory glared at him. He was conscious the little bitch may be listening so tried not to give much away.

"Do you have him?...Good…What has he told you?...Yes. And?...yes you have my authorisation to do whatever it takes. Finish this!"

He jabbed at the phone and disconnected the call then threw it back to the bedside table and switched his attention back to his lover. A man, who moments before had bought him to the brink of climax, but now showed him nothing but disrespect. If there was something he hated more than anything else, it was disrespect. He deserved respect. He did not deserve the hateful look that Gregory was giving him - the whore.

"Don't you ever use that tone with me again," he curled his fingers into a fist, flexed them and contemplated his next move.

Gregory had such a beautiful and perfect face. He was lithe, supple, flexible – all qualities that appealed to him. He did make him feel good. Made him feel amazing. He had done it just moments ago. Those delicate artists fingers, sensitive to every nuance, every curve and crevasse of his body. But it hid the boy's vile inner core. He had only ever wanted his money, and now he had dared to curse him in the most offensive of terms. Lessons must be learnt.

"Baby, you know you love it when I talk dirty to you," said Gregory; affecting flirtatiousness. But his perfectly quaffed hair, his devious blue eyes, thin pink lips and shapely cheekbones hid a fear and contempt that enraged the Turk.

"How dare you! How fucking dare you interrupt me when I am doing business! You know my rules."

He glared at Gregory, who tried to hold the gaze and hide his terror. The man was a coward, but the red rimmed eyes, the look of submission in them, he felt his penis swell and harden. It felt so good to hold such power over him. He could almost smell the fear and it was delicious. A spark of vengeance ignited, Gregory needed to be punished. Osman imagined the beauty of retribution, to see Gregory bleed for his sins, as the prophets bled for Allah. He flexed his fingers, balled them into a fist, and with lightening reflexes, he planted a fist into the side of Gregory's jaw. There was a satisfying crack and the boy screeched with agony. He was thrown to the floor by the force of it, losing his balance and toppling from the bed with a cry and a thump.

The white heat of adrenalin surged through Osman. His heart rate quickened. Beads of sweat leached from the craggy wrinkles of his brow. He panted and bared his teeth, letting the wild beast that gave him his power work through his senses. Bringing him power, blood of the righteous.

He surged from the bed with a snarl and landed squarely astride Gregory, who lay dazed below him. The ripple of the impact curled along his naked flesh, making him feel invincible.

He raised a fist, balling it tighter and more determined than the last. An urge washed through him to destroy the beauty of that mocking face, to pummel him into the wretch he made himself. He bared his fist down onto Gregory's face, sinking his curled fingers into the soft, resistant warmth. Gregory's nose crunched under the impact, folding sideways. As he screamed out in agony, Osman was balling another fist. He plunged it into Gregory's eye socket, the sound of the fist on flesh, wet and heavy. Then the punches came thick and fast. Blood erupted and oozed, Gregory's helpless form flailing and whimpering under each impact. His head pounded left and right, blood splattering across the Kashmir carpet in red fireworks. When Gregory stopped whimpering – Osman paused for breath. He stepped back from the naked and bloody body, enjoying the sport of it. As abruptly as the anger flared up, it died away. He felt the arousal swell once more at the sight of his vengeance.

"I told you not to interrupt me when I'm doing business. Maybe now you'll learn," he scoffed, satisfied with his handy work. He curled his hand around his hard penis and tugged repeatedly, bringing himself to a satisfying climax and throwing the contents hand across Gregory's crumpled body. He planted a kick into Gregory's ribs and walked away, rubbing his torn knuckles with contentment.

MONT BLANC SUISSE BANK, ZURICH, SWITZERLAND

July

Günter Roth lifted his cuff and glanced at his Rolex – they would be here any minute. His fountain pen danced across the bottom of the document, then he flapped the page to dry the ink before sliding it into a leather document wallet, emblazed with the Mont Blanc Suisse livery.

It always made him suspicious when a client he had heard nothing from in years emerged from nowhere. His job, however, was dependent on discretion. The customer was King – often his customers actually were Kings, Sultans, Nobility or Hollywood Royalty.

He had not been made aware that this particular client was deceased. Hearing from the daughters' lawyer certainly explained the 12 year gap in his dealings with the professor.

Günter supped the last morsel of syrupy coffee from his bone china cup and looked up at the oversized wall clock. He drummed his neatly trimmed fingernails on the desk pad, then straightened it. He hated it when it slid crooked on his antique mahogany desk.

His desktop phone blared impatiently, it made him jump, he lifted the receiver. His secretary informed him that his visitors had arrived and he thanked her. He lifted himself out of his big leather chesterfield chair, which creaked in protest. He brushed down and straightened the creases in his pin striped Armani suit, adjusted his wire-rimmed spectacles and left his private office. His hand stitched Italian leather shoes clapped on the polished marble floor, which gleamed from the reflective constellation of the chandeliers suspended high above.

He found his visitors waiting in the grand receiving hall of the bank, sat in a row on one of the long couches, like blackbirds on a telephone wire.

Günter painted his trademark smile in place and stepped forward with his hand outstretched.

"Good day. Welcome to Mont Blanc Suisse Investment Group. I am the Client Account Manager, Günter Roth," he said, in Swiss German.

Of the three visitors, the first to stand and take his hand was a tall and imposing man.

Günter scanned him and made an assessment. The man was dressed in a well-cut black suit, with a lilac silk tie and matching cufflinks. He was clean-shaven, his hair slicked back with gel, tanned and tough looking. A sharp pair of designer glasses perched on his nose. Younger than he, perhaps in his 40's, and he supposed that women would find him handsome.

The man took his hand and shook it with a definite and firm grip. Günter could see the man was serious and professional, which filled him with confidence. A businessman, European, but without hearing him speak it was difficult to tell what nationality. Then the man introduced himself and his two female companions.

"Good day. My name is Thomas White, I am the family's translator," replied the man in crisp and well enunciated German. He could tell that German was not the man's first language, it was too perfect, but from the accent, he couldn't place the man's nationality. Perhaps Belgian or Dutch.

The two smartly dressed and attractive women who had accompanied him then stood and they traded handshakes while Thomas White introduced them.

"This is your former clients' Daughter, Georgina Morgan – her married name. And my colleague Sasha Green, the family's lawyer."

Both the women bid him good day and wished him well in English. Günter looked them up and down. The women were slim, dressed in smart dress suits with simple jewellery and court shoes. The lawyer was taller, with a mass of blonde curly hair swept into a knot and pinned up. Her eyes were a savage shade of green, keen and inquisitive. Her suit was well fitted and flattering, resting at the knee, her shapely long legs shrouded in seamed stockings. She carried a tidy leather satchel at her side with brass buckles. The Daughter looked frail somehow. Her skin like alabaster, her features pointed and birdlike, her chestnut hair cropped short and orderly. Her suit was distinctly more high street and he couldn't help but wonder how much the hawkeyed lawyer and her mean looking companion were ripping her off for their services.

It seemed clear from their glazed expressions that neither woman spoke any German.

Günter spoke and understood English well, but he was glad of the presence of a translator, sometimes it just made things much easier when agreeing complex business transitions, he need only speak in his native tongue. At least the Daughter may get her money's worth from the Translator.

"This way please," he said.

Thomas translated it for the women, but Günter's motion to the meeting room at the back of the hall and hand gestures made it unnecessary. The three visitors followed, a chorus of noisy shoes echoing around the restored baroque interior of the bank, which had been operating for almost 200 years from this building.

A bank once used by Tsar's and Emperors - these days used by celebrities, sports stars and entrepreneurs looking for a secure place to deposit their vast wealth.

"*Bitte*," he gestured towards the big soft chairs around a highly polished conference table.

"Could I offer you a drink?" Günter asked - Thomas translated and all three asked for glasses of water. He pressed the intercom on the wood paneled wall and asked his secretary to oblige.

Once the three had sat, he unbuttoned his doubled breasted jacket and swept the flaps back behind him like a raven landing and tucking its wings in.

He looked to Thomas, then addressed the women in German, waiting between sentences for Thomas to translate.

"Here at Mont Blanc Suisse, we are proud of our discreet and comprehensive security. As you can understand, we have many wealthy and important clients, not least of who was your late father," he smiled sympathetically at Georgina, "I am sorry for your loss. Although I understand it was some time ago?"

After the translation, Georgina replied with a meek smile, "That's right. My father had kept the key to the safety deposit box in his office and after his death my mother would not allow anyone in there to disturb his things. It was only recently, when my mother died and we were clearing out the house, that we found it."

Thomas translated the response.

"I see," Günter peered over his glasses at her and sat with his legs crossed widely and hands folded together over his knee. "My condolences on losing your mother."

Georgina thanked him for his sympathy.

"I will need to see any documentation you have related to the box, the key, and of course some identification from each of you," as Thomas translated, he looked at the three of them and smiled expectantly.

"Of course," responded Thomas in his crisp German and collected their passports. Sasha Green placed her satchel on the table top and opened the buckles.

She slipped out an anonymous file and opened it wide on the table, then took out a large crumpled envelope, opened it, and shook the key onto the table.

Günter adjusted his spectacles and pulled the paperwork towards him. He scanned the papers in the document wallet, his face set in a contemplative frown.

As he read, there was a light knock at the door and his secretary walked in carrying a tray, on it a cut glass water jug and matching glasses.

After she had distributed the glasses and topped them up with water, in German, he asked her to hold on for a moment. He scanned the passports, looking at the three visitors with appraising eyes. His face stretched into a small smile "*Wunderbar*," he said, then handed the passports to his secretary and instructed her to take copies.

He then turned his attention to the documents the Lawyer had bought. The three visitors sat quietly and patiently, sipping at the water while he read through the paperwork.

He looked to Thomas to translate; "This is a copy of the Will, yes?" The Lawyer nodded, "And also the clients copy of the agreement and the key, yes?"

"That's right. My client is keen to find out what is in the box, this is one of the few things she has left to remember her father by," she said.

Thomas Translated again; "Of course. I do understand," said Günter, "This all seems to be in order. I need to ask for your client to sign this agreement," he pushed the document he had prepared earlier in front of Georgina with an eager smile and handed her a pen printed with the bank's logo. The young woman, he guessed she was in her late 20's, opened the wallet and her face sank.

"I am afraid that all of our documentation must be kept in German, for audit purposes. It can be translated into English for a fee, but as you have a translator here, perhaps he can help." Thomas translated Günter's words then took the file and shuffled his chair closer to Georgina. He explained the terms of the agreement and she signed it. The Lawyer then witnessed it with an illegible squiggle that passed as her signature.

"*Sehr gut*," he said, taking the wallet back from them. Thomas translated as he explained the next stage.

"I will call for an escort and show you down to the vault room where you may inspect the contents of the box in a secured area. Do excuse me."

He nodded politely, offered his best customer service smile and left the visitors alone.

"*Edith?*" he called across the hall to his secretary who was sat behind a sweeping reception desk tapping into her computer.

"*Ja, Herr Roth?*" she stood up, smiled and shuffled around the side of the Reception desk.

In German, he asked, "Please could you fetch Hans and have two members of his team escort my guests to the safety deposit box vault room."

"Very good, sir."

She scuttled away.

He brushed his suit down, rearranged his spectacles and clasped his hands together in satisfaction. They were the last appointment of his day. An early finish. Excellent - it meant he could go to the driving range before meeting his brother-in-law, Jan, at the clubhouse for that long awaited rematch. This time, he was confident he'd beat him, and leave Jan licking his wounds at the 18th hole.

MONT BLANC SUISSE SECURITY BOX VAULT ROOM

July

It was almost as if his spirit was watching them. She'd always believed that bodies always fail before the soul. In moments of contemplation, she asked herself why things were as they were. She could feel him near, could almost imagine the sensation of his warm familiar breath on her neck.

The thick walls of the vault muffled all external sound, all she heard was her pulse in her ears and the breath of the others, but there seemed to be more than the three of them in the room. Was he watching over her? Or was it in her head?

In the centre of the claustrophobic room that was isolated from the outside world, like the airlock of a space craft, was small square table.

In the middle of it was a box, reminiscent of an army strongbox. The brushed aluminium sparkled with promise.

Gina glanced back at her companions. Tom and Sasha were both stood by the sealed door, their hands clasped in front of them, as if they were praying at a grave. Sasha gave her an encouraging nod – it was her box, she should be the one to open it.

She slotted the small key into the lock and turned it. The lid relaxed and sprang open a tantalising slot, as if it could breathe, holding stale air in its metal lungs waiting to be set free - waiting for her. She folded back the lid on its hinge and leaned over to look inside. The inside smelt of dirty money and neglect.

Slowly, silently, she appraised the items first with her eyes, then with her other senses as she took them out one by one. Tom and Sasha moved in closer and the three of them gathered around like excited children around a pile of presents on Christmas day.

First she pulled out a chunky and old fashioned Nokia, examining it as if it was a curio, a throwback from a bygone age that should have been in a glass cabinet at a National Trust exhibition of weird and wonderful medical contraptions. She set it down and Sasha picked it up, she turned it on and it sang an optimistic Nokia welcome like an old friend shouting across a room. The buttons bleeped as Sasha examined the menus.

"Perhaps you should switch it off and save the battery?" cautioned Tom. Sasha did as she was told with a sheepish grin, like a child who had been scolded.

Next Gina pulled out wads of cash, wrapped in paper waistbands.

Tom picked up the stacks and flicked through them, as if he were mentally counting. He gave a verbal infantry as he did it.

"Ten thousand Swiss Francs. Ten thousand US Dollars. Ten Thousand Australian Dollars. Ten thousand Pounds."

"A slip for ten thousand pounds," interrupted Gina, lifting out an empty labelled sleeve and waving it around.

Surely her father hadn't died with ten thousand pounds in his pocket, and left another ten thousand behind? Where had the money gone?

Next out of the box came two passports. One in a US binding, one in an Australian binding.

Gina peeled open the US one, it was static, and smelt new and unused.

"My father's name wasn't Jack. This ID is fake!" her voice seemed to echo around her as if the walls were pouring scorn on her naivety.

"May I see?" Tom took the passport from her and flicked through it. A US driving licence also fell out of the booklet, with the same name and picture, "It's him."

Tom held up the picture to show Sasha. Smiling back was an image of David Thornton.

"We should get someone at The Agency so run the name Jack Riddler through their databases, see if there is any trace of him?"

"Good idea. It might tell us where Thornton went after Budapest?"

"Budapest?" Gina's face screwed up.

"The last sighting of your father between leaving Varna with the bronze box and being killed in a car accident was a few days before his death, at Budapest airport, but we couldn't find him on any of the flight manifests. It's possible he travelled under a false name."

She nodded, as if it made perfect sense her father would do such a thing, too numb with confusion to question it.

Tom studied the passport while she pulled the last items from the box.

"This is good work," he mumbled.

"Sorry?" Sasha looked up.

"This ID. It's professional. There's nothing to indicate that it's fake. There are not many people out there who do work this good. This would have been pricy," he fanned the passport around then placed it on the table.

Gina took an envelope from the box, then passed it to Sasha, a sick feeling lodging itself in her throat.

"This is for you."

Sasha's face screwed up with confusion as she took the envelope. Her eyes widened with shock to see her name handwritten on it.

"Do you mind if I take it?"

"Sure, why not. It was never meant for me," Gina replied, but inside she was fuming.

What had this woman mean to him before he had died? She'd said he barely knew her? Why would she lie?

She'd meant enough to leave her a note in a safety deposit box – more than he'd done for his own children.

Was it anger or was it jealousy she was feeling?

Both sensations felt unpleasant.

The last item she took from the box was another Moleskine notebook.

A favourite of Hemmingway's – whenever she saw a

battered Moleskine she remembered the fat commission she had made trading some of Hemingway's books on behalf of a Canadian Billionaire. The commission had all but paid for her and Rees' lavish wedding. It seemed somehow poignant to her that her father favoured the books too – he hadn't lived long enough to see her get married.

She flicked through the pages, like a child's flick book, she was disappointed, as if she expected to see a stick man jumping up and down in the corner of the page.

"More nonsensical doodles and scribbling's," she tossed the book onto the table.

Sasha picked it up, an almost wounded look in her eye. She too flicked through it.

"I wonder if these sketching's are somehow connected to the other books?" she mused. She didn't seem to be addressing anyone in particular but both Tom and Gina looked at her, their curiosity peaked.

"We should take all of this with us, it may be useful to the investigation," said Tom. He piled up the contents of the box.

"You take the money – it's your inheritance," he pushed the stacks of money towards Gina. She eyed it suspiciously, as if it would bite. She offered a wide smile to the Agents,

"I don't have big enough pockets!"

Sasha opened up her satchel, glanced at Gina for permission, who nodded, then scooped the money into the satchel as if she were pushing dirt with a brush into a dustpan. Tom looked over to her and a silent agreement passed between them. Sasha opened the bag wide and piece by piece Tom dropped each item into it.

"Right," he declared, clapping his hands together, "is that it?"

Gina closed the box, locked it, even though it was empty, it seemed somehow respectful to leave it that way after they had gutted it, and they made for the door.

"Aren't you going to open the letter?" asked Gina, watching Sasha slide it into the satchel before buckling it back up.

"Later," she said with a somber smile.

BAHNHOFSTRASSE, ZURICH, SWITZERLAND

Sasha was the first to step out of the bank and onto the boulevard. Her feet throbbed in her once-worn stilettos, the sooner they got back to the car so she could change into her trusty pumps the better.

She waited impatiently while Tom exchanged niceties at the door of the bank with the stout bureaucrat they had conned into allowing them access to the safety deposit box. She wasn't sure if she'd ever be comfortable deceiving people like that, but found consolation by telling herself that Gina had inherited the box, and its contents, and they had just helped her to retrieve what was rightfully hers. Whether she chose to share the money with her brother was down to Gina's conscience.

As Tom stepped out into the sun-soaked street she held a hand out, "keys."

Tom opened his mouth to argue, then snapped it shut when he saw the stern look in her eyes.

"Thank you," she said tersely as Tom tossed the keys to the hire car into her hand.

"I'm happy to drive," he said, with the hint of a smile.

"After the drive here, I'm not going to be a passenger again while you're behind the wheel of a three litre BMW!" she raised an pinched eyebrow then she and Gina exchanged a conspiratorial look.

Sasha mirrored Tom, scanning up and down the street for surveillance, suspicious looking characters among the bustle of shoppers, tourists and commuters, as well as traffic. It had become second nature now. At first she had thought Tom was being paranoid, but after what happened to Gina, she was taking her training more seriously now.

"Clear," muttered Tom and they crossed over, heading for a side street opposite that would lead them back to the car.

The people thinned out as they moved further away from the shops and street café's.

Tactically, Tom had taught Sasha that quiet side streets had both advantages and disadvantages. When somewhere was deserted, it was easier to spot an assailant and therefore their element of surprise would be lost and you can better defend your position. On the other hand, a target would also be seen by an assailant more easily, so it worked both ways. In a crowded place, it was easier to hide in plain sight, and rule number one of covert work was not to create a scene and draw attention to yourself – unless, of course, the mission depended on creating a diversion.

Tom and Sasha exchanged wary glances. They were both unarmed. She could see that Tom was nervous without his side arm. He was twitchy, hyper alert. Watching his reactions made her anxious so she turned her attention away and kept watch over Gina. Tom would look out for all of them, she would look out for Gina.

Tom's footsteps quickened behind them.

"Pick up the pace ladies, I think we're being watched."

A flicker of panic streaked across Gina's face. Sasha touched her arm reassuringly. They closed in to flank Gina, a tight defensive pack, and hurried on.

The opening at the end of the alleyway was close now, just a few metres. Her gaze went beyond the end of the street, looking for signs they would be cut off. She wasn't prepared for something closer.

A figure stepped out of the shadow of a doorway into their path. Gina flinched, Tom stiffened.

"Deutsch? English?" he said, Sasha glared at the man, startled. He had a mass of shaggy dark hair, a grubby face and dirty jacket zipped up to his chin, "Spare a little change?" he said, holding out a filthy hand.

Sasha shook her head, Tom said no and apologised, then stepped around the man, but Gina smiled politely and reached into her inside pocket for her purse.

The man's eyes widened, then he lunged forwards and

grabbed Gina with both arms, pulling her to the ground. Gina tried to scream but the man stifled it. Sasha kicked her shoes off and bent down to grab one. She wielded it like a weapon and swung into the fracas. While she was crouched, and before she could bring the shoe high enough, she felt a heavy thud plough into her side. Losing her balance, she dropped the shoe, then swung around to see a hooded figure looming down on her.

Tom kicked the tramp, who was grappling with a feisty Gina, and caught the man in the crook of his knee. He balled a fist. As the man fell, he plunged it into the side of his face. Blood exploded out. It gave Gina the chance she needed. She dug her teeth into the hand that was attempting to gag her then pulled herself from the assailants grip. He wailed with pain and span around, swinging a fist towards Tom with all his weight behind it. The punch caught Tom in the stomach and he folded over, clutching his middle before coming at the man with a left uppercut into his jaw. The attacker ducked away, lessening the impact of the blow and came back at him. They traded frenzied punches and kicks. Gina scurried out from under the tirade, like a crab, and dashed across the alley.

Sasha landed on her hip, sending pain ricocheting through her. She cried out, her legs flailing in the restrictive pencil skirt of her dress suit. She scrabbled to reach for the shoe with one hand and tried to haul herself up with the other. Fierce eyes glowed under the shadow of the hood and big hands reached for her. The attacker straddled her, forcing his weight down on her thighs, crushing her into the cobbled pavement. She writhed under his weight, kicking her legs out. She felt the seam slowly give from the slit in the back of her skirt but the sound of ripping was muffled by the grunts and growls of the struggle. The floor was cold and damp on her flesh, but far from the usual embarrassment, she was glad her legs were released, it gave her extra strength and purchase to resist him. She tried to punch the man, but couldn't get leverage. He gripped her wrist, squeezing it hard. He dashed it repeatedly onto the ground, the pain was unbearable and she screamed.

"Sasha!"

The sound of her name was watery and distant, but she glanced towards it and saw Tom, grappling with the tramp and trying to reach for her. Seeing he too was in trouble, her mind sharpened. She looked back up at the man on top of her, their eyes locked. His were cold and malevolent, and in the shade of the tall buildings, under the cowl of his hood, his features were indistinct. He was so close now she could feel his hot, moist breath on her face. Like two enormous spiders, his hands drew in either side of her face. Her breath caught and she felt the excruciating pressure of her windpipe being crushed. The blood thundered in her head, desperate, she rasped for air. Her head felt like it was swelling up, her eyes bulging. She clawed at the hands choking her. Kicked and writhed but she could feel herself weakening with every frantic wheezing, gasp. It was futile trying to pull his hands away, they were too strong. She reached for the shoe, her fingernails scratching at the cobbles. Just centimetres away, she felt the rough tip of the heel on her finger. With a decisive surge of energy she managed to shift herself enough to get closer. She clasped the toe-point of the shoe and with the last vestiges of her fading strength she channeled all of her adrenaline into the defence. She swung the shoe up and slammed it as hard as she could, heel first, into the side of the hooded man's head.

He froze on impact. His muscles loosening. She tore his hands from her throat and rolled out from under him. His eyes wide and fixed, in slow motion, like a tree being felled, the attacker flopped sideways. An ooze of gelatinous blood rolled across his wide eye and down his nose, he didn't blink or flinch. With a sickening thud he fell to the ground, his gaze fixed on his killer.

Sasha scuttled backwards on her bottom, the back of her skirt and stockings shredding. Her face cold and contorted with horror. Her shoe was stuck proudly out of the side of the hooded head, the heel sunk to its girth.

Tom's scuffle with the assassin disguised as a tramp dissipated as the two men tired. It ended with Tom driving the mans' skull into the pavement and knocking him unconscious. Tom stumbled away from the scene. His face bloodied, his knuckles torn, his suit bedraggled, shirt stained and shredded. The glasses that had been part of his disguise had long been abandoned, crumpled in the gutter like a crane-fly.

He span on a heel, wild fury in his eyes, trying to locate the team he had vowed to himself to protect at all costs. He saw Gina, curled up, hugging her knees, rocking on her coccyx between two dumpsters, panting. She looked terrified and shocked but fine. He whipped his gaze around, trying to locate Sasha. He found her, sprawled in the middle of the street, coughing and urging, rubbing her neck. A noxious cocktail of relief and horror chased through his veins. Despite his exhaustion and aching limbs he ran the few metres towards her and skidded into a crouch beside her.

"My God, Sasha, are you all right?"

She nodded in silence, her eyes fixed on the dead mans. Tom wanted to pull her into his arms and hold her close, but there was no time.

He gripped her shoulders, "Sasha, it's all right, you're safe, but not for long. The other guy is unconscious, we need to get out of here."

Tom helped her to her feet. She seemed so frail under his arm and leaned into him as she stood. Sasha's stunned gaze was still fixed on the carcass.

"Sasha."

She didn't respond. A cold silence gripped the street.

Tom pressed a hand into her cheek and pulled her gaze away, directing her eyes to his, "Sasha, focus."

"Where's Gina?" she asked. She seemed to be in a trance.

"She's fine. She's over there," Tom nodded towards the dumpsters.

He took off his jacket and wrapped it around her shoulders, protecting her modesty.

"Gina. Come on. Let's go," he shouted, as he pulled Sasha away, her feet barely holding her weight, "Now!"

Gina unfolded herself, like an origami bird coming apart, and stood up. She nodded and stepped out into the street.

Tom reached for her and gently took her arm, leading them both away from the scene.

"I thought he was a homeless guy. I was going to give him some change. Why would a homeless man attack us?" Gina was shaking, she looked numb, her eyes like concrete.

"He wasn't a homeless man. The minute you reached into your inside pocket he attacked because he thought you were about to draw a gun. It's a classic sign of a trained killer."

"Oh God, so this was my fault?" Gina's eyes stretched wide, her skin so pale it was almost transparent.

"Of course it wasn't," said Tom squeezing Gina's arm, "They were sent here to kill us and capture you."

"How do you know that?"

"Because that's what I would do."

Sasha shook herself from his grip. He flexed his fingers to feel her again, as if he needed the contact as much as she did. She leaned over and picked up her satchel from the gutter where it had fallen and pulled the car keys out of the side pocket. She passed them to Tom.

"Let's just get back to the hotel," she said, her tone flat and defeated.

MARRIOTT HOTEL, ZURICH

"Milton Harkett." The voice on the end of the phone sounded cheerful yet professional.

"Who's the client?"

A low sigh issued down the line, "Tom," instant recognition.

"You know I can't tell you that."

"Who's the client?"

"No matter how many times you say it, it doesn't change the fact that I am bound by the confidentiality agreement with the client."

"That's convenient."

"Enough, Tom," Milton sounded agitated now. Tom smiled to himself. When Milton was irritated he made things happen and got results, "why do you want to know?"

"Because we've just been attacked."

"Are you all okay?" Milton sounded concerned.

"Fortunately, yes, but Gina is shaken up, she's not trained for this."

"Well, it was your call to bring her along."

"And a call that has proved fruitful. We've accessed Thornton's safety deposit box."

"Great. Some real progress. What did you find?"

"That's not the reason I'm calling. The details will be in my report, I'll email you later, but my pressing concern is the safety of my team."

"How will knowing who the client is help with that?"

"Because we're being played."

"How can you be sure? Were you followed? Have you taken all the necessary precautions?"

"Milton," Tom scowled down the line, "How long have I been doing this?"

"Okay, fine - point taken. So how do you think you were

tracked down?"

"Whoever they are, and whoever they are working for, they seem to be one step ahead of us. They know where we are and what we're doing."

"Is it The Libyan?" asked Milton.

"That's my suspicion. I take it you have been giving the client regular updates on our progress?" Tom wanted to clarify it, for all their sakes.

"Of course, that is in our standard terms of business."

"Then the way I see it there are two possibilities, since I'm confident that we've not been followed. Either, there is a mole in The Agency or the client is double crossing us, they are in The Libyan's pocket."

"I trust your instincts, Agent Sheridan. I'll do some discreet digging inside The Agency and see what I can find out from the client."

"Thank you. That's all I ask. And one more thing…"

"So it's not all then?" Tom could imagine the wry smile on Milton's face.

"Not quite! As a precaution, we'll leave the city, they may know where we're staying. I'll swap the car and we'll drive further into Switzerland and hole up until we can plan our next move."

"A wise precaution. There's an Agency safe house in Geneva. I'll send you the details."

"Thank you."

"Good luck, Agent. Keep me posted and I'll edit and delay my updates to the client, to give you a head start!"

"I appreciate that. Speak to you later."

They closed the call. Tom turned to Sasha, who had a reassuring arm draped over Gina's shoulder, and offered them both a small, encouraging smile.

"Milton's going to deal with it. It'll give us some breathing space."

"Breathing space for what, Tom?" he looked back at his partner, her eyes filled with rage.

"We need to work out our next move," he rubbed his chin,

appreciating how soft it felt, he was used to a layer of spiny hairs being there, "Pack your things – we're leaving."

ISTANBUL, TURKEY

July

Dr Hakan Kamel hobbled down the steps of the museum and into the car park. The heat and dust of the day seemed to coalesce there. Before he'd reached the bottom of the short flight of steps, his shirt was soaked with sweat. It clung to his spine and armpits relentlessly. He trudged across the dusty and crumbling concrete towards his battered old Fiat Panda, rust eating up the sills like dry rot. He paused by the car and fumbled around in his worn leather satchel. The distant rumble of traffic was the usual soundtrack of the choked city streets and it was nothing more than white noise to him these days - but he looked up, when tyres screeched into the car park. A yellow post van wriggled its way up the narrow track and Kamel ignored it. He returned to trying to locate his keys in his bottomless bag, cursing to himself they had probably fallen in between the leaves of one of his many text books.

The van screeched across the car park, pulling up next to his car. It seemed strange to Kamel the postman had pulled up so far from the building, but he was too occupied to concern himself with such things. He lost patience and shook it angrily to loosen his keys from wherever they were lodged.

He heard heavy feet crunching on the dust behind him and stopped to look up. Before he could see who had approached, he felt a strong hand clamp something soft and sour smelling over his mouth and nose. He panicked and tried to escape the grip, but in vein. Blackness descended.

*

Hakan Kamel blinked his eyes open with a terrified gasp. They slowly focused. It was dark. He felt cold - a rare sensation in Istanbul at this time of year. Perhaps he was underground? He heard the echo of dripping water. His whole body ached, his face slack with bewilderment. As he regained full consciousness he tried to move. Pain seared through his hands and feet and he clenched his jaw to keep from crying out. Hard, clammy plastic glued to his flesh. With a frightening clarity he realised he was naked, and bound to a chair. He gave in to the urge to scream but his voice failed. He cleared his throat.

"Hello?" he murmured. His eyes flicked around the room. It was big. The walls were hidden in shadow. It smelt old and damp like a cellar or the cistern. There was no natural light, only a dim emergency light, over a closed metal door a few metres ahead of him that cast a faint antiseptic pool. The silence was unsettling - no noise penetrated the room but the sound of his own breathing and the incessant dripping water. He rattled the chair, testing the bonds. A surge of adrenaline pumped through him and he began to bounce around in the chair shouting and screaming.

"Hey! Hey! Help…Help me…" he screamed and shouted, in both Turkish and English. His cries reverberating around the empty room, until his voice failed him.

The grind of a lock being opened cut through his shouts. The door ahead of him opened, bright light spilling around it and illuminating two men entering the room. The two silhouettes approached him. One of them slammed the door behind him and the other reached for a light switch on the wall.

A buzz scattered around the room, followed by a series of clunks as a relay of florescent strip lights whirred into life. Kamel squinted, his eyes used to darkness. The blurry silhouettes began to fall into focus as they approached him, their faces indistinct.

"Who are you? What's going on?" he demanded, panting with desperate fury.

The two men were robed in black; dressed from head to toe in black combat fatigues with balaclavas pulled over their faces.

Four wide, white, eyes burned through menacingly. The men closed in silently.

One of them grabbed Kamel's shoulders, his gloved fingers gouging into his bare flesh, he filled Kamel's view as he tipped the chair onto its back legs. Kamel cried out, but the other man stifled it with a towel. He held the towel with one hand, winding the ends together tightly around his head, covering his mouth and nose. With his other hand he reached for something behind Kamel. The first assailant was now astride of him, holding him firmly.

The next sensation he felt was cold and wet and excruciating. One of the men was pouring jugs of water over Kamel's face, soaking the towel. The icy water splashed into an old steel bath under his head with a sinister metallic trill. The sound rang in his ears. His eyes stung in the torrent. He thrashed and writhed but the men and the duct tape around his ankles and wrists were holding him. He felt like he was drowning and had never been more terrified in his life. He felt a warm, wet sensation around his thighs and buttocks – he'd pissed himself.

With a crash, he was thrust upright again and the towel was released.

He coughed and spluttered, desperate, gulping for air.

"Our mutual employer says hi!" the first man spoke, in English, with an Egyptian accent, while the second man wrung the towel out over the bath. The sound made Kamel feel like he wanted to piss himself again, but his bladder was already empty. The first man took his hands off Kamel and stepped back. He folded his bulging arms over his broad chest.

"What do you want from me?" coughed Kamel, speaking the language they all seemed to understand here - English. Drool trickled along the deep jowls around his mouth and beads of water hung on his bushy eyebrows and pointed beard like diamonds.

"My colleague and I have some questions for you," said one of the men, his voice muffled by the woolen balaclava.

"Then why not ask me. Why all the drama?" Kamel amazed

himself with his new found courage.

"Where is it?" the first man asked.

"Where is what?"

The second man span the damp towel in his hands to form a rudimentary garrote. He pulled it around Kamel's throat and squeezed.

Kamel choked and heaved for air, feeling his consciousness slipping away. The man released the towel, just as Kamel's face reddened and his eyes slid back into his head.

Kamel coughed and spluttered violently, thrashing around in the chair with what little strength he still had.

"The box, you fat fuck," spat the man who was stood in front of him, his arms still folded around his chest.

"What box?"

He unfolded his arms and drew in a deep and disappointed sigh. He thrust his hand forward and grabbed Kamel's neck, pushing it into the back of the chair. Just as Kamel had recovered from the first near-strangulation, his breath failed him once again. He felt himself letting go, embraced by a warm darkness. It was strangely inviting.

"Don't fuck around old man. Surely it's obvious that we're serious."

He let go of Kamel, who gulped for air, feeling giddy.

"You mean the Varna Box?" asked Kamel, looking bemused.

"No, your mothers fucking jewellery box. What do you think?" hissed the interrogator. His companion chuckled and slapped the damp towel across his hand like a club. Kamel glanced around to see what the wet thumping noise was, and gulped hard, causing another bout of coughing.

"David Thornton stole it in 1998 and no one has seen it since."

"Tell me something I don't know old man," scoffed the interrogator. He sighed and glared at Kamel. "All right," he continued, sounding defeated, "let's try something else. What do you know about the box?"

"I know it was stolen!" Kamel grinned.

"Fuck you!" yelled the interrogator then balled his fist and thrust it hard into his face. His nose made a horrific crack and Kamel wailed in agony. Blood spewed down his face, diluted by water and sweat, it spread and dripped down over his shoulders and neck.

Kamel sobbed for a moment before taking control of himself. He glared at the interrogator, who was nursing his knuckles.

"Why don't you just kill me and have done with it," anger seared through Kamel with a fresh wave of adrenalin.

"Well that depends on you," the man took on a diplomatic tone, trying to create the impression he was being reasonable. "You can either answer my questions and we will confer with our mutual employer and ask him if he will spare your life - depending on how useful your information is. Or, Ali and I can have a little fun. We have a whole array of tools and techniques we can play with."

He could imagine the smile on his face, his tone proof enough he was a man who loved his work. He began to pace a short, repeating path, back and forth in front of Kamel and explained in glorious Technicolor about the tools and techniques he and Ali were versed in; "We've done a little water boarding already. How did you like that, fun wasn't it? It was such a laugh, in fact, you pissed yourself," he paused the pacing and sneered at Kamel before continuing, "Ali loves water boarding, don't you Ali?"

"I do, Rehu. But you know what I prefer…?" responded the second man, in such a matter of fact way they could be comparing favourite TV shows.

"Yes I do. But maybe you should share it with our friend here."

Ali grabbed a handful of Kamel's thinning hair and yanked his head back to look him in the eye. Kamel cried out and stared back at the man.

"I failed dental school, but I still have my tools. I do enjoy ripping out teeth," he threw Kamel's head back upright and chuckled.

Rehu, the interrogator, grinned at Kamel with satisfaction, "Speaking of trades. You are lucky, old man, you found your calling. Me," he prodded himself in the chest as if everyone should feel sorry for him and his lack of direction in life, "I tried many trades. I tried the army, but they said I had anger issues when I sliced off the dick of a man I was questioning." he winked at Kamel, who gulped, and glanced down at his own exposed penis, as if he was checking it was still intact, it had certainly withered somewhat. Rehu continued, "So I retrained as an electrician. But that never worked out for me. I kept my equipment through. I'll show you later," his voice took on a sinister tone, "Should I go on? Ali and I can do this all day long. In fact, we have so many tools at our disposal we can go on for days, weeks, months even. Slowly stripping you of yourself, causing you unimaginable pain. You think this hurts," Rehu prodded Kamel's smashed nose and he screamed, "We've not even started."

Kamel's face throbbed, his head was pounding, he was shivering, his whole body hurt as he stiffened and seized up.

"The choice is yours old man. I could kill you," Rehu nodded as he contemplated the alternatives, "but it would be slow and very, very, painful," he chuckled and shook his head as he said it, "and slowly, bit by bit you will talk to us and give up the secrets in that thick-head-of-yours," With each of the final words, he prodded Kamel's temple, "Or, we can be civilised and sensible and you can give us the information we seek. You might then stand a chance of living through this, and although you will have lost your dignity, you would still have your miserable fucking life."

Kamel closed his eyes and explored the inside of his skull for a moment. There was no sense in his impossible situation getting worse and there was a chance the men would be true to their word and he'd live through this. He had neither the strength or the stamina to withstand much more - "All right!" he blurted it out in desperation.

"Good choice," Rehu gripped Kamel's clammy and bloody shoulder as if he had just negotiated a successful business deal.

"So your name is Rehu?"

"What of it?"

"Good and evil personified," Kamel made an amused noise through his bloody nostril, "interesting."

"What can I say? My parents had a sense of humour," said Rehu, folding his thick arms around his chest again and glaring down at Kamel, "So talk to me about the box old man."

"Well it depends what you want to know?"

Ali then interrupted, grabbing a scruff of Kamel's hair again and used it to shake his head. Sprays of blood, water and sweat sparked into the air, "we ask the questions," he hissed.

Rehu threw a look at Ali that implied an order to stop. "So what's in the box?" he asked.

Kamel saw that Rehu seemed to be the more senior of the men, it was him he needed to appeal to if he was to get out of this alive. He surprised himself with how calm and logical he was being. Given reasonable alternatives, the hypothesis would be to take the path of least resistance. And what harm would it do to share knowledge with these thugs? After all, they had only chosen such a dark path through lack of education and choices? This is how the scientist in Kamel justified what he was about to say.

"The question is not what is in the box, rather what it is," he began, "There are several theories about what the box is. Throughout history there have been containers purporting to possess mysterious powers; the Ark of the Covenant, Japanese Puzzle Boxes, Pandora's Box. Thornton and I believed it to be Pandora's Box."

"What?" said Rehu, his eyes narrowing.

"Surely you know the story? The story goes that a long time ago in a world before any cares or troubles Epimetheus was sent a playmate, a young girl called Pandora. Epimetheus had been given a box to look after by a mysterious wanderer called Quicksilver who would one day return to claim it. But Pandora was curious. She was desperate to know what was in the box. One day her curiosity got the better of her. She lifted the lid and opened the box. She released into the world all of the troubles that have dogged mankind ever since; War, famine, disease, unhappiness, old age and death…"

"I know the story," interrupted Rehu, "but that's ridiculous. It's just a myth. Like dragons and unicorns and shit."

"Of course," huffed Kamel with a superior tone, "Let me finish. How will you ever learn anything if you do not listen? It is certainly not a true story. But as humans, we are always trying to explain the world around us. History is littered with the misinformation of ignorant people making sense of their world by accepting stories told to them that explain what they cannot explain. A fine example is the medical humours; Before biologists understood how the human body worked they had a theory of four temperaments. It is a theory of proto-psychology that suggests that four bodily fluids affect human personality traits and behaviours; sanguine (pleasure-seeking and sociable), choleric (ambitious and leader-like), melancholic (introverted and thoughtful), and phlegmatic (relaxed and quiet). Of course we know better now."

"And your point?" Interrupted Ali, who had been listening but was losing patience.

"It's rude to interrupt. Didn't you go to school and learn manners and respect."

"No actually," said Ali, defiantly.

"Well, respect, my boy, is an important skill. You go much further in life if you respect people, especially your elders," Kamel drilled a stern stare into Ali, who shrank in stature.

"I'm going to find a chair. I think we'll be here a while," Ali announced and trudged off like a puppy who'd just been kicked.

"Fetch me one too!" shouted Rahu after him. Ali made a mock salute and left the room. Kamel noted the door was unlocked. Perhaps he had a chance to escape?

"I am cooperating with you aren't I?" he asked.

Rehu shrugged.

"Perhaps you could loosen these binds and fetch me something to keep warm?"

"Don't push you luck, old man. Keep talking," Rehu leaned

close to Kamel then backed off. Kamel had managed to shift the balance of power in the room, but Rehu was keen to remind him who was in charge and reclaim the high ground.

"Where was I?"

"Humours or some shit," grunted Rehu.

"Ah yes! My point was the story of the world's troubles being stored in a box that were released by Pandora is nonsense. But it is a way of explaining something that could not be explained given the knowledge of the time. Men have always told stories. Knowledge has been spread through generations using the medium of stories. In fact, our whole lives are seen by us as a narrative in which we are the central character. The trouble with stories is that each new narrator tells it in a different way. Before people had ready access to education, and only the wealthy classes could read and write, people spread knowledge through storytelling. The story would have been distorted over the years. And in fact, would have been made up in the first place by someone who did not have the knowledge that modern science gives us today."

"Like Chinese whispers?"

"Exactly!" Kamel grinned triumphantly. He almost forgot his predicament. He was in his element now - hearing the sound of his own voice imparting his vast knowledge - that was the narrative he had assigned to his own life.

"Then what's the true story?" asked Rehu. His posture had slackened and he looked interested. He shifted from foot to foot, "where's this chair?" he muttered to himself. They both looked towards the door as it creaked open and Ali appeared with two cheap plastic chairs stacked together.

Ali thumped the chairs down, parted them, then slid one to his companion. It roared across the concrete flood before being stopped by Rehu's firm hand. Both men sat and dragged the chairs in front of Kamel.

"How long do you intend to keep me like this?" he asked.

"Until you've told us the whole story then we will call our mutual employer for a decision."

"You keep saying our mutual employer, who are you talking

about?"

"Who's your boss?" asked Rehu.

Kamel's brow crinkled, "Dr Osman Elmas. Director of the Istanbul Archaeological Museums, of course."

"Bingo!" said Rehu with a wide grin.

Kamel fell silent. He felt sick and dropped his head in disbelief, "I want to speak to him," he demanded.

"You'll speak to us first."

"Osman can't possibly know what you are doing to me. It's preposterous!"

Rehu gave a slow nod.

"Ring him! I must talk to him and settle this. He's got it all wrong. Does he think I've stolen the box? Does he think I've sold it? He needs to understand. There is no need for him to punish me like this. I don't need to be taught a lesson. I would never, never sell our heritage. It's not me who has been stealing artefacts from the museum – I was the one who discovered it and reported it to the authorities. Why would I do that if I was responsible? I need him to know the truth," Kamel struggled in the chair once more, rocking it from side to side in desperation.

"Listen, Hakan," Rehu settled a reassuring hand on Kamel's shoulder and he stopped struggling, mostly out of the offence taken to Rehu's assumption that it was acceptable to use his given name, "If you tell us, we can pass it on to Elmas. You have my word."

Dejected, Kamel drew in a deep breath and sighed. He had sworn an oath, but knew that if Elmas didn't hear the truth, he would have him killed by these thugs. His stomach churned as he questioned whether he was willing to betray a dead man to save his own skin. He was the last of them; perhaps Elmas could take up the flame and be the next in the order? Perhaps he'd been wrong about Elmas and it was someone else who had been smuggling artefacts out of the museum?

"All right," Kamel dropped his head, allowing it to loll against his chest for a moment, almost as heavy as his heart. He looked up at the two men.

"What I am about to tell you is known only to a handful of people. David Thornton and I swore an oath. We are the last of an ancient order of knights, for want of a better description, who through the generations have promised to keep the box hidden."

"Hidden? From what? And since when?" Ali leaned closer, resting his elbows on his knees to get closer and look Kamel in the eyes.

"The first guardian of the Pandora Order was Democritus. A Greek scholar, who was a student of Leucippus, at the time of Plato.

'Democritus, made the connection between the Pandora story and an ancient box he acquired during his extensive travels across the middle east. Democritus is famous for proposing the first theories of atoms…"

"Atoms? You mean like nuclear stuff and the A bomb," Ali was so excited he was salivating.

"Exactly, my boy! You are right!" Kamel was triumphant, "You should have gone to school. I think you are cleverer than you let people believe!" he grinned at Ali. Although Rehu and Ali were masked and swathed in black, like harbingers of death, Kamel had deduced that Ali was quite young. He had the spark of youth in his eye. Eager to please and to be accepted. Malleable. He must have been in his late teens or early twenties. The perfect age to be susceptible to radicalisation by extremists. The thought crossed Kamel's mind that perhaps these men were corrupting the teachings of Allah. He had always been uncomfortable about Elmas's extreme views but had kept it to himself for the sake of the job he loved. But he had said so much now, he might as well finish the story and stand a chance of walking away.

"Democritus, although a pioneering thinker and often referred to as the father of atomic science, feared the box. The word atom means invisible and until the turn of the 20th century it was believed to be the smallest possible constituent of matter and it was Democritus who first proposed this. To him, the box, in his limited view of the world, oozed death. It shook the very foundations of his beliefs. For him, only Zeus could possess such power. He was determined to hide the box from the world and started the Pandora Order, by passing his knowledge on to his apprentice who in turn kept the secret safe. To this day the order has continued. Of course, today, we know the power of splitting atoms, from the first experiments by Marie Curie in the 1930's to the detonation of the first Atomic Bomb in 1945. Pierre Curie, incidentally, Marie's husband, was also in the Pandora Order, and he first proposed to the order that perhaps Democritus had discovered the world's first naturally occurring radioactive power source – what we today would call a fission reactor."

"A nuclear reactor?" Rehu sounded baffled. Kamel suspected that Elmas had told them none of this.

"Are you listening?" demanded Kamel, staring at Rehu. Rehu snapped himself out of a trance in which, Kamel suspected, that the man was thinking about what to do with it if he found the box before his employer.

"Carry on old man. In fact..." Rehu stood up and walked back towards the door where a crumpled rucksack had been dumped. He reached in and drew out an aluminium thermos flask. He returned to the chair, but before sitting he uncapped the flask. It hissed and a warm cloud of mouth-watering coffee filtered out.

"Here," he held the flask to Kamel's mouth and tipped. Kamel drank deeply of the warm liquid, closing his eyes in pleasure. It was the best coffee he'd drunk in his life, he prayed to himself that it wouldn't be his last. As Rehu took the flask away, replaced the cap and put it down, Kamel sighed.

"Thank you, son. You have a good heart. I know it. Men do terrible things when they are desperate."

Rehu seemed to rebuke himself for allowing Kamel to form such an opinion. It pleased Kamel he seemed to be getting to him. Perhaps there was still the opportunity to turn the situation to his advantage. Hope gave him a renewed sense of confidence.

"Just keep talking you fat fuck," said Rehu.

"Where was I?" said Kamel, put off by the insult.

"Nuclear bombs!" said Ali, as excitable as a kid in a toy shop.

"No, my boy. Not nuclear bombs. A naturally occurring nuclear power source. Do you know the rest of the Pandora story?"

Both men shook their heads.

"After Pandora opened the box and she and Epimetheus argued and cried about whose fault it was, they heard a kindly voice and noises from inside the box. They had already opened the lid once and there was a chance that if they opened it again the troubles would find their way back in, so she opened the box again. This time a fairy flew out. The fairy was called Hope. The Pandora myth is morality tale. Wherever there is trouble, death and tragedy there is always hope. There is always a ying and a yang, a good and an evil, a black and a white – for every action is an equal and opposite reaction – that's physics 101. It is a nuclear power source. It can be used for good and bad. It can generate cheap and clean energy, enriching our lives, driving economies, growth and prosperity or it can wipe out humanity. The Pandora Order understands that people have a predisposition to destroy each other. Darwinism – survival of the fittest and all that. Democritus, who was well educated and well-travelled, understood this and we still know it to this day. I mean look at us? Look what you are doing here, right now, to me? People are horrible to one another. An infinite source of power. Think what would happen if that fell into the wrong hands?" he stopped for breath, "During the second world war the Nazi's were seeking the box. But it wasn't only the Nazi's who were obsessed with ancient history and mysticism - General Patten was too and was a member of the order. Part of the real reason he took such an interest in the Nazi's looting activities was because he was terrified they would find the box. There is evidence that Himmler wanted to use its power to develop weapons, to rival that rumoured to be being developed by the US. Patton set up the Monuments Men, a team of allied specialists in preserving European culture and art. Their secret agenda, that few men in the MFAA knew, was to keep the box out of Nazi hands, at all costs.

'The box had remained hidden at the Varna Necropolis for thousands of years before Thornton's team discovered it in 1998. Thornton took the box and hid it and took the secret to his grave."

"What do you mean he took it to his grave?" Rehu looked exasperated, having listened to the professor. Kamel feared the consequences, for he had nothing else to tell them and they were no further forward. In a last desperate pitch, he tried to separate himself from Thornton, in the hope they would spare him.

"I had no part in Thornton's actions, he never told me where he'd hidden the box," Kamel smiled jubilantly but he feared the rage that was tangibly building in Rehu. Rehu flexed his fingers and balled his fist, his face reddening. He drew his arm back and readied a punch and was about to release. Kamel winced, panicked, he couldn't take any more, he had to think fast.

"No, no. Wait!" Kamel ducked his head aside - shuddering, expecting to be hit again.

Rehu loosened his shoulders, "Make it good old man," he bared his teeth and leered over him. Kamel was sure that this was his last chance before the two men unleashed their fury on his naked, bloody and miserable body. They would pummel him into wet fleshy gore if he couldn't think of something convincing to say.

"I'm telling you the truth!" He was crippled by a visceral fear. He was running out of things to tell them which meant he was running out of time. He wracked his brains for anything else he could offer them in exchange for his life. He remembered the conversation he had had the day a Bulgarian Detective rang him to tell him they had tracked David back to the UK and he was dead. The Detective had said Thornton had flown to Budapest then on to Amsterdam. Kamel knew that David's brother lived in Amsterdam. They had played golf with Michael once, they'd posed for Michael while he took a picture of them. As he was lining up the shot he had boasted about his beautiful house and Dutch wife, his second, who was 20 years younger than him and a former model. David's older brother was so talkative and irritating he was hard to forget. Could Michael be the next in the Pandora Order?

"I think I know where David took the box?"

"You think?" sneered Rehu.

"I know. I know where it is."

"Where?" barked Rehu, a rabid wolf, salivating over a carcass.

"Amsterdam."

"Where in Amsterdam?"

Kamel could no longer control himself. The terror welled up and although it shamed him, he couldn't help himself, he broke down into floods of desperate tears, "I don't know. Please. Let me go. I've told you all I know. Please," he begged.

Rehu kept Kamel hanging there, in desperate terror.

"Will you call Osman for me. Please?" Kamel pleaded with Rehu, glancing at Ali too to gauge the balance of sympathy between them. He could see only blackness in their eyes and they glared at him with menacing silence. He sobbed bitterly, hanging his head, willing to do anything to get himself out of his predicament. He knew Osman Elmas - a man he had been loyal to, whom he had spent his whole career trying to impress, a man notorious for his intolerance – held his life in his hands.

"Please," he wept.

Rehu stared silently. Pity in his eyes. He glanced at Ali and he slid his phone from his trouser pocket.

His fingers danced across the screen. It rang more times than was usual and just as he was about to disconnect the call, it was answered.

"Selam!" Kamel overheard the voice on the other end of the phone. Elmas sounded irritated. That was always a worrying sign, it meant that someone, somewhere would suffer his wrath.

"Sir, it's Rehu."

"Do you have him?" said Elmas.

"We've got him and he's been talking, sir."

"Osm…" Kamel cried out, in the hope of pleading with him, but Ali wrapped the wet towel around his face, gagging him. Kamel fought for a moment but Ali tugged the towel so that it pressed on Kamel's broken nose. The agony was so intense that Kamel froze, on the verge of losing consciousness, knowing that if he moved or tried to speak it would be excruciating. He listened hard to the conversation, grateful that Elmas spoke so loudly on the phone.

"He has asked for leniency," said Rehu, his eyes burning into Kamel's.

"What has he told you?"

"He's told us where to find it."

"Yes. And?" Elmas urged Rehu to elaborate.

"The box is in Amsterdam, we'll send some guys to get it. Can we get rid of this bastard yet?"

Kamel knew what it meant. He was hyperventilating, his eyes bulging, whatever they did next would hurt.

Kamel didn't hear the last part of the conversation, Rehu had turned away. His future had just fallen from a cliff and was hanging on with one hand.

"And? What did he say?" Ali urged Rehu to tell him the decision.

"Elmas has given us the go ahead."

Ali let the towel go and the two men stepped away.

Kamel had done his best to eavesdrop, "Go ahead for what?" he asked. All he had now was hope.

Had he got through to the men? He had told them more than he should have, he had got their respect – surely?

Ali and Rehu ignored Kamel's desperate tears.

"He told us to do whatever it takes, and to finish this," said Rehu.

"So we can finally get rid of this fucker then?" said Ali.

Rehu nodded. He threw a sly smile at Ali.

Was this how it would end? He had worked his whole life to leave a legacy, to be respected, revered even. He could hardly believe that it would all end here - wretched and naked, duck taped to a chair in a damp cellar covered in his own piss and blood.

There was no sense in denying it, he knew what was coming. If he had any hope of salvaging a shred of dignity in his final moments, he wanted to look his killer in the eye. He used the last of his strength to lift his head and look at them. His eyes sallow and defeated, moist with despairing tears.

Rehu slid his hand into a pocket on the chest of his combat fatigues and took out a pistol. He aimed. He fired.

One bullet impacted the centre of Kamel's forehead. The thump rocked the chair, his head slumped to the side, a thick ooze of blood dribbled down into Kamel's eye socket. His dead eyes staring right into Rehu's.

AGENCY SAFEHOUSE, A SECRET LOCATION SOMEWHERE NEAR GENEVA

July

"It's a good job we stopped at that petrol station and got some supplies, these cupboards are bare," said Sasha.

Gina watched her systematically bang doors and rummage through the kitchen looking for anything they could eat or drink.

"Pass me the bag will you," said Sasha, "I'll stick the kettle on." She wasn't addressing either of them in particular, but Gina picked up the carrier bag and took it over to her. It helped, feeling like she could contribute something, she'd never felt so small and vulnerable.

"I'll see if I can get the heating going," said Tom who disappeared through a side door off the main room.

The safe house was a squat single story building, set back from the road and hidden from it by an unruly strip of hedgerow. It occupied the corner of a scruffy square of meadow, with far reaching views to the foot of the basin of hills that lined the plateau. Gina imagined that it had once been a farm workers house, she wondered why they would have left, assuming they'd had a choice.

It was quiet, a faint chill in the air. After she helped Sasha to unload the groceries she went exploring, leaving Sasha to fuss around in the kitchen, playing mum.

She stopped and looked around, breathing slowly and deeply, trying to get a sense of the place.

The front door opened onto the main living room, laid out as a seating area, dining area, with a kitchen in the corner. It was comfortable and clean but gloomy with the blinds closed and the energy saving light bulbs yet to brighten. She could have stepped onto the set of an Ikea Catalogue shoot demonstrating the cheapest way to furnish a room with flat-pack Formica. There was a thin film of dust over everything. She ran her finger along a blocky white side table, leaving a trail, like feet dragged through snow. The whole place smelt clean but neglected. Off the main room were three doors, two leading to bedrooms and one leading to a bathroom. Each was furnished simply and neutrally, utterly impersonal, utterly characterless. Bland but comfortable.

She glanced back to the kitchen and watched Sasha for a moment.

What was her story? And why had she lied to her about how well she knew her father?

She didn't want to trust the woman, but knew she had little choice. She was all alone and completely dependent on Sasha and Tom, at their mercy. It didn't sit well with her, she'd always felt in control. Even when she and Rees had been running, she'd felt more in control than she did now. Okay, so the agents had just saved her life, but they had put her in harm's way in the first place. She didn't know what to think.

She wished Rees was with her. He'd be holding her hand and oozing platitudes about what her father had been involved with and offering her advice on how to handle the two agents. She felt numb and wondered if the shock of what happened in that alleyway in Zurich was still affecting her.

She chose her bedroom and went back for her carrycase. She tugged the string on the blind that covered the front window, to let the diffuse autumnal sunlight in and open a window.

"Don't do that!" Tom shouted across the room. She jumped in her skin. The heating system thrummed and rattled in the cavity walls, as if it too was warning her.

"But I was just going to let some light in and open a window?"

"Why do you think I parked the car behind the house, hmm?"

She shrugged, "Because that's where the parking space was?"

"Because we don't want to advertise the fact that we're here!" he snatched the cord from her hand and let the blind drop.

She backed away, wounded, and grabbed her bag. She scurried into her room and flung the bag on the bed, slamming the door behind her like a disgruntled teenager.

"The same with the bedroom!" he shouted after her.

She understood, but it didn't mean she had to like it. She stuck her middle finger up at the closed door. She was no more than a prisoner. As long as they were being pursued, as long as the box was hidden, it held her freedom. It also held her family captive - all her faith and trust placed in Danny's capacity to be subtle, not something he excelled at. She told herself her sensible, dependable Rees would keep them all in perspective. God she missed him.

She star-fished the bed and kicked off her shoes, staring up at the artex ceiling. She drew imagined patterns in the swirls of plaster, letting her mind wander to anywhere but here.

Her limbs felt heavy, her senses numb. She must have drifted off. The next thing she knew she was roused by the muffled sound of raised voices from next door. Tom and Sasha seemed to be arguing about something, or at the very least, engaged in a heated debate. She swung her legs around and climbed off the bed, then padded across the plain beige carpet and peered around her door.

Sasha was sat in an armchair and Tom slumped across the corner of one of the settees. On the coffee table was a mess of paper and books, dotted with empty coffee mugs. She stepped out, enjoying the different textures from the soft carpet to the rough timber floor, playing on the soles of her naked feet.

"What are you talking about?" she asked, sliding into the corner of the other settee. Sasha offered a smile but seemed to be in the mid flow of making a point. Tom just glanced at her then ignored her, listening irritably to Sasha.

"...We get most of our knowledge of ancient history through text written years, sometimes millennia after the events," continued Sasha, "How can we possibly take it at face value. The sad truth about the way ordinary people lived their lives, even just a couple of centuries ago, is that most people were illiterate. Reading and writing was the domain of the wealthy and therefore the educated, and ergo the powerful. History is written by the victors and the scholars, not by the common man."

"It doesn't mean we should disregard the historic record," said Tom, his eyebrows knotted together.

"Well of course not, that's not what I'm saying."

"Well it's what you seem to be saying."

"Oh for God's sake, Sheridan. All I'm saying is that Archaeology helps fill the gaps and build up an honest picture. History is in the earth we stand on not in books on shelves in dusty libraries!"

"Well I'm sorry but I disagree. Of course history is in books, that's why they call them history books." He shot an angry look.

"Now you're just being petty!" Sasha said, her face red with frustration.

Gina, whose patience was now fibre thin, halted the exchange, "HEY!"

Stunned, they broke off and glared at her.

"Guys, why are you arguing?"

The two of them looked at her blankly.

Now she had their attention, she took her opportunity. She knew how they felt, she saw it. Whenever they were close to each other, their body language changed. She saw how they looked at each other when they thought no one was watching, yet when they spoke to each other it was always in denial.

Why couldn't they just be honest with each other?

The way they danced around each other exasperated her.

"What can you agree on?" she said, although the double meaning in her question fell on deaf ears.

Tom and Sasha glanced at each other and shrugged.

She would get no admissions from them today, so she mediated their pointless argument instead. It was as if the two of them would deliberately wind each other up, just to disguise what they were thinking. They were as bad as each other.

"It seems to me you can at least agree both methods are valid? But both have their place," she said, now she had their attention, "So rather than argue over minutia, let's talk about something related to the case shall we? I'll start writing things down."

She reached across to the coffee table and rooted around in the jumble of papers and pictures until she had found Sasha's notebook and pen. "May I?" she waved the book at Sasha, who nodded then took it from Gina.

Sasha flicked through to the middle of the book and handed it back to her. Gina thanked her, out of politeness rather than any level of acceptance.

"I'm just going to mind map what we have," said Gina, "You two are the investigators, you can start putting the pieces together. Just tell me some ideas, I don't care if you don't agree with each other," she fired a stern look between them, "Let's just capture all of it then sort through it later - Agreed?"

"Fine," said Tom, sulking, his pride wounded. Sasha nodded enthusiastically, masking her frustration as best she could.

"Okay - so what have we got?" Gina glanced expectantly between the two agents, waiting for someone to start.

"A stack of worthless notebooks," Tom waved dismissively at David's notebooks, like an aristocrat shoeing away a beggar. The books were strewn across the table like a tower of cards that had collapsed, next to a file bulging with scraps of paper and surveillance images.

"They're not worthless!" Sasha scowled, Tom looked at her defiantly.

"Enough! You're supposed to be professionals. We've all had a fucked up few days. Let's not take it out on each other!"

Tom sat up straight, as if he'd been called to attention. Sasha folded her arms but her eyes said she was willing to listen.

"Well," he took a deep breath, as if he were about to embark on an epic storytelling session, "In the folder are pictures of the characters we can link to the box, as well as addresses, maps, notes relevant to the case…"

"Yes, yes," Gina was impatient for him to get to the point, "Sasha filled me in on the case so far on the flight while you were snoring!" Gina offered Tom a wry smile, which he willingly returned.

"All right, then I'll paraphrase; We travelled to Bulgaria where Sasha spoke with the curator at the Varna Archaeological museum. We went to meet with a colleague of your father and Sasha's but found him dead. Next we went to Istanbul where we met a cagey Dr Kamel. Osman Elmas wasn't there. You then called Sasha and you know the rest."

"So other than the two Turkish archaeologists and some anecdotal stuff from a museum worker in Varna, all you have is what's on this table?"

"That about sums it up. The key is among the clues left by your father I'm certain of it."

"Okay, let's see," muttered Gina, thinking aloud, she mumbled an inventory, "Four notebooks left at our old house, one notebook in a safety deposit box, some money, a phone, passports and …a letter," It dawned on Gina the letter wasn't on the table.

"Have you read the letter yet?" she asked Sasha. This would give her the perfect excuse to find out what Sasha was hiding.

Sasha flushed crimson. Gina narrowed her eyes, her reaction spoke volumes. She felt sick for a moment, her mind playing out all sorts of unpalatable scenarios. She put it to the back of her mind – maybe she was jumping to conclusions?

"Not yet," Sasha admitted.

Gina was sure there was more to it. Did Sasha know what would be in the envelope? Was she keeping secrets from all of them?

Tom fired a look at her, Sasha chose to ignore it.

"I'll get it," she quickly got up and made for the coat rack. She rummaged through the pockets and dragged out the crumpled envelope. Tom and Gina both twisted around in their seats to watch, while Sasha opened the letter and read it.

Her eyes moistened.

Tom's expression pinched with impatience, "What does it say?"

Sasha looked up and forced a smile. She could see in her eyes she had just read it for the first time and something in it had upset her. She folded the letter up and slid it back into its envelope then bought the precious package back to the table.

"He left this for me because he suspected his life was in danger. He wrote three bullet points, I can only assume they are clues," Tom and Gina stared at her in quiet anticipation. The crumpling of paper as she unfolded the letter to read once more, broke the silence. She read the points aloud, "The first one - 'I was going to buy you a diamond, but now that I can't, you will need to find one for yourself'. 'The old name for Varna is the key' and 'Nokia will let you in'. Any thoughts?" she folded the page up again and put it away.

"Nothing else?" pressed Gina. She suspected that Sasha was hiding something from her.

Sasha shook her head, seemingly oblivious to her suspicions.

"Great. More puzzles!" Tom blew out a frustrated breath, "Let's take it one at a time shall we. 'I was going to buy you a diamond, but now that I can't, you will need to find one for yourself'?" he pursed his lips and looked to Sasha for an answer.

Her face folded in confusion. She seemed wrapped in thought for a moment, before shrugging.

"I don't know. I need to think on it some more."

Tom sighed, disappointed, "So, 'The old name for Varna is the key'?"

"Odessus," said Sasha.

Tom gave a satisfied nod, "What does it mean though?"

Gina and Sasha shrugged.

"Well we know the box is no longer in Varna, so it could just be something in the name?" suggested Sasha.

"But do we know for sure the box isn't there? How can we be sure you've not been on a wild goose chase?" Gina posed the uncomfortable question.

"We can't," said Tom, "But it is a reasonable assumption. We have no further evidence of Thornton returning to Bulgaria."

They exchanged glances that silently drew a line under the doubt and Tom continued.

"Nokia will let you in? Nokia will let you in…" he repeated, trailing off into thought.

Gina and Sasha exchanged a puzzled look.

"It must be something to do with the phone?" suggested Sasha.

The others nodded in agreement.

"Diamonds? Diamonds?" mused Tom.

"My uncle Michael is a Diamond Trader?" Gina suggested, although it seemed tenuous.

"Uncle? As in David's brother?" asked Tom.

Gina nodded, she thought about her Uncle Mike, pictured his pompous face, remembered his drunken ramblings at her mothers' funeral.

"Where will we find your Uncle?" asked Tom.

"Amsterdam!" she blurted it out. "What about if dad flew from Budapest to Amsterdam and then back to England?"

"Or rather, Jack Riddler did?" said Sasha, her eyes wide with excitement, as if she'd just made a discovery.

"Let's find out shall we?" said Tom, reaching across the table and extracting his laptop from under the paperwork.

He booted it up, and tapped at the keyboard while the others waited, their eyes focused on him.

"And there we have it!" he said and span the screen around for the others to see. On an EasyJet flight manifest, the agency had managed to acquire he found the name.

"Looks as though I'll be taking up my Uncles offer of a visit. Maybe Dad took the box to Amsterdam? It makes sense. Castell Diamonds has reputedly one of the most secure vaults in the world. That's where he took it."

GENEVA, AIRPORT

July

"Wait here, I'll go to the information desk and see if there are any flights available to Amsterdam Schiphol," said Tom, before striding off.

Gina took a seat and Sasha sat down beside her on the cold steel bench, it pressed into the back of her thighs harshly. They sat in awkward silence for a moment. Sasha was sure that Gina was suspicious of her.

She could never tell her the truth, it would destroy her - 'Hey, by the way, I had an affair with your dad?'

She fidgeted on the icy seat and felt the letter crumple in her trouser pocket.

"I'm going for a wee, will you watch my bag?" said Gina, getting up.

"Sure."

She watched, and as soon as Gina was out of sight she pulled the letter out and opened it once more.

Dearest Sasha

If you are reading this, it probably means I am dead. If I am, and it seems like an accident, look into it, it probably wasn't.

There are some things you need to know, that will help you get to the box:

- I was going to buy you a diamond, but now that I can't, you will need to find one for yourself

- The old name for Varna is the key

- Nokia will let you in

I want you to know that I'm sorry and that I love you.

David x

She cradled it in her hands like a precious child. The only thing she had left of David.

The guilt at the horrible things she'd said to him and the things she'd thought about him, this grudge she'd harboured for all these years, it burned. Like her heart was spontaneously combusting in her chest. She clutched the letter there, between her breasts.

The sound of footsteps getting closer interrupted her. She quickly stuffed the letter back in her pocket and smiled awkwardly at Gina as she retook the seat beside her.

They didn't speak. They barely acknowledged each other. Like strangers on a train, forced to sit together, neither having the courage or will to strike up a friendly exchange.

The raucous squeal of Sasha's mobile interrupted the uncomfortable silence.

"Hello."

"Hello, this Dr Blake?" the caller asked in stilted English, with a thick Bulgarian accent.

She skipped a beat, wondering if the call was anything to do with Tsvetan's death; "Yes, how can I help?" she replied.

"Dr Blake. This Dr Ivanov from Sofia St Anna Hospital. We have admission a patient who has given your name and number for emergency contact."

Sasha was confused. She had no close family, and couldn't think of anyone in Bulgaria she knew well enough to be their emergency contact.

"A patient? Who is it? What's happened?"

"A Gregory Lepton. He say he has no family but you are close friend. He asks to see you."

"Gregory?" she said in disbelief.

"You know this man?"

"Yes. Yes of course. I am in Geneva but will get the next flight. Okay, yes…Thank you Dr Ivanov…*ciao*."

"What is it?" asked Gina, her eyes glazed with concern, it was obvious to anyone around her that Sasha had just received some disturbing news.

"Change of plans. We need to find Tom. Before we go to Amsterdam, there is something I must do in Sofia."

SOFIA, BULGARIA

July

"Oh God!"

Horror lodged its fist in Sasha's throat and moistened her eyes at the sight of Gregory, lying there looking so pathetic. Blood stained bandages swaddled his head like entrails.

"Hey, Sash," he muttered in a watery voice.

Because he was found by a chambermaid in the Presidential Suite of the Sheraton Hotel, it was assumed Gregory was a man of modest affluence and he was taken to the best hospital in Sofia. His modern and private room resembled a budget hotel; with a kitchenette, lounge area and en-suite bathroom. The difference was the array of bleeping and flashing medical machinery surrounding Gregory's bed. He had been propped up by the nurses, and was conscious but groggy.

Sasha plunged across the room and threw herself onto the bed beside him.

"Oh Gregory, what has he done?" she caressed his swollen purple cheek softly.

"At least he's still alive," said Tom.

Sasha glared a warning shot at him..

"Who's that guy?" asked Gregory, eyeing Tom.

"This is…" she didn't quite know how to introduce Tom, she had to think quickly, "This is an associate of mine from the British Museum. We're working together on a project."

Tom nodded in acknowledgment and leaned into the doorframe, staying out of it. Gina was at the hotel resting.

"Oh sweetie, I'm so sorry," said Sasha, sobbing lightly.

"It's okay," muttered Gregory, his voice gravelly, as if he were chewing on stones, "You can say it. You told me so," he flashed his eyebrows but even that caused his eyes to water.

"Why did you call me, of all people?"

"Because you knew him once. And he seems to know a lot about you now."

Tom and Sasha exchanged an anxious look. Tom, who had been watching from earshot propped himself up and paid attention, "What are you talking about?" he said. He began to stride towards the bed, his arms folded tightly across his chest.

"He has files," said Gregory.

"Files? What do you mean, files?" Sasha's face tensed.

"And who's 'he'?" asked Tom.

"He's been my benefactor for a number of years. We have a…relationship…But he's a connected and influential man. I hear things, see things – he calls it business. I saw a file on you. Both of you," Gregory threw a slow look between them that hung in the air like smoke.

Tom glared at Gregory with one eye wider than the other in suspicion; "Who are you talking about?"

"Dr Osman Elmas," Gregory dropped the name like flatulence, and Tom and Sasha screwed up their faces in disgust.

"He's your homosexual benefactor?" Sasha's pulled a face in incredulity. Gregory responded with a slow nod.

"Interesting," mused Tom.

"This can't be a coincidence, Sheridan," said Sasha.

Tom snapped out of his pensive stare and nodded gruffly to Sasha, "I don't believe in coincidences," he said and pulled a cheap plastic chair to the side of the bed; "These files. What's in them?"

"Pictures of you both and some scribbled notes in Turkish that I didn't understand. Osman has always tried to keep me out of his business, but we've been seeing each other for many years. It's taken him a long time to trust me. When we have been together he has left stuff lying around. I've always suspected he was more than the Director of the Archaeological Museum and an advisor to the Turkish government. Over the last few months especially, I've overheard suspicious phone calls," his voice faded and he tried to reach for a glass of water by the bed but his movements were stiff and slow. Sasha helped him so he could continue. She was sat on the edge of the bed now, holding his hand lightly.

After taking a sip and thanking her for her kindness he continued; "At first I thought maybe Mafia. He seems to do a lot of business here in Bulgaria. But I'm not sure now. He harbours extreme Islamic views so disapproves of any business that exploits people's vices. I think he uses Bulgaria as a route into the European market, selling stolen antiquities to wealthy European investors."

Tom and Sasha stared at each other in disbelief for an instant. Sasha had never considered that what she was involved in was so close to home.

"Has he used you for any of this?" quizzed Tom, suspicion lacing his voice.

"No," said Gregory, sounding adamant, almost insulted by the suggestion, "But he has contacts all over Europe, in some of the worlds most respected institutions. He contacts me when he's travelling on business and I escort him. In exchange he supports my art."

"Do these institutions include the British Museum?" asked Tom.

Gregory nodded. Tom narrowed his eyes at the information and he seemed to be avoiding looking at her. She felt strangely guilty.

"Osman is a man of great influence – it has its advantages and disadvantages," continued Gregory, oblivious to the tension between Tom and Sasha, "but when I saw your face in one of his files, Sash," his voice broke and tears rimmed his eyes, "He can do what he likes to me, I can take it. But you? No fucking way! I had to call you, I think you might be in danger," he gripped Sasha's hand as tightly as he could manage and fixed her with a serious look, his eyes moist with fear.

"I know, Gregory," she offered him a reassuring smile, "I know there's someone after us, but until now we didn't know who. So thank you."

Tom and Sasha's nameless quarry now had an identity. They both wanted their revenge on Osman Elmas, on that at least, they did agree.

"Gregory," began Tom, with a serious frown, "I am about to tell you something that you must promise not to repeat."

She fired a wary look at Tom, who ignored it. Gregory agreed to the conditions.

"I am an investigator and Dr Blake is assisting me. There is someone higher up the food chain than Osman Elmas. A man known only as The Libyan. Have you ever heard Elmas mention him?"

Gregory was lost in thought for a moment, while Tom and Sasha waited for his response.

"I think I have heard the name mentioned when he has spoken to his contact in Sofia."

"There is a contact in Sofia?" asked Tom, as if he needed to be sure.

"There's a businessman that Osman works with in the city. A Jewish man who has business interests across Europe and North Africa. I met the man once, he's shifty," said Gregory.

Sasha knew from the subtle signals she noticed in Tom that he was desperate to press Gregory more on it but they could both see that Gregory was getting weaker. He looked pale, his stature had shrunk into the bedcovers and the machines seemed to be bleeping more erratically.

"Gregory," said Sasha, squeezing his hand, "I know you're tired, but for all our sakes. Who is the Jew? He could take down Elmas and lead us to The Libyan."

"His name is David Ishmael. Elmas invited him to an exhibition launch I had here in Bulgaria at the National Palace of Culture in Sofia."

"Do you know where he works from in the city?" asked Sasha.

"Not exactly…" Gregory paused and thought about it for a moment, "but I remember him commenting he was lucky to have his office opposite the Palace of Culture but the building he was in was ugly and falling down?"

"A falling down ugly building in Sofia, well that narrows it down," grumbled Tom. Sasha fired a disapproving look.

"Thank you Gregory. That's really helpful. Get some rest." She planted a kiss on Gregory's forehead, and harried Tom out of the room. She let the door fall closed and they stepped into the sterile corridor with that familiar hospital stench.

Tom glared at Sasha, "Have you been keeping things from me? Did you know about any of this?"

"Oh course not! How dare you!"

She was so incensed by the insinuation she raised her hand and struck Tom hard across the cheek. He was stunned into silence. His bottom lip trembled as if he had something to say, but he was in too much shock to form any words. They were in a state of stalemate in the empty corridor. It was Tom who interrupted the awkward silence.

"I need to get back to the hotel to check this Ishmael character out. Are you coming?"

"I have nowhere else to go," Sasha held a hand out, "come on, Sheridan, give me the keys - this time I'll drive. The other drivers in this city are almost as crazy as you behind the wheel."

For once, he backed down. He reached into the pocket of his jeans and handed Sasha the car keys.

The rain hissed down hard on the road ahead and the wipers struggled to keep up with the deluge. The puddles were getting deeper as they ploughed through them, the few blocks back to the hotel. Inside the car Tom and Sasha remained silent, the windows misted up from their heavy breathing.

They dashed into the hotel lobby, their jackets over their heads. As soon as they stepped inside the storm that brewed from nowhere stopped, Sasha glanced back, the sky was still a stodgy and uncertain shade of grey.

When Tom let them into the hotel room, Gina was sat upright on the bed, wrapped in a hotel robe, her legs folded across themselves. She was wielding the TV remote like a cudgel, her face as dark as the sky outside.

"I didn't expect to see you in our room," said Tom, relieved he would not have to suffer more uncomfortable silence with

Sasha.

Gina looked up and smiled bleakly, "I guessed you wouldn't be long so I thought I'd wait in here."

"You all right?" asked Sasha, sliding onto the bed next to Gina and resting a reassuring hand on her shoulder. Gina nodded reluctantly.

"But I can see that you guys aren't all right. I'm getting bad vibes from both of you. What happened?"

"Nothing," barked Tom, still feeling the after effects of a throbbing face.

Gina glanced at Sasha for a straight answer, who shook her head.

"Well, perhaps I should leave you kids to sort this out?" sighed Gina, like the hapless mediator in a broken marriage.

As Gina got up Sasha said, "Before you get settled, pack your things. We're leaving for Amsterdam first thing in the morning. Let's see your uncle and end this," Gina's mood visibly lifted.

Tom offered a repentant glance but could see from her cold eyes that Sasha wasn't ready for that. "I'm going to take a shower," she said and disappeared into the bathroom.

As soon as she was out of earshot, Gina pressed him, "What did you say to her?" she hissed.

Tom felt the irritation festering. Everything he'd done was to try to protect them yet neither of them seemed to have a high opinion of him

How dare she challenge him like that? He was the one with the red face.

"Me? She was jumping to conclusions again."

"Tom?" Gina stretched out his name cynically, her tone chiding his dishonesty.

He breathed through the frustration of feeling so isolated and misunderstood.

"Fine! The friend of Sasha's we went to see, Gregory…."

"Gregory Lepton – yes," interrupted Gina, "I'm familiar with his work. She mentioned before she was friends with him. Is he all right?"

"He'll live," said Tom dismissively, "anyway," he continued, "Lepton has been in a relationship for some time with a man called Osman Elmas."

"Isn't he one of the Turkish archaeologists? He knew my father?"

"That's right. After speaking with Gregory we now think it is his men who have been chasing us."

Gina's tone changed, she seemed thirsty for revenge, a healthy reaction for a soldier, but not for an office girl with no means to defend herself in a fight, "Is he the fucker that sent those guys to kill you and capture me?" she continued.

"Perhaps," replied Tom, wincing a little, he'd never heard her speak like that before and it made him nervous, "But it goes higher than him. And Gregory gave me the name of a Jewish businessman in the city who can lead me to the man at the top of the tree, a wanted terrorist known only as 'The Libyan'."

"So that's who you are planning to see?"

Tom nodded. Gina swallowed hard, as if she was experiencing Tom's apprehension first hand.

"And Sasha has a problem with that?" Gina sounded surprised as she asked.

"Not that, something else," said Tom, staring into the middle distance.

How could he say it without sounding like a complete arsehole?

He probably should apologise to Sasha, he thought. The last time he was slapped across the face by a woman, it was his father's girlfriend - he was fifteen and had just 'borrowed' his car.

Fortunately Gina took the choice away with her next comment.

"You know, the two of you need to start being honest with each other."

"I am honest with Agent Blake, with both of you!" protested Tom, almost too vehemently.

He didn't need her schoolgirl psychoanalysis. Besides, what

business was it of hers?

"I think you know what I mean, Tom."

Enough, he wanted rid of her so he could work. He was in no mood for her mind games.

"What is this? Why do I always feel like you girls are ganging up on me? Perhaps you should leave. I need to get online and find out about Elmas's contact in Bulgaria and you should go and pack," he said and waved accusingly at the interconnecting doors between their rooms.

Gina fired an exasperated look at Tom and took herself back to her own room, slamming the door behind her.

He opened up his laptop and stared vacantly at the screen, his mind scattered and a heavy guilt descended. Why, whenever they got closer, did he always have to push Sasha away? He rubbed his temples then shook himself out of it typed.

When Sasha came back into the room - having hastily thrown on the clothes she'd been wearing, and rubbing at her hair with a damp towel - Tom was crouched over his laptop tapping away furiously.

"What are you looking at?" she asked as she approached the desk. Tom flinched, almost imperceptibly, so focused he hadn't noticed her.

He turned in the chair and looked up at her, gazing at her a little too long for colleagues, "I know how to find Ishmael."

"Great! When do we leave?" she said, anything to change the subject and push the investigation forwards.

"I'm going alone."

Sasha threw the towel onto the bed and jabbed her hands into her hips, "I'm your partner, Agent Sheridan, or have you forgotten that? Milton bought me in on this thing because you need me. He has placed his trust in me, why can't you? And after everything we've been through!" Her head was throbbing with anger.

What did she need to do to prove herself?

"No, that's not it," he said with self-conscious earnestness,

"That's not what I mean. I do trust you. Look, I'm sorry I was so crass with you earlier. I don't always think before I speak. I'm going to see Ishmael alone because I don't know what to expect from the man and our time is running out. I need to find The Libyan and stop this from escalating."

She fired a cynical look at him. At least he'd apologised but it felt somehow dismissive. She released the tension in her arms and folded them lightly around herself, resting a hip on the desk to listen to him, "What do you mean our time is running out?" she asked.

"The Libyan is going to want the box before the elections," began Tom, adopting a serious tone, "We have no way to know what his plans are for it, but if he is going to use a legitimate process to take power, it will be during the elections and the box will be his symbol of power," he was breathless with urgency, "We need to split up. I'm sending you to Amsterdam with Gina precisely because I do trust you. Elmas and The Libyan's men could be in Amsterdam already. You two should go ahead to Amsterdam."

"But…" she began to plead. They had come this far as a team, she didn't want to split up now. The truth was, she was afraid to be without him, to find herself having to use some of the self-defence techniques she learnt while in The Agency training programme. She always felt safe when he was close.

"There's no time. There's a giant street chess board in the Casino Square in Amsterdam, we'll meet there. When I've done what I need to do I'll text you a rendezvous. It should take no more than forty eight hours."

"Who are these people?" She slouched against the desk, exhausted by the complexity of the web they were caught in, "You know," she began, a distant look in her eye, "I heard someone say once that; 'society is like a stew, if you stir it up once in a while, a layer of scum floats to the top'," she offered him a defeated smile and he smiled a warm, genuine smile back. It suited him, if only he'd have the courage to show it more. He hesitated, as if he had forgotten something. He logged off and got up, leaving Sasha perched on the desk. For a fleeting moment, in that rare smile, she saw something in him – a sadness. A regret.

"I'd better go," he said

"What, now?" she said, with an edge of antagonism, anything to get another reaction from him.

"It's almost four," he said, refusing to be drawn in, glancing at his watch, "Ishmael won't be in his office much longer and then it will be the morning before I can see him. I need to go now."

He got up, grabbed his rucksack and quickly stuffed his clothes and things into it then reached for the laptop. Sasha watched, knowing he was right but chewing over the consequences in her mind. Fear jabbed at her insides. What if something happened to him? She couldn't bear the thought of it.

Tom slung his rucksack over his shoulder.

"I have to go. Bye," and he walked out, barely making eye contact with her. The door clicked closed behind him.

She wavered, and regretted letting him leave so abruptly. She bundled towards the door, slipped the card key from the slot and stepped out into the corridor after him.

"Tom!" she called down the corridor. He was at the far end, about to step into the lift. He turned, surprised to hear his name.

"Tom, wait," she yelled and jogged towards him. The door closed, the noise echoing behind her.

She stopped short, caught her breath and fixed her gaze on his.

"Be careful," anxiety swam through her. Tom's shoulders loosened and his face softened. A smile threatened to betray him. Although he often infuriated her, she would miss him and was terrified of having to say goodbye. She had vowed to never let anyone she cared about leave on sour terms again. She fought the urge to throw herself at him but still longed for the connection to be real and physical. She stepped closer, opened her arms and drew them around his shoulders. At first he stiffened, unprepared for her affection towards him. He wrapped his arms around her and drew her in closer. An exhilarating suggestion of intimacy. He brushed his hand down her hair and pressed his face into her neck. She pulled him in a little tighter, longing to feel his skin, it was warm and comforting against her cheek. She breathed in his delicious smell. They held each other for a moment, longer than friends. She had to force herself to pull back and break the connection and he didn't seem ready to let her go either. He loosened his hold but before she could step back he cupped a hand around her cheek. Her whole body shuddered with anticipation, her blood flowing hot like molten metal. She enjoyed the feel of his rough, warm fingers on her face. Her smile swelled her cheek to fit the curve of his palm.

"Sasha, I..." he stopped himself, paused and filled in the blank, "I'll see you in Amsterdam."

His hand dropped and it was as if he'd taken a plug away, she immediately deflated.

"The White Queen and the Black Knight," Sasha winked, trying to sound positive. It made Tom chuckle, a delightful sound she would give anything to hear again.

"Look after Gina. Keep each other safe," he said, his voice laced with authority, as if he were giving a command to a soldier. She was no soldier, but she accepted the advice in the spirit it was intended.

"I will," she nodded, and the connection broke away. Tom called the lift and Sasha turned back to towards the room. Both looked back over their shoulders, their gazes locked once more, they shared a smile and walked away.

*

In the lift, Tom leaned on the mirror and thumped the back of his head against it. Either punishing himself for allowing his vulnerability to show or knocking some sense back in, he wasn't sure.

"Stupid," he cursed, "get a grip."

He wrung his fingers through his hair, turned and looked in

the mirror. He looked weary, his eyebrows starting to permanently knit together, like two train carriages colliding. He took a breath and asked himself if he should go back. Her smell still lingered. He didn't need her advice; he was always careful, wasn't he?

But deep in his guts was the festering knowledge that where he was about to go, who he was about to see, could be a one way trip. It ate at him, hurt his head and ached in his bones.

Should he have been honest with her? As Gina had urged him? Would he regret not seizing the opportunity?

He sighed, lifted his hand, hesitated then pressed the button for the ground floor. The lift announced he was 'going down' and he snorted at the irony of it.

He was committed.

SOFIA, BULGARIA

July

"I am intrigued," said the thin, pale man. He barely filled his grey suit, as he examined Tom closely with bulging eyes that looked too big for his head.

"Intrigued?" said Tom, affecting a light hearted tone, "What about?"

The waif of a man wagged a bony finger, gesturing him to follow down the utilitarian corridor. They passed a line of frosted mesh windows that suggested a watery view over a car park and the man led Tom through a thickly painted door into a small office.

"Intrigued about how you found me?"

"You can thank our mutual acquaintance, Dr Osman Elmas for that."

"Elmas?" the man's eyes seemed to bulge more as the name registered, "I see," he muttered and waved Tom into a worn office chair, it's yellow foam seeping out like a squashed custard tart. The man retreated behind the desk. The room smelt faintly damp but the overwhelming smell was of recent paint. Its high ceiling was criss-crossed with pipework, yet another dreary former soviet office block, crumbling since the 70's. Everywhere Tom went in this city was the same depressing sense of a place no one cared about. A city whose former glory was still yet to recover from soviet occupation. No amount of paint could cover the scars of the communist regime, and the people who made their lives here in the crossroads between east and west looked weary from it. Sofia seemed soulless compared to the holiday atmosphere in Varna with its beaches and parks.

"I am simply here to do business. Dr Elmas assured me that you were the man who made things happen."

"You flatter me Mr Sheridan. I have been doing business with Osman Elmas for many years. We have many mutual friends."

"As I understand," said Tom, nodding respectfully, "I am sure an agreement can be reached between you and I. I am a man of means."

"I know who you are Mr Sheridan," the man's eyes narrowed and he leaned closer to Tom, his long back arched like a vulture picking at a carcass.

"You doubt my sincerity?" said Tom. He sat tall in the chair and glared at him.

"I pride myself in doing a little research before any business deal. It is always important to know your opponent, wouldn't you agree?" he responded.

"Indeed," said Tom.

The skinny man reached for a glass of water that was set on top of a desk pad. There was nothing else on the desk except for an old mug stuffed with chewed biros. He was a man who liked to keep his house in order, he left no mark and no clues about his business.

"Thomas John Sheridan," began the man, taking a pen from the pot and twiddling it between his fingers, "son of Elizabeth and John Sheridan, both deceased. Educated at the University of Reading. Mentored in History and the classics by Professor Frank Fitch, a close friend of the family, in your home town of Oxford. Joined the British Army in the 1980's where you were stationed in Germany, serving under Colonel Falkner. Briefly seconded to the UN force in Croatia, during the Yugoslav wars, where you helped protect the cultural heritage of Dubrovnik, before returning to Germany. You reached the rank of Captain and were the Team Leader for an elite unit tasked with finding artefacts, stolen by the Nazi's, hidden behind the Iron Curtain - things claimed by Stalin as reparations. You were discharged in 1995, for reasons that have been classified. You were then recruited by a specialist agency. For years you have used your knowledge of antiquities and your special forces training to retrieve artefacts for your country or your employers. And now you would have me believe that you want to do business?"

"You have done your homework, I see?" the question was rhetorical. But being such a private person, Tom was shocked at how much the man knew about him and tried to disguise it, "What you forget to mention is The Agency is a business, they exist to make money. With more than 15 years of experience, I now only work on the most lucrative contracts on behalf of my employers. Right now, I have something to trade and I want to take it to the highest bidder."

"Then this is just about money?" his voice was laced with cynicism.

"And the hunt," said Tom, with a grin.

"And what makes you think I am interested in bidding?"

"I don't, but I think your employer is. Besides, I'm alive, speaking to you. If you, or your employer, weren't interested I'd be dead."

"And Osman Elmas led you to me?"

"In a manner of speaking."

"And why do you think I can help you? Or indeed, who you believe to be, my employer?" he squinted at Tom, stooping further across the table as if he were short sighted and couldn't quite focus on him.

"David Ishmael, born in Beirut to a Libyan mother and an Israeli father - a volatile combination. Educated in England at Oxford, then at UCLA where you graduated in International Business Studies. A business Advisor to Colonel Gadaffi until 1998. Some say you know who really bombed flight 103 over Lockerbie in 1988. But essentially, you are an entrepreneur and The Libyan has recognised your talents and ability to negotiate winning business deals."

"You have done your homework too I see."

"I have a high level of clearance at The Agency. I can find out many things, for the right price."

Ishmael sat back in the seat, he still seemed skeptical but confident enough in Tom's motives to want to know more. He crossed his long legs and focused his steely eyes on him before asking, "And this artefact you are selling - what is it?"

"The bronze box."

Ishmael's eyes expanded to wide moons, flooded with light, "I'll make the call."

AMSTERDAM, THE NETHERLANDS

July

"What was he like?"

"I'm sorry?" Sasha peered over the rim of her steaming coffee cup, confused.

"My father," continued Gina, "What was he like?"

Sasha felt her cheeks warming.

How could she possibly answer without appearing guilty?

She took a deep drink of syrupy coffee to buy her mind time to form the words.

"Well, he was passionate about his work. I didn't know him well. We worked together for a few weeks but I had studied his work for some time, so knew him mostly by reputation."

Gina's eyes gave nothing away as she listened and waited for more.

"You said he'd mentioned me?"

"He mentioned his children, yes, as any Father away from his family would. I'm sure he missed you."

"He was absent on international quests for most of my life. All I ever knew of him was from letters he would write and gifts he would send. His letters were always about his work and what exciting things he'd discovered. Never anything more."

Gina sounded melancholic as she recounted the memories.

"Then, I'd say, you knew him pretty well. His work was his life," said Sasha in a chirpy tone.

"Is that supposed to reassure me?" Gina's tone darkened, a palpable mood-shift, "And I know you are lying. I see it," she hissed.

"Lying? Why would I lie? Gina, you're mistaken," she directed her traitorous eyes into the contents of her cup.

"Then what about the letter? I know there is something you are keeping from …"

"Wait," Sasha lifted her hand and cut Gina off, "Don't look, but we're being watched."

Gina sipped at her coffee.

"Two O'clock, creased sweatshirt and stonewashed jeans. Finish your coffee and we'll leave quietly," said Sasha.

They both drained their cups. Gina scowled and propelled herself away from her and towards the door. Sasha took five euros from her purse and slid it into the wallet containing the bill. She was not going to wait for her change.

"Ready?"

Gina nodded and stepped into the street. Sasha's wooden chair ground noisily on the tiled floor, disturbing the hush of the half empty brown café.

"*Tot ziens en bedankt* (goodbye and thanks)," called the waiter across the room as he polished glasses, drawing attention to the women as they left. A bell chinked on the door as they left and filtered into the crowds on Damrak.

"This way," Sasha scurried down the street, trying to disappear into the crowds of students and tourists and Gina followed, glancing back. They merged into a huddle of students but the group began to disperse. Sasha glanced back over her shoulder and saw the man was still following them. They weaved across the wide pavement, dodging cyclists and shoppers. The man kept coming. A tram roared past, the tracks rattling, the wheels screeched along the steel. As it passed, they looked back. The man had closed in and was just a few metres away. He reached for something inside his jacket pocket.

"Come on," she grabbed Gina's arm and pulled her under a tram shelter. The rails began to whistle and vibrate, this time in both directions, a sure sign a tram was coming down each track. The man was closer still, a small group of tourists gathered around a tram timetable was all that stood between them. The man was pulling his hand out of his jacket, something bulging against the fabric. Sasha kept checking the distance of the two encroaching trams, and then saw their chance. She silently communicated the plan to Gina. The clattering of the trams was louder and the wheels scraped and screeched towards them.

"Now!" she shouted above the din and pulled her across the tracks. The first tram slammed on its breaks to avoid them, and as they crossed the first track, the next tram was fast approaching. It rang its bell furiously, narrowly missing them as they jumped back onto the safety of the pavement. They ran along the cobbles and rounded a corner down an alley. Not stopping to look back, Sasha led them through another alleyway, then right and left and left again. She pulled in under the canopy of a hotel and they stopped to catch their breath. Glancing up and down the street they relaxed again.

"I think we lost him," said Gina.

"Let's hope so," panted Sasha.

"How long have we got?"

Sasha took out her phone, "about an hour."

"How far are we from where we're meeting Tom?"

"It's only a ten minute walk to the Casino square from here. The chess set is behind it."

"Chess set?" Gina's face was folded in confusion.

"Black Knight to White Queen, three," Sasha looked at Gina with a smile, "He's the black Knight, I'm the white Queen. He's talking about the giant chess set behind the casino. We're meeting at three."

AELEXANDRIA, EGYPT

July

"The Libyan will see you now."

Tom blinked as the sunlight assaulted his eyes. The air-conditioned car had shortened his memory of the oppressive heat and he wiped his brow with the back of his hand.

"I am sorry about the blindfold," said the burly man, dressed in an expensive black suit, who had picked Tom up from Alexandria airport an hour ago, "The Libyan insists on it." he offered Tom a rueful smile.

"I understand," Tom smiled politely at the man and tidied his hair where it had been ruffled. His escort had been sat with him in the back of the car and had chatted to him throughout the journey. He had told Tom stories about his beloved home city and Tom shared his knowledge about its namesake. Of the three hired goons who had bought him here, all wearing the uniform of lavish suits hiding expensive firearms and bloodied hands, only this man had spoken to him. He glanced at the sullen faces of his companions as they climbed out of the car and waved him towards the lobby.

Tom had been bundled into a black Mercedes, grey with desert dust, and buffeted along endless roads to get here. He was alone, unarmed and about to call the bluff of an international criminal and terrorist. He swallowed hard, feeling his Adams apple twitch while keeping his face emotionless and the fear from his eyes.

"This way Mr Sheridan," the friendly guard smiled and accompanied Tom into the cool interior of the Villa.

Tom glanced at the ornate colonnades and stepped through the intricately carved double wooden door. Inside, a pool of light cast by a stained-glass window sprayed a mess of colours onto a polished marble floor.

The hallway was larger than any apartment he had ever lived in. A wide expanse of dim space lined with studious looking statues in Grecian or Egyptian attire, like an ancient tomb. It reminded him of an exhibit at the British Museum. He was led down the hall and registered at least 10 doorways leading to other rooms in the single story villa - it was more of a miniature palace than a summer house.

"Here we are," the man smiled at Tom, knocked once on an oversized door that could accommodate a giant, and opened it wide for Tom.

"Thank you….urr?"

"Asim," replied the man and held a hand out to Tom.

"Asim? Doesn't that mean protector?"

"It does, beamed the man."

"Hmm, appropriate," Tom smiled, shook Asim's hand and stepped inside. The other two guards who had accompanied them in the car, were a few paces back and hovered in the corridor behind him.

"Close the door," a voice Tom recognised, ordered from a tall leather chair, facing away from him, "Come in Mr Sheridan."

He walked across the shimmering floor. Light cascaded into the room through archways lining the wall in front of his host. Organza curtains billowed in the breeze and potted palms lapped up the whitewashed walls. The room was huge, more of an auditorium than an office. The only furniture was arranged like an oasis in a desert of marble. The occupied chair was behind a thickly carved ebony desk, a couple of easy chairs in front of it, a globe Tom assumed to be a liquor cabinet and a line of bookcases filled with historic volumes on a far wall.

From beyond the archway, three security men stepped into the room, glaring at him with itchy trigger fingers, they fanned out quickly.

"Don't mind them Mr Sheridan. Come here so I can see you."

He moved towards the chair and a leathery face appeared around the wing of it.

"Hamed?" Tom knew it, but struggled to hide the incredulity in his voice.

"Welcome my friend," grinned the man, then waved him over.

Tom offered him a polite smile and moved around to the front of the desk to look the man in the eyes.

They reached a hand to each other across the desk. Tom took the big leathery hand, bejeweled with a ring on almost every finger, and shook respectfully.

"So, Hamed. You're The Libyan?"

"I have been known as such."

"But aren't you half Afghan? What about your Afghan heritage?"

"I am Afghan on my mothers' side. It makes me more Libyan than Afghan, but I have lived in both countries."

"And now you are in Egypt."

"Allah's law is universal. The teachings of Islam transcend national boundaries. This is my vision for a new world we can be proud to hand down to our children and grandchildren. All people living by the natural order of things."

"A lofty goal?"

"But a worthy one," he bowed his head, as if praying to a higher power.

He lifted himself out of the high backed chair. He was wearing a loose white kaftan and leather sandals, he looked more like a pilgrim than a businessman. He was a slight man, his face brown and gristly, peppered with liver spots. Wisps of grey hair scraped back across his scalp, poorly hiding his bald patch.

"David Ishmael said you had something important to discuss with me?"

"I'm calling in a favour," said Tom, folding his arms lightly across his chest and watching The Libyan moved slowly out of the chair and towards him.

"Our debts to each other are settled, Tom," he said, drawing up to look him in the eye.

"Are they? I overlooked certain things in exchange for the

lives of my men, it cost me my career, yet you live here like a King?" he gestured to the grand room around them with its marble shod floors and warm sunlight spilling in between the columns leading to a swimming pool.

"Because I am a successful business man you think I owe you?" The Libyan's face pinched with irritation.

"No, you owe me because if it weren't for me you'd be rotting in Guantanamo Bay and I'd be a General in the British Army by now."

The Libyan chuckled meanly, and offered a sly grin to Tom, "I suppose you are right," he conceded. A broad smile split his hard face and he offered Tom his hand again. He hesitated, then took it. The Libyan's grip was rigid this time, and lingering, he accompanied it with a slap on Tom's shoulder.

"Come, my old friend. Let us take a walk around the garden and talk, I'll arrange some tea," he flicked a gaze at one of the guards hovering ahead of them, who nodded and stepped out. Tom had counted six security guards and Asim so far, the odds were stacking against him.

They moved from the cool interior of the villa and out onto the scorched terrace, had it not been for the fine mist of water floating from the fountains, the heat would have been suffocating. The fierce sun seared the earth. The *tick tick* of a sprinkler over the incongruously lush lawns and the twittering of birds from the neighbouring olive grove were the only sounds. The air was heavy with pollen and dust. The Libyan stepped down the terrace towards the kitchen garden. Bees droned around the lavender and the scent of roses mingled through the air.

"I hear you have been working for a private agency for some time?" began the Libyan, affecting a casual tone. He held his hands together behind his back as he descended the short flight of stairs.

"That's right" said Tom, walking alongside him stiffly, his hands clasped behind his back. His military discipline had become too ingrained to forget, the only person he ever felt he could be anything but wooden and emotionless around was

Sasha. His thoughts drifted to her for a moment, missing her, hoping she was all right. He forced himself back into the moment, reminding himself to always be guarded around Hamed Moktari, aka, The Libyan.

"Still a man of few words I see, Tom," The Libyan turned to offer him a crooked smile, and led the way between the lawns and flowerbeds, "please," he gestured for Tom to follow him to a gazebo at the bottom of the expansive formal gardens. Beyond a low fence was a paddock, and surrounding the property were olive and orange groves, stretching over low rolling folds and towards an outcrop of rocky hills. There was no one and nothing for miles around and Tom had no idea where they were in relation to the city, it could be an hour in any direction.

"You have a beautiful place here," he said. Pleasantries made him feel less exposed.

The Libyan offered Tom an impatient smile and gestured him into the shade of the gazebo. Inside the pavilion was a mosaic-topped café table, set with four matching chairs. The two men sat opposite each other across the table. Tom glanced back down the path and two burly men in black suits were approaching them. Eight of them now. He glanced about, checking his exit points.

Hamed never went anywhere without at least a couple of bruisers in suits. For the first time, Tom questioned his motives. He cursed himself for stepping freely into the lion's den and felt exposed. Having been stripped of any weapons, all he had was his own guile and brute strength, should things get ugly.

"I know you don't have it, Tom."

"You know I don't have what?" he responded, innocently.

"The box. You tricked Ishmael into granting you an audience with me. What I want to know is why?"

"Honestly?" replied Tom, "So I could see who we were up against."

The Libyan chuckled, "Really?"

Tom's face remained unwavering, "But what about you,

Hamed. Why do you want the box so badly?"

"I think you know."

"Sorry to sound cliché, but with great power comes great responsibility. Do you think possessing the box will realise your lofty goals?"

"That is the plan," The Libyan grinned.

"The Agency will get to the box before you, we know where it is."

"Is that so? And what if I tell you I know too and it is only a matter of time before my men get to the box. They will stop at nothing. There will be collateral damage."

"Is that a threat?" Tom narrowed his eyes and stood.

"Well that depends on many things," a cruel smile licked across Hamed's face. Tom tensed, glanced around at the two security men who were now within a long stride of the gazebo. They were closing in and he would make sure he was ready for them.

"What do you mean?"

"We both want the same thing, Tom."

"What makes you think you know what I want?"

"Because we are not so different you and I. I'll tell you what you want, because it's also what I want."

"Enlighten me," he folded his arms and glared at The Libyan.

"You want to win."

He was right, he always wanted to win. He always liked to have the last word, and he always wanted to outwit his opponent.

"We can't both win."

"Ah!" Hamed pointed a finger at the sky, as if he were having a revelation, "I beg to differ. There can be a win-win here."

"How is that?"

"Bring the box directly to me, we cut out that sweaty Turk, Elmas, who frankly I do not trust anyway – I hear he likes boys, which sickens me to the core and offends Allah," Hamed seemed to silently rebuke himself for going off topic before continuing his proposition, "Come directly to me with it and I shall pay you more than The Agency and guarantee the safety of your lovely partner."

"My partner?" he affected an innocent look.

"Come now. Dr Blake is a beautiful, intelligent woman and I know you don't like boys, Tom," he chuckled to himself and then broke into a fit of coughing. One of the security men moved closer to Hamed with urgency, but was batted away with an irritated wave. Hamed recovered and fixed a cunning look on Tom.

"My men are thorough but can also be quite clumsy. I cannot guarantee the safety of Dr Blake or Thornton's daughter while they remain in Amsterdam."

Tom gulped and masked his horror, feeling his face reddening. He had thought The Libyan was calling his bluff, but he knew where Sasha was and had been watching them for some time.

Damn Milton for not dealing with it. Sometimes Milton seemed more interested in bureaucracy and pleasing his clients than watching out for his agents in the field.

The Libyan grinned menacingly, knowing he had backed Tom into a corner.

Tom pushed the chair away and it screeched against the tiles. The Libyan flinched and it pleased him to see the old man's discomfort.

"I need time to think about your proposal, Hamed," he said and stepped out of the gazebo onto the path.

"Sheridan," demanded Hamed. He glanced back over his shoulder but sensed it before he saw it. The two guards were closing in, both reaching inside their jacket pockets. "I'm afraid time is not a luxury you or I have. I will need your answer before you leave here," The Libyan flicked a gaze at the men - an implied order.

Tom's military instincts kicked in. One of the men drew a pistol from his shoulder holster and aimed it at him.

Tom ducked and then threw an adrenalin powered punch into the man's gut. He groaned and crumpled over. The second man came at him with a gun.

"Shoot him!" ordered The Libyan, then picked himself up from the chair and scurried off up the path, like a rat escaping the flood.

The second shooter aimed but Tom kicked his arm, clearing the shot harmlessly out into the paddock. A horse whinnied in the distance.

The first attacker came back at Tom, who caught his movement in his peripheral vision and kicked back like a bucking horse, knocking the man sideways. The second man span on a heel and held his gun with both hands. He tried to take a steady stance to get a shot off but he kicked his shin, then sent an uppercut into his jaw. His head jolted to one side and a spray of blood exploded from his split lip.

The first attacker held his weapon up again but Tom kicked it clean from his hand. The gun clattered onto the flagstones. The attackers eyes were wild, he gripped at his throbbing fingers, realising he could no longer hide behind a gun, he formed his other hand into a fist. He struck Tom hard on the side of his head. Dazed, he whirled around and got a lucky kick into the gut of the second attacker who was still startled and stumbling about, having dropped his gun in the melee. The first attacker then punched Tom hard in the kidneys. A hot pain streaked up his spine and down his legs, they threatened to fold beneath him. With all his strength Tom stayed on both feet. The assailant looked pleased with himself and rubbed his torn knuckles, getting ready for another go. The other man scrabbled about on the floor and took hold of the gun once more. Tom registered the movement quickly and grabbed for the man's hand. He squeezed his hand around the gun with all his strength. The man wailed in agony. There was a satisfying crack and he lost his grip on the gun. Tom went to reach for the gun but the other attacker threw a punch into his side. Tom almost toppled over, but span upwards and hit the man hard in the throat. Struggling to breathe, the first attacker staggered backwards, clutching his neck. The remaining attacker was on his hands and knees on the ground at Tom's feet. Blood oozing around his teeth, he fumbled about to find a gun. Tom picked up one of the guns and aimed it between the man's eyes. The guard was prone at his feet, it would have been an easy kill, but he hesitated.

"Please!" through bloody spit and tears the man begged for his life, "Please. I have a f..family," he stuttered. Tom lowered the gun but then noticed the man glance towards the house.

Four more suited security men came running down the path towards them.

"Shit!" he cursed. The man at his feet was now clutching for Toms ankles sobbing like a child. He kicked him aside then turned on a heel to face the new threat.

A shot rang wide and ricocheted off the gazebo. Tom crouched out of the way, "fuck, that was close," he swore then ducked behind one of the gazebo's pillars and aimed in the direction of the men heading towards him. They were shouting and firing wide.

Tom let off a shot. He caught a lucky hit. A gush of blood flew from one of the men's shoulders' and he was knocked back on his feet, but the remaining three were fast approaching and would soon be in range to get a clean shot at him.

Tom looked around, remembering the exit points. He ducked and ran towards the back fence. Behind him, the shouts and gun shots were getting closer. He vaulted over the low fence into the paddock then ducked and ran its perimeter. Shots pinged and ricocheted around him, spitting up dust and sparks. He kept his head down and ran.

He took shelter behind an old olive tree with a reassuringly thick trunk. "What's my plan?" he said to himself, his subconscious given voice in a moment of crisis. He caught his breath and allowed the train of verbal thought to continue, "I don't know which way to run. If I just run I'll find myself out in the desert and the sun will kill me. The car!"

He assessed the distance of the three attackers and saw two of them bundling over the fence. Behind them, in the grounds, a further four men had joined the hunt.

He had to move. Laying out some cover fire he ran from

tree to tree, gradually making his way around to the front of the house.

In front of the house was a blur of activity. As he rounded the corner he saw The Libyan being bundled into a black Range Rover. His white gown flashed and disappeared into the car. Its back wheels span in the gravel and with a screech it sped down the track towards the road. Tom crouched at the corner of the house and aimed. The shot missed the car and spat into the dust and gravel. The black Mercedes was still there, its engine running, the doors open as two more brutes in suits barked unintelligibly to each other in Egyptian. The men were distracted, this was his chance. He ran out from behind the house, his gun held at arm's length ahead of him. He fired one shot and it struck with deadly accuracy between one of the men's eyes. The other man looked around in shock.

He hesitated.

"Sorry, Asim," he said, and shot the man who had been kind to him in the foot. Asim screamed and fell to his knees, blood pooling around him.

Tom ran across the driveway, the voices of his pursuers getting dangerously close. Now men were spilling out of the lobby and towards the car. He leapt into the driver's seat and gunned the accelerator. The tail end of the car danced then gripped, sending clouds of dust back towards the house. As he pulled away, he leaned over and pulled the passenger door shut. A gun shot ricocheted off the door with a spark "fuck," he cursed, shaking his hand as if he'd burnt it. He sat back upright and leaned to the driver's door, tugging it shut. As he sat up and settled in the seat he shifted up the gears and didn't look back. Until, with a terrifying bang the back window disintegrated into a million safety-glass shards. He looked over his shoulder and through the gaping hole where the back window had been. Three men gave up their pursuit and stopped to catch their breath on the track behind him.

He slumped against the headrest, closed his eyes briefly to compose himself then tugged across the seatbelt and clipped it in. He smiled to himself, took a few deep breaths and refocused.

He pumped the accelerator and careered onto a main road. One word rang clear as a peel of Sunday bells in his mind, his only goal now, he said it out loud; "Sasha."

A SECRET LOCATION SOMEWHERE IN LONDON

July

"Milton Harkett," he announced as he lifted the receiver, his voice tripping up in pitch.

"Selam, Milton," the deep authoritative voice responded. Milton recognised it. The caller then asked how he was in Turkish.

"Selam - You know my Turkish is Rusty! I'm well. How are you?"

The caller switched to heavily accented English, "Good, good, but I did not call to exchange niceties. I call for an update on our arrangement."

"Our arrangement still stands. My Agents find the box, The Agency gets paid for the job. There is little else to say," Milton stiffened and he hardened his tone. The reports from his Agents had made for grim reading, "Call off your dogs Osman, before someone else is killed."

"My dogs, as you call them, are necessary to expedite the process. My employer has a small window of opportunity - you must understand this. You have seen the western news, you will know there is a power vacuum since Gadaffi was murdered. Libya is in crisis and the box is a symbol from the dawn of civilisation. Born of the heart of Babylon. Your methods do not work."

"My methods?" Milton tried to hide his incredulity, "Osman, old friend," he said, with veiled cordiality, "You hired The Agency because your methods have not worked for the past, I-don't-know-how-many years! My Agents are making good progress, they are close, I know it, but having your men follow them isn't helping."

"My friend, I beg to differ. While my men follow your

Agents they are kept motivated. Motivation gets results."

"How is having Agent Blake's key contact executed helpful or motivating?"

"I know nothing about this," Osman sounded genuine in his defence and it planted a seed of doubt in Harkett's mind. He had been chewing over what possible motivation Osman would have for having Tsvetan killed, but now he doubted his complicity.

"Then who did kill him?"

"I have no idea," this time his defence sounded more desperate.

"You have some nerve, ordering my team to be attacked in the street - You do have control over your pack of baying dogs I assume?"

"That must have been a street robbery. Whoever who had the Bulgarian killed is working against me, not for me. And he shall pay for that mistake."

"So you do know?"

"I swear to you. This is not our doing. And my employer is also not responsible."

"So someone else is seeking the box?" said Milton, his eyebrows creasing together.

Milton shuddered. Perhaps Tom had been wrong about the leak? There was another player at work, someone who was yet to show their hand.

He had known Osman Elmas for some years. He had proved a powerful ally but he was also a dangerous one. Milton remembered the old adage; 'keep your friends close, but your enemy's closer' - he liked to add to it – 'preferably in your pocket.' The balance shifted while he was in Elmas' pocket.

"Osman, when you have the box, you will be rich beyond your wildest dreams. Save yourself some money and hassle now and let my guys do their job. Do this, and my fees remain the same. Past...indiscretions...will be behind us. My fees will prove to be peanuts when you have your prize. But, and I say this as a friend, sincerely, if I, or my Agents suffer any collateral damage, my costs will go up. I hope you understand."

"Perfectly," said Elmas.

"Let's speak of it no more," he affected a light hearted tone, wishing to end the conversation on a positive note, he could ill afford to upset a man like Osman Elmas, he could only guess at what someone like him was capable of, "Our interests in this venture are mutually beneficial, let's keep it that way."

"Agreed."

"So how is Zenab? Is she keeping well?" asked Milton, seemingly innocently.

"She is well," Osman's response was stilted.

"And you daughter, Aisha. I understand she is applying to Oxford?"

"You understand correctly," grunted Osman, failing to hide his suspicion.

"I have many sources," Milton said, his tone chirpy, "I have some influential contacts at Oxford."

"Indeed. And I understand Agent Blake has lectured there and Agent Sheridan's family have strong links there," replied Elmas.

"There are plenty of opportunities for foreign students there, if of course, they pass the rigorous selection criteria. Perhaps I could be of assistance?"

"That's kind of you, but my Aisha is a resourceful and capable young woman."

"I'm sure she is. But it will always help her if she has friends in the right places."

"She can make friends."

"I'm sure she can. Life at Oxford will be difficult if she doesn't."

"Quite," said Elmas, refusing to be drawn in by the veiled threat.

"Wish her luck from me. Let's hope she doesn't need it."

"Thank you. You must excuse me, I have a meeting to attend. *Ciao.*"

"*Ciao*," replied Milton and hung up the phone.

As soon as the receiver clicked into place Harkett voiced

his irritation. 'Goodbye and good riddance. You fat fuck.'

AMSTERDAM, THE NETHERLANDS

"Blake!"

Sasha turned at the sound of her name, knowing who had called to her immediately. His velvety voice carried across the square and she span on a heel to locate it.

"Tom," she said under her breath, never more relieved to see him.

Sasha waved across the square, then turned to look for Gina. She was preoccupied looking at the menu of a street café. Knowing Gina was all right, Sasha hurried across the square to meet him.

Tom quickened his pace and jogged around the chess board to meet her.

They stopped short of contact. Standing a respectful distance apart.

"Are you all right?" he asked, his eyes filled with unease.

She wanted to hold him in her arms and never let him go. She resisted - back to work.

"We were followed down Damrak but we lost him. What about you? You look knackered."

"It's been a long day," he offered her a small smile, "Where's Gina?"

"Over there," she pointed, "We've not eaten yet. You?"

"Just some cardboard bread and rubbery cheese on the plane. I could use a decent meal."

Tom led Sasha back to where Gina was stood, his hand brushing the small of her back lightly - enough for her heart to quicken and muscles to tense. The delicious feeling of arousal coursing through her. If only she had the courage to act on it.

"Hey, Tom!" chirped Gina as they approached her, "You look awful."

"You should see the other guy," he said.

Sasha hummed, knowing there was some truth behind his

comment.

He flicked her a grin.

"After you Agent Blake," he gestured.

"Thank you Agent Sheridan," she smiled politely and followed Gina to a table at the front of the terrace overlooking the giant chessboard.

"Oh come on!" said Gina. "What's all this *Blake* and *Sheridan* nonsense? It's insufferable watching you too avoid each other," she huffed dramatically then go up. "When you order, I'll have a beer. I'm off to find the bathroom. For God's sake just talk to each other will you. I see it. I see it in both of you. Just bloody well say it!"

Gina stamped off and disappeared into the café.

Tom and Sasha froze in silent shock. They looked at each other in bewilderment then burst into spluttering laughter. She enjoyed the rare sound of his laugh.

"What was that about?" said Tom, bemused.

Sasha shrugged, "search me!"

The waiter attended them, in perfect English with a mixed Dutch/American accent, asked for their drinks orders and handed them three English menus.

"Drie bier... please," said Tom. After confirming the size the waiter left them.

"Drie?" sniggered Sasha.

"I almost slipped into German," confessed Tom, "I'm pretty sure we're more welcome here as English speakers than as German speakers!"

Sasha folded her hands under her chin and rested her elbows on the table, fixing her attention on him. She offered him a soft smile and could hardly keep her eyes off him. She had thought of him every moment since they'd been apart.

"So are you going to tell me where you've been, Tom?"

He smiled at the sound of his name, as if it sounded good when she said it. He seemed nervous. He fidgeted in the hard metal patio chair, ran his fingers through his hair and glanced around him, as if trying to decide how much, and indeed what, to tell her. Either that or he was checking his exits to make a quick getaway from having anything other than professional contact with her.

"Perhaps we'll wait for Gina and I can tell both of you."

Sasha huffed but knew it made sense.

"So, what else do we have?"

"The notebooks, what do you make of them?" he asked.

"While you were away I went through them and compared them. A lot of it seemed to be coded."

"Odessus is the key?" he said.

"I thought that but it still didn't quite make sense. I think it's worth taking them back to The Agency and having their code breakers work through them."

"Good idea," nodded Tom, "do you have any ideas from his notes? You knew the man, how did he think?"

She laughed a little, "No one knew how David thought, he was almost as bad as you when it came to revealing anything personal."

She offered him a crooked grin, then pulled a serious face, "I'm not convinced there are any clues in them about the box, but I do think they contain clues about other missing artefacts."

"Interesting," hummed Tom, with a distant looking frown.

"What about the rings?"

"Rings?"

"The picture of Kamel and Thornton, wearing matching rings?"

"Oh yes. An Analyst at The Agency looked at the picture. It was inconclusive but according to his reports both rings were forged at the same time using old techniques. It was hard to see from the image but they seemed to be ancient. They depicted slightly different images, but were created by the same goldsmith. The Analyst speculated the images represented two of the old elements – fire and water."

"Okay," said Sasha, with a contemplative look.

"I know, interesting, but not sure how it's relevant?" said Tom, as if he'd plucked the thought from her head.

They sat silently for a moment, she was happy to be in his

company again and hoped he felt the same. The way his chocolate eyes penetrated hers filled her with a warm sense of calm - she could disappear into those eyes. There was a reassurance in the proximity, even if it was not as close as either of them dare permit. A gust of wind whipped through the square and flapped the tablecloth, bringing a raft of fallen leaves to the feet of their table, surrounding them in a pool of copper.

The waiter returned and three beers appeared on their table, Gina joined them a second later.

"Oh yes!" she declared as she sat down.

Gina wrapped her hand around the wet cold glass, seeming to enjoy the feel of it as she drew it up to her lips.

"Cheers," said Tom, grabbing his glass and taking a deep drink.

"Cheers," echoed Sasha, holding her glass up to her companions.

"So what were you talking about?" asked Gina, blinking hopefully over the lip of her glass.

"Nothing really, we were waiting for you," replied Tom.

Gina looked dejected.

"Tom was about to tell us where he'd been. Weren't you?" Sasha smiled expectantly at Tom.

"Yes," Gina congratulated herself on the fact Sasha had used Tom's first name. Tom glared at them both. He took a deep breath and another gulp of ice-cold wheat beer, he seemed to be resigning himself to being up front with them.

"Shall we order food first?" he suggested. Sasha grumbled to herself, impatient to find out what Tom had done, then reluctantly agreed. They waved the waiter over and all ordered from the menu.

Once the waiter had gone Tom told them how he'd followed the lead from Gregory about David Ishmael. How he had met Ishmael in Sofia and set up a meeting with The Libyan. He left out the part about having known 'The Libyan' in a former life.

"Alexandria?" said Sasha, once Tom had told his tale. "He

calls himself 'The Libyan' yet he is in hiding in Egypt?"

"He has a lot to hide. I imagine supporters of Gadaffi aren't popular in Libya right now. I think he's lying low, until he can get his hands on the box and make his move."

"And what do you think his next move will be?" asked Sasha, sipping her beer as she looked at him.

"His ultimate goal, he told me, was 'the teachings of Islam go beyond borders and there is a natural order of things'."

"Some kind of radical Islamic super-state?" said Sasha.

Tom nodded solemnly.

"No doubt he has a lot of passive support for his ideas among the Muslim Brotherhood."

"Muslin Brotherhood?" Gina lowered her brows.

"The democratically elected rulers of Egypt. Ironic they are so anti-western."

"This Libyan - What is he, some kind of comic book bad guy who tells the hero his plan before letting him escape!" commented Gina, a big smile on her face.

"If only!" smiled Tom back, "Arr, and I didn't realise I was your hero?"

It was the first time Gina or Sasha had ever known Tom be anything other than serious. Gina looked so startled she froze, her pint glass raised, her mouth agape, lost for words. Sasha and Tom sniggered like pranksters.

"Every girl needs a hero," Sasha fired a cheeky wink at Tom, who tried to disguise a blush.

She let his words sink in and gazed out into the square, watching the chess match that had started when they arrived and seemed to a have progressed no further. A crooked old man with small eyes and bushy brows was frowning and rubbing his chin as he assessed his possible moves. His opponent, a tall old gent in a smart linen suit with Germanic features and square wire rimmed glasses, glared back at him, looking equally serious. The crooked man reached down with a groan and shuffled a giant white rook a place, prompting a tut and a sigh from the other man.

"I could watch this all day," commented Gina, who joined

the audience, "So what's our next move?"

Sasha and Tom exchanged quizzical looks.

Tom responded, "We're here on your hunch Gina. What do you think?"

MOZARTKADE, AMSTERDAM

The steps up to the house might as well have been a mountain, they were just as insurmountable. The very idea she had to ask a favour of her obnoxious uncle made life on the run from international terrorists seem preferable.

She had seen pictures of this house so many times, Mike always boasted about it at family occasions, she felt like she already knew the place, despite it being her first visit.

It was a tall mock 17th century merchant's house – built in the 1980's - a twee reproduction of the old city.

She took a deep breath and ascended the short but steep flight of stone steps, terracotta pots of red flowers lined up on the low redbrick walls either side of her.

She glanced behind her, still paranoid she was being watched or followed, although her senses had given her no warning signs. The grand house faced a glassy canal, a dark speck broke the silver sheen on the surface as a lone Canadian goose, like a sentinel, drifted past effortlessly and seemed to crane its neck round to watch her.

The damp evening chill carried the scent of the canals and noise of distant traffic as she psyched herself up to ring the doorbell. She held her breath then pressed the button.

An impatient chime echoed through the house and she heard heavy footsteps walking down the hall inside. The door clicked and swung open.

"Georgina! My, my, what a wonderful surprise!" said Mike with a flourish of his arms. He was wearing a designer sweatshirt, rolled to the elbow, exposing his flabby and hairy forearms, and beige chinos' – he looked like a fat businessman who fancied himself as the next Tiger Woods.

"Come in, come in," he beckoned.

Gina stepped into an expansive hall, shod with black and white checkerboard flooring. It reminded her about the set-up she had conceived for her pompous uncle, and made her smile.

"Hello Uncle Mike," she said, trying to sound happy to see him.

He leaned his bulk into her, gave her a crushing hug and planted a wet kiss on her cheek. She held him lightly back, enough to be polite. He smelt faintly of alcohol and expensive cologne, as ever.

"I was so excited when you called from the airport. Ursula and I are delighted to see you. Do, do, come through. Welcome, welcome. Come on in."

He pressed the front door closed and she glanced back.

So jumpy now.

A mess of sunlight was speckled across the tiles from the cut glass door panels, like a monochrome kaleidoscope. The smell of fresh flowers wafted thought the space. In an alcove under a grand processional staircase was an oversized vase bursting with lily's and paradise flowers. She smiled and followed him down the long hall.

"So you are in town for a few days I understand?"

"That's right."

"And where's Rick?"

"Rees."

"Yes, yes," he grumbled.

"He's had to work I'm afraid. Actually Uncle Mike, I'm here on business."

"Business you say?" he looked over his shoulder to her with inquisitive eyes.

She nodded and they walked through an ornamental plaster archway and into a large drawing room at the back of the house.

The room had a high ceiling, with tall long windows lining one wall, draped with swags of rich copper coloured fabric. White wood paneling with framed sections of yellow silk painted wallpaper depicting birds and willow trees. The floor was a vast expanse of gleaming oak parquet, dotted with islands of Persian rugs, each with their own collection of furniture. One island had two massive red leather chesterfield settee's facing each other, another had four big claw footed chairs surrounding a sleigh style coffee table, another had a shiny white grand piano in the centre with two antique damask armchairs arranged as an audience. There was room to spare between the islands. In a nook, beside a huge fireplace was a grand bookcase with glass doors sealing off an enormous collection of books with a ladder on a runner. The other side of the fireplace was a big antique armoire; she suspected it was his liquor cabinet.

Michael waved her towards the settees and they sat opposite each other. In the middle of the wide coffee table between them was a half full cut glass decanter and set of matching glasses. In the decanter was a sweet smelling liquor and a crumpled, half read newspaper. She glanced at it.

"You have today's telegraph?"

She was surprised to see it, when she had looked on newsstands for English newspapers they were always a day out of date.

"Ah yes, the editor is a friend, he always arranges for me to have a copy, it doesn't usually arrive until late afternoon, but I mustn't grumble," he said, casually, although it still sounded like a grumble.

"Is Ursula home?"

"I must give you her apologies. She has popped out to the deli to get some bits for dinner – we insist you at least stay for dinner my dear. It's so nice to have guests, and family too. It's so rare we have family come to visit, even Bobby doesn't come out to see me and his step mother much," he said, enthused but masking a sense of sorrow.

I wonder why? Thought Gina, smiling to herself.

"Funny how my Bobby looks so much like David and Danny, don't you think?" he mused, not addressing her in particular, his eyes seemed to drift into some unidentifiable space in the distance.

"You don't need to go to such trouble for me. Really. It's fine," interrupted Gina, impatient, and keen to get him back to the point, she didn't want to be here any longer than was necessary. But she knew it was futile, once Michael had made a decision, it was always final. Partly why he was so unpopular in the family but everyone was too scared to acknowledge it.

"Stuff and nonsense," he puffed his chest up, like a cock about to get into a fight, "I'll hear nothing of it. We'd love to have you. In fact, you are welcome to stay."

"That's really kind of you Uncle Mike, but I'm booked into a hotel."

He mumbled something approximating I understand, and reached for the decanter. He poured two glasses, without checking and passed one to Gina, she took it but resented he hadn't offered her a coffee instead, he had a way of assuming everyone drank as much as he did. She sniffed the contents of the glass and sipped it. A fine Port she found surprisingly pleasant.

"You said you are here on business. What sort of business?"

"You know I work for an alternative investment company?"

"Of course," he said, sounding offended, as if he would never forget such an important piece of information - yet it was okay to always forget the name of her husband of three years?

"Well, I am in town to meet two clients. They are a lovely couple, very much in love, who have run very successful enterprises and are looking to spread their investments. They have already invested in artwork and fine wine and are interested in investing in diamonds."

Gina let the suggestion hang for a moment and watched Michael's reaction. He was nodding, rubbing his close shaven chin contemplatively.

"I am sure I can arrange for them to meet with myself and my partners. What's their schedule?"

"I'm sorry to be so restrictive, but Mr Knight has already set up a meeting with Costa Diamonds tomorrow morning, before their flight. I managed to persuade them to meet with you before they make any decisions, I'd rather give you the business, Uncle Mike," she offered him a persuasive smile over the rim on her glass.

"Hmmm," Michael thought out loud then fixed his eyes on her, "For my brothers little girl I'm sure I can arrange something for this evening."

"Oh, thank you Uncle Mike, I really appreciate it. You've always done so much for the family, I wanted you to have the business."

Flattering Uncle Mike always worked. He'd never done anything for the family, but she knew money always talked to him.

PRINSENGRACHT, AMSTERDAM

"At least this room is a twin! No more arguing over who gets the bed?" Tom flashed a smile, but Sasha seemed unmoved.

"What?" he said, frustrated she was being so cold.

"Nothing," she mumbled and disappeared into the bathroom.

The last time he had been alone with her, they had held each other. The memory of it was irresistible. The way she felt stretched against his body, the warmth and silky softness of her hair at his cheek, her fresh scent. It was powerful and real. The desire to feel her against him again was stronger now than ever. They had been apart for no more than a couple of days and he had thought of little else. His thoughts so filled with her he let his guard down and left himself exposed. Alexandria had been the only fire fight he'd been in where his first thought wasn't for his own self perseveration. He was driven by the fear of never being with her again, of never looking into her emerald eyes, of never having told her the truth, of never knowing for sure she felt it too.

He hovered around in the room waiting for her, feeling worthless, it felt like purgatory.

He heard the toilet flush and shortly after she stepped out and moved past him as if he were a ghost.

"Talk to me Sasha," he said, his hands clenched on his hips.

She stopped, span on a heel and fixed him with a serious look.

"Why are you stood there like a lost puppy?"

She seemed to be mocking him and his pride got the better of him.

"I'm not! You're being evasive and I want to know why?"

"I..." her eyes glowed with indignation, "How can you

look at me with a straight face and say that? You live your life being evasive! It's all secrets and lies with you!"

"Lies! I've never lied to you!"

"Oh you have! But that's not what I meant."

His resentment still festered, "Why do you do this?"

"Do what?"

"Find ways to punish me. It was eight years ago and you are still treating me like your enemy."

"Punishing you? Where is this coming from?"

"You know what, forget it," he turned away and considered leaving the room before he said something he'd regret.

He hesitated.

What the hell am I doing? He said to himself. Tight fingers gripped his elbow.

"Where are you going?"

She sounded angry. He was afraid if he turned around to face her she'd slap him again.

If she did, he deserved it. Better to take it like a man and be sorry after.

He turned to look at her, winced a little.

She gazed up at him, looking beautiful and vulnerable, her eyes filled with frustration and confusion.

"Why are we doing this?" he asked, relieved when she hadn't hit him.

"Doing what?" she snapped.

Tom was tired of arguing, he didn't want to leave, he just wanted to be with her.

"We're fighting over nothing instead of saying what we really want to say."

"And what do we 'really want to say', hmm Tom, What?" Sasha dug her knuckles into her hips.

He stifled a smile. He could see it infuriated her, his serene, disaffected, response to her temper. He wondered if she provoked him because she couldn't resist the drama; but he was writing the script for the next act. If it was drama she wanted, he had his own ideas.

Without a word, he stepped closer. Sasha's eyes widened

and before she could react he had already made his move to take the White Queen.

He slipped one arm around her waist and with the other reached for her cheek. He brushed his fingers around the curve of her jawline and took her head in his hand.

She stiffened, trembling from fear or anger, it didn't matter, he enjoyed the reaction. He claimed the power back. Her thick hair cascaded through his fingers like warm flowing water and he pulled her in hard.

He sought out her lips with his. He had wanted this since the day she walked back into his life, had longed to feel her close. His lips danced against hers for a moment, before she responded. She tasted divine. Sweet, warm and soft.

It paid off when she reciprocated. The surge of adrenalin was erotic and enlivening, locked together in pure desire. Her eyes drifted closed and she hummed. Tom's arousal grew as Sasha relaxed into his arms and folded hers around him. His shirt rippled under her precise fingers as she gripped and spread them across his back. Her hands were definite but soft, he longed to feel his skin against hers. She dragged the shirt out of his waistband and slid her slender fingers up his spine while he trembled with desire.

Her hands felt exquisite as she stroked the soft downy hairs in the small of his back and the contours of his muscles. The tips of her fingers slipping below his belt, dancing along the top of his buttocks.

Every part of him ached to feel himself inside her, he held her tighter. The thrill hummed through him. He massaged his fingers into her scalp and slid his other hand along her curves, resting it on her round bottom, he gipped lightly and she responded with a moan of desire. He sunk his fingers into the soft, resistant warmth; like dough in his hand, moving in slow circles, massaging progressively lower and moving his hand between her thighs, under the hem of her skirt.

His desire was so intense now, it overtook his other senses. The room around them melted away and the two of them became everything. He had been wound so tightly for so long, he wanted nothing more than to release it. Every molecule in his body tuned into focus and awakened.

He slid a hand over her belly, hesitating as it moved across the firm mound of her breast. Her shallow breathing quickened, her head tilting to the side as he move his lips away from hers and tasted the skin on her cheek, along her jaw and across the bitter sweet taste of the perfume on her neck.

His heart drummed against hers. His hands moved down her hips. He lifted her skirt, pulled her hips against his, feeling her weight press against his penis, enjoying the feel of her there. Enjoying her curious hands travelling down his tight muscles and over his belt.

Sasha's breath warm on his neck, her sighs enthralling and absorbing, a silent chorus cheering him on. Tom traced kisses around her neck, across her shoulders as she tipped her head back to allow him access to the contour of her neck and reveal an enticing glimpse of cleavage. He moved the kisses back along her jawline, seeking out her delicious lips once more.

But the moment was stolen.

Sasha's mobile blared through the silence. She hesitated.

"Leave it," mumbled Tom, his lips still occupied with hers.

She relaxed back into the embrace and eventually the irritating whine of the phone stopped.

He stroked his hand along her thigh and drew up her skirt, revealing a small pair of lacy knickers. He pressed his fingers deep into her soft buttocks and held her firmly against him, his free hand dancing up her body where it stopped at the top button of her blouse. He undid the button with nimble fingers and progressed down to the next, and the next, until her breasts pressed through the folds of cotton. He slid his hand under the lace of her bra, brushing the side of his finger along her hard nipple. He was drifting into a heady state of arousal as she grappled with his belt, their lips never separating.

Again, the blare of a mobile phone interrupted them.

This time it was Tom's.

With his tongue dancing around hers, he grumbled, "for fucks sake."

His eyes drifted towards his jacket pocket, but she pulled him back with her nose and mouth, keeping him locked in the kiss.

The cantankerous phone stopped and they relaxed again, tugging at each other's clothes with urgency. Sasha had fumbled open Tom's belt and was busy undoing his trousers, while Tom slid his hand around the lace of her knickers and began to slide his fingers inside, his other hand now holding her jaw and keeping her locked into the kiss.

One final disruption broke the spell. This time it was the hotel phone blaring.

"Dammit!" cursed Tom.

They released each other, and exchanged glances, waiting for the other to make the decision to break this long awaited foreplay.

"We should answer it. Someone is clearly desperate to get hold of us. It could be an emergency?" she sounded unconvinced, but they both knew she could be right.

He heaved a heavy breath, offered her a defeated smile and went for the phone beside the bed. Sasha was reluctant to release him and stroked her hand across his back. He hitched up his trousers and did the fly up, picked up the receiver and perched on the edge of the bed, devastated and defeated.

"Hello."

"Finally! I was beginning to worry about your guys, neither of you answered your mobiles."

He glanced up at Sasha, who was watching intently for clues about the call. She slid onto the bed next to him.

'Gina,' he mouthed.

She slid her arm around his back and rested her head against his shoulder. He longed to drop the phone and press her into the bed where he could tear her clothes away and finish what they'd started.

"Is everything all right?" continued Gina when Tom didn't respond immediately.

"Yeah, fine. We were both…busy," he tilted his head to rest it against Sasha's, enjoying the sensation of her soft hair on his cheek and the weight of her resting upon him.

"I've just been to see Uncle Mike," continued Gina, "He can meet us this evening. He has made arrangements to stay late so he can offer a *private tour for my clients*," Gina sounded triumphant.

He rolled his eyes, "Great," no conviction in his tone.

'Tonight', he mouthed to Sasha.

'*I know,*' she mouthed back, straining to listen in to the conversation.

"You will need to look the part," said Gina, "I've told him the cover story. That you are a wealthy couple who own several businesses and are looking for an alternative to the bank to invest some of your money. I've told him you can only see him tonight and you are meeting with his competitors tomorrow. I told him I trust you and you're a lovely madly in love couple," he imagined the playful smile on Gina's face. After all Gina's intentions to match make them, he stifled a smile at the irony - If only Gina had realised what she had interrupted.

"Oh, is that so?" he replied, trying to lace his voice with disapproval.

"Yep!" Gina was sounding more and more jubilant, she had clearly enjoyed spinning a yarn for her uncle. He wondered what other narrative she had concocted around the fictitious relationship.

"I told Uncle Mike I've been working with you both for some time. You are Mr and Mrs Knight."

"Mr & Mrs Knight?" he tried to sound incredulous - Gina had gone to town creating these fictional characters.

"I got the idea from the chess board. It seemed somehow appropriate. You are both my Knights in shining armour after all!" She sounded like a mischievous school girl.

Sasha laughed quietly to herself. He offered her a crooked smile and affected a serious tone for Gina. He imagined Gina must have thought she was playing some joke on the two of them, and he was happy to play along.

"I see," he said. If Gina was the school girl, he was happy

to take the role of headmaster, "What else do we need to know about Mr and Mrs Knight, hmm?"

"You have a portfolio of properties and I have advised you on several other alternative investment opportunities, such as wine and artwork. Uncle Mike is primed to do his utmost to impress you, he wants the business."

"And we're madly in love?"

"That's right! Rich and wildly in love," Gina failed to stifle a snigger. As did Sasha, while Tom played the role of disproving authoritarian.

"I see," he grumbled, "Then I imagine he would be expecting to meet a couple who are wrapped up in each other's affections?"

"He will," this time Gina didn't even try to disguise the mischievous joy in her tone.

"Though I must admire your creativity, Gina, you have made this quite awkward for us, you realise this don't you?"

"I'm sorry, Agent Sheridan," said Gina, who plainly wasn't sorry, "You will just have to swallow your pride and play along I'm afraid. It's the only way."

"Very well. And what time is this farce taking place?"

"7pm. But we need to get you guys kitted out first."

"What do you mean?" he was puzzled, wondering what other trick Gina had up her sleeve.

"You're a wealthy couple. People who have so much money they can afford to spread their investments on expensive things like diamonds. We only have a couple of hours and you guys need to dress the part. Come on, we need to go shopping!"

Tom groaned. What was it with women and shopping?

Sasha laughed out loud; he wasn't the kind of man who enjoyed shopping. He gave her a stern look before ending the conversation.

"Fine," he huffed, "I suppose that means we need to leave now while the shops are still open?"

"Yep," said Gina, gleefully. "I'm just going to freshen up quickly and I'll be there in a minute."

Tom dragged his feet along the herringbone red brick of Wolvenstraat, following Gina and Sasha as they strolled along, gazing wide eyed at the brightly lit plate glass shop windows.

"Can we stop for a beer yet?" he asked, losing patience already, like a child being dragged around a supermarket who'd had just been told to put the sweets back on the shelf.

"Not until we've bought our outfits. Then we'll stop," said Sasha in her most maternal tone. Tom grimaced.

"Then let's get a frigging move on and buy something. We're not tourists, we're here on business."

Gina's response was to offer him a serene smile, she seemed to be enjoying his discomfort.

"What's our plan when we get to your Uncles office? I trust you have a plan, beyond humiliating us!"

Gina fired a sarcastic look, "We'll discuss it over a beer once we've got everything we need."

He rolled his eyes at her.

"What about here?" Gina stopped in her tracks, he almost walked into her in his haste to escape the claustrophobia of shopping.

"Well," he sniffed, "They only seem to have about four outfits on display so it must be expensive."

Sasha smiled and waved him into the shop with them.

A skinny shop assistant eyed them down her nose. Tom in his jeans and creased T shirt, the girls in light summer dresses and neatly made up, having made an effort to look the part. In a heavily accented voice, the assistant pretended to care, "*Guten abend. Deutsch, English, Svenska…*" she said through her false smile.

"English," grumbled Tom.

The shop assistant saw his resistance and joined the conspiracy, smiling at Gina and Sasha, genuinely, for the first time.

Why was it then when a gaggle of women got together they

took such pleasure in ganging up on the token man?

He felt more of a pawn than a Knight.

"Forgive my husband, he does so hate shopping," Sasha affected her most well-to-do English.

"He refuses to wear anything but jeans much of the time, but we are meeting an important business associate later and both need new outfits for the occasion. I wonder if you could help?"

"Of course, madam," the assistant offered a curt nod to him, "Sir."

He nodded politely to disguise his utter contempt.

"Follow me," she led the three of them through the narrow shop towards the back. The white walls and high ceiling were sparse and bright. Everything sparkled. An ostentatious purple velvet chaise long dominated the bare room. Behind it was an antique chest, piled with glistening accessories. Along the walls was a sprinkling of clothing - silk shirts and dresses, well cut suits and crisp jackets, all hung on padded coat hangers or arranged onto dead eyed mannequins. The smell of fresh flowers and the shop assistant's expensive perfume suffused the air. Soft, barely audible, cool jazz, rippled around the room from secret speakers.

At the back of the shop was a white chiffon curtain. The woman swept it back and revealed two white leather couches facing each other over an ornate coffee table. On the table was a tall purple vase of white and yellow calla lilies and a couple of glossy books, like fabric swatch files but with pictures of beautiful people looking brooding on the covers.

"Do take a seat sir. I'm sure we can find something suitable between us. Can I offer you a coffee?"

Tom blinked at the shop assistant, dumbstruck by her helpfulness, "Ur, yeah. I'll take a black coffee please."

"Of course," nodded the skinny woman, "Greta?" she shouted, in a lyrical voice, and from an almost invisible door at the back of the shop, another skinny and heavily made up young assistant came trotting out. The two women exchanged a few words in Dutch and the young girl scurried out again.

Tom shrugged, looked around for an alternative and sat on one of the sofas. Sasha offered him a smile then proceeded to flit about the shop with Gina and the first shop assistant.

He picked up one of the fashion books and thumbed through it, almost choking at the prices, then fumbled about in his pocket to check his wallet. Imagining moths fluttering out of it, he slid it back into his jeans and furtively watched Sasha sweeping around the shop. The way her toned curves pressed against the cut of the dress, its light fabric floating around her shapely calves like petals around their stamen. Her blonde curls bounced around her shoulders. She glanced back at him, not expecting to lock eyes with him.

A small smile crept across her face, an earnestness in her eyes. He felt his chest swell with warmth and wished he could scoop her up and finish what they had started.

He distracted himself with the inane fashion books once more, trying to take his mind off of sex and back to work.

SOFIA, BULGARIA

July

"*Shef...* (boss), the body is through here."

The uniformed officer spoke to the Detective in Bulgarian.

"Thank you Officer. Has anyone else been down this alleyway beside yourself and the man who reported it?"

"No sir."

"Good. Where is the witness now?" asked Detective Vladislav Violinov.

"At the station, sir. Waiting to be questioned," replied the local policeman.

"Good, keep him there, I will need to speak to them myself later."

"It's just a man out walking his dog sir," said the policemen, shrugging, "I doubt he can help."

"Still, he is an important witness. What's his story?" said Vladislav, he didn't get to be a Detective by casually dismissing potential witnesses.

"He said he had picked up his dogs' shit in a bag and went to throw it into the dumpster when he saw a hand sticking out. He lifted the lid of the dumpster and found the body. Then called us."

"All right," he jotted some notes in his pad, flapped it closed and looked up at the young, keen eyed, policeman, "Show me."

The officer guided Detective Violinov down the alley between two concrete tower blocks. Vladislav zipped his leather jacket over his black polo neck shirt against the cold wind ripping between the tower blocks. Stepping over uneven paving and between litter and bags of rubbish torn open by wild dogs, the first thing he noticed was the smell. He took a handkerchief from the pocket of his black, arrow straight, trousers and held it to his nose. When he lifted the lid of the dumpster he was assaulted by the powerful stench of decay.

A light pool from a street lamp in the twilight bought the full horror of what had happened into sharp focus.

"It looks like he's been here for a couple of days. Mind you, in the summer heat, bodies decay quickly, it could be under 48 hours," said Vladislav, talking himself through the crime scene.

He took his baton from his belt and flicked it to its full extension, still holding a handkerchief over his face with one hand he prodded at the squidgy body.

He gave a running commentary as he examined it, his voice muffled by the handkerchief, "The pockets have been turned out. It looks as if he's been strangled with something; there are thin bruises around his neck from a garrote. He's a big fellow so whoever did it must have been strong to have lifted him into here. More likely it was a couple of men. He looks familiar…"

"Sir!" another uniformed officer jogged down the alley towards him and he turned to look over his shoulder at the man, "I found this," he said, as he approached, he was waving something.

Vladislav took his baton out of the dumpster and leaned it against the outside before stepping closer to the man.

"What is it?"

"A wallet, *shef*."

"Let me see."

Before he took the wallet he tucked the handkerchief into his pocket and screwed up his nose. He removed a pair of rubber gloves from his pocket and snapped them on.

He examined the expensive looking leather wallet closely and opened it. Inside was a Turkish driving licence with a photograph of the wallets owner. Below the Turkish the name was translated into English.

"I can read English, sir," said the young officer keen to be helpful and impress the well-respected Detective, "No cash or credit cards, sir. A street robbery?"

"I can read English," he said, "And I'm not so sure it was

just a robbery, not this man."
　The name on the ID was Dr Osman Elmas.

CASTELL DIAMONDS, AMSTERDAM, NETHERLANDS

July

"Mr and Mrs Knight. My niece here has told me all about you, it is such a pleasure to meet you," Michael held out his stout hand and they shook it in turn.

"Thank you, Mr Thornton, for agreeing to meet us at short notice. I appreciate we have put you at rather an inconvenience. I fear Mrs Morgan does get a little carried away from time to time. But I am sure she only has the best interests of her clients at heart," said Tom, in his best Oxford English, offering Gina a fierce smile. She fired a look at him but he could see in her eyes she knew he was enjoying taunting her.

"Not at all, and please, do call me Michael, we are all friends here," he pasted on a salesman's smile, then held out a hand to usher them onwards, "Please."

They followed him through a series of security doors, which he accessed with a swipe card, and pretended to be interested while he gave them a commentary on the history of the company.

"Castell Diamonds has been in this building since 1890 but the city has had a thriving diamond trade since the 17th century. Diamond polishing has traditionally been one of the tradesmen's guilds open to Jews and it was Jews who settled in the city, allowed to practice their religion during the reformation of the church across Europe, who established a prosperous diamond market place here. It was during the 19th century when the Dutch colonised South Africa and diamonds were discovered there the trade flourished and that's when Castell Diamonds was founded. This way."

Mike led them down a short but steep flight of narrow steps leading into the dark underbelly of the old building. They followed him down a narrow corridor of chiseled walls, illuminated by a long string of buzzing lights.

At the end of the corridor was a massive reinforced door, leading to the vault. A wheel, like something from a navy ship was fixed to the middle of the reinforced steel door.

"This is where our clients store their investments," he said, with a glint in his eye, swiped his card in a keypad next to the door then took the wheel in both hands and heaved it clockwise.

There was a hiss, as cool air seeped around the door. Michael pushed it open, the door helped along by a runner, like a curved tram rail, set into the polished concrete floor.

"We are fortunate to be built on one of this city's few natural rock beds. This vault is carved out of the granite so it is impenetrable except through this door," he said as he beckoned them into the vault, "If there was ever a nuclear threat on the city, this is where I'd come! Of course, we do have an emergency release button if anyone should find themselves trapped in this room," he nodded at a big red button inside a glass box on the wall.

The room was large, but with no natural light and only one way in or out, still felt claustrophobic. It was walled with concrete but set into the wall on three sides were safes, like a bigger version of the one in their hotel room, with a number pad on each. In the centre of the room was an incongruous polished wooden table, a folded piece of black velvet at one end. The table was surrounded by four padded wooden chairs of the same beautifully polished walnut.

"Please, do take a seat. And we can talk about the services we offer."

Michael held his hand up to wave them around the table and then pulled chairs out for Gina and Sasha.

"If you chose to invest in rough diamonds, this is where they would be kept," he began, shuffling in the chair to get comfortable and waving at the room around them.

"So how does the investment work?" asked Tom, buying some time to assess the room and decide how to execute their move, and keep up the pretense.

"We import the rough diamonds and they are graded. Investors buy the rough diamonds and store them here. When we receive an order from a client for a diamond to be cut and polished, we put a message out to any investors who own rough diamonds of the appropriate grade and you can then decide whether or not to sell."

"So, it is prudent to invest in rough diamonds in a variety of grades so that you increase your chances of selling?" asked Tom.

"Correct," said Michael, rubbing his hands together.

"Or we could just buy a diamond cut and set to order for our own use?" asked Sasha, joining the ruse.

"Indeed. But of course, once it's cut and made to order there is less opportunity to add value to the piece, but if you would like a beautiful gift for your lovely wife, you could of course just purchase that," he fired a wink at Tom, who kept up the charade by smiling adoringly at Sasha. Although he was playing a role, he meant the smile.

"Would you like to proceed?" said Gina.

Tom and Sasha exchanged a knowing glance. That was the signal. Next it was Gina's turn to put her acting skills to the test.

Gina stretched across the table to look her Uncle in the eye.

"Uncle Mike. I need to ask you something."

She put on her most forlorn sounding voice and painted a matching expression across her face.

"Of course, whatever is the matter dear?"

"It's about my father."

"Gina my dear, can this not wait until later, we are here to do business," he offered a rueful smile to Mr and Mrs Knight.

"Actually Mike," began Tom, "It is appropriate to ask now," he allowed his expression to cloud and glared viciously at Michael.

Michael shifted in his seat, he swallowed hard, fiddled with his tie, his face a map of anxiety.

"What is this?"

"Please Uncle Mike. I need you to tell these people which of these safe's belonged to my father." Gina's voice was pleading, she even managed to manufacture some tears. Tom couldn't help but be impressed by how convincing her fear seemed to be, it was palpable.

"That's preposterous; you know I can't do that!" Michael's face reddened and he puffed up his chest.

Tom slowly lifted himself from his chair and loomed over Michael, who sat back and stared at him in sheer horror and disbelief. Tom placed his phone on the table in front of them with a flourish.

"Uncle Mike. Please. They have Rees. If you don't do as they say they'll kill him, then go after Danny," Gina leaned over the table and grasped for her uncles hand. He held her for a moment, stunned.

"I just have to make the call," said Tom, glaring at him.

"Urm…I…" beads of sweat bubbled up on Michael's forehead.

"Please!" Gina let out a sob.

Tom picked up the phone, "I'm not a patient man," he said and scrolled through the menus of his phone for show.

"My God!" Michael's breath seemed to catch in his throat, as if he didn't dare even breathe.

"Number 17," he said, letting go of Gina's hand and waving frantically to the back wall of the room.

"Thank you," Gina heaved out a thick breath as she said it, slumping in her chair.

"We can't have you causing any trouble for us," said Tom, walking around to the back of Michael's chair, he unbuckled his belt. Michael looked over his shoulder at Tom.

"What the devil…"

"Please Mike, can I still call you Mike? Put your hands behind your back."

Mike hesitated.

"Miikke!" said Tom, menacingly drawing out his name.

Michael did as he was asked and clasped his fingers together for security.

Tom pulled the belt from the last of its loops and wound it as tightly as he could around Michaels wrists. Michael winced and whimpered in pain. Tom was satisfied he would have difficulty breaking loose.

"Thank you," he said and walked back around to look his captive in the eyes. He pulled his silk handkerchief from the breast pocket of his expensive pinstriped suit, crisp with a straight from the shop smell.

"Open," he said to Michael, dangling the handkerchief in front of his face, "Time to shut you up I think."

With a wicked flash of a smile he then stuffed the handkerchief deep into Michael's mouth, who mumbled and groaned in protest. He playfully slapped Michael's flabby jowls and joined Sasha, who was now stood in front of number 17, appraising it carefully as if she were working out how to extract an artefact from centuries of compacted dirt.

"What do you think?" he said softly as he stepped in behind her. He hesitated for a second, he couldn't resist it any longer, he placed a hand on her shoulder, and squeezed gently. Sasha peered over her shoulder at him, and blinked her big green eyes at him. He could swim in those eyes forever, like a paradise lagoon.

"I keep thinking about the clues in the letter."

"You have everything in your bag right?"

She nodded, "I have it all. The notebooks, the letter, even the old phone."

"Well what numbers might be significant to David?"

Sasha shrugged.

Tom turned back to look at Gina. She was sat opposite her uncle. He seemed to be trying to persuade her to untie him, with a series of nods and flicks of his head and eyes, shaking his hands against the chair.

Gina seemed to be doing a good job of whispering platitudes to him.

"You girl!" said Tom, enjoying the mock violence in his tone.

Gina looked up and narrowed her eyes at him.

"Come here girl, we need you. And you," he waved an accusing finger at Michael, "Mike. Just relax, it'll all be over soon."

Horror pooled in Michaels eyes, as if Tom had implied a death threat.

Gina joined Tom and Sasha, with her back turned to her uncle she mouthed to Tom, 'girl?' he flicked her a crooked smile.

"Can you think of any numbers that might be important to your father?"

Her eyes glazed over as she thought for a moment, "Dates of birth? Wedding anniversaries?"

"No, too obvious," said Tom, "it would need to be more obscure than that."

"Well perhaps if I look at the evidence, I might see something?"

"She's right, Tom," said Sasha, her tone filled with hope. She reached for her handbag and carried it over to the table where she tipped the contents. Lipstick, pens and coins skittered across the wood then with a thud, the notebooks and the phone plopped out, as if the bag had laid an egg.

Michael just watched in incredulity, hardly seeming to believe what was happening.

Gina spread the items out and watched them, as if they were about to start dancing.

"The letter?" she said.

Sasha reached into the side pocket of her handbag and took the letter out. She seemed afraid, worried Gina would ask to see the letter. Tom saw it in her eyes and his instinct was to protect her from any harm.

"Can you read out the clues again for us?" he asked.

Sasha unfolded the letter, her eyes looking more relieved now;

"One; 'I was going to buy you a diamond, but now I can't, you will need to find one for yourself' – well I think we can tick that one off," Sasha offered a smile to the others but they were all staring so intensely at her it went unacknowledged.

"Two; 'The old name for Varna is the key' – Odessus. But how does that help us?" she looked defeated but sincere looks from Tom and Gina urged her to continue.

"Three; 'Nokia will let you in'?"

Gina became animated.

"That's it!" she declared, "I have an idea!" she seemed to be excited.

"What are you talking about?" Tom said, his brows stitching together.

"The phone. The numbers," she said, as if it should be as clear to them as it was to her.

Gina grabbed the phone and flung herself towards number 17. The safe was set into the wall cavity at chest height. She reached out and stroked its smooth cold door.

"Odessus, how do you spell it?"

Sasha and Tom exchanged a puzzled look and they joined Gina at the safe.

"O D E S S U S," said Sasha. They watched as Gina mouthed the letters and looked at the phone.

"What?" asked Sasha, desperate to understand what Gina had discovered.

"The numbers on the keypad. Odessus – look!" she showed the keypad to Sasha, then recited the numbers, "The numbers corresponding to those letters on the keypad are; 6336686."

The three of them looked at each other, and shared a triumphant laugh.

Sasha stepped up to the keypad, took a breath, exchanged encouraging glances with the others and tapped in the sequence.

The door buzzed, a spring released and it popped open.

THE PAST

ABDERA, THRACE - 370 BC

'Word is a shadow of a deed.'

Democritus

Draco's throat felt dry and brittle, each breath a pale shadow of the last.

"Take them," insisted Democritus, pressing the small leather pouch into his hand.

"What is it?"

"These four rings, they are a promise. A promise to protect humanity," he said, fixing a steely look on the boy with his hollow grey eyes.

"No sir, I cannot. It is too much. What am I to do with them?"

"You know what you must do, boy, now is the time to act. Choose who are to be the guardians of the box. You must, there is no one else," Democritus hissed and clenched his frail firsts, the blue veins popping out as if to emphasise his insistence.

"But sir, I cannot," Draco's voice faltered, meek sobs following each breath.

"You must, boy. I have no sons, I have no heir. You are as a son to me my young apprentice. You know all I know, the fate of the world lies in that truth. Do what is right. Do what you must."

Democritus' face reddened, and he heaved a succession of laboured breaths, clinging to his last vestiges of strength. His old body had shrunk to little more than a skeleton draped with rags. The candle at the old man's bedside flickered, and threatened to extinguish, then as if it had found a new fuel source, the flame grew and brightened.

Democritus had withdrawn to his bed two days ago, his body so frail and rotting from the inside outwards he could no longer support his own weight. Draco had tended to him ever since. Sleeping by his master's bedside, feeding and cleaning him.

"Let my theory of Atoms be my legacy, not this abomination," continued the old man. He grasped with his skeletal fingers for the boy, who held them with his plump young fingers, "I have always said I would rather discover one scientific fact than become King of Persia – Atoms are that fact, they come into being and perish. You know this, I have taught you this. I am no different, my time has come boy. Atoms are unlimited in size and number, and they are borne along in the whole universe in a vortex, and thereby generate all composite things; fire, water, air, earth. For even these are conglomerations of given atoms. And the elements, they are part of us too. You know the teachings of the four humours are linked to the elements and make up all of us. The rings are for each of the humours, choose your guardians wisely to keep them balanced. This box, Pandora's Box, it is death incarnate. It burns away the other elements, leaving nothing but destruction. I can only think to call it the anti-atom. I have even speculated its power lies in splitting atoms and releasing only an unearthly fire, the essence of death. It is the gateway to the eternal fires of the underworld. It must never, ever be loose in the world, or we all meet our end. Do as I ask you, boy, it is my final wish."

Democritus' face turned from red to purple now, as he fought for breath.

"Please sir," sobbed the boy, pleading with his master, "Without you I am all alone. Don't leave me sir. I need you. I have so much more to learn from you."

"Don't cry for me boy. Think only of the laughter."

Democritus tried to reach for Draco with his free hand, barely the strength remained to lift his arm. The boy leaned in closer, resting his head on the old man's chest. Democritus pressed his thin fingers into the nineteen year old lads' thick dark curls.

The world seemed to be rushing away as he gripped the

boy's hair like it would anchor him to life. The strength to even open his eyes had failed him and they hooded the last blurred light from his senses. An echo of Draco's voice washed over him from some distant plain. His senses were failing him but he focused as hard as he could on the boy, the only one to be there with him so he would not have to die alone.

THE PRESENT

CASTELL DIAMONDS, AMSTERDAM, NETHERLANDS

Gina stared into the opening. This was the climax. It was as if everything in her life before had led to this point. Everything around her melted away as she gazed through a window into the rest of her life. The feeling hummed through her body, her limbs burning deliciously. She felt herself drifting, the world falling away. Images of her father rushed into her mind, memories both her own and imagined. Her heartbeat grew louder and louder, reaching a crescendo in her mind. Then it seemed to slow, each beat a definite punch but the space between expanded. As if time itself were slowing down, her heart seemed to only drum a couple of times a minute, the thud and pulse drawn out in the extreme; but there was no pain; only a sense of elation as if she had grown wings and could fly high to the heavens.

"Gina? Gina what's wrong?" the voice was willowy, as if it were calling her from another reality.

She felt drawn to the dark opening, as if it were a doorway to another universe. A black hole, leading to a singularity of absolute clarity and harmony, a point in space and time where everything begins and ends. Her hands reached out, almost involuntarily, bound by some witchcraft. She saw them ahead of her, white and fluid as if they were being stretched into a time warp. They melted into the black square pool of the opening and it seemed to suck the rest of her in.

Her hands landed on something solid, and cold, with rippling contours, smooth to the touch. She pulled the weight towards her, dragging it to the centre of her chest, as if her heart itself would only be complete and find its beat again with the box as part of it.

A box of solid bronze. Intricately depicting scenes of death and destruction, woven with scenes of joy and life. The sun and moon, monsters and flames, water and flowers, skulls and cherubs - all merging together to form a frieze of Creation and Armageddon in the same frame. Lines, spirals, and geometric shapes carved into the lid.

It was beautiful but frightening. Gina took it from where it had laid dormant and dragged its bulk into her. She sagged under its weight but then found a balance. She turned around slowly and in an instant, like a clap of thunder, the room returned, the colours faded, the dream dissolved and the spirits that had drawn her in vanished from her conscience. She carried the box to the table.

"Sorry, Uncle Mike," she said as their eyes met across the table.

Gina stroked the box reverently.

"Is there anything else in the safe?" asked Sasha, her eyes not sure where to focus, the box or the safe. She tore herself away and walked to the hole in the wall, like exploring a crypt. Gina was too absorbed with the box to respond.

Tom joined Sasha. They exchanged a wary look. Of the two of them, Tom was the one brave enough to put his hand in. Sasha winced, half expecting a booby trap to close on it and slice off his hand.

She felt a deep sense of relief as he pulled out an innocent looking envelope. A4, manila, bulging with papers and something small and hard. He dragged out the envelope and held it up to the light.

"It's for you," Tom smiled at her, and handed her the envelope, her name was scrawled across it. Her stomach summersaulted. It was David's handwriting, more messages from beyond the grave.

She glanced at Tom, puzzled, then opened it.

Sasha tipped it up and out slid a gold ring. Examining it quickly, she made the decision to sit down and look at the contents of the envelope more closely.

She put the ring on the table and Tom picked it up, inspecting it closely as if he were a goldsmith making sure it was genuine.

Sasha pulled out some photocopied pages of an ancient manuscript and a few handwritten notes. She flicked through the small bundle.

"How's your ancient Greek?" she pinched up an eyebrow and looked at Tom. He gave a small laugh and joined the others at the table.

"All right there Mike?" he said, clapping their hostage on the shoulder. The trussed up diamond dealer huffed and puffed and fidgeted in his chair, red in the face with frustration.

"Good!" smiled Tom. He hesitated for a moment then reached for Sasha's hand. She was scrutinising a sheet of scrawled notes and read them with growing fascination.

He rested his fingers lightly on hers and dipped his head to capture her eyes.

"What is it?"

Gina, who had been obsessively exploring every image carved onto the outside of the box, looked up, as if suddenly aware she wasn't alone.

"It's from your father," said Sasha, looking at Gina, who's eyes widened with interest.

"And?" urged Tom, all three of them now stared at Sasha expectantly, even Michael had calmed down and was fascinated by the proceedings unfolding in front of him.

"It seems there was truth in some of the gossip going around the Varna Archaeological Museum," she began, tracing the text with her fingers as she read and then paraphrased it for the benefit of her audience.

"The ring is a symbol. There are four of them. These manuscript pages are copies of lost texts by the Greek Philosopher, Democritus. He and Leucippus developed the Atomic Theory. He was the first to suggest all matter is made of up of particles, his ideas were so radical and revolutionary he was denounced by Plato. Later, of course, as science's knowledge of the world around us increased, his ideas were given new weight. He seems to have come into possession of the box and realised what it was. He believed it to be the fabled box of Pandora."

"But that's ridiculous! It's just a legend!" Tom scoffed.

"You know as well as I do history is distorted by the opinions of its writers, and it is often written hundreds of years, even millennia after the fact. Like Chinese whispers, the message is skewed as it passes down the chain of time. Are you willing to take the risk there is not at least a shred of truth to the story? Wonder weapons and all that?"

She glared at Tom.

His repentant look implied she continue with her tale.

"Democritus passed the rings to his apprentice, four of them in total, each representing one of the four medical humours and also their twinned elements. They are the rings of the Pandora Order – an ancient order of 'knights', for want of a better word, who swore they would protect the box. He and Kamel had two of the rings. This one is for me. Here," she pointed to some scribbles and sketches of each of the rings, "He explains what each of the rings mean."

Tom read the text over her shoulder.

Gina looked at the ring and at the pages then back at the box. Her hands cradling it like a precious child. She ran her fingers around its perimeter.

"So what's in this box that people will die for, or kill to protect?" Gina mused, not addressing anyone in particular, she seemed to be in some form of trance.

A clarity shot through Sasha. It was terror. Pandora's Box – all the evils of the world contained in it – confined in a room with it would be the last place on earth she would want to be if it was opened.

"No! Gina stop. Whatever you do, don't. Don't open the box!"

Gina glared at her, as if she didn't care. Sasha, pleaded with her, "Don't. Please. Whatever you do, don't open it."

Gina's eyes glazed over, as if a requiem to her long dead father were playing out the final chords in her head. They could all understand why she was so drawn to the box. Her father had died to protect it.

Gina smoothed the surface of the box with her fingers as it waited. As if she believed it had been waiting for her, as if her father's soul was imprisoned inside it, like it was calling to her to look inside and free him from all the secrets and lies.

Tom, always airing on the side of fatalism, reacted to Sasha's pleas. He tugged Gina's arm away with unexpected violence. The grip sent a shooting pain down his arm as if Gina was somehow transmitting it from the box and through herself into him. He cried out and let go.

Sasha continued to plead with her, as Gina's eyes seemed to grow wider, like she had been possessed by some unknown force making her its marionette.

"Gina. Please. Just believe me. If you open that box, you'll never be able to go back."

"Why should I listen to you? You and Tom. You've lied to me Sasha, I see it. Yet you ask me to trust you now?" she fired a petulant look at her and gripped the box, as if she were protecting it, she pulled it against her heart.

Even her Uncle Mike shook his head, joining in the chorus to stop her from doing it.

"We're on your side Gina, if we weren't you'd be dead by now!" insisted Sasha, anger fuelled her words and darkened her expression.

"I need to know. I need to know what my father died for."

"Is there nothing I can do to change your mind?" Sasha made one last attempt to persuade her.

Gina shook her head and stared in awe at the box, under its a spell.

"Then I'll go. I'll leave you to do this, because I can't stand here and watch while you betray everything your father believed in."

"How would you know what my father believed in. He was my father!"

"And he was my lover!" Sasha blurted it out, then regretted

it. Pressing her fingers against her lips to stop further betrayal falling from them.

Gina's face reddened and tears of hate and fury burned into her eyes.

"I'm sorry, Gina."

"Sorry...I..." Gina was lost for words.

"Enough!"

Tom put himself between the two of them, "Enough of this madness. Come on."

He pressed a heavy hand into Sasha's shoulder.

"What about the box?" she said, staring at it. She knew she had to walk away but something stopped her. This was an amazing discovery. It should be studied, understood, respected; but it was dangerous.

"It stays," said Tom, fixing both of them with an earnest look, "This is the safest place for it."

"What about the Agency?"

"No one should have this box. Least of all The Agency. Thornton died to keep it hidden and he left this ring to you as its keeper," he picked up the thick band of gold, intricately stamped with the mark of air and blood, "This is yours Sasha, you are the Artisan – courageous, hopeful and amorous. David wore Phlegm and Water, he was Rational - calm and unemotional. Kamel wore Black Bile and Earth, he was Guardian – despondent, sleepless and irritable. Three of the humours..."

"...And one still remains – Yellow Bile and Fire, the Idealist," said Sasha, completing his sentence, they'd both read it in the photocopied pages – a facsimile of a world long forgotten.

"This ring is a vow," said Tom, presenting it to her, his face painted with sincerity, "It is your vow now. This is your call."

"Gina. Will you come with us?"

Gina glared at the woman who had saved her life but had lied to her since that first meeting in the coffee shop. The cruelest of lies.

"I need a minute," she said, stroking the box like a cat on

her lap.

Sasha gathered up the papers, slid them into the envelope then folded it into her handbag. She made for the door.

Michael tried to shout and fidget himself free, his cries still distorted. He was the silent onlooker, his eyes terrified and confused.

Tom moved towards Michael and hope shone in his tear rimmed eyes; but Tom wasn't about to release him. That would be Gina's decision. Instead, he reached into the inside pocket of Michaels jacket and slid out the pass card.

He followed Sasha to the door. Sasha turned back to Gina.

"Goodbye Gina."

Gina did not respond, and the Agents slipped out of the room, leaving Gina alone with her uncle and the box.

Tom and Sasha exchanged a knowing look.

"That box can't be let out of that room," said Tom, his voice grim.

"Agreed," Sasha nodded, giving him implied permission to do what they were both thinking.

He stepped forwards and took the wheel of the door. His eyes made contact with Michael's. Dread filled the hapless man's scarlet edged eyes and he shook his head desperately.

"Sorry Mike. Your fate lies in your niece's hands now." Tom saluted Michael and tugged the wheel. The massive door groaned and slowly tracked back along its rail closing with a reverberating thud. Tom spun the wheel.

Gina slid her hands around the join between the box and its lid, caressing the crack with her fingers.

*

EPILOGUE

Two Days Later

Wrapped in heavy coats to protect against the biting winds gusting along the canals, they turned down the side street. They passed between the tall and pretty merchants houses, towards the black scar of destruction at the end of the street.

Red and white plastic tape whipped and fluttered across the street ahead, two police incident vans were parked precariously on the side of the narrow street, butted up against buildings and beyond them was a swarming dark mass of activity.

As they approached the scene, the dark mass became a crowd of police and men in suits making notes, talking in huddles and nattering on mobile phones. Closest to them was a tall blond officer. He glanced over his shoulder, aware there were people approaching the crime scene and turned a serious gaze to their direction.

"I'm still at a loss as to how you managed to persuade Milton to indulge you in this farce!"

Tom frowned at Sasha, who responded with a grin. She strode ahead, approaching the officer, a professionally courteous smile painted across her face.

Seeing her, the officer ducked under the plastic tape and challenged her.

"I am afraid this road is closed. This is a crime scene," he said, his Dutch accent somehow lyrical, yet off key.

Sasha held out a hand and smiled to pre-empt him.

"Excuse me Officer," she began. Out of some baffled sense of courtesy the officer accepted her hand and shook it firmly, "Are you in charge here?"

"I am Madam, but I am afraid I will have to ask you to leave the area. I cannot give you any information on this incident. We have had reporters asking all day and I have said the same to them too," he said, polite but abrupt. His eyes told her he had long ago lost patience with snoopers.

"Officer. You misunderstand me. I am Agent White and this is my partner Agent Black," she waved Tom into the conversation. He stepped forward and acknowledged with a polite nod.

"Agent White and Agent Black?" repeated the officer, a spark of amusement flashing in his eye, an air of doubt in his voice.

"I know," Sasha made a small laugh, "We are with Interpol. I sometimes think the Director only partnered us out of entertainment value!" she flung a smile between Tom and the Officer, "I have my ID," she said, reaching slowly into the inside pocket of her flatteringly fitted dress suit. She handed him the ID and Tom passed his over too.

She held her breath. No matter how many times she assumed another identity for The Agency, she always hated the lie. Sooner or later she was sure she'd be discovered. The officer studied the ID cards carefully and passed them back with a reassuring nod.

"If you will follow me Agents," he said, holding an arm up to indicate permission for them to approach the scene. He dropped away a section of tape and waved them through.

"*Danka*," said Tom, his eyes telling the officer they no longer needed him. The officer nodded back respectfully and left them alone.

"What the hell do you think happened here?" said Sasha, as they picked their way over the charred remains of the old town house that had been the headquarters of Castell Diamonds since the nineteenth century.

Tom replied with a shrug.

A cold slick of sweat covered her body, dread pulling at her breath. What if Gina had opened the box? What if she'd caused the fire and taken herself and Michael's lives with it? She felt sick for a moment. Should they have stayed? Could she have done more to stop this? The guilt ached in her bones.

She and Tom had been about to board their flight back to London, just forty eight hours after they'd left the diamond house, and then they'd seen the reports of the fire on the breakfast news.

"I overheard a couple of guys talking about arson. At least, I think that's what they were saying, they were speaking in Dutch, it was similar to German but I couldn't be sure. Whatever happened, it has to do with the box," he paused and turned to her, his eyes filled with darkness, "It's too much of a coincidence otherwise. And you know how I feel about those."

An eyebrow flicked up, then he strode on ahead of her, kicking up charred piles of destruction.

"Allo!"

Sasha turned to look over her shoulder towards the voice. The blond officer was calling out and waving to them.

"Hang on," she said to Tom, brushing his arm lightly then retracing her steps towards the police line. She smiled and waved at the officer.

"Your colleagues have just arrived!" he shouted, smiling, and pointing to three men in dark suits approaching from the other side of the wreckage.

"Thanks!" she smiled then turned back. Her heart lodged itself in her throat and rattled her ribs.

Oh shit. She cursed to herself and picked up her pace to get back to Tom.

He glanced back at her, his eyes heavy with concern. He'd seen them too. He headed towards her, his steps long and resolute.

"We need to go!" he said, grabbing her arms and pulling her away.

"Wait! Who the hell are those guys?"

"I don't know and I don't want to hang around to find out. Let's go!" he tugged at her.

Reluctantly, she yielded and followed him back across the site. They moved away from the officer and the three suits, who had now disappeared into what remained of the building.

Sasha looked back and hesitated. She grabbed Tom's arm.

"Stop, Tom. Look!"

He huffed and turned.

"What?"

"They're taking something away," she gestured to the three men in suits who were leaving the ruin, carrying some sort of plastic crate between them. They were too far away for them to see what the men had, but they both suspected.

"Fuck!" hissed Sasha.

"You don't know that it's the box," said Tom, his brows knitted together, "It could be anything. It looks like they're carrying a standard evidence box to me."

"Oh come off it, Tom. It has to be the box!"

"We can't be sure. We need to get out of here before our cover's blown."

"We should follow those guys. If they have the box we have to stop them."

"Don't be stupid, Sasha. Are you trying to get us both killed? We have no idea who they are. They claim to be Interpol, whether they are or not, we can't take them on alone. I can't believe I let you talk me into coming here at all. Now come on!"

He grabbed her arm and pulled her away.

"Let go of me!" she shook him off. He gave her a look. A look that said, in no uncertain terms, that this was not the time to argue.

She hesitated, balled her fists.

"Fuck!" she said, then made a show of following him. She was brimming with frustration, her head pounding, her mind racing, it burned.

"We can't just walk away, Tom. Not after everything that's happened."

"Yes we can!" he stopped, swung around and glared at her, "and that's exactly what we're doing, understood!"

He turned back, ducked under the perimeter tape, holding it up for her. She frowned at him, then followed him.

He led her around the corner and down a side street, their footsteps heavy, fast and determined on the cobbles. The alleyway opened up onto a square. Tom walked into the middle, by a dormant fountain and waited for her to catch up.

"So that's it? We just walk away?" she said, scowling at him, her hands on her hips.

"That's it," he folded his arms and gave her a withering look.

"So now what? Hmm? You seem to have all the answers!"

"It's over."

"No. It's not over."

"It is! Get it in your head. This is where it ends, Sasha, I mean it."

Spittle gathered in the corners of his mouth in angry beads. A vein on his neck throbbed like a trapped earthworm, his Adams apple bouncing around like a pin ball.

"Ends? Where what ends?" a hot feeling of dread began to build. She knew the meaning behind his fury but didn't want to believe it. She had to hear it from him.

"All of it!" he unfolded his arms and made a slicing gesture through the air.

"This. We're done. Mission fail. Job done. The fucking end. Get it?"

"What about the other night? You and me? What was that?"

A fist of formed in her throat, tears pricking at her eyes.

"It was a mistake. It should never have happened. We were colleagues, that's it…"

"Were?"

"Were. Past tense. Nothing else matters. And now we're done."

He said *done* as if he'd just fired a gun. The word like a bullet in her chest.

He turned away.

"Tom?" she didn't want to sound like she was pleading with him, but his name fell from her mouth.

He looked back, bobbed towards her then pulled away. He tugged the lapels of his jacket tightly around himself, as if he was activating a force field, keeping her at bay. His eyes were dark, cold and cruel. His mouth set into a frustrated frown.

"We're done. The job is done. Go home, Sasha."

He reached into his trouser pocket, opened his wallet and slid something out. She felt like a whore, about to be paid off. He handed her a room key. She took it and they both held it for a moment.

"Get your stuff from the room. Your passport and plane ticket are on the dresser, then go," he released the card and backed away from her.

"Forget me, forget the box, forget The Agency and go back to your life."

He turned away and crossed the square. He took a couple of steps then glanced back at her. He plunged his hands deep into his pockets and said, "Goodbye, Sasha. Maybe we'll meet in another life?"

A small smile flickered across his lips, then it melted into a look of defeat and sadness.

He walked away.

The end…

WHAT'S NEXT?

Did Gina open the box?

Did Sheridan and Blake *really* walk away?

Solomon's Secrets

The Second Sheridan and Blake Adventure

Dunhaung, China 1908 – an archaeologist discovers an ancient temple, but the legendary library rumoured to be at its heart is what he really wants to find.

The present - archaeologist, Dr Sasha Blake is studying a replica of an ancient manuscript at Bristol University. Offered sponsorship by a wealthy silk trader, Jon Solomon, she is desperate to locate the original document and four powerful rings that accompany it.

However, Sasha's investor is hiding terrible secrets and when she becomes his next victim, Sasha seeks revenge.

She agrees to work as a double agent for a covert organisation, The Agency, and becomes the bait in a web of conspiracy to catch Solomon. Once again, Sasha's life collides with Agent Tom Sheridan, and the stakes are raised as their relationship deepens.

Can Sheridan and Blake find the manuscript in time to stop Solomon, or are they about to fall into his trap?

Solomon's Secrets - Chapter One

SECRET LOCATION SOMEWHERE IN PARIS – PRESENT DAY

Tom Sheridan gazed down the corridor, an unlit cigarette dangling between his fingers.

He watched while his men dragged the hooded and bound detainee towards the holding cell. She fought them as they bundled her towards him.

He didn't know why he'd taken up smoking again, all he knew was he enjoyed the head rush and warmth in his throat. It made him feel alive, when most of the time all he felt was numb.

His hands trembled, he needed the reassurance and the kick right now, but would have to wait until after the interrogation.

He slid the cigarette into his shirt pocket and folded his arms, steadying himself, building up courage.

He'd done this a thousand times. Usually the people he questioned were real scumbags, they deserved what was coming to them. But not this time. This one would be the worst of his career. This one meant something.

Gabriel's Game
Part 1: The White Queen

The Third Sheridan and Blake Adventure

Bristol, 1205 – a Templar Knight returns from the crusades seeking forgiveness. He failed to retrieve a sacred manuscript from the Library of Constantinople.

The Present - archaeologist, Dr Sasha Blake is being hunted by an unseen enemy.

Her only chance is to locate and ancient manuscript and trade it for her life.

Tom Sheridan is at her side, but is he being hunted too, or is he one of the hunters?

They are offered shelter and assistance by a wealthy businessman, Gabriel Fletcher.

Can Gabriel be trusted, or is he playing games with Sasha?

Gabriel's Game
Part 2: The Black Knight

Will Sheridan and Blake make it out alive?

ABOUT THE AUTHOR

Amy Morse, writing as Amy C Fitzjohn (her maiden name), was born in Swansea in 1976. Growing up in the East Midlands and later in Somerset - Amy is a cider-drinking Westcountry girl at heart, but now lives between Bulgaria and Bristol.
The Bronze Box is her fourth novel but the first to be published. One day, she intends to bring the first three books up to scratch. The three books are part of a series of fantasy novels for young adults; 'The Chronicles of The Colony'.
Amy has been writing and telling stories for as long as she can remember but it was only when living overseas she found the time, and motivation, to write novel length fiction.
Amy's day job is a business trainer, coach and entrepreneur, she is also on the organising committee of Bristol Festival of Literature.
Look out for future works from this promising new writer.

www.AmyCFitzjohn.co.uk

Amy also writes non-fiction books in her married name, Amy Morse, and provides writing support services to business

www.AmyMorse.co.uk

NOTES AND INSIGHTS

A few personal touches…

This is my debut novel - I hope you enjoyed reading this story as much as I have loved telling it to you.

I first started forming it in my head back in 2010, drawing on ideas from many sources. It then took a year to get onto the page. It really has been a labour of love.

People ask me about my writing process and I think for every writer it's a very personal thing.

I wrote the first chapter, then the last chapter and I had a series of scenes in my imagination but they had no particular sequence. I wrote those scenes in fits and starts then stitched them together, played with the narrative, poked the characters to provoke a reaction and then let the book take me along the course it needed to go.

The editing process has been long and sometimes painful but I am lucky to have such a tolerant and amazing husband, so thank you Graham (who I have dedicated the book to).

Like all artists, I take my inspiration from many sources:

-   I have chosen to write in my maiden name 'Fitzjohn'. It's my small contribution to keep the family name going.

I have memories of spending many hours being dragged to registry offices and libraries as a kid in the 80's while my dad researched the family tree. In this internet age, his genealogy work has come on in leaps and bounds.

I hope that my book(s) will be my legacy, since I don't plan on having any children!

- In the book, Tom Sheridan holds great affection for an old family friend, a war hero; Frank Fitch.

I named him after my Granddad's, both of whom I view as war heroes. In WWII my father's father, Frank Fitzjohn, was in the RAF and was a Liberator Navigator. My mother's father, Albert Fitch, fought in North Africa. They both came back and went on to have happy lives and families.

- The story spans 2 places where I have a home, Bulgaria and Bristol.

I spent 18 months living a few miles inland from Varna and first learned about the Necropolis at the Varna Archaeological Museum, as featured in the book. It fascinated me that little known Bulgaria has such a rich and ancient history and that much of its archaeology is still undiscovered. That was the initial spark for the book – the 'what if' something terrifying lies buried and undiscovered there?

Writing a book about it - What a great excuse to do research!

- Anyone who knows Bristol will appreciate the comedy value of a 'car chase' down Gloucester Road. Possibly one of the most congested roads in, reportedly, one of the most congested cities in the UK!

- The Nokia 5110: for the technology geeks, this model featured in the book, is the same as my first ever mobile phone (showing my age now!)

- Sasha Blake and Tom Sheridan are re-inventions of two characters from a series of unpublished books I wrote previously.

Printed in Great Britain
by Amazon